THE RECIPE BOX

This Large Print Book carries the
Seal of Approval of N.A.V.H.

THE RECIPE BOX

A NOVEL WITH RECIPES

VIOLA SHIPMAN

THORNDIKE PRESS
A part of Gale, a Cengage Company

Farmington Hills, Mich • San Francisco • New York • Waterville, Maine
Meriden, Conn • Mason, Ohio • Chicago

Copyright © 2018 by Viola Shipman.
Thorndike Press, a part of Gale, a Cengage Company.

ALL RIGHTS RESERVED
This is a work of fiction. All of the characters, organizations, and events portrayed in the novel are either products of the author's imagination or are used fictitiously.
Thorndike Press® Large Print Women's Fiction.
The text of this Large Print edition is unabridged.
Other aspects of the book may vary from the original edition.
Set in 16 pt. Plantin.

LIBRARY OF CONGRESS CIP DATA ON FILE.
CATALOGUING IN PUBLICATION FOR THIS BOOK
IS AVAILABLE FROM THE LIBRARY OF CONGRESS

ISBN-13: 978-1-4328-4985-6 (hardcover)

Published in 2018 by arrangement with Macmillan Publishing Group, LLC/St. Martin's Press

Printed in the United States of America
1 2 3 4 5 6 7 22 21 20 19 18

To my grandmothers,
for teaching me to bake,
open doors, and say thank you.
For encouraging me to become a writer
and the person I am today.

To our elders,
whose sacrifices and journeys
made us who we are
but whose stories are being forgotten.

This book is a thank-you
and a reminder to stop and listen,
talk and bake.

Put in the extra effort in life and baking.
The end result is always worth it.

— MY GRANDMA, VIOLA SHIPMAN

PROLOGUE:
APPLE CRISP

Fall 1939

Alice washed her hands in the kitchen sink, looked out the window, and smiled.

The last of the day's light filtered through the brightly colored leaves of the sugar maples and sassafras, basking the kitchen in an otherworldly glow. One good storm off the lake, one sweeping windstorm, and the leaves would be gone, the trees would be bare, the orchard's twigs and limbs just silhouettes, the land ready to hibernate once again.

But, for now, she thought, *the leaves remain.*

She smiled again.

As do the apples.

Alice could see two figures moving in the orchard.

"Leo," she whispered to the kitchen window, unconsciously twirling her wedding ring. She watched the dog circle the man, its tongue and tail wagging. "Oh, Mac." She laughed.

The angle of the sun cast their shadows down the hillside, their silhouettes making them look like giants. The man held a basket, and when he reached to pick an apple, the light made it seem as if he were hugging the tree, caressing its limbs, saying good night.

Just like he does with me, Alice thought, leaning even farther to look out the kitchen window.

Alice could feel the chill in the approaching night air creep through the gaps in the windows and the chinks of the old logs. And as Mac circled Leo in delight, his barks echoing through the orchard, causing birds to scatter, Alice turned on the oven to preheat.

She pulled a carving knife and pastry blender out of the kitchen drawer as well as a baking dish and a red speckled enamelware bowl from the cupboard. Then she arranged flour, sugar, and cinnamon on the old wood counter. She opened the refrigerator and reached for the butter.

Her husband came through the door and handed her a basket of apples.

"You don't have to do that," Leo said, looking around the kitchen, seeing the items lined up on the counter. His smile, however, belied his words.

"I know," Alice said, "but I want to."

"OK then," he said happily. "I'll build a fire. Getting chilly."

He started out the door with Mac, then turned and said, "We make a great team, don't we?"

"Like cinnamon and sugar?" She laughed.

"No," he said. "We made it through the Depression somehow, this orchard intact. We've been married over thirty years." He stopped. "We complement each other, bring out the best."

"Like cinnamon and sugar?" she repeated.

This time, he laughed. "Yes, like cinnamon and sugar."

He and the dog went back outside, and Alice began to peel and core the apples, her knife pirouetting in quick circles, leaving curlicues of bright red and green skin in the bowl. She sliced and diced the apples, then started her topping.

She worked from memory. The recipe was ingrained in her mind. She had been taught by her mother and grandmother. This dessert was the family's favorite, the one everyone requested while the apples were fresh, ripe, and just off the tree.

But now everyone is gone, Alice thought.

On their own, leading their own lives. She stopped. *Away from the orchard.*

As she tossed the apples in sugar and cinnamon, she no longer saw her hands but those of her mother and grandmother: knuckles that were beginning to resemble the sassafras trees out the kitchen window, the skin more and more like waxed paper. Alice didn't like the look of her aging hands, but today she appreciated their beauty, their imperfections, their character and history.

How many times have I made this apple crisp? she wondered as she continued, not bothering to measure, just going by instinct: a dash of this, a little more of that, eyeing the topping to ensure it resembled little pieces of gravel, not too big and not too small. She stopped for a moment and did some quick math in her head: *What, ten times a year multiplied by forty-six if I started baking at ten? Four hundred sixty times? How many times will I make this before . . . ?*

The thought ended as her husband came rushing back into the house carrying an armful of wood and twigs for the potbellied stove.

She finished the dessert and slid it into the oven, setting an old timer on the counter. Within minutes, the scent of apples, cinnamon, and sugar filled the little cabin.

"Smells good," Leo called from the front room, where he was sitting in his favorite chair by the stove, the dog curled up on a blanket in front of the fire. Mac lifted his nose and sniffed the air. "He thinks so, too."

"The dog knows his apples." Alice laughed. "He should. He's named after one." She smiled at her two boys, their noses twitching with excitement.

"Soon," she called. "Be patient."

As Alice washed dishes, the sun slunk behind the orchard, and the world was quickly cast in darkness. The thought she hadn't finished moments ago came rushing back into her mind as she studied the soapsuds on her hands.

Suddenly, she flicked bubbles from her fingers, grabbed a dish towel to dry them, and pulled an index card and a pen from a kitchen drawer. The card said *RECIPE* at the top and was adorned, appropriately enough, with little apples. She had received these as a gift from her church and had kept them forever but never used them.

Until now.

She steadied her hand and began to write, her hand dragging over the wet ink as she imparted the secrets that had never been divulged before:

Alice Mullins's Secret
Family Apple Crisp

A big smile engulfed her face, and she added an exclamation point at the end, giggling at the audacity of it.

Alice Mullins's Secret
Family Apple Crisp!

And then she wrote, step by step, ingredient by ingredient, her beloved family recipe, adding her own directions: *May call for a few more dashes of cinnamon,* or *If apples are especially tart, add another quarter cup of sugar.*

When Alice finished, she realized her handwriting was the same as her mother's and grandmother's — same slant, same formal *F*s, and *Q*s that looked like the number 2. Again, she smiled and, as the timer went off, she gave the index card a little kiss.

She put on an oven mitt featuring a few scorch marks and poked the crisp with a toothpick. It came out clean, and she smiled.

Perfect, Alice thought.

She pulled the dessert from the oven, set it on top of the oven to cool, and started in on some homemade whipped cream, adding a dash of vanilla and whipping it until it formed a soft peak and was as pretty as a cloud on a northern Michigan summer day. Alice dragged a finger through the whipped cream and tasted it, and then did it again just for good measure, accidentally dropping a dollop onto the index card, the fat from the heavy whipping cream leaving an immediate circular stain in the middle.

No, she thought, trying to clean it off. *Too late.*

Alice shook her head and grabbed two plates and a spatula to cut the crisp. She placed a big piece on her husband's plate, the apples steaming and sliding to the sides, before topping it with whipped cream, which began to melt as soon as it hit the hot dessert. She made a second, smaller plate for herself and then joined her husband by the fire.

Leo dragged his fork through the crisp, shut his eyes, and smiled like a child.

"You didn't have to do this," he said yet again.

"I know," she repeated. "But I wanted to."

Alice took a bite, sat back as the plate warmed her hands, the fire warmed her aching body, and the apple crisp warmed her soul, and watched her husband finish his dessert.

That is the thing about baking, she thought. *You bake for someone because it is familial and familiar, new yet ancestral, a way of connecting generations.*

Mac sighed and rolled onto his side. Leo lifted a fork filled with apples and streusel topping to his lips and again shut his eyes.

You bake for someone because it is an act of love, she thought.

A few days later, Alice walked into the kitchen after a day of working the orchard and raking leaves to find a small wooden box sitting on the kitchen counter. The wood was shiny and new, and it smelled as fresh as the outdoors. On the front was carved *RECIPE BOX.*

"I made it for you," Leo said, startling her. He walked over and picked up the recipe card that was still sitting on the counter and slid it into the box. "See? Fits perfectly. A place to keep your family recipes." He stopped and smiled, pulling a key from his pocket. "And secrets."

He continued: "I added a lock, just so you can keep them a family secret. Here you go," he said, handing her the key. "All yours."

Tears filled her eyes, and Alice grabbed

her husband and held him tightly, the wool from his jacket tickling her face.

"Everyone's gone from here," she said. "Just us now. This orchard. And these memories."

"Write them down," he said. "That way, they'll never die."

"Who'd want to make these old recipes?" Alice asked. "My farm cooking?"

"Anyone with a heart and a family," Leo said. "Our family." He stopped and said in a hush, "Anyone who wants to remember."

"Remember what?" she asked.

"You," he said, his voice husky with emotion. He kissed her cheek. "Better get busy."

For the next few weeks, Alice wrote every recipe she could remember and filled the box with cards. She added the key to a chain she wore around her neck, just to keep it near to her heart, and locked her recipe box up every night to keep her secrets safe and sound.

One night, her husband brought in the last batch of apples, and she made another crisp.

Alice guessed it was not only the 461st crisp of her life but also the best one she'd ever made.

It would be her last.

FAMILY APPLE CRISP

Ingredients for Filling

5 medium-large Granny Smith apples
3 medium Honeycrisp apples
4 medium McIntosh apples
1 stick unsalted butter
1/4 cup light brown sugar, packed
1 teaspoon ground cinnamon
1 teaspoon baking spice
1 teaspoon apple pie spice

Ingredients for Topping

2 cups granulated sugar
1 1/2 cups all-purpose flour
1 teaspoon ground cinnamon
2/3 cup butter, room temperature

Directions for Filling

Preheat the oven to 350°F.

Peel the apples and cut them into wedges. Place the wedges in a large bowl.

In a large skillet or saucepan, melt 1 stick butter over medium heat.

Add the apples. Slowly stir and turn over the apples in the butter.

Add the brown sugar, cinnamon, baking spice, and apple pie spice to the apples and butter and stir. Continue to stir until the sugar and spices are incorporated and have coated the apples.

Reduce the heat to low. Cover and cook 10 to 12 minutes, stirring occasionally. (The apples should still be firm, but slightly softened. They will finish cooking in the oven.)

Directions for Topping

While the apples are cooking, butter a 9 × 13-inch baking dish.

In a large mixing bowl, combine the sugar, flour, and cinnamon and blend together with a fork.

Cut the butter into large pats and add to the dry ingredients.

Use a pastry blender to cut the butter into the mixture, until it resembles loose crumbles, about 2 minutes; there will be some pea-sized pieces, but the mixture should largely be an even, coarse crumble.

Assembly

Transfer the cooked apples and sauce to the prepared baking dish.

By hand, sprinkle the topping mixture over the apples, distributing it evenly.

Firmly pat the topping onto the top of the apples.

Bake 50 minutes, or until the crust is golden.

(Note: The apples will bubble a bit into the

topping.)
Serve warm with whipped cream or vanilla
ice cream.

Serves 12 to 16

■ ■ ■ ■

PART ONE:
PEACH-BLUEBERRY
SLAB PIE

■ ■ ■ ■

ONE

Summer 2017

Sam Nelson sipped her latte, staring out the window of the coffee shop, waiting for the rain to stop. She watched garbage men in yellow slickers jump out of trucks to pick up the trash, the deafening noise causing her head to throb. She was still bleary-eyed with sleep, and the scene looked blurred and too bright, as if it were a paint-by-numbers portrait.

Sam shut her eyes to still her mind, and her head suddenly whirred with colorful images of apples, the kind a child might draw — smiling, dancing, hanging from trees. A coffee grinder and milk frother roared to life, accompanied again by the sound of trash trucks, and Sam's eyes popped open. She realized she was unconsciously rubbing the necklace she wore every day that was hidden under her uniform. She pulled it free and ran her fingers over the key that hung from the chain.

Starbucks was jammed with those who, like her, rose at dawn to start their day: construction workers, Wall Street traders, emergency room doctors, eager assistants.

And struggling pastry chefs like me, she thought, looking around the coffeehouse.

But mostly others like me who were so sleepy leaving this morning they also left their umbrellas at home, she realized, her face breaking into a slight smile.

Sam watched the rain slide down the window in great sheets, the sky heaving, the city stopping for once — even at dawn, when everyone was waking and had somewhere to be — Mother Nature forcing everyone to halt for one brief moment. And then, as quickly as the rain had started, it stopped, the surprise summer thunderstorm over. Sam rushed out onto the sidewalk, the crowd dispersing in different directions like water bugs on a lake.

The humidity of the summer day suddenly smacked Sam directly in the face, *like being hit with a warm, wet washrag,* her grandma used to say.

Sam was rushed along in the wave of those who were now late and had somewhere to be.

I do, too, Sam thought, *but I don't want to*

get there.

Sam walked briskly downtown, sipping her latte when she slowed to cross the streets. She could already feel the first of three espresso shots coursing through her veins.

She looked at the city streets coated in rain, the early light illuminating their inky blackness, their darkness beautifully framed by the lighter concrete gutters and side-walks.

Broadway looks just like a big blackberry galette, Sam thought, before shaking her head at the terrible analogy.

That would have earned a C minus in English lit, she thought, *but my instructors at culinary school would be proud.*

Sam slowed for a second and considered the streets. *So would my family,* she added.

New York had its own otherworldly beauty, stunning in its own sensory-overload sort of way, but a jarring juxtaposition to where Sam had grown up: on a family orchard in northern Michigan.

Our skyscrapers were apple and peach trees, Sam thought, seeing dancing fruit in her mind once again. She smiled as she approached Union Square Park and stopped to touch an iridescent green leaf, still wet and dripping rain, her heart leaping at its incredible tenderness in the midst of the city. She leaned in and lifted the leaf to her nose, inhaling, the scents of summer and smells of her past — fresh fruit, fragrant pine, baking pies, lake water — flooding her mind.

Sam's knees suddenly felt like the jellies her family made, and she took a seat on a nearby bench and took out her phone, guilt overwhelming her as she clicked on the e-invite she had received a dozen times over the last few months.

HAPPY BIRTHDAY TO . . . US!

CELEBRATE OUR CENTENNIAL (AND GRANDMA WILLO'S BIRTHDAY)!

MULLINS FAMILY ORCHARDS & PIE PANTRY IS TURNING 100! AND OUR MATRIARCH IS TURNING 75!

WE HOPE YOUR FAMILY WILL JOIN OURS FOR THIS ONCE-IN-A-LIFETIME CELEBRATION!

PI = 3.14159
(WHO ARE WE KIDDING? PIE = LOVE!)

Sam stared at the last line. *Are they still using that same old slogan?* she thought, but the word *FAMILY* stuck in her vision, and when she shut her eyes, it floated in front of her eyes, just as the images of apples had earlier.

She clicked on messages from her grandma and parents: *Hope you can make it! Miss you! Love you!*

Sam's family hadn't officially pressed her to return for the celebration — *too proud, just like me,* Sam thought — *but what am I supposed to do?*

I can't ask for time off to go home, she continued. *He would never give it to me. And opportunities like this don't just fall in your lap in New York City.*

Sam opened her eyes and, as usual, passing New Yorkers were shooting her second glances as they passed, confused as to why a woman would be wearing all white in a city that typically outfitted itself in the darkest of colors.

Sam had to confess that she looked like a Disney character — *some sort of ice princess perhaps* — in her chef's whites and blond hair.

"You the last virgin in the city?" a man yelled as he zipped by on his bike.

"You wish!" Sam yelled back.

Subtlety was not New York's strong suit,

and the city had taught her to be tough.

So did my grandma, Sam thought, touching the tree's branch as she stood, thinking of her Grandma Willo. *She taught me to bend but never break, just like her name, just like this tree.*

Sam shook her head, checked her watch, and groaned. She picked up her pace, zipping past the Flatiron Building before turning and skirting Madison Square Park to head east on 23rd.

She kept her head down, sipping her latte and counting every single step as she did every morning to avoid reality — *48, 49, 50, 51* — glancing up every so often just to avoid running into someone and to check out familiar window fronts.

208, 209, 210 . . .

Sam stopped and lifted her eyes to see the bright yellow awning jutting out over the rain-slicked sidewalk, smiling brightly, falsely, just like . . .

Sam tried but couldn't halt the thought that had already formed, the one that popped into her head every single morning.

. . . an insipid reality star.

"Move, lady!" a passerby said to Sam, who was still stopped directly in the middle of the sidewalk — much to the chagrin of other New Yorkers. "It's called a bakery."

A kind-looking woman walking her dog slowed and asked Sam, "Are you hungry? Do you want something from the bakery?"

For some reason, Sam shook her head no and showed the woman her Starbucks cup. The woman looked at Sam and said very seriously, "He's famous, you know," pointing to the bakery.

"I know," Sam said, staring up at the awning. Happy-faced pies dotted the fabric, like little baked suns, the venting on each crust designed to make the pies look like they were smiling with adorable deep dimples.

Her stomach lurched as it did every morning when she read the bakery's name: DIMPLES BAKERY.

Sam walked up to the door of the shop and gave it a yank, her arm reverberating. *What the . . . ?* she thought. Sam placed her face against the glass and held her hands around her eyes, her breath steaming the window. *Why is it still dark?*

She began to fish for her keys when she heard, "Hey, Michigan!"

Sam turned and smiled.

"Hey, Jersey!"

This had become their greeting since Sam and Angelo Morelli, the deliveryman for a well-known East Coast organic produce company, met a year ago. Although Angelo was born and raised in Brooklyn, Sam first met Angelo when he was delivering Fresh Jersey tomatoes for a classic southern tomato pie Trish was making. Between his accent and the tomatoes — which Sam instantly fell in love with — Sam had inadvertently referred to Angelo as "Jersey," and the nickname had stuck.

"How were the Hamptons?" Angelo asked through the open window of the delivery truck. He jumped out, ran around to the back, and threw open the corrugated door. Boxes of fresh fruit and produce — a rainbow of bright colors and rich textures — were piled up in crates and boxes, ready to be delivered.

"Montauk," Sam corrected. "Girls' weekend was fun. Four of us crammed into a little motel room by the beach. It had a two-burner stove, and I somehow managed to make the most beautiful galette for breakfast."

Sam smiled. The Hamptons reminded her of where she had grown up in northern Michigan: the beaches, the cute shops, the farm stands selling fresh fruit and produce right off the highway.

"Mets took the Tigers last night!" Angelo said, breaking Sam from her thoughts.

"But the Mets won't make the playoffs," Sam said. "Tigers will."

"That hurts," Angelo said, acting as if Sam had just won a sword duel with him. He grabbed his side and nearly fell to his knees.

"You're a real peach," Sam said, laughing at his theatrics.

"Speakin' a' which," Angelo said, excitedly jumping to his feet, his dark eyes wide and his black curls bouncing as he gestured to the back of the truck. "Voilà!"

Sam walked over to the truck and inhaled. "Smells like heaven," she said.

"That's somethin' in New York." Angelo laughed.

Sam smiled and looked at Angelo.

Now those are some dimples, she couldn't help thinking.

"How's school?" Sam switched subjects.

"Slow and steady. One night class at a time," he said, moving crates. "I think I'll finish when I'm a hundred and five."

"No time frame on passion and dedication," Sam said.

Angelo turned and smiled. "Thanks for saying that," he said. "I need to be reminded. Not easy working full time and going to school." He hesitated. "I'm glad you encouraged me to go back to school. I'm enjoying my business classes."

Angelo picked up a crate and smiled at Sam, the effort causing his biceps to flex. He put the crate down and caught Sam staring at him.

"Maybe we could go to a game sometime?" Angelo said quietly, considering Sam's blue eyes.

Yes, Sam wanted to say. *I'd love to.* But then she remembered Michigan — and Connor, the high school boyfriend whose heart she had broken because he never wanted her to move away from home.

Sam realized she was nervously touching the key on her necklace again, and she tucked it under her chef's whites. She wanted to say yes but she'd feel guilty starting something she didn't have time for with her job.

"No problem," Angelo said quickly, taking her silence as a no and leaping into the back of the truck. "I get it. A girl like you and a guy like me . . ."

He seemed embarrassed and Sam could tell he was disappointed.

She wanted to explain, but Angelo was already out of the truck with another crate in hand and at the front door waiting for her with a full dolly.

"What do you think's going on?" Sam asked, partly to divert his attention and partly to understand why Trisha, the head pastry chef, wasn't already at the store. "Trish is usually here before four A.M."

Angelo jiggled the doorknob and knocked as Sam got her keys. She opened the door, and the duo walked in. Sam turned on the lights.

"Hello?" Sam called. "Trish?"

Sam scanned the bakery. A black-and-white checkerboard floor led up to walls covered in pink-and-white-striped wallpaper featuring black-and-white posters from *Gone with the Wind, Steel Magnolias, The Notebook,* and *Cat on a Hot Tin Roof,* but mostly the walls were filled with photos from Chef Dimples's fame-making stint on the insanely popular reality matchmaking show *With This Ring.*

Too-big ornate iron tables filled the space, while the bakery area was lined with old-fashioned cupboards, supported by ornate finials and overflowing with pink Depression glass plates. The glass bakery cases were lined with pink-and-yellow shelf paper and filled with muffins, cookies, cakes, pies, especially all things Southern: pecan pie, lemon meringue pie, sweet potato pie, red velvet cake, pecan tassies, pralines, bread pudding, cobblers, strawberry shortcakes. The windowsills held boxes filled with bright petunias.

The place was brand new, and it looked like a movie set, a fictionalized version of real life, just like . . .

Chef Dimples, Sam thought. *The place is just like him: no real history, no real character. And he doesn't even know how to make one of the desserts in here he takes credit for. It was all created for TV.*

Sam thought of how different this bakery was from her family's pie pantry, her grandmother's watercolors — of apple trees, fresh-baked pies, the bay filtered through the orchard — painted on the bakery's cement floors and old, warped wood walls, and the barn-wood counter where she had sold pies.

Sam never sold the pastries she helped create here. They were sold by Chef Dimples's former bachelorettes — those who hadn't received the final ring. Customers flocked in for a social media photo op rather than the baked goods.

"Sam?" Angelo asked, his voice causing her to jump. "Sorry. I found this."

Angelo was standing by the register and holding a folded piece of paper. Sam walked over and took the note from him, grimacing as if she already knew the outcome. She began to read:

" 'Chef, and I use that term loosely,' "
Sam started, before stopping to look up at
Angelo. "Oh, this is *not* going to be good."

She continued reading the note: " 'I not
only quit, effective immediately, but I wish
you nothing but a ring of bad luck for the
rest of your so-called career. You are an
energy vampire, a soul-sucking vacuum, a
soulless human with a Hindenburg-sized
ego that will eventually crash and burn. I
want to see you stand in the kitchen and
actually make something . . . use your hands
to do something other than slap your staffs'
rears, comb your hair, put bronzer on your
cheeks, hand out fake rings to customers,
or count your money. Look forward to seeing you soon on *TMZ,* a tragic episode of *E!
True Hollywood Story,* or *People*'s *Where Are
They Now?* Love, Trish.' "

"That's some real reality TV stuff right
there," Angelo said, his dark eyes wide, a
bemused smile crossing his face. "She
pulled out the big guns. He deserved that,
right?"

Sam nodded, her face frozen as panic
began to set in.

"But you don't?" Angelo asked, suddenly
understanding. He walked over and gently
put his arm around Sam's back. "I'm so
sorry," he said.

Sam leaned into him. "Thanks," she said. "I'm now on the firing line. And I mean that literally. He's going to go ballistic when he finds out. And I'm the only one left standing . . . for now."

Angelo took a step back, grabbed Sam's shoulders, and looked her deeply in the eyes. "Maybe this just means it's your time to shine," he said. "Maybe this means it's your time to take a stand and show him what you've got. You trained at that fancy school, right? You come from a family of bakers, right? You're from Michigan. That's the Show Me State, right?"

Sam laughed. "No, that's Missouri, Angelo."

"Neighboring states, though, right?"

"You New Yorkers." Sam continued to laugh. "No sense of geography once you're off the island."

"What the hell is going on?"

Sam and Angelo both jumped at the sound of a booming Southern voice behind them. They turned, and Chef Dimples was standing — not smiling, dimples still intact — one arm holding a cell to his ear, the other gesturing angrily.

He looked, as always, camera ready — a bulked-up version of Matthew McConaughey with grass-green eyes, tousled blond hair, and one of those mischievous smiles that melted mothers and girlfriends alike, no matter if he had just stolen money from their purses or broken their hearts. Those dimples had made him famous.

Deep enough to plant an apple seed, Sam remembered her grandmother saying after she had told her she got the job and to watch the show.

And even Mother Nature seemed to highlight his beauty: this morning, the city's early light splayed into the bakery and surrounded his body, seeming to illuminate him as if he were a religious figure.

His moniker, Chef Dimples, had caught on after *With This Ring,* and he had begun to appear on morning shows — baking sweets with Hoda or Rachael and handing them out to screaming women on the streets — before getting his own cooking show on the Food Channel. He was the Southern male version of the Barefoot Contessa. Or, at least, that's what he told everyone.

But Ina Garten actually worked hard at her business, Sam thought. *And she knows how to cook. No, strike that: She actually cooks.*

Even more irritating to Sam was that her boss *only* answered to the name Chef Dimples.

Yes, Chef Dimples.

No, Chef Dimples.

Of course, Chef Dimples.

Sam always had trouble saying his name, forcing herself to utter it, always with a mix of embarrassment and repulsion. Worse, saying it made her feel as if she were acting in an awful kids' show, and that he had this alter ego everyone could see through, like Hannah Montana, although he didn't seem to realize it himself.

"Hello?" he asked sarcastically. "Is anyone going to answer?"

"Good morning, Chef Dimples. What are you doing here?" Sam didn't mean to say the last part, but the morning's drama had cleared her edit button.

"I own the place," he said. "Remember?"

Sam could see Angelo's face burn with anger at his tone toward her.

Chef Dimples said into his cell, "I'll call you right back," before looking at Sam. "I'm doing a live segment on *GMA* in two hours. Trish knows that." And then to Angelo, "Who are you, and what are you doing here?"

"I'm Angelo. I deliver your fresh fruit and produce. Every day for the last year." He held out his hand as if to shake Chef Dimples's hand and smiled innocently. "What's your name?"

Sam's head spun wildly toward Angelo, surprised at his question. He turned and gave her a subtle wink.

"I'm Chef Dimples."

"Nah, man," Angelo pushed. "Your real name. Doubt you were born Chef Dimples, right? My friends calls me Bocce, 'cause I never been beat at the game, and Sam calls me Jersey, but my real name is Angelo Morelli. See where I'm headed?"

Sam watched Chef Dimples's green eyes go wide, and the flush that seemed to permanently remain in his cheeks spread over his entire face, as if he had been overtaken by measles. Sam had seen this look before when she had binge-watched his season on *With This Ring* and a woman named Tara had called him out, claiming that both his Southern accent and culinary skills were half-baked. She had become the season's villain, of course, and Chef Dimples had only stepped up his game to impress the other contestants, constantly baking cookies for his dates.

"The way to a man's heart may be through his stomach," he became famous for saying on every date — in his heavy, syrupy, praline-sweet Southern accent — as he fed his bachelorettes, "but the way to a woman's heart is sweetness."

How many of those desserts did he make?
Sam had wondered as she watched, considering the show only seemed to show one clip of him over and over dumping flour into a mixing bowl, which would billow onto his shirt, forcing him to take it off and wipe down his face. *Please.*

"You don't get to ask questions of me in my own bakery!" Chef Dimples screamed, knocking Sam from her thoughts. "And you call me Chef Dimples when in my bakery!"

Angelo shook his head, wheeled his cart through the swinging doors and into the kitchen, and returned, turning to Sam.

"Lots of fresh blueberries to go with those peaches today," he said. "Brought them in honor of your trip to the Hamptons." Angelo stopped. He leaned in to whisper to Sam. "You don't have to put up with this, you know. You got mad skills. I've tasted everything in here that you've made." He hesitated. "You also got grace."

This time, Sam's face flushed.

Angelo wheeled his cart directly up to Chef Dimples, causing him to take a big step backward. "See you later, Dwight Lilliputh," he winked, using Chef Dimples's real name, the one that was used in the first few episodes of *With This Ring,* the name he never allowed anyone to use, in person, in

TV interviews, on press releases. "See? I watch TV. And we got Google in Brooklyn."

"My name is Chef Dimples! Now get out!" He turned, aiming his full wrath at Sam. "Where in the hell is Trish?"

Sam sheepishly stepped forward and handed him the note. As he read it, Sam swore she could see steam billow from his ears, as if he were Wile E. Coyote. When he finished, he crumpled up the paper and threw it at Sam's feet.

"She'll never work again," he said. "Of all days. With *GMA*." He stepped forward to consider Sam. He was wearing one of those too-tight suits young, in-shape New York City men liked to wear — fitted jacket, tapered pant legs that stopped short to show off brightly patterned socks — and light suede shoes that showed not a speck of dirt.

You obviously didn't take the subway, Sam thought, looking down at her chef's whites that were already beginning to show the city's grime.

"You'll have to do until I get a real pastry chef," Chef Dimples said dismissively.

"I realize my role has been more of a sous chef, assisting Trisha —" Sam started.

"And me," he interrupted.

When did you make anything, besides a list of your celebrities who were stopping by?

Sam thought.

"Of course, Chef Dimples," she said. "But I trained at the Culinary Institute, I interned for pastry chef Jon Paul DeGaude at The Farm, and my family owns its own orchard and bakery."

Chef Dimples rolled his eyes. "Really?" he asked. "About seven million people are going to be waking up to watch me in two hours, and they want to be bowled over by a great dessert. They could care less if your family made donuts in a barn. Just make me look good."

Sam's head spun in fury and her stomach lurched, but she willed her tears to stop from reaching her eyes.

"Of course, Chef Dimples."

He stormed into the kitchen and looked around. Suzette, a young dishwasher wearing earphones who always came in through the back, eyed him warily, ducking her head and continuing to put up mixing bowls, pans, and dishes.

Chef Dimples looked at Sam, his dimples deepening. "I don't care if it tastes like crap," he said. "Just make it pretty for TV. And make it Southern."

Sam nodded.

And, with that, he hit call on his phone. "I'm back," he said, striding out, the swinging doors cueing his exit as if he were in a bad Western.

"I'm gonna need some help," Sam said to Suzette, who was still trying to remain as invisible as possible. Sam gestured to Suzette to remove her earphones and then repeated herself. "I'm gonna need some help. If you can help me wash the fruit, get all the stems off these blueberries, and pluck out the bad ones, I'll get started skinning and pitting the peaches," Sam continued in a rush, picking up a peach. "We should have enough baked goods to get us through this morning's rush — and we have a lot of dough frozen and ready for muffins and cookies if you want to start baking those. I'll handle this."

Sam stopped, shut her eyes, and took a deep breath.

The scent of peaches — sweet, nostalgic — filled her nose, and once again images of her family orchard and bakery filled her mind.

"Do you have a recipe in mind?" Suzette asked in a meek voice.

Sam opened her eyes and smiled. She had, without knowing, pulled her necklace free and was rubbing the key around her neck once again.

"I do," she said, walking over to wash her hands. "I do."

Two

Summer 2006

Sam Nelson sprinted between the rows of peach and apple trees, her arms out-stretched as if she were soaring over her family orchards like the ancient crop duster her grandfather used to fly.

In one hand, she held an old wooden basket, in the other a half-eaten peach, the juice dripping down her arm. U-Pickers, who flocked to the Mullins Family Orchards and Pie Pantry every summer day and fall weekend to wander the lush hillside, pick their own fruit, and gorge themselves on apple pies and cider donuts, jumped as the thirteen-year-old girl flew past them, a blur like the bees and hummingbirds that darted from tree to tree.

"You're supposed to pick some, Sam," she could hear her grandmother call in the near distance, "not eat all our profit and scare away all our customers!"

Sam laughed, finished off her peach, and tossed the pit far into the air, watching it roll down a hill. She continued to dart in and out of the fruit trees before stopping in front of a tree to watch an urban family dressed in pressed shorts and colorful polos fill their baskets with apples.

"Excuse me," Sam said, using her free hand, still sticky with peach juice, to tuck her long, blond hair into the back of her T-shirt. To the shock of the family, Sam began to scale the tree, climbing with one hand and holding on to the basket with the other, until she was entwined in its upper branches. She looked out at the orchards and then down at the family. "There's an even better tree . . . one, two, three . . . six rows down and on your right."

As the family continued to stare, Sam said, "See you later. And thank you for visiting Mullins Family Orchards!"

The family walked away, turning every so often to consider the girl hidden in the tree.

Sam sighed.

Another birthday stuck here working on this orchard, she thought. *Every birthday. Every summer. Why couldn't I have been born somewhere else? Or in the winter?*

Sam scanned the orchards. U-Pickers laughed and posed for photos with apples on their heads, babies in the baskets, hugging trees. She lifted her head to study the sky, blue as her eyes. The clouds moved across the sun, blocking it out for long distances at a time, causing the landscape in front of her to become illuminated one patchwork piece at a time: the rolling hills lined with grass and endless rows of trees, peach, tart cherry, apples of every variety; blueberry bushes sitting at the bottom of the hill where the rain pooled; the old red barn where high school kids doled out baskets for fruit, which Sam's father weighed when they returned; the old shed where more high schoolers handed out free donut samples and sips of apple cider to arriving cars; the farmhouse with shutters — designed with apple cutouts — where her grandparents, Willo and Gordon, lived; the blue-green waters of Suttons Bay stretching out beyond the trees, the Old Mission Peninsula jutting into it; the family cornfields that sat across M-22 and would soon be cut into an intricate corn maze filled with spooks and goblins to scare fall visitors.

This slice of northern Michigan was Sam's home, her whole world.

And yet, she thought, squinting her eyes and watching a large boat drift across the horizon on the bay, making it look as if the world were indeed flat, *there has to be so much more out there, doesn't there?* Sam watched the boat get smaller and smaller as it drifted through the bay and out toward the big lake, wondering if her "boyfriend" Connor — who had asked her to go steady by giving her an old mood ring — was on it with his dad, taking tourists out on a fishing charter.

"Sam?" she suddenly heard her grandma call. "Sam?"

"Now where could she be?" her mother asked.

Sam shut her eyes to block out the world, held her breath, and squelched her giggles. Suddenly, she screamed when she felt her leg being tugged.

"Grandma!" she yelled, opening her eyes to find her grandma Willo partway up the tree and pulling on her leg.

"I've never picked an apple this big before," Willo said, continuing to tug on her granddaughter's bare leg. "Seems like it's stuck on the tree."

"Grandma!" Sam continued to laugh. "Stop!"

She looked down at her grandma. "And *you* look like the one who should be picked!"

Willo was sporting her customary outfit: a

floppy crocheted red cap that resembled a ripe apple, with a green stem and two little leaves on top. It was something a parent might dress their toddler in for a photo shoot, but Willo had the innocence, enthusiasm, and excitement of a child, qualities Sam adored in her grandma.

"Thank you, Sam," she said, bowing with a flourish of her hat, her cropped salt-and-pepper hair flat against her head. "That's a compliment! I'm a new version of a Red Hat Lady."

Sam smiled at her grandma. She sported an oversized T-shirt with the Mullins logo on the front — *PI = 3.14159 (WHO ARE WE KIDDING? PIE = LOVE!)* — which hung down nearly to the bottom of her capri pants; her bright purple tennis shoes were the exclamation points on her outfit. She was quite the contrast to Sam's mom, Deana, who still looked like a girl herself in cutoff overalls and blond ponytail, her lips shiny with gloss.

"What are you doing up there, young lady?" Sam's mom asked. "You could hurt yourself."

"Never have before," Sam said. "I just wanted to get a better view of the world."

"Today's a big day for you," Deana said. "Thirteen! You're officially a teenager!"

"What do you want for your birthday?"

Willo asked, before adding with a laugh, "and if it's different than what we already got you, pretend to like it anyway."

Sam looked out over the gently rolling hills and sighed. "I want what's out there," she said.

Willo and Deana glanced at one another.

"What do you mean?" her mom asked.

"I want the world," she said.

Willo continued to look at Deana, sadness etched on her face. "But your roots are here, sweetheart," Willo said, "just like these trees."

"I know," Sam said, exhaling loudly, tapping her basket against a branch nervously. "But shouldn't we be able to grow wherever we want?"

No, Willo wanted to scream. Instead, she took a deep breath, smiled, and willed herself to say cheerily, "Yes, of course."

Willo put one arm around her daughter and squeezed her, before jumping up to tug on her granddaughter's leg once again.

"It's a big birthday, and we have a big surprise for you," she said, changing the subject. "So go get cleaned up."

Sam climbed down the tree, handed her basket to her mom, and took off running, her arms again outstretched, her mom and grandma watching her fly away until she was no bigger than an apple on the tree in front of them.

At dusk, Sam walked into the family room of her family's brown-shingled cottage that sat on a rocky point of beach overlooking the bay and called out, "Hello?"

She scurried barefoot from room to room, calling out to her mom, dad, and younger brother, Aaron, but her voice was the only one that answered back.

"Hello?" came the echo.

Sam slipped on a pair of fancy flip-flops — bejeweled with shiny blue stones — and slipped out of the cottage, stopping at the last moment to give her image a final once-over in the little mirror shaped like a ship's wheel mounted by the front door. Sam was wearing her favorite dress, the sweet summer blue one that her mom said matched her eyes and that featured little eyelet sleeves and hem. She had pulled her long, blond hair into a pretty fishtail braid and swung it over her shoulder, a look she had seen in a fashion magazine.

Sam scurried up the hill to the edge of her family's orchards, the light growing dimmer as she entered the hobbit-sized forest of fruit trees. She squinted and her heart began to pound.

I'm thirteen! she suddenly thought. *A teen-ager!*

Sam slowed her pace. *Why did everyone leave?* Suddenly, she got angry. *Are they still working? Did they get tied up with stupid tour-ists?*

She made her way up another gently roll-ing hill — apples trees now replacing sweet cherry trees — and that was when she saw it: lights had been strung between rows of trees and, in the distance, lights twinkled in the barn.

Sam suddenly began to run, her braid swatting her back as if she were a racehorse, and she sprinted until she was standing under the lights in the orchard and could see her entire family — aunts, uncles, cousins — and many of her friends from school.

"There she is!" she heard her grandma yell. "Sam's here!"

Sam's mom and dad rushed out of the barn to hug her, followed by her nine-year-old brother, Aaron, who gave her a half-hearted side hug and a soft punch in the arm. Everyone in the barn clapped.

"You're old now," Aaron teased. "Hurry up and turn sixteen so you can drive me around."

"You'll have to ride in the trunk," she

teased back, messing up his already-messed-up hair.

"Happy birthday!"

Sam turned, and her grandma and grandpa were standing, arms outstretched.

"Thank you," Sam said. "Did you do all this?"

"Let's just say it was a joint effort," Willo said.

"That means she did," Gordon laughed, "along with your mom. I love you to the moon and back, Sammie!"

"Me, too, Grandpa," she said.

"Me, three," Willo added. "Now follow me."

Willo was sporting two party hats, both angled on her head, giving her the look of a demented dragon. She was wearing so many colorful leis that they made it seem as if she were wearing a neck brace. She walked Sam over to a long table in the back of the barn strewn with party supplies, carefully placed a hat on Sam's head — "Don't want to mess up your beautiful hair!" she said, moving the braid over Sam's shoulder — hung a blue lei around her neck, and tucked an electric-blue hydrangea behind her ear.

"Hungry?" she asked.

Sam lifted her nose like her grandparents' dog, Doris, a happy old yellow Lab who was standing guard by the barbecue grill. Doris believed she truly ruled these orchards, and it was her duty to keep them rid of pesky, unwanted animal visitors.

"We made all your favorites," Willo continued. "Barbecued ribs, corn on the cob, foiled potatoes, fresh tomatoes with basil, and iced tea."

"You're forgetting the most important part," Sam said with a smile. "Dessert. It's what we do best."

"That's a surprise," Willo said, matching her granddaughter's smile.

I hope it's a cake this year, Sam thought. *For once. Not another pie.*

"Go say hi to Connor and all your friends," Willo said. "They're waiting."

Sam took off in a flash and ran to her girlfriends, all screaming, jumping up and down, and chanting, "You're a teenager!"

The girls parted like the Red Sea as Connor approached carrying a small gift topped with a tiny bow. "Happy birthday," he said, holding out the box.

"For me?" Sam asked.

"Of course," he said.

Sam opened the box. Her hands trembled nervously. A delicate gold chain sparkled. Sam lifted it out. "A necklace," Sam said.

"See?" he asked, cupping the end of the

chain. Two small gold pendants sat in his palm. "One is the state of Michigan," he continued, "and the other is an apple."

Sam looked at Connor, her eyes wide.

"One is for home, and the other is because . . . well" — he stopped and scanned the orchards behind them — "it's home, too."

"Oh, Connor, it's too much," Sam said.

"My mom picked it out," he said nervously, smoothing his sun-lightened bangs across his forehead. "I wanted to get you Justin Timberlake tickets, but they were too expensive. And my mom would have had to drive us. My mom really likes you." Connor hesitated. "So do I."

He smiled shyly, and the hanging lights sparkled off his braces.

"Thank you," Sam said, giving him a quick hug as her friends giggled.

Sam wanted to tell Connor she liked him, too, but she couldn't get the words to come out.

What's wrong with me? she wondered.

Her friends immediately broke into applause and circled around her to see the necklace.

Saved by the bell, Sam thought, forcing a smile at Connor, who retreated to talk to the boys clustered together in the corner.

After dinner was over and Sam had opened endless gifts, the lights suddenly went off.

Happy birthday to you . . .

Sam turned, and her mom and grandma were carrying a huge platter. Candles flickered on top, a huge *13* candle towering over them. They set the platter down on an old wooden picnic table in front of Sam.

When the singing ended, Willo said to her granddaughter, "Make a wish, and blow!"

Sam shut her eyes, made a wish, and blew.

"What did you wish for?" her brother yelled, causing everyone to laugh.

"She can't tell," Willo said, leaning over and yanking out the dripping candles. Then she whispered into her granddaughter's ear, "But I bet you wished you could already help us run the bakery and orchard."

Sam's heart felt as if it had been cracked in two. She turned away from her grandmother to hide her expression, remembering what she had said earlier in the day.

What if I don't? Sam thought.

"What is this?" Sam asked, as her mom and grandma began to cut the dessert. "I kind of hoped there'd be a cake."

"Here?" Willo laughed. "That's heresy."

"This is a peach-blueberry slab pie," Deana told her daughter. "It's an old secret family recipe."

"It's kind of . . ." Sam stopped, unsure of how to finish the sentence she'd already started. ". . . ummm, not pretty."

Deana kneeled next to her daughter. "You never try it," she said. "You always say the same thing: that it's not pretty enough to eat." She stopped and looked up at her own mom. "That kind of hurts our feelings."

"I'm sorry."

Willo kneeled on Sam's other side, her knees popping. "Think of how our trees look in the winter before they become so beautiful in the spring," she said. "The apple blossoms, the fruit, the green leaves are hidden until they're revealed. And yet they're still beautiful, even in winter. The beauty in the world is more than skin deep."

Deana stood and opened a gallon of vanilla ice cream. She picked up an old scoop and dipped out a huge circle of ice cream that she placed on top of the still-warm pie. It began to melt immediately. "Taste it," her mom urged.

Sam picked at the pie for a second before digging her fork into the crust and the fruit and tasting it. Her eyes widened, and she dug her fork back into the pie.

"Told you," Deana said.

"And your mom and I still have our gift

to give to you," Willo said, "but we want to do it after everybody leaves, OK?"

Sam nodded and continued to eat, asking, "Can I get another piece before it's all gone?"

Willo and Deana smiled broadly and chuckled, cutting another piece.

After everyone had cleaned up and said their goodbyes, three generations sat in front of an empty platter, the lights in the orchards swaying gently in the summer breeze. In the distance, they could hear the waves from the bay and the big lake, Lake Michigan, while crickets hummed in unison in the orchard, tree frogs moaned, and a whip-poor-will called.

Willo stood and walked to the table in back, where she pulled out a wrapped box that had been hidden under her jacket.

"Happy birthday!" Willo and Deana said in unison.

The present was wrapped in brown paper stamped with pies and apples, and it was tied in string. It was the way the Mullinses always wrapped their fresh and frozen pies for customers.

Sam untied the string and ripped open the paper. Her mouth fell open, and she looked up at her mom and grandma, confused. "What is this?" she asked, unable to hide her disappointment.

"It's our family recipe box," Deana said. "We made a new one for you."

"And it's filled with our treasured family recipes," Willo added. "All of our special pies and desserts. We copied some of the original recipes, and your mom and I hand-wrote some of them, too, just for you."

"I don't understand," said Sam. She looked at her mom and grandma. "I was sort of hoping to get my first cell phone. Or even tickets to see Justin Timberlake in Traverse City."

Willo nodded and Deana placed her hand on her daughter's back. They both took a seat next to Sam, as Deana produced a small key from her pocket.

"Here," she said, handing her daughter the shiny key. "We had this made for you, too. Open it."

Although new, the box's wood looked old and burnished, and it glowed in the light. Apples had been carved onto its top and then hand-painted, but the red and green had been scraped and flecked to make it look worn. On the front of the box, under-neath the small lock, was a little sign that read *RECIPE BOX.* Sam took the key and inserted it into the lock, which popped when she turned the key fully. Sam opened the box, which was crammed with index cards. Little tabs reading *PIES, COBBLERS, DONUTS, COFFEE CAKES, COOKIES,* and *JAMS AND JELLIES* marked different sections of the box. Sam pulled out the first card, which read *Peach-Blueberry Slab Pie,* and studied it closely. The recipe was handwritten, in cursive — in the same looping style Sam used — and the ink had been faded and smeared, the words ghosted next to each other. The card was flecked with flour, and there were darker stains, perhaps from vanilla or eggs, as well as clear stains where butter and grease had soaked into it.

"It tells a story, doesn't it?" Willo asked. "Sort of like my face. Like our orchard. That's the original recipe — and recipe card — from your great-great-grandmother, Alice."

She continued: "We have a tradition in this family: my mom passed along her mother's recipe box to me when I turned thirteen, and I gave your mom her own recipe box on her thirteenth birthday. This box continues that tradition." Willo took a deep breath and looked at her granddaughter. "This recipe box is the story of our lives, of where we came from, how we got here, and where we are now." Willo hesitated, her faded blue eyes filling with tears. "These recipes were handwritten and passed down by the women who came before us. These aren't just recipes, Sam. They're our family history. There is nothing more important than family and food. They represent our sustenance and our soul. Food represents how we celebrate, how we come together, how we rejoice, how we mourn, and how we remain one."

Sam looked at her grandma and then at her mom, whose eyes traversed the lighted branches of the fruit trees dancing before her. "The roots of these recipes go back as long as the roots of these trees," Deana said. "And this gift comes with a sacred pact. No one has these recipes. Only the three of us hold keys. We must protect these and pass them on, because they can never be re-created."

"And," Willo added, "the other part of the pact is that the birthday recipient must make the slab pie for the first time alongside those who are passing it along. You've helped us crimp pies in the pantry before, but this will be the first pie you make all on your own. Are you ready?"

Sam nodded.

Willo grabbed a flashlight and Deana a bucket, and the three went out into the dark orchards — the light scanning the rows and then the trees as if they were playing a nighttime game of hide-and-seek. They picked fresh peaches and blueberries and made their way to the kitchen of the pie pantry that sat in an old barn on the other side of the orchard.

Willo placed the recipe card in front of Sam and tied a *Mullins Pie Pantry* apron around her waist, while Deana began to gather ingredients. Finally, the trio started in on the dough.

"Here's how to use a pastry blender," Willo said, showing Sam the old utensil with its wooden handle. "Keep cutting in the shortening and butter until it looks like gravel," she said.

"This is a lot of dough," Sam said, her face already dusted with flour.

"It is," Deana said. "Double crust. For a reason. Right, Mom?"

"That's my cue for a story," Willo laughed. She put her hands on top of Sam's, and the two began to form balls of dough. "We nearly lost all of this — our orchards, our home — many times over the last hundred years. The Depression, family illness, the rise of corporate farming, which threatened small family farms like ours," she said, her voice soft. "And then came the worst winter of our lives: we lost all of our fruit, and many of our trees. We had no way to make a living."

Sam carefully finished rolling the balls of dough, and then the three grabbed paring knives and began to skin, pit, and slice peaches.

Willo continued: "But your great-grandma and I refused to give up, despite the odds. We took all the frozen and preserved fruit we had from the year before and began to make pies. We sold them out of the barn and to churches and local restaurants, and then tourists started showing up. Then we got orders for holidays, and it kept going. It allowed us to get through that horrible year and keep the farm. A few years later, we opened the bakery in the barn and started the U-Pick."

Willo stopped, set down her knife, and picked up the recipe box. "*This* saved our orchard," she said. "The women in our family saved our legacy."

Willo then picked up the index card for the slab pie. "And this was one of the first desserts we made. Did you know your great-great-grandfather started as a baker in Chicago after he emigrated from Germany?"

Sam shook her head.

"Our love of baking is in our DNA. He

made this slab pie because it was what the women in his family made for the men when they worked in the mines and the factories," she continued. "They didn't need a fork or spoon to eat it. They could just eat it with their hands, like a sandwich. And the workers in Chicago — especially the fire-fighters and cops — loved it for the same reason. I had to translate many of these recipes, including this one, from German."

Willo picked up the knife and began to peel a peach in quick, deft motions, finishing one and starting on another before Sam had even gotten halfway around hers.

"But the amazing thing is this pie represents the essence of summer in the Great Lakes," she said. "It is simple and yet so, so rich. It celebrates our bounty in the most delicious way. And the glaze that goes on top . . . it's truly the icing on the pie! It's one of my favorites, and your grandpa just loves it. Now, I'll show you how to roll out the dough. It's not as easy as it might seem."

When they finished, Willo and Deana handed Sam a paring knife and said, "Time to vent the crust. You have to do this so the pie won't explode and run over into the oven. But you have to create your own design."

Sam thought for a moment about creating

her own design, but instead she carved an *M* into the middle — like the Mullins pies always featured — before adding her own mark: three vertical lines underneath the *M.*

"What do those represent?" her mom asked.

"Us," Sam said. "The three of us."

As the slab pie baked, and Willo and Deana cleaned up the kitchen, Sam picked up the recipe card and ran her fingers over the words. She looked around the old kitchen — the stoves, the industrial-sized mixers, the vintage enamel mixing bowls, the worn rolling pins with red handles, the mason jars for jellies and jams, measuring cups stacked everywhere, seared oven mitts hanging off old nails — seeming to see it for the very first time.

When the pie came out of the oven, Sam sliced three pieces and topped them with vanilla ice cream. Just as they were about to slide their forks into the pie, Sam asked, "Can I make one more wish?"

"Of course," her mother said.

"I wish to be the best baker in the world," she said.

Willo and Deana beamed and then took a big bite of pie, their faces exploding in smiles.

"I think you will," Willo said. "I think you

just might outdo all of us."

Willo looked at Sam and asked, "Promise me one thing?"

Sam nodded tentatively. "OK."

"Promise me," she said, thinking of her granddaughter in the tree earlier in the day, seeming to read her thoughts, "that even if you leave to go out into the world, you will make this pie whenever you want a taste of home and a reminder of our family and our history."

Willo hesitated and continued. "And promise you will make this if you want to prove to somebody it doesn't matter what anything or anyone looks like, but that it's what's inside that counts. Promise?"

"I promise," Sam said, before her face fell. Her eyes scanned the recipe card. "Oh, no. I got a big blueberry stain in the middle of the card."

Willo picked it up and showed it to Deana, and the two women smiled.

"Now it has your history on it," she said, her voice emotional. "Now the recipe has new memories. Blue ones."

Sam laughed.

"Just like your teeth, Grandma."

THREE

Sam pulled the slab pie out of the oven, testing it with a toothpick.

"Comes out clean," she said to herself. "It's done."

She looked at Suzette, crossed her fingers, and sighed, just as Chef Dimples stormed into the kitchen, followed by a cameraman and producer.

"What's that?"

"A peach-blueberry slab pie," Sam said, nervously straightening the apron over her chef's whites. "It's a family recipe." Sam thought of her grandfather. It had been one of his favorites, and her grandma had made it for him on every special occasion.

"Why isn't it one of *my* family recipes?" Chef Dimples asked.

You don't have any family recipes, Sam wanted to yell. *There isn't one recipe written down. Your family owned banks. You had a full-time cook.* Sam's stomach clenched. She knew what he was going to say next, the line he told everyone.

"My family invented blueberry pie," he said, staring at her.

That's not just a line, Sam thought. *That's a bold-faced lie.*

"I know, Chef Dimples," Sam said.

"And what is this?" Chef Dimples asked, pointing a finger, which Sam couldn't help but notice had clear polish on it — *so* not *the hands of a baker,* she thought — at the *M* and the three dashes she had cut into the crust to vent it.

"It's supposed to be dimples," Sam lied. "I'm a terrible artist. My apologies, Chef Dimples."

He glared at Sam, his green eyes flashing in the lights the cameraman was testing in the kitchen. "I'm not eating that," he said. "It's ugly. It will look terrible on TV."

"Taste it," Sam pleaded. "Please."

He continued to stare at her.

"Please, Chef Dimples," Sam corrected.

He smiled like a snake, his dimples flashing, and glanced at Suzette, who immediately rushed over carrying some plates.

Sam cut three slices before topping it with whipped cream — "Homemade," she said — the cream melting on top of the golden crust, the steaming fruit sliding across the pink Depression glass. Suzette handed out forks, and Chef Dimples slid his into the pie.

With the very first bite, his eyes widened and for the briefest of moments, he shut them, savoring the taste.

Sam's heart leapt as she immediately recognized the reaction.

It's the same one I had when I was thirteen and tasted the pie for the first time, she thought, containing a smile. *He knows it's good.*

Chef Dimples held out his plate to Sam.

"I can't serve this," he said, unable to look at her. "It won't look good on camera. Hurry up and bake me a blueberry pie . . . and *don't* vent it. Put one of those cardboard cutouts of my face over the pie." He turned to the producer. "Have Lara Spencer say something like, 'That looks way too good to eat. People will eat that up. Literally. And let's shoot in the bakery. It's too dirty back here."

He turned to Sam. "Get my pie ready," he said. "And clean this mess up."

The producer and cameraman didn't move as Chef Dimples exited the kitchen. They were finishing their pie.

"Can I get another slice?" the burly cameraman asked. "Been up since four. This is

71

crazy good."

Sam nodded, still in shock, and began to cut him another piece.

"This is the best pie I've ever had," the producer — a middle-aged woman in jeans and a blazer — agreed, her lips and teeth tinged blue. "Seriously. This is amazing. Tastes like . . . heaven. Like something my grandma would have made."

"Thank you," Sam said, suddenly picturing herself as a girl high in the peach tree.

"Where did you learn to bake?" the producer continued, holding out her plate for another piece. "You just can't learn to make this kind of recipe, or bake like this. It's a gift. It's been handed down to you."

The sincerity of her words caused Sam's eyes to well with tears. "Thank you," she said. "The women in my family taught me. This is a recipe from . . ."

"Clean this mess up now," Chef Dimples shouted, rushing into the kitchen once again when he realized no one was following him. He grabbed the dish out of Sam's hand. "And throw that pie away. Nobody wants to eat that."

He reached for the cameraman's plate, but the stocky man squared up his shoulders and gripped the dish even more tightly. "You're not taking this away from me," he said, his mouth full.

Without warning, Chef Dimples picked up the slab pie and slid it into the trash as everyone watched in shock.

"Ow!" he yelled, forgetting the tin was still hot from the oven and rushing over to the sink to rinse his hand in cold water. "Now make *my* blueberry pie."

Sam looked into the trash, her pie a heap of blue and peach rubble. Suzette slinked into a corner, while the producer and cameraman watched, their mouths — still full — open wide.

Sam could feel her spirit leave her body. Her eyes seemed to go blank in front of her. Her ears began to ring loudly as they had earlier when the trash trucks went by, but — just as quickly — they went silent, and she could hear her grandmother say the following very clearly, as if she were standing beside her in the pie pantry:

Promise me that even if you leave to go out into the world, you will make this pie whenever you want a taste of home and a reminder of our family and our history. And promise you will make this if you want to prove to somebody it doesn't matter what anything or anyone looks like, but that it's what's inside that counts. Promise?

"You didn't invent blueberry pie."

Sam heard the words leave her mouth, but she couldn't feel herself saying them.

"What did you say?"

"Have you ever even picked a blueberry?" Sam continued. She could feel her mom and grandma beside her, giving her strength. "Have you actually ever cooked something for someone simply because you loved them and wanted to give them a piece of your heart?"

"Excuse me?"

"You're a fraud. You're a flaky crust with nothing inside."

Sam stopped, took off her apron, and tossed it on the floor.

"I quit," she yelled, walking toward the swinging doors leading to the bakery. "Make your own damn pie." Suddenly, Sam stopped cold and turned.

"I'm sorry," Sam added. "I should have said, 'I quit, Chef Dimples.' "

And, with that, Sam exited, the scent of the slab pie trailing behind her, out the bakery and onto the streets of New York.

Peach-Blueberry Slab Pie

Ingredients for Pie

3 1/4 cups all-purpose flour
1 teaspoon salt
1 cup butter, cold
1 large egg yolk
3/4 cup plus 1 to 2 tablespoons 2% milk
1 cup granulated sugar
3 tablespoons cornstarch
5 cups sliced fresh peaches
3 cups fresh blueberries

Ingredients for Glaze

1 1/4 cups powdered sugar
1/2 teaspoon vanilla extract
5 to 6 teaspoons 2% milk

Directions for Pie

In a large bowl, combine the flour and salt; cut in the butter until crumbly. Whisk the egg yolk with 3/4 cup of the milk; gradually add to the flour mixture, tossing with a fork until the dough forms a ball. Add additional milk, 1 tablespoon at a time, if necessary.

Divide the dough into two portions so that one is slightly larger than the other; wrap each in plastic wrap. Refrigerate 1 hour or until easy to handle.

Preheat the oven to 375°F. Roll out the

larger portion of dough between two large sheets of lightly floured waxed paper into an 18 × 13-inch rectangle. Transfer to an ungreased 15 × 10 × 1-inch baking pan. Press the dough onto the bottom of the pan and up the sides; trim the pastry to the edges of the pan.

In a large bowl, combine the sugar and cornstarch. Add the peaches and blueberries and toss to coat. Spoon into the pastry.

Roll out the remaining dough and place it over the filling. Fold the bottom pastry over the edge of the top pastry; seal with a fork. Prick the top with a fork to vent.

Bake 45 to 55 minutes, or until the crust is golden brown. Cool completely on a wire rack.

Directions for Glaze

Combine the powdered sugar, vanilla, and enough milk to achieve a drizzling consistency; drizzle over the pie. Cut the pie into squares.

(Note: Your favorite seasonal fruits may be used for this slab pie. Raspberry-rhubarb is particularly delicious. Some fruits, such as raspberries and rhubarbs, will require more sugar in the filling.)

PART TWO:
CIDER DONUTS

FOUR

Summer 2017

Sam checked her boarding pass, smiling at the fruitful irony of the words stamped on it, indicating her final destination: *Cherry Capital Airport.*

She was heading home — *Tail between my legs,* Sam thought. *I feel like a complete failure. How did the job of my dreams turn into such a nightmare?*

As the plane took off and Sam watched New York City grow smaller, she recalled how big it had seemed when she arrived to start culinary school. The city had even made her bigger-than-life grandma — who had accompanied her to New York to get her settled — seem tiny and out of place.

Sam remembered that after her mom and grandma had left Sam on her own, she had pulled down the creaky Murphy bed in her studio apartment, which was one quarter the size of her bedroom at home, and begun to cry. Sirens wailed, people screamed, taxicabs honked, construction noise echoed. As Sam sobbed, a scent — so powerful, so familiar, so reminiscent of home — enveloped her tiny apartment. She stood, sniffing, trailing the scent like Doris used to do in the orchard when she was tracking a varmint. Sam followed her nose until it led her to one of the two cupboards that stood guard over a small sink, two-burner stove, compact refrigerator, and oven barely big enough to hold a frozen pizza. A grease-stained bag, emblazoned with the orchard and pie pantry's logo, sat atop the set of new mismatched plates her mom had just bought her at Fishs Eddy, an adorable home-goods store they had stumbled on while wandering the city. The vintage-inspired dishes, glassware, and linens reminded them of the dishes they used in the pie shop and bakery back home.

The bag was tied with string, and a hand-written tag dangled. Sam untied the package and lifted the tag to her eyes. Her grandmother's looping handwriting read, *Know your heart feels it has a big hole in it right now. So does ours. Here's a taste of home. These should help fill it. You will never be a misfit as long as you follow your heart. We love you and are so proud of you. Mom &*

Grandma.

Sam opened the bag and screamed in delight to see that it was filled with one of her favorite treats: homemade apple cider donuts and donut holes. The bottom of the package was scattered with donut remnants, misshapen pieces of dough that fell apart in the fryer that the pie pantry had nicknamed "misfits." A recipe card for the donuts, written in her grandmother's same looping cursive, was inside. Sam lifted the recipe card and ran her fingers over the writing, remembering her thirteenth birthday. The card smelled like cinnamon, sugar, apples, and fried dough. She popped a donut hole into her mouth and shut her eyes, savoring the sweet dough, which melted in her mouth.

How did they sneak this here without me knowing? Sam had wondered.

Sam had made the donuts for her schoolmates one evening after they'd had too much wine and sneaked back into the school's kitchen to make something to quell their munchies.

"These are amazing!" her friends had all said, as she made and fried the donuts. "Why didn't you ever make these before now?"

Sam couldn't admit to them that she was

a bit embarrassed by many of her family recipes: the donuts and dump cakes, the slab pie, the penchant for either too much sugar or too much rhubarb. Her goal was to be a pastry chef, a first-class baker, not . . .

Sam winced at the thought that always crossed her mind, the one that made her feel like a traitor: *a self-taught pie maker.*

"Would you care for something to drink, ma'am?"

The flight attendant's voice shook Sam from her memory.

"Water," she said. "Thank you."

Sam smiled, once again paralleling the irony of the flight attendant's words and her final destination: *Michigan. The Great Lakes,* Sam thought. *Water, water, everywhere.*

Sam sipped her water and suddenly sat up straight, one thought she'd never had before suddenly filling her mind, making her heart beat faster.

How hard must it have been for my mom and grandma to leave me in New York, alone, all on my own? I wasn't the only brave one. They were, too. They wanted me to fulfill my dreams.

Sam looked down at her water, and then at the words *Cherry Capital Airport* on her boarding pass, jutting from the seatback pocket in front of her.

Even if it meant leaving home and never coming back.

Sam felt her cell vibrate, and she reached into her jacket pocket to fish it free.

Miss you, Unicorn! Lily, one of her two roommates, texted. *It's already too quiet.*

Miss you, too, Sam texted back immediately.

And we're hungry!!!! Fiona, her other roommate, added to the group text.

Sam laughed. The two girls, who were born and raised in New York City, couldn't microwave a bowl of soup or fix a grilled cheese sandwich. Lily and Fiona were so used to eating out their whole lives, they believed food simply arrived in front of you whenever you wanted. When Sam began to cook for them, they were astonished to see an actual meal prepared from scratch.

You're like a unicorn, Lily had said, wide-eyed, the first week after they'd moved into an apartment together in Brooklyn, Sam thrilled for the company and more square footage than her studio had provided. They were drinking wine, celebrating new jobs and their new place, and Sam was making roasted whitefish with capers and lemons and an apple pie. The three had cracked up at Lily's statement, more so after a few drinks when Fiona made a tinfoil horn and attached it to Sam's forehead. The nickname had stuck, just like the horn.

I'll send food, Sam texted, *and money to help with rent until I get my head on straight and am ready to look for another job. I promise!!*

No worries, Lily texted. *My dad said he'll kick in extra because you saved him so much $$$$ cooking for us all the time! Have you told your family yet?*

Sam's heart quickened. *No,* she texted. *Will be a big surprise.*

Next time it will be your shop, your rules, your pie, Fiona added. *Pie = Love. WE WILL SEE YOU SOON! HAVE A GREAT VACA WITH THE FAM!*

Sam's eyes filled with tears. ♡ ♡ ♡, she texted.

She wiped her eyes with her jacket sleeve and felt her cell vibrate again.

C'mon, girls, Sam thought, before looking down at her phone. *You're killing me.*

Trish told me what happened and gave me your number. I'll miss you but don't blame you. Let me know where you end up. And I'll root for the Tigers this fall in the playoffs.

Sam's heart quickened. *A text from Angelo?*

She was still staring at the phone, and a photo of Angelo wearing a Tigers ball cap popped up, with a text that read, *Mets vs.*

Tigers! He was standing in front of Citi Field, pointing at the Detroit logo on his head, laughing like a kid, his dark eyes twinkling, his dark curls bouncing.

And those dimples, Sam thought. *Now those are some dimples.*

Looks good on you! Sam texted. *I'll make you a Tigers fan yet!*

My friends said they'll kill me if I wear this the whole game, Angelo replied. *People are yelling bad names at me, Sam! I blame you! Lol.*

And then: *Keep in touch. Please.*

Sam's heart again quickened.

Please, he wrote. Please. *What do I say?*

Without thinking, Sam found a thumbs-up emoji and hit send. As soon as she did, she immediately began to beat herself up.

You idiot, Sam thought. *An emotionless emoji?! A thumbs-up? Am I a ten-year-old?*

Angelo sent a matching thumbs-up back, and Sam's stomach sank, even more so as the plane began to descend.

"We need to take your cup of water, ma'am. We'll be landing soon."

Sam jumped again at the flight attendant's voice. She handed her the cup and then looked out the airplane window at all the water below.

"Lake Michigan," Sam sighed, her breath fogging the window. "Truly a great lake."

She snapped a photo and texted it to her roomies, who immediately responded, *Is that the ocean? Where are you?*

Most East and West Coasters had the same reaction to Lake Michigan: it was so grand in size, so beautiful, its beaches so sandy, its dunes so spectacular, it had to be an ocean.

About to land, Sam texted. *Not an ocean. Lake Michigan. This used to be my swimming pool.*

The plane banked left and started its final descent. As it did, the entire coast of northwestern Michigan's Lower Peninsula came into view. It was early morning, and the summer sun made the water sparkle as if the state were wearing a rhinestone gown. Water not only surrounded the state but also ran through it: big bays and winding rivers, little creeks and ponds, marinas filled with bobbing boats and sailboats whose white masts matched the gulls that soared overhead.

Sam held up the cell to snap another picture and, as she did, realized her hand was much like her state. Not only was Michigan called the Mitten because it was shaped like a hand, with Traverse City and Suttons Bay sitting where the pinkie was located, but its water resembled the veins in Sam's hand, traversing the state, giving Michigan — its people, its produce, its land, its bounty — life. Water was Michigan's lifeblood.

Sam looked at her hand — dry, red, nails boyishly short from her work.

They look more and more like my mom's and grandma's hands every day, Sam thought. *When did that happen?*

When the plane landed, Sam waited to grab her tiny bag from the overhead bin, suddenly realizing how little she had truly accumulated during her time in New York. Sam always wore a uniform to work, and had little money for extras and nowhere to store anything if she bought it. She lived mostly outside her apartment, spending time either at work or in the city after spending most of her time at school. Her only big acquisitions had been a few expensive pieces of bakeware and cookware she'd picked up at specialty shops in the city.

I was Tiny House *before people thought it was cool,* Sam thought. She immediately pictured her family's home and orchard, grand, wide open, breathtaking.

Distracted in thought, Sam pulled the

small suitcase from the overhead compartment, bumping a man behind her and knocking his reading glasses from the bridge of his nose. She waved an embarrassed *Sorry* at him and began to wheel her small bag off the plane.

So cute, so small, so clean, so quiet, Sam thought, walking into the terminal. *So not LaGuardia.*

Indeed, the little airport was the perfect *Welcome to Pure Michigan!* hug for first-time visitors. The terminal was an Arts and Crafts–inspired design, which encompassed the openness and natural setting of the Grand Traverse region. A welcome area reminiscent of a northwoods lodge, complete with a glowing stone fireplace, greeted visitors, and the airport's homage to Frank Lloyd Wright was visible in the cherry wood, copper light fixtures, stone wainscoting, and stained glass.

I gotta give it to you, Michigan, Sam thought, her face breaking into a slight smile. *You have the trademark on quaint.*

Michigan, Sam repeated in her head, this time hearing Angelo's voice saying the word to her.

Sam stood in a small line, waiting to get her rental car, and exited a few minutes later to find it, one of many compacts lined up in the lot. She tossed her suitcase into the trunk, jumped in, started the car, began to back out, and then suddenly braked, her heart racing.

I think I've not only forgotten how to get to the highway but also how to drive, Sam thought, her hands clutching the wheel. *What's it been? Two years?*

Sam suddenly remembered her thirteenth birthday, when her brother had begged her to grow up so she could drive him around town, free them both of being reliant on their bikes, their legs . . .

Our imaginations, Sam added. *We wanted to be anywhere but here.*

A car honked and Sam jumped. She looked in the rearview mirror, and her rental was still in park, halfway out of the parking spot and jutting into the lot's driving lane. She quickly put the car into drive and hit the gas too fast, and the car jumped forward. Sam slammed on the brakes and then put her face into her hands and started to laugh. When she lifted her head, Sam caught a glimpse of herself in the mirror. Her blond hair was pulled back into a ponytail, long wisps having worked loose and trailing down her neck and the side of her face. She blew her bangs out of her eyes, an annoying habit she had acquired from having her hair controlled underneath a chef's hat or hairnet for so long. She was paler than she had ever been, especially during the summer, and red rimmed her blue eyes from the recent stress and early morning flight.

But there was also something different about her appearance that Sam couldn't quite put her finger on. She looked at herself in the mirror, staring intensely for so long that she scared herself.

Do I look different? she thought. *Or do I just look different in a different setting? Have I changed that much?* She averted her eyes but looked at herself one more time. *Who am I?*

Sam shook her head, nabbed her cell, pulled up her map app, and waited for the voice to navigate her to the highway.

As Sam drove through Traverse City, she immediately noticed there was also something different about the largest city close to where she had grown up. Summer traffic was snarled, cars barely moving, and the city's once-empty blocks were filled with ethnic restaurants, wine bars, craft breweries, and ritzy condos. It wasn't New York City — nothing was — but it was bustling, alive, energetic.

Sam slowed in traffic, her head bobbing

left and right like one of those dogs people put in their back windows, and again caught her reflection in the mirror.

Maybe the city's just grown up, Sam thought. *Like me.*

Sam neared the coastline and looked at the endless blue water. She opened the car window, inhaled, the smell of water filling her lungs, then stuck her head out of the window like her grandparents' happy Lab, Doris, used to do and said, "Hello, Michigan!"

She turned onto M-22 and headed north toward home, Suttons Bay.

M-22 was the name of the old highway that looped along Lake Michigan and through many of its prettiest resort towns. The road, which ran directly alongside the water, offered breathtaking views of the lake and its bays and was a popular drive for tourists. The moniker itself — M-22 — was now a popular Michigan trademark and was featured on bumper stickers, T-shirts, sweatshirts, and ball caps. For many Michiganders and tourists, though, the symbol represented something even deeper, something nearly spiritual: that this was as close to heaven as they might actually come every year, in terms of both northerly direction and beauty. The resort towns that dotted

M-22, like Northport, the summer home of chef Mario Batali, and Leland, known as Fishtown, were throwbacks, as quaint as Mayberry and as pretty as a vintage post-card.

Sam continued to drive in slow-moving traffic, her jaw dropping as billboard after billboard screamed the area to be one of the nation's most beautiful and popular tourist destinations.

TOP 10 MUST-SEE!
NEW YORK TIMES

YOU HAVEN'T SEEN SUMMER
UNTIL YOU'VE SEEN MICHIGAN!
USA TODAY

HEAVEN ON EARTH!
GOOD MORNING AMERICA

The world is now screaming our praises, Sam thought, chuckling, before realizing her choice of pronoun. *Our? Do I have the right to say* our *any longer after leaving?*

Sam turned on the radio to distract her mind, and an oldies song blared through the speakers. She looked down to see that the radio was tuned to Oldies 101.

No, Sam thought. *It's a sign.*

She gripped the wheel.

Or a warning.

Oldies 101 was the station that filled the pie pantry every day of Sam's life. The music — Elvis, Rosemary Clooney, Dean Martin, Frank Sinatra — was the sound-track to her childhood. Her grandma used to sing nearly every old tune out loud — *and out of tune,* Sam thought — as she made pies, swaying her hips and dancing as she crimped crusts.

Sam held her hand over the radio dial, nearly changing the station, but she turned it up instead when the song changed to "Tutti Frutti" by Little Richard.

How appropriate, Sam thought. *Do you sense I'm in the area, Grandma?*

Drivers began to pull off the highway to take photos or get gas, and the traffic slowly thinned. Sam picked up the pace, the wind sending her hair flying, and, before she knew it, she was singing along, suddenly feeling like a tourist.

The sights were familiar to Sam, but they seemed new to her, brighter, prettier, quainter. As she neared Suttons Bay, she slowed her car and, like other tourists, pulled off to the side of the road to enjoy the view.

The water in the bays that sat inland from

Lake Michigan were the color of the Caribbean: emerald green fading to aqua near the shoreline, which darkened to navy as the water deepened. Sunlight illuminated the flat, sandy bottom of the bay, and docks jutted straight out past the shallows — hundreds of yards into the water — and held boats, big and small, moored in the deeper water, alongside Jet-Skis and kayaks. Some homeowners had built little bars in the water, where they could sit and watch the sunset, while others had blown up giant rafts big enough to hold ten people.

As if pulled by a magnet, Sam suddenly got out of the car and went running toward the water. She kicked off her flip-flops and walked into the bay, forgetting how cold the water was even in summer, letting out a surprised yelp. Though this water was chilly, the bay was still warmer than Lake Michigan and significantly warmer than Lake Superior, where reaching seventy degrees was considered spa-like. The bay water got a chance to warm, especially in the shallows. Sam dipped her hand into the water and watched it run through her fingers, little diamonds sifting through them. Minnows, no bigger than a comma, nibbled at Sam's toes. Sam looked out over the bay and her heart leapt.

It's so beautiful, she thought. *So pretty it almost looks fake.*

Sam stepped out of the water, let her feet dry on the sand, picked up her shoes, and headed back to the car, driving north until she finally turned away from the water and onto Bayview Point. The little two-lane road disappeared at the top of a winding hill, which was deceptively tall. Her tiny rental slowed, chugged, and groaned as it drove up, up, up until the view opened up to a 360-degree panorama: the little town of Suttons Bay sat in the near distance at the bottom of the hill, while farmland and vineyards stretched out around it like a patchwork quilt. The blue-green bay sat in the foreground, with the tip of Suttons Bay pointing into the water as if it were hitch-hiking. Glacially formed Old Mission Penin-sula separated Traverse Bay into east and west bays, and the tourist haven, which was filled with top-notch wineries, sat in the distance. Sam smiled.

Old Mission Peninsula resembles a sea horse swimming, she always thought as a kid.

On the other side, Lake Michigan shim-mered in all its glory, sparkling in the sum-mer sun, stretching to infinity.

Sam slowed her car, and dust swirled, as

if Pig-Pen had come to greet her. The pavement suddenly ended at the top of the hill and became a dirt road.

I'm home, Sam thought, looking at the sign directly in front of her car.

Nothing's changed.

Welcome to Fruit Heaven!
Very Cherry Orchards — First Right
Mullins Family Orchards and Pie Pantry
— Straight Ahead

Bayview Point was filled with orchards; the glacier-formed ridge was the ideal spot — in terms of temperature, moisture, and location — in which to grow the very best fruit.

God took His time to carve out the perfect place, Sam remembered her grandma always saying.

Indeed, the hilltop was akin to a real cherry on top of a stunningly picturesque sundae. Bayview Point was home to two of northern Michigan's most popular orchards and tourist stops: Very Cherry Orchards and her family's Orchard and Pie Pantry. The first half of the hill was dense with rows of tart cherry trees, and the limbs of the small, bushy trees were bursting with cherries, red arms waving at Sam as if to greet her home.

In the spring, these trees were filled with white blossoms that slowly turned as pink as a perfect rosé, their beauty so tender that it used to make Sam's heart ache when she would run through the orchards as part of her high school cross-country training.

Often, when Sam ran, the spring winds would tear at the tender flowers and make it look as though it were snowing in the midst of a beautiful warm day.

Like every good native, Sam knew cherries had a long history in northern Michigan. French settlers had cherry trees in their gardens, and a missionary planted the first cherry trees on Old Mission Peninsula.

Very Cherry Orchards grew nearly 100 acres of Montmorency tart cherries in addition to Balaton cherries, black sweet cherries, plums, and nectarines. They sold their fruit to U-Pickers as well as large companies that made pies, but they had also become famous for their tart cherry juice concentrate, now sold at grocery and health food stores across the United States. People loved it for its natural health benefits, rich in antioxidants. When Sam was growing up, all the old locals used to sit around the pie shop drinking coffee and gossiping about how the cherries made their joints feel better, whispering how they hoped "the outside world" never discovered their secret.

Sam would refill their cups, silently scoffing at such insular thinking.

A car honked, and Sam jumped. She looked in the mirror, and a snaking line of traffic disappeared down the hill. Sam checked her watch; it was only ten A.M.

Maybe they were right, Sam thought, easing her car into drive. *Maybe some things should remain a secret from the outside world and stay as they were.*

Sam eased her car down the dirt road. Her mouth fell as she took in the natural beauty, her mind used to the concrete and steel of New York City.

It was an achingly beautiful day: the red cherries on the green limbs set against a backdrop of blue skies that only a lack of humidity could create and, in the distance, clear water as far as the eye could see.

Sam drove past Very Cherry's orchards, still taking in the scenery, and that was when she saw it, the scene causing her to hit the brakes too quickly, her rental spitting gravel.

Her family's orchard and pie pantry stood before her, and Sam felt herself catapulted back in time.

Greeting visitors was a mammoth, wood-carved sign, MULLINS FAMILY ORCHARDS

AND PIE PANTRY, the name appearing in the branches of a large tree, accented with smiling apples. The sun over the tree was a pie. *Pie = Love* was written in the roots of the tree's underground.

Set back from the driveway, behind the sign, was a tiny log cabin and an ancient Ford Model T truck that still looked brand-new. The back of the truck was overflowing with baskets of fresh apples and peaches, along with petunias trailing over the side. The log cabin, with its lopsided front door and old wood bleached gray from the weather, was Sam's great-great-grandparents' original home, the one they had lived in when they began to settle this land.

At the edge of the entrance sat a small shed. The shed was actually an old bus barn that Sam's mother and grandmother used to take cover in when waiting for the school bus in the never-ending snow that blanketed northern Michigan from November through April. The shed had been salvaged and restored, and high school kids now served samples of apple cider and homemade donuts to the snaking lines of tourists waiting to park.

"Misfits!" two smiling teenagers in aprons called from the shed as the cute curtains —

made from vintage fabric featuring cherries, pine trees, happy deer, cardinals, and boats bobbing on the water — fluttered in the breeze. "Who wants a misfit?"

Sam smiled, slowed, and waved at the teenagers.

"Want a misfit?" a boy with braces yelled from the shed.

They have no clue who I am, Sam thought. Before she could say a word, the boy sprang forth like a baby deer, his legs too long for his body, making it seem as if he might tumble at any moment. He was carrying a red plate lined with a paper towel. As he got closer, Sam could see that the plate was filled with odd-shaped pieces of dough covered in cinnamon and sugar.

"Misfit?" the boy asked with a smile and slight lisp, the sun glinting off his silver teeth.

"Sure," Sam said, taking a piece that was shaped like a parenthesis. Sam put the warm fried dough into her mouth, and it melted. She licked the cinnamon sugar off her lips. "Thank you."

"Delicious, right?" the boy asked. Sam had to force herself not to chuckle at the boy's braces-induced lisp. "They're making the apple cider donuts fresh right now. You can park in the Fuji Apple lot near the door."

Sam knew what he was going to say next, and she said it out loud and in unison with the teen.

"Follow your nose," they said together.

"How'd you know that?" the boy asked.

"ESP," Sam laughed, nabbing another piece of misshapen dough.

Sam pulled forward. *How many times did I say that,* she wondered, thinking back on her high school summers when she did anything and everything: giving out samples, crimping pies, handing out baskets, weighing fruit.

Sam parked in the Fuji lot — every parking area was designated by a different type or variety of fruit — and when she emerged from the car, the smell of fresh, frying donuts filled the summer air.

Sam checked her appearance in the mirror, took a deep breath, and headed inside. Picnic tables sat on a large concrete patio underneath a bright awning outside the pie pantry, an old barn painted, appropriately enough, barn red. Sam opened the heavy, old wood door with a grunt, and the smell of donuts intensified. The corridor that led to the pie pantry was lined with antiques and memorabilia from the orchards and the bakery: vintage cooking utensils, farming equipment, baskets, old photos, antique orchard ladders. Uneven wooden shelves were filled with mismatched cups and saucers, as well as empty Ball jars, which the pie pantry used to serve their apple cider.

Sam walked into the pie pantry, a cavernous space with a concrete floor. A mix of Formica and wood tables filled the space, along with even more memorabilia covering the walls and hanging from the ceiling. The tables were filled with visitors and locals eating donuts, drinking coffee and cider, steeling themselves with sugar before they headed to the U-Pick or walked out with pies for their summer visitors.

The cement floors were painted with childlike images of smiling apples, dancing peaches, waving trees, and happy pies, all forming a Yellow Brick Road–esque path leading to the back of the barn, where the pie pantry and kitchen were located. Sam followed the cartoonish path, which always made her feel like a little girl playing hopscotch, and into another huge, open space, separated by an ancient barn-wood counter that spanned some thirty feet. A series of girls were stationed behind cash registers, and the counter was lined with free samples of desserts: apple pie, peach pie, jams, and apple cider donuts. A sign overhead read: EVERYTHING IS HOME-MADE! BY HAND! JUST LIKE GRANDMA MAKES!

Another large, hand-painted sign reading DON'T LEAVE WITHOUT A SLICE OF HEAVEN! hung over a doorway that led to a room filled with desserts, just baked and ready to take home, lined up on wooden shelves and labeled *FRESH APPLE, FRESH CARAMEL APPLE, FRESH APPLE CRISP, FRESH APPLE TURNOVERS, FRESH APPLE CIDER* while freezers were filled with frozen pies. More shelves were filled with the pie pantry's jams and jellies as well as their famed homemade caramel and chocolate sauces. And wood crates and cute baskets were overflowing with apples, peaches, and plums.

Women worked in a kitchen behind the registers, rolling dough, crimping pies, slicing apples, frying donuts, proving that every single thing was, indeed, handmade, just as the sign said.

This might have been one of the first open kitchens, Sam finally realized, thinking of how trendy it was in New York restaurants for diners to see their food prepared in front of them.

That was when Sam saw her grandma,

shimmying to an old song as she fried donuts, her behind moving, her head bobbing. A big smile engulfed Sam's face, and she watched her in silence for a moment.

The women making and baking pies worked separately but in unison, an assembly line of humans instead of parts, each handling a different task expertly. Oldies music played in the background, and, from a distance, the scene resembled a beautifully choreographed routine by Pilobolus, a dance group Sam had seen in the city.

The women all chatted and laughed as they worked. The workers were as varied as the pies they made: some were round and red, some blond and peach complexioned, some as long and firm as a rhubarb stem.

They seem so happy, Sam thought, watching them work. *Was I ever this happy at my job?*

"May I help you, ma'am?" a teen asked Sam.

"No," Sam started. "I'm here . . ."

Before Sam had even gotten the first few words out of her mouth, she saw her grandmother stop cold, and, without turning, she called, "Sam? Is that you?"

"Hi, Grandma," Sam called.

Willo turned and blinked in disbelief, before plopping a pile of dough she was holding onto a table dusted with flour. The flour rose into the air like a ghost. "Our baby's home!" Willo yelled, running toward her granddaughter, arms wide. "What a surprise!"

Willo hugged Sam, squeezing her until Sam had to say, "I can't breathe, Grandma."

They both laughed, and Willo held Sam at arm's length and studied her closely, her eyes filling with tears.

"You look tired," Willo said.

"Got up before dawn," Sam said. "Early flight."

"How's your job?"

"Fine," Sam lied.

"Is he treating you OK?"

"Yes, Grandma," Sam lied again.

"What are you doing here?"

"I got some unexpected vacation time," Sam said. She hesitated. "Chef Dimples said I had earned a few days off."

Willo eyed her granddaughter warily. She opened her mouth but then clamped it shut, inhaled, and smiled.

"Chef Dimples," she muttered under her breath. "What a name."

Willo studied her granddaughter's eyes.

"Am I on trial, Grandma?" Sam said with a laugh. "This feels like the time everyone thought I made that peach pie for Jimmy

Jenkins."

"And didn't remove the pits," Willo interrupted. "Or add sugar. But did add lots of salt. And put pieces of newspaper in the crust . . ."

"Why would I do that?" Sam asked, eyes wide, hands in the air.

"Because he stole your bike, remember?" Willo said, a smile crossing her face.

"OK, Grandma, OK," Sam said. "But I'm not lying this time."

Willo nodded. "Good. Well, it's a wonderful, unexpected surprise." She stopped. "How long are you here for?" Before Sam could answer, Willo said, "Doesn't matter. I don't want to know how long, I just want to celebrate every moment you're here." She stopped again. "My baby," she said in a voice choked with emotion. "My baby's home."

For a moment, the two studied each other closely, no words spoken, as if they were at a museum and standing before a painting they had never seen. Willo was dressed in a version of her standard attire. She wore a crocheted cap that resembled a cherry pie resting on her head, complete with a lattice crust and crimped edges. A too-big apron engulfed her body and hung like a drape down to her shins. As always, a colorful pair of sneakers — these, white with pink laces — adorned her feet.

Her grandmother was cute as always, but Sam noticed she looked different, too: Willo's eyes were faded blue now, the color of blueberries picked too early, and her shoulders were slumped, her back hunched, the years of labor showing on her tiny frame. And yet there was a strength in her presence, a light that seemed to shine forth, and Sam could feel her grandmother's love and energy vibrate and shimmer like the light that filtered in through the wavy glass windows of the barn.

Sam glanced at her grandmother's hands, red and dry. Arthritis and hard work had made the knuckles resemble tree roots and yet her ring finger remained largely unaffected, as if she'd made a secret pact with it so she would never have to remove her wedding ring.

How long has it been since Grandpa died? Sam thought, doing quick math in her head. *Can it be six years already?* Sam's heart dropped. She thought of all she'd done in the past six years, the friends she'd met, the places she'd been, everything she'd experienced, all new, exciting. *I'm just starting,* Sam thought, looking closely at her grandma, before glancing down. *She's continuing without the love of her life.*

Willo caught Sam looking at her ring. "Anyone special in your life?" she asked. "Besides Chef . . . Oh, I can't even say his name without rolling my eyes."

Sam immediately thought of Angelo.

His dimples, Sam thought, her heart racing. *I wonder if he texted me again?*

"No," Sam said. "Too busy between work and insane roommates. Not lots of time for love."

"Always time for love," Willo said with a wink, before changing the subject. "I wish I had known you were coming. I would have planned a party, or made all your favorites."

"I think you have your hands full with the big party coming up," Sam said.

"I hope you stay for it," Willo said.

Sam didn't answer.

Willo turned, her eyes searching the bakery. "Your mom must be in the office. We have a lot of restaurant deliveries scheduled today," she continued. "Want to go find her? And your dad is in the orchards. And your brother just left again for college last week. He started school already."

"I know," Sam said. "He's so excited to move into the fraternity house at Michigan. Been texting me pictures. His room's already trashed. Don't tell Mom and Dad after all the cleaning and decorating they did for him. It'll have to be fumigated in May."

Willo laughed. "Are you tired? Do you want to go unpack and rest for a bit?"

"No, I'm sort of jazzed from the drive, the coffee, and the sugar I just had eating the misfits."

"Speaking of which," Willo said, nodding toward the kitchen, "I have to finish donut duty. Do you want to help?"

"I'd love to," Sam said.

Willo grabbed Sam's hand and walked her back to the open kitchen. A group of women who had seen Sam grow up before their eyes swooped in for hugs, asking about her job and life in the big city.

Sam began to share stories of her life, the women listening as they made dough, cored apples, and deep-fried donuts.

"Remember how to make these?" one of the women asked Sam.

"You eyeball the cider," Sam said in unison with a half-dozen women, who all broke into a fit of giggles when Willo said, "Hey, that's not funny."

"Your recipe was never detailed," Sam joked. "And you must have repeated that line to all of us a million times."

"That's how it was written in our recipe

box," Willo protested, stopping and looking around at the group, who were still chortling. Willo turned and looked at Sam. "You know, sometimes that applies to life, too. You think you need to live it as precisely and as detailed as how we often bake, but sometimes you just have to eyeball it, follow your gut, change a recipe or ingredient or direction because you know it will turn out better."

Sam stopped and stared at her grandmother. *Does she have ESP?* Sam thought again, feeling guilty for lying.

"Remember how to fry these?" another woman called to Sam, waving her over.

"I was never very good at this," Sam said.

"Don't you worry about the misfits," Willo said, looking up from a fryer. "Mistakes happen."

Again, Sam's heart pinged. She picked up a donut and dropped it into the sizzling oil, the delicate dough falling apart and creating a series of misshapen pieces.

"Lots of misfits," a woman said, and laughed. "Kids out front got lots more to sell now."

Sam stared into the oil, which hissed and spat, and watched the misfits float around like deflating life rafts.

FIVE

"Misfit?" Sam called out the front door of the tiny shed.

A father in a minivan slowed as he pulled into the drive of the Orchard and Pie Pantry and rolled down the windows. Screams, music, and the sounds of video games rolled forth, and four kids scrambled to the windows, hands reaching into the air.

"A little more sugar can't hurt, right?" he called to Sam, giving her an exhausted smile.

Sam jogged out and held a plate of apple cider donut pieces up to the windows.

"Yeah!" the kids screamed, grabbing for the donuts and shoving them into their mouths, sugar and cinnamon ringing their lips and coating their fingers.

The mother removed sunglasses, revealing dark rings under her eyes. "They look forward to coming here every year," she

111

said. "The beach, the lake, the sweets."

She leaned toward her husband and whispered to Sam, "I think I'll enjoy it more when they're all in college."

Sam laughed.

"How do you stay so thin?" the mother asked.

"You must love it here," the father said, grabbing another misfit.

Sam nodded politely.

A honk blared behind them, and the children screamed. The father looked into the rearview mirror: a group of teenagers in a shiny red convertible, top down, engine revving, music blaring, were waiting. The driver raised his hands in the air as if to ask, *What's taking so long?*

"You can park in the McIntosh lot," Sam said.

"See you next summer," the father said. "We're off to pick apples and buy a hundred pies."

"Yeah," the kids screamed. "Sugar!"

"Follow your nose," Sam called.

The minivan slowly pulled forward, and the convertible roared to life, racing ahead before suddenly braking so hard, the car fishtailed, spitting gravel, a cloud of dust engulfing Sam.

As the dust dissipated, Sam heard, "Aren't

you going to say it to us?"

Sam stood a few feet behind the convertible and slowly began to approach it. When she got within arm's length, the convertible again sped forward a few feet, leaving Sam in another dust cloud.

She stood there and watched the car slam its brakes yet again. Two young men in the front seat were laughing, and the two young women in the back were giggling wildly as they played with their hair.

"Just playin' with you," one of the guys yelled. "Come here."

The convertible gleamed in the summer sun. It was foreign and expensive, and looked as if it had just been washed and waxed. The four passengers looked the same, too: they were tan, drinking iced lattes, wearing colorful shorts and trendy T-shirts. Everything to Sam resembled a mirage as the dust continued to settle.

"We just wanted to hear you say it," the driver said, running a tan hand through his long, gleaming dark locks, which slid through his hand and fell into his eyes.

"Say what?" Sam asked.

"Ask us if we want a misfit?" the passenger said, turning his ball cap around backward on his head and looking directly at Sam.

"Do you want one?" she asked.

"Want one of what?" the driver asked innocently.

"A misfit?" Sam asked.

"Looks like there's a big one standing right in front of us," the driver said, an evil smile crossing his face, peals of laughter echoing from the car. The driver high-fived the guy in the passenger seat and again sped off, leaving Sam in the dust as the girls snapped photos with their cell phones.

"Follow your nose," they yelled at her.

Sam stood there in shock, unable to move, her eyes filling with tears. She realized the platter of donuts was shaking in her hands, the little pieces rolling to and fro as if they were passengers on a life raft who suddenly got caught in a storm.

She zombie-walked back to the shed, set down the tray, and tried to calm herself. Sam caught a reflection of herself in the window. Everyone told her she was a pretty girl — "naturally pretty," they always said.

But what does that even mean? Sam thought now.

She was wearing an oversized apron with the pie pantry logo on it that hung almost to her knees and an old pair of tennis shoes already dirty from the endless dust, mud, flour, and cider. Her hair was in a ponytail; she wore no makeup or jewelry, just a bright red coiled key chain around her wrist that resembled an old telephone cord and held an assortment of keys to the bakery, freezer, U-Pick, Kubota, and van.

She leaned into the window and could see that her face was already dusty and her teeth were flecked with blueberries that she kept in the shed as a snack.

I am *a misfit,* she thought.

A car honked in the drive.

I live in the middle of nowhere working on a stupid orchard that people visit and then immediately leave to go back to the city to a normal life. I have a boyfriend who will eventually take over his family's charter fishing business, just like I'll take over my family's business. Where am I even going to be in five or ten years? Right here? Doing the same thing? Doling out donuts and baking pies the rest of my life?

Sam suddenly tore off her apron and tossed it on the floor, rushing out of the shed, the keys around her wrist jangling.

She took off running as cars continued to honk, and ran until she was out of breath, in the middle of the orchards, away from the crowds. She found an apple tree and lay underneath its arcing branches. She looked up at its green leaves, the limbs heavy with apples.

I can't escape my family, Sam thought, as the apples bobbed softly on the trees. They were cartoonishly red and shiny, like the apples her grandmother painted all over the pie pantry. *I am a misfit.*

Sam closed her eyes, shiny apples still floating in her eyes.

All summer long, teenagers from Chicago, Detroit, St. Louis, and Cleveland would roll into town, their families with summer homes right on the beach. "Cottages" they called them, though many were like compounds. They drove their huge SUVs and sporty convertibles; everything was perfect, polished, and shiny, from how they looked and spoke to their futures.

What's it like out there? Sam thought. *What's it feel like to have your own identity, to reinvent yourself?*

Sam worked most summer days from sunup to sundown. When she was in school, she worked weekends when she wasn't studying or running cross-country. Life here followed the seasons, but it never really slowed: while the orchards hibernated, the pie pantry came to life, hiring even more seasonal bakers to help make pies for the holiday rush.

Sometimes I feel like I'm suffocating, Sam thought.

"Need a little room to breathe?"

Sam jolted upright. Her mother and grandmother were standing in front of her.

How do they always know what I'm thinking and where I am?

She nodded.

"Wish you had told us," her mom said, folding her arms. "Had a line of cars a mile long waiting for donuts and parking."

"Oh, it's OK," her grandmother interrupted. "Mind telling us what happened?"

Sam shared the story, and then Willo and Deana took a seat on the grass beside Sam.

"Same thing has happened to us both," they said in unison, before sharing similar stories of run-ins with rude people.

"Unfortunately, that's just part of life in the service industry," her mom said, rubbing her leg.

"Unfortunately, that's just part of life," Willo added.

"How did the name *misfit* even come about?" Sam asked. "It's so . . . dumb."

Willo laughed. "Well, it's really not," she said. "We used to call them all sorts of slang terms: kooks, greasers, killjoys, chumps, and we had to keep changing the name as times changed. We used *nerds* for a long time, and then we started calling them dweebs."

Willo hesitated. "And then a group of kids

wasn't so nice to your mom."

"I had braces," Deana said. "I had pimples. I had a perm. You do the math."

She smiled briefly, but Sam could tell the pain was still there. Deana continued: "And I worked here most of the time so I didn't really get a chance to do a lot with friends after school. It was hard."

This time, Willo reached out to rub her daughter's leg. "Your mom was pretty down one Christmas," she said. "All of the kids were going on a ski trip to a resort in Boyne City, but she had to stay here and work during the holiday rush. She was moping around one night, lying on the couch and watching TV . . ."

". . . stuffing holiday cookies in my mouth," Deana added.

". . . and *Rudolph the Red-Nosed Reindeer* came on. She was about to change the channel, but I made her sit back down and watch it with me. Remember the part about the Island of Misfit Toys?"

Sam nodded.

Willo continued. "All of those toys that were tossed away and didn't have a home because they were different: the Charlie-in-the-Box, the spotted elephant, the train with square wheels, the cowboy who rides an ostrich . . ."

". . . the swimming bird," Sam added with a laugh.

"And I told your mom that all of those toys were magical and perfect *because* they were different," Willo said. "What made them different is what made them unique."

Sam looked at her mom, who gave her a timid smile.

"I walked in early the next morning to open the pie pantry, and your mom was already in there making donuts," Willo said. "She had a big plate of donuts that didn't turn out perfectly, and she looked up at me and said, very quietly, 'I want to start calling them misfits.' When I asked her why, she said, 'They're as good as all the others, even if they look a bit different.' We haven't changed the name since."

Without warning, an apple fell from the tree and landed with a great thunk just inches from where they sat.

"Is that a sign?" Willo laughed.

"A warning perhaps?" Deana added, reaching over to grab the apple. "You know, this may look perfect on the outside, but you don't know what's happening to anyone on the inside, unless you ask. That's why people act the way they do."

Deana stood, Willo stretched out her hands, and Deana helped pull her mother to her feet. Willo again reached out her hands, and Deana playfully tossed the apple to her.

"You know what they say?" Willo asked, showing Sam the fruit. "Apple doesn't fall far from the tree."

She looked at Sam, who rolled her eyes with great drama as she stood up.

"I think I've heard that one before, Grandma," Sam said, beginning to walk away. "Especially here."

"I know, I know, it sounds so — what do you kids say — lame?" Willo continued. "But we all think that's such a bad thing when we're young. And then we get older, and you know what? We realize it's really not."

Six

"How's it going?" Willo asked Sam, knocking her from the memory.

Sam checked the fryer. "Oh, my gosh," she said. "These don't take very long to fry, do they? Hope they're not too brown."

Willo grabbed an ancient metal strainer from the counter and fished out the donuts. "Perfect," she said. "Golden. Brown as a berry. Like me."

Sam laughed. The summer sun turned everyone who worked at the orchard "brown as a berry." Sam had no idea where that phrase had originated, but her grandma used it all the time, and it seemed fitting for a family who grew fruit. Indeed, her grandma's face was tan, but it couldn't cover the dark circles under her eyes, and it made the skin on her hands look even more translucent when she touched her own cheek.

"I have so many questions for you," Willo said, catching Sam watching her.

"I bet you do," Sam laughed.

"But we'll let those slide for now," she continued. "You look . . . well . . . a bit lost."

"I'm fine, Grandma," Sam said, pulling her shoulders straight and raising her voice. "I'm home, aren't I?"

"Are you?" Willo asked, walking away to take some fresh donuts to the front of the pie pantry before returning and kissing her granddaughter softly on the cheek. "I'm sorry. I don't mean to pry. I love you," she said.

"Me, too," Sam added.

The two let the remaining donuts drain for a few seconds on thick paper towels and then began to toss the hot donuts in cinnamon and sugar. For a few moments, Sam worked in unison with her grandma, and she watched the other women do the same.

Some were making the dough, mixing cake flour, sour cream, cinnamon, and nutmeg, before pouring in the sweet apple cider, eyeballing it just so, until the dough was moist but not wet. They rolled the donuts and then put them on trays under plaid dish towels to rest.

Sam wondered how much things had changed since Willo's own mom and grandma had worked on the orchard.

There was a beauty in working silently.

No one felt a need to talk; just knowing that friends were nearby filled the silence and Sam's heart. As she began to fry more donuts, she felt a peace in baking that she hadn't experienced in a long while.

"Can I ask you a question?" Sam finally asked.

Willo stopped, raised her eyebrows, and then squared her shoulders as Sam had done moments earlier. "Depends," she said. "I'm just teasing. Of course."

"Why did you and Mom decide to smuggle donut holes and misfits into my first place in the city when I started school?" Sam asked, before turning and looking around the pie pantry. "Of all the desserts you could have brought as a surprise. I've always wondered."

Willo didn't even consider the question before answering. "The donut holes were because we had huge holes in our hearts because you wouldn't be here anymore," she said. "And the misfits were because I never wanted you to change to be anything or anyone other than who you are and who you were meant to be." She hesitated, and her voice broke. "Even if it meant that hole in my heart would never be filled again. We only want what's best for you, Sam."

Sam's heart leapt into her throat, and all

she could do was nod. The two set to making donuts once again, working quietly, but the silence was filled with the sounds of women chopping, mixers whirring . . .

And love, Sam thought.

She thought of working for Chef Dimples and of working here right now, and her heart again expanded.

Ironically, for the first time in a long time, Sam thought, *I don't feel like a misfit.*

Or maybe I do, she reconsidered, looking around at all the women in the bakery before sneaking a glance at her grandma. *And maybe that's a good thing. Maybe there's a reason apples fall close to the tree.*

LUE CRANE'S OLD-FASHIONED FRY CAKE CIDER DONUTS

Ingredients

3 cups granulated sugar
1 stick unsalted butter, melted
2 tablespoons baking soda
2 tablespoons salt
1/4 cup ground cinnamon
2 teaspoons ground nutmeg
6 eggs, cracked and beaten
9 1/2 cups bread flour
2 tablespoons plus 2 teaspoons
  baking powder
1 cup whole milk
3 cups sweet apple cider
1 quart oil

Directions

Cream the first seven ingredients for 3 minutes in a mixer on medium-high.

Turn the mixer to low and slowly add the bread flour and all the baking powder to the creamed ingredients until evenly blended (do not overmix).

Slowly mix the milk and cider into the dough until smooth. Dough will be thick. Let dough rest for 20 minutes.

Turn dough onto floured surface after it has rested. Using flour as needed, pat or roll dough out to a thickness of half an inch.

Cut with a donut cutter. Heat one quart of oil in an electric frying pan to 375°F. Drop donuts in hot oil, about 8 at a time. Fry for about 2 minutes then flip over and fry until done. Remove donuts with a slotted spoon and place onto paper towels to drain.

If the dough is too hard to handle, just drop small spoonfuls into the hot oil for donut balls.

Dust with powdered sugar or cinnamon-sugar when donuts are almost cool. Eat with abandonment!

Yields about 2 dozen donuts

■ ■ ■ ■

PART THREE:
CHERRY CHIP CAKE

■ ■ ■ ■

SEVEN

Summer 2017

As twilight began to flicker, summer resorters scurried to the ends of their docks toting bottles of wine and picnic baskets. From Sam's vantage point on her family's deck on a hill overlooking the bay, the scene resembled a live-action animated cartoon of ants.

I need some perspective right now, Sam thought. *I feel pretty small, too.*

People flocked like lemmings to the water's edge all across Michigan's vast coastline every pretty summer evening to watch the spectacular sunsets. They were marvelous spectacles, a fireworks display most nights — a kaleidoscope of color and light in the sky, white clouds turning cotton candy pink, Superman ice cream blue, and plum purple, the sun a giant fireball that seemed to melt in the water as it began to slink behind the wavy horizon.

Sunsets are one of our simplest and most profound gifts, Sam remembered her grandma telling her years ago as they walked the shoreline looking for witches' stones — the ones with holes in them — or pretty Petoskeys to make matching necklaces. *They remind us that we were blessed to have enjoyed a perfect day, and they provide hope that tomorrow will be even better. It's God's way of saying good night with His own brand of fireworks.*

Sam could feel someone staring at her, and she turned her head. Her dad — tan but tired — was watching her.

"It's so good to have you home, Sam," he said, though his serious tone belied his words.

"Thanks, Dad," she said.

She turned, and her mom and grandma were watching her closely, too.

"Where's my wine?!" someone yelled in the distance, and Sam's family laughed nervously.

The family had hurriedly gathered for dinner to celebrate Sam's surprise return — asking employees to stay on to cover the long summer shifts at the Orchard and Pie Pantry — but there was a palpable unease. No one seemed to be buying Sam's explanation that Chef Dimples had rewarded her with a sudden vacation.

"Why didn't you call us?" her father had asked. "We would have picked you up from the airport, so you didn't have to rent a car."

"You just told me that you wouldn't have any time off until next year," her mother said. "You didn't even know if you'd make it for the holidays."

"Or my or the orchard's big birthday parties," her grandmother had added.

"Am I on trial?" Sam asked. "Isn't anyone happy I'm here?"

Silence ensued.

"Now where's *my* wine?" Willo suddenly asked to break the tension, and everyone laughed a bit more easily.

"I'll get another bottle," Sam said too quickly, jumping up from her deck chair.

She walked into the cottage, shutting the screen door to keep out the mosquitoes, and headed to the kitchen. Sam opened the refrigerator, scanning every shelf.

What? she thought. *No wine?*

Sam turned, and hidden under the expansive island sat a wine fridge, hunkered away like a stainless steel chipmunk.

When did my family get so fancy? Sam thought. *A wine fridge? We used to drink out of Solo cups.*

She kneeled down, opened the wine

fridge, and scanned the shelves, filled with a variety of white wines. Sam began to pull each bottle out and read the labels; all of the wines were products of the dozens of vineyards that dotted northern Michigan, including the two peninsulas that ran north from Traverse City into Grand Traverse Bay. There was a wealth of whites — chardonnays, sauvignon blancs, Rieslings, rosés, and dessert wines.

All of these were produced within a few miles of here, Sam thought, a feeling of pride filling her soul.

Sam pulled out a pinot gris and stood. A few bottles of red gleamed in the fading day's light: a cab franc, a pinot noir, a merlot. Robust reds were a bit harder to come by in northern Michigan because of the weather and growing season, but Sam was happy to see such a selection.

Sam had had the pleasure of meeting famed Italian chef Mario Batali at culinary school, and the two had bonded over Michigan. Batali owned a summer home in Northport, not far from Suttons Bay, and he had been influential early on in touting Michigan's summer produce and fruit, fresh fish, and local farms and wineries. When someone in class had mocked Michigan wines, saying they believed it was too cold to grow grapes, Batali had pointedly reminded them that Michigan was on the forty-fifth parallel, just like Bordeaux, Burgundy, and Alsace.

Sam had then added that Lake Michigan acted like a big blanket or air conditioner along the state's coastline, and the effect created perfect temperatures and growing conditions for grapes and, of course, apples, cherries, asparagus, and so much more. Batali had winked at her, and Sam had purchased a pair of orange Crocs not long after in his honor.

Sam opened the drawers and scanned them for a corkscrew.

Nothing?

That was when she saw a brand-new electric opener sitting on the counter.

And a fancy bottle opener, too?

Sam felt a ping of guilt at her better-than-everyone-else urban attitude. She began to cut off the seal at the top of the bottle and then realized the top screwed off.

Sam chuckled at herself and then stopped cold, as Shakespearian whispers were carried along softly by the summer breeze through the screen door and floated into the kitchen where they hit Sam like a brick:

Has she seen Connor?

I don't know. Does she even talk to him

anymore?

I don't think so. But did you see she's still wearing his necklace?

And the key to the recipe box.

Is she dating anyone now?

Why is she home?

She seems too stressed to be on vacation.

Sam felt her knees buckle, and she took a seat on the wood floor of the kitchen still holding the bottle of wine. The whispers continued.

Did she get fired?

Did she quit?

Did she give up?

Sam leaned back against the wine fridge, the door cool on her now-flushed skin.

Why am I here? she thought. *Why did I quit? Have I given up?*

The late evening's light shone off the old pine planks of the kitchen floor, illuminating every ancient dog scratch and dent, the footpath worn from refrigerator to kitchen sink, seemingly every memory and every step of Sam's life embedded in the floor.

Sam screwed the top off the wine and lifted the bottle to her lips.

"Hard day?"

Sam spewed a stream of white wine from her mouth, startled.

Sam nodded, and Willo took a seat next

to her granddaughter, her knees creaking as she bent.

"Do you mind sharing?" Willo asked once she was next to Sam. "Or was it a bottle for one?"

Sam winced more than she smiled.

For a moment, the two sat in silence, handing the bottle of wine back and forth, taking small sips.

"I raised you to be a real class act, didn't I?" Willo asked.

This time, Sam smiled.

"We're all so happy you're home," Willo said gently, "but we're . . . well . . . we're just surprised to see you."

"Should I leave?" Sam asked a bit too defensively.

"Of course not," Willo said. "We want to support you, but we need to know how. I know, in due time, you'll tell us what's going on."

Willo stopped and touched Sam's arm. "We just want you to be happy." She hesitated. "And you certainly don't seem like your old self."

"Maybe that's a good thing," Sam said, again a bit too defensively.

"Maybe," Willo said. "Change is good. But sometimes you can't run from something, some place, or someone. Sometimes you have to run toward something."

"Is that a bumper sticker?"

"Sam," Willo said, following it up with one of her trademark under-the-breath *tsk-tsks.* "It's the foundation for a happy life."

Willo took the wine from Sam's hand and raised it to her mouth, taking a healthy drink.

"Grandma!" Sam said, her face in shock.

"I'm girding myself to tell you a story I haven't told anyone," she said. "Only my mom knew."

Sam's eyes grew wide, and she took the bottle back and matched her grandmother's healthy drink with her own chug.

"I think I need to gird myself to hear this," she said.

Willo waited for Sam to finish. And then she said, "I almost didn't marry your grandfather."

EIGHT

Willo Beck stood on the runway of the Charlevoix Airport, eyes as big as the sun, mouth open, scarf billowing in the wind. She was clutching her suitcase tightly, her knuckles white, refusing to give up her bag.

"It looks like a toy plane," she said, her blond hair whipping in the warm summer breeze. "My friend's little brother has one just like it."

The pilot, a tall man with a square jaw and gray eyes whose face looked worn and rugged, looked at Willo and cocked his head at the plane. "We've been flying to Beaver Island since 1945, miss," the pilot said. "Plane goes up, plane goes down. Birds fly farther in a day."

"It's the 'down' part that makes me nervous," Willo said, looking at the tiny plane with big wheels and propellers on each side.

The pilot smiled. "I flew a fighter in World

War Two, miss. This is like takin' your dog for a walk."

Willo's hand eased on her suitcase. Blood flowed back into her knuckles.

"I promise," he reassured. "Never lost one yet." He looked up at the sky. "And look at this day. It's perfect. It'll be like flying in heaven."

Willo handed her bag to him. The pilot walked to the back, tossed in her suitcase, and then reached for her hand.

"Step here," he said, helping Willo climb into the plane. "Watch your head. And buckle up."

Willo fastened her seat belt and then watched the pilot circle the plane, checking doors and hatches. He jumped in and checked all the gauges.

"Am I the only one on the plane?" Willo asked.

"Looks like it," he said. "A lot of people boat over to the island. You're lucky. You'll be there before any of them."

A man on the runway gave the pilot a thumbs-up. "Watch your ears," he said. "Gets kinda loud. And make sure your seat belt is tight. Sometimes one of the doors will just swing open."

The engines revved to life, drowning out Willo's screams. Before she could unbuckle her seat belt and run, the plane was scooting down the runway and then, shakily, slowly, unsteadily, taking flight.

Willo clamped her eyes shut. She could feel the plane bank left, then right, and then climb higher, her ears popping at its ascent. Her stomach dropped and lurched as the small plane was buffeted by the wind. Images of Willo's mother and father popped into her head, and she said a little prayer, the one her parents had taught her when she was a young girl to say every night before she went to sleep so she would wake up safely again in the morning.

Now I lay me down to sleep, I pray the Lord my soul to keep . . .

Willo panicked as she started to recite the next line about dying before she woke.

I never thought about what it meant until now, she thought. *What a terrible prayer for a child!*

"Open your eyes," she thought she could hear her mom and dad say to her.

"Open your eyes!"

Willo finally realized the pilot was yelling at her, his voice barely audible over the roar of the engines.

Willo opened her eyes, and the pilot turned his head. "Life's an adventure, miss," he said. "You have to keep your eyes open or you'll miss it."

He scanned the panoramic view beyond the plane. "It's beautiful, isn't it?"

Willo slowly turned her head and leaned toward the window. Her heart leapt into her throat. The plane was much closer to the water than Willo had dreamed it would be, and she felt as if she were in a dream. She took a deep breath, shut her eyes, and then quickly looked again. The waters of Lake Michigan were a mix of aqua, turquoise, and emerald.

It looks just like the photos of the Caribbean in National Geographic, Willo thought.

The sunlight illuminated the sandy bottom of the lake, revealing an intricate, striated pattern below the surface of the water. The shadowy silhouette of the plane appeared on the water's surface. It looked like a black bird winging its way to the island.

"It is beautiful," Willo whispered to herself, before lifting her voice and calling to the pilot. "It is beautiful."

"Why are you headed to Beaver Island?" the pilot called back.

Willo looked at him, and then out the window. "I don't know," she said.

"Beautiful few days to find out then," he said.

As the plane approached Beaver Island,

Willo saw that dense forests of pines enveloped the island, hugging the entire perimeter up to its sandy shores. The island looked largely uninhabited, unexplored, and Willo felt as if she were dropping into a remote jungle. That was when she saw the waves gently lapping the golden shores. Willo relaxed all at once until the plane suddenly lurched lower, and the pilot called, "Hold on!"

Willo saw no apparent runway, just a thicket of trees as the plane crouched lower, lower, lower to the ground. Then, out of nowhere, a runway no bigger than a driveway appeared in a clearing, and the plane just dropped as if it had run out of gas.

Willo screamed and checked her seat belt, and then, quickly, the plane's wheels were on the ground, and it was screeching to a bumpy halt.

"You kept your eyes open," the pilot said after he turned off the engines. "Proud of you."

He scrambled out of the plane and helped Willo off before grabbing her bag from the back of the plane. "Where you headed?" he asked, setting her small suitcase on the ground.

"I don't really know," Willo said.

"You don't know?" the pilot asked, a look

of amusement and concern crossing his face.

"I'm headed to my friend's cottage by the lighthouse," she said.

"That's quite a ways from here," he said. "South end of the island. Need a ride?"

Willo looked at him and shook her head. "I think I need some fresh air," she said.

"Head down this road and go into town," he said. "Keep walking until you hit the end of the island. Lighthouse is the biggest thing around. Can't miss it . . . unless you get lost."

He laughed. "Everyone knows everyone here," he said. "Someone will always help you out . . . if you actually come across another person."

"Thank you," Willo said, picking up her suitcase. She began to walk away from the minuscule airport — one small building that served as arrival and departure gate — but stopped and turned. "And I'll keep my eyes open from now on." She smiled.

Less than a mile into her walk, Willo was kicking herself that she had worn a pair of cute saddle oxfords instead of her sneakers. She had yet to see a car, much less a person, and felt as if she were the last person on earth.

I have never felt so alone, Willo thought,

despite . . .

The whole island smelled like pine and water, and she could hear the wind and roar of the lake all around her, as if she were in a movie theater. Her shoes crunched on sand and gravel, and she switched the suitcase from arm to arm each time her shoulder began to ache. Finally, she stopped at a little picnic bench along the side of the road, where a small, shallow creek burbled through lake stones, carrying pine needles slowly downstream. She set down her suitcase and looked into the creek, catching her reflection in the water.

Who am I? Willo asked herself.

Willo took a seat at the table, opened her suitcase, and pulled out a sandwichlike piece of slab pie her mother had made and stored within a pillowy safe haven of shorts and T-shirts.

Thanks, Mom, Willo thought. *Slab pie. My favorite.*

Her mother and her best friend, Sally, were the only ones who knew of her escape to Beaver Island, which sat roughly thirty miles off the shores of northern Michigan. Sally had told Willo she could borrow her parents' cottage.

"You'll have it all to yourself," she told Willo, giving her a hug. "The quiet will give you time to think."

Willo knew the island had a certain unusual history and lore to it, but the isolation was what appealed to her at the moment.

I'm like an escaped prisoner, Willo thought. *On the run for my life.*

Willo's heart ached as soon as the thought entered her mind.

How can I be so heartless? she wondered.

As she took a bite of her pie and continued to think, the sun glinted off the ring on Willo's finger. Her heart ached again.

She lifted her hand and studied the engagement ring, turning it in the light.

Why did I say yes? Willo thought.

Two cardinals landed near the creek, dipping their beaks into the water. They stopped and began splashing one another in a playful manner. The birds fluttered their wings, water droplets glimmering in the light, and danced around in playful skips. Then they grew still for a moment, tossed back their heads, and began to sing a chorus to one another.

That's love, Willo thought. *Look how they complement each other, enjoy being in each other's company.* She stopped and asked herself again, this time out loud, "Why did I say yes?"

Willo watched the birds flap their wings,

singing as they took flight. *I did what I thought society expected,* she thought.

Willo had dated Fred since he asked her to homecoming junior year in high school in Suttons Bay. Fred was steady, hardworking, earnest, quiet, and introspective. He wanted to stay in Suttons Bay, one day take over Mullins Family Orchards with Willo.

Ants began to march onto the picnic table, picking up crumbs of crust as large as their bodies and then silently turning to trek back home.

Yes, Willo thought. *Fred is just like an ant.*

After high school, Willo had gone to college to study business while Fred had stayed home to work his family's small farm. College had changed Willo's life, opened her mind and her way of thinking. Learning about the world had made her own world seem small, and she wanted to travel, move, make her mark on places she had yet to see.

Is a life on the orchard the life I want? she asked herself. *Is Fred the man I want? Forever suddenly seems like a very long time.*

And at her graduation dinner — just hours after she'd gotten her diploma — the waitress brought a cake to the table, one slice already cut. When she served it onto Willo's plate, a ring was sitting atop the icing. When Willo looked up, Fred was already on his knee, their families applauding, Fred's mother in tears.

What was I supposed to do? Willo asked herself again.

Willo finished her pie, picked up her suitcase, and continued her journey, eventually making it into "downtown" Beaver Island. She trudged through the tiny street that arced around the lake, until the sidewalk ended and she was on a dirt road that ran through a thicket of woods. Finally, she could see light, a clearing, and when she came out of the woods, the majestic end of the island greeted her, the lighthouse standing guard over the shoreline and the beautiful waters of Lake Michigan.

A lone, low-slung cottage covered with weathered, graying shake shingles sat on a grassy knoll, with the lighthouse and sandy shoreline just beyond. Little pink roses climbed a trellis, a hammock gently swayed between two knotty pines, and three rockers sat on the small front porch.

It looks just like in a storybook, Willo thought.

She set her suitcase down on the front porch and dug out the key to the house. Willo smiled when she entered: a floor-to-ceiling lake stone fireplace engulfed the living room — the whole house smelled of smoke — and the front of the house was filled with windows overlooking the lake. Suddenly energized, Willo skipped into the kitchen, bright linoleum on the floors and bright red laminate making it sparkly. Two small bedrooms, connected by a blue tiled Jack-and-Jill bath, sat on the other side of the house, both with views of the water.

Willo placed her suitcase on Sally's bed. She looked at all the photos on the wall: Sally as a baby, Sally walking the beach with her mother, Sally as a teenager swimming with her friends, Sally growing up right in front of Willo's eyes. Willo walked back into the kitchen and opened the icebox; there were some staples in there, for the family's upcoming Labor Day visit, and Willo knew her mom had packed a PBJ and another piece of slab pie for dinner.

Enough until tomorrow, she thought.

Willo walked to the front of the house and stared out the living room windows. There were no curtains.

No need for them, Willo thought. *No neighbors.* Willo scanned the stunning expanse. *And this view!*

The lake extended as far as Willo could see — a watery blue fabric that moved in the wind, the lighthouse watching over everything. Willo looked up at the lighthouse, and it seemed to call to her. Willo stepped onto the front porch, kicked off her shoes, and walked down to the shoreline. The lighthouse was built of white stone, and it had a few steps leading up to a door. Willo tugged on it, but it was locked. She took a step back and covered her eyes against the sun. There was a circular walkway surrounding 360 degrees of glass near the top, and an American flag whipped in the summer wind from its summit. Willo peered into the windows of the lighthouse.

Looks dark inside.

She circled around it and found, on the side closest to the water, a semicircle stone wall to which a series of plaques had been attached. One plaque told the brief history of the lighthouse and the dates it had first opened and finally closed. The other plaques commemorated those who had died in Lake Michigan just beyond the lighthouse. Willo read of people who had perished in plane crashes and shipwrecks, fishermen who could not be saved, children who had been caught in riptides, families out for a summer boat ride, and rescue officers who had died trying to save all of their lives.

People like me, Willo thought, reading the plaque, *whose lives just ended without warn-*

*ing, never to return home to their loved ones
again.*

The final lines of the plaque read:

They . . . left our hearts with sorrows
   aching,
Still our lamps must brightly burn.

Willo walked to the shoreline and took a
seat on the sand, looking into the distance,
the lake serene and flat.

What were their lives like? Willo wondered
of those who had died. *What had they been
thinking and doing right before their lives had
been so quickly taken?*

She lay back and looked up at the lighthouse.

Were they happy?

Willo's eyes opened and closed, then fluttered, and before she knew it she was fast
asleep, dreaming of perishing just beyond
the lighthouse. When she awoke, it was dusk
and her skin was chilled. She stood, still
drowsy, her mind still filled with her fitful
dreams.

I need some rest, she thought. *I'm exhausted and emotional.*

Willo headed to the cottage, turning back
to look at the lighthouse every few steps as
if it were still beckoning her, before shutting

the door, eating her PBJ and pie, and going to bed.

The next day dawned sunny, warm, and bright.

Perfect beach day, Willo thought. *And perfect beach reading day.*

Willo put on a swimsuit and then some shorts and a cute sleeveless top, grabbed a dollar her mother had given her and a little beach bag, placing a towel in it, and headed back toward downtown, stopping at a little sandwich shop to grab a donut and cup of coffee, as well as a pimiento cheese sandwich and a Coke for later. She sat on the front porch of the shop, ravenously downing her donut and coffee, asking a local passing by where the prettiest and quietest beach was located.

"Long walk," said the old man with skin like pine bark, spitting a dark rivulet of Skoal off the porch.

"I expect heaven to be a long walk," Willo said with a serious nod, drinking her coffee.

The man roared. "You got a story, ma'am," he said. "I can tell."

He kneeled down, pulled a pencil from the front pocket of his overalls, and grabbed a napkin from Willo, then drew a map to the beach.

"Go lay your story to rest here," he said

with a wink, grunting as he stood, then headed into the shop.

Willo stood, stretched, studied the man's map, and headed out on foot.

The map the man had drawn led Willo through a maze of Beaver Island natural wonders. She trudged through dense pine forests and across clear streams with only stepping-stones or fallen limbs as bridges; she walked through fields of wildflowers, the buzz of bees filling the air; she climbed a dune, the sand hot from the summer sun, emerging atop a peak that offered a breathtaking view of Lake Michigan and its pristine, undeveloped coastline.

Willo hiked down the hill, the dune grass scraping at her legs, and — out of breath — emerged at the shoreline. She kicked off her shoes and walked into the water, the chill of Lake Michigan taking her breath away as it always did. Willo washed her legs and turned, scouring the beach.

Not a person in sight, Willo thought, smiling. *The man was right.*

She pulled out her beach blanket, gave it a flip in the wind, and tossed the latest Agatha Christie novel on top, using her shoes to anchor the ends. Willo wiggled out of her shorts and top, rubbed some Coppertone onto her arms and legs, and plopped onto the blanket with a big sigh. She sat watching the waves, which instantly lulled her.

Lay your story to rest here.

The man's voice reverberated in her mind.

It's not that easy, she thought. *Because my story has no happy ending.*

Without warning, Willo began to cry. Big tears rolled down her cheeks and plunked onto her thighs. She lay back, the sun drying her tears, and lifted her paperback.

Take me away, Agatha, she thought.

Despite the suspense surrounding Hercule Poirot, Willo's eyelids grew heavy, and the book swayed in her hands. Slowly, she dropped the book, closed her eyes, and succumbed to her weariness.

You're getting red.

Willo dreamed that Agatha Christie's eccentrically refined Belgian detective was standing over her, his mustache twitching.

Why are you wearing a tuxedo on the beach? Willo asked him.

You're getting red, he kept repeating.

Willo opened her eyes and screamed. Standing over her was not Poirot but a shirtless young man whose skin and hair were as golden as the sand, his stomach rippling like the water.

"I didn't mean to startle you," he said, backing away. "You look like you're starting to get a little sunburned."

Willo sat up and put her arms around herself, trying to gather her wits.

"How long have I been asleep?" she asked groggily.

"Let's put it this way, if I hadn't shown up, you'd likely have slept long enough to look like a lobster," the boy said with a smile. "Which aren't common around here. Right now, you have time to get some more lotion on."

Willo studied herself and grabbed the lotion. "Who are you?" she asked, more than a slight tone of indignation in her voice.

"Who are you?" he mimicked with mock indignation.

She laughed. "Sorry," she said. "I'm Willo. And I'm not myself today."

"I'm Gordon," he replied. "And this beach is the perfect place to lose yourself." He stopped. "Or find yourself."

He walked to the shoreline and stood ankle deep in the water. To Willo, he resembled Troy Donahue, and her heart skipped a beat.

"What brings you to this beach?" he called over the waves. "Not many people know about it. Just the locals."

"A man at the sandwich shop in town told me about it," she said. "Are you a local?"

"Sort of but not really," he said.

"What's that mean?"

"My dad and I come up here every few weeks to fish," he said. "We have a friend who owns a little cabin here, a shack really, and we boat over here from the mainland. Beaver Island used to be the largest supplier of freshwater fish consumed in the United States."

"You're a regular treasure trove of information," Willo said, standing up and walking over to join him in the water.

"Treasure trove?" Gordon asked. "You must be a college girl."

"Just graduated," she said. "Michigan State."

"Congratulations," he said, nodding in admiration. "Must have big plans for your future."

Willo ducked her head, turned away from him, and looked out over the water without answering.

"Sorry," he said. "Didn't mean to be nosy."

"I . . . I . . ." Willo started, unable to get out what she wanted to say.

"No need to explain," he said. "A lot of people escape to this island for many reasons. Do you know the history of Beaver Island?"

Willo looked at him and shook her head.

Gordon walked out of the water and took a seat on the beach, patting the sand for Willo to join him. She walked over and sat, her legs just inches from his.

"At one time, it was the site of a Mormon kingdom," he said.

"A what?" Willo asked, sitting straighter.

"A Mormon kingdom," he repeated, nodding emphatically. "After Joseph Smith, the founder of the Latter Day Saint movement, died, most considered Brigham Young to be Smith's successor, but many followed a man called James Strang, who moved his followers to Beaver Island over a century ago. They helped build the island and became a force here."

Willo's blue eyes grew larger as Gordon recounted the tale.

"Strang proclaimed himself king, and he was crowned by his followers. But others on the island didn't like his self-declared status as island ruler, or the fact that he was a polygamist with five wives and fourteen children," Gordon continued. "Two men were flogged after their wives refused to follow Strang's edict to wear bloomers. As they recovered, they began to plot against him."

"This is like a movie," Willo said.

"One summer day, the USS *Michigan*

entered the harbor here and invited Strang aboard. As he walked down the dock, two men shot him from behind and then ran onto the ship, which departed and let the men out at Mackinac Island. They were never convicted, and Strang died shortly after that. Mobs came from Mackinac and drove Strang's followers off Beaver Island."

"Wow," Willo said. "That's quite a story. How do you know all that? You a college boy?"

This time, Gordon ducked his head, his bangs brushing his sun-bleached eyelashes. "No," he said shyly. "There's a history museum downtown, and all the locals talk about the island's history when we go fishing. I'm just a kid from Traverse Bay who helps work on and restore boats with my dad. Small family business. Always wanted to go to college, though."

"I'm from Suttons Bay," Willo said. "My family owns an orchard."

"What orchard?"

"Mullins," she said.

"Oh, my gosh," he said. "My family used to drive over there all the time."

"Used to," Willo said, repeating Gordon's words in a sad tone, her eyes shifting from his to search the water. "We're having some problems right now, to be honest. Farms are getting bigger, corporations are running them. Groceries have nice fresh produce in stock all the time." She hesitated. "People watch TV or go to the movies now. Spending a day at the orchard doesn't sound as fun as it used to for a lot of folks. I'd hate for my family to lose what they started so long ago." She hesitated. "And I don't know if I want to be a part of it, to be honest. Such a different life than I imagine now."

"Your family won't lose it," Gordon said. "Sometimes you have to realize that the only constant in life is change."

"Wow! Very profound," Willo said with a chuckle. "Did you know Heraclitus, a Greek philosopher, said that a very, very long time ago?"

"No," Gordon said. "You learned a lot in college."

"I guess I did," Willo said. Then she laughed. "But if knowing a dead Greek philosopher is all I know, I'm in for big trouble in the real world."

"My dad says, 'Give a man a fish and you feed him for a day; teach a man to fish and you feed him for a lifetime.' "

"That's a Chinese proverb," Willo said admiringly.

"Sort of my family's philosophy in life and work," he said. "I tell my dad, 'If we don't catch fish, we're having a Swanson TV dinner.' "

"I don't know if that proverb will catch on," Willo said. She laughed and, without thinking, reached over and hit Gordon's leg. She quickly removed her hand and stood, walking into the lake in hopes that it would cool the heat she felt when she touched him.

My hand is tingling with electric shock, she thought.

"That's why I came out here . . . just to forget for a while," Gordon said. "I'm going through the same thing as you. My dad's business is struggling, too. The boat industry is changing . . . no one buys, wants, or restores the vintage wooden boats anymore. They want aluminum. New, new, new!" He hesitated. "I feel a lot of pressure to do what everyone expects. I've forgotten what it's like to just be young."

Willo could feel her cheeks quiver with emotion. She turned and looked directly at Gordon, nodding. "Then let's forget," she said. "Let's swim, lay out . . ." She stopped and poked her skin, which had quickly turned from pink to brown. ". . . get a little more tan . . . be young."

Gordon stood and ran to the water. "OK!" he said, before running with abandon into the lake and then diving into the water headfirst. He emerged with a resounding *whoop* that echoed along the beach.

Willo laughed and followed suit, screaming as her body dove into the chilly waters. She stood, water cascading off her body in shimmering droplets, and ran her hands through her hair. She saw Gordon staring at her.

"You look like you're wrapped in diamonds," he said.

Her heart stopped. *That may have been the most romantic thing anyone has ever said to me,* she thought.

"I wish I had met you before . . ." Gordon hesitated, and Willo saw that he was staring at her ring, wet and glistening in the water and sun. ". . . *that* diamond."

The only constant in life is change, Willo thought, before she again heard the old man's voice from the sandwich shop. *Lay your story to rest here.*

Willo retreated to her beach blanket and lay back, the sun drying her skin. In the haze from the beach, Gordon looked like a beautiful ghost who had appeared out of the towering dunes that surrounded them. He walked toward her and took a seat too close to her on the sand. She felt paralyzed.

"I like the key around your neck," he said. "What's it for?"

"This silly thing?" Willo asked, lifting her necklace and grabbing the key that had swung backward around her neck.

"It's not silly if you're wearing it," he said.

"It's a key to my recipe box," she said.

"You cook?"

"I bake," she said. "But I don't know if I want to."

"Maybe that key holds the answer," Gordon said. "Where are you staying?"

"Why?"

He laughed. "Don't mean to intrude," he said. "Just didn't know if you were planning to spend the night out here. You seem . . . lost."

"I am," Willo said, shocked the words had come out of her mouth. "I'm staying at my friend's cottage. It's right next to the lighthouse."

Gordon tilted his head back and laughed.

"What's so funny?" she asked.

"It all makes sense now," he said. "The lighthouse has a history, too. Want to hear it?"

"You're full of stories," she said.

"Better than being full of you-know-what," he laughed. "One dark and stormy night less than a century ago . . ."

"A ghost story?" Willo asked, her voice rising.

"You decide," he said. "A woman named Elizabeth was married to a man named Clement, who was the lighthouse keeper. When he became ill, she looked after the oil light, which was not easy in the winter. One night, the couple heard a loud flapping of sails in the distance and could barely make out the flashing lights of a ship in distress, which they soon realized was sinking."

Gordon continued. "Clement and a first mate rowed out into the darkness in a rescue boat. Neither of them was ever found again. Elizabeth was heartbroken but dedicated her life to the lighthouse, once saying that there would always be others in treacherous waters who would need the rays from the shining light of her tower to guide them to shore. Her motto was . . ."

Willo sat up. "I just read the plaque. Something about her keeping the lamps burning brightly."

"That's right," he said. "Some people say they can still see the oil lamp burning even though the lighthouse has been closed for a long time."

"That gives me goose bumps," she said, rubbing her arms and legs.

"Meet me for dinner?" Gordon suddenly asked. "I'm frying some fish my dad and I caught . . . maybe you can offer us some college business advice about our family business."

"I don't know," she said. "It doesn't seem right."

The two sat in silence for a long while, and then Willo said, "OK." Gordon smiled, and there was a moment of awkwardness, before Willo added, "I'm hungry anyway."

She leaned back and grabbed her sandwich, damp and warm from the water and sun. She eyed it closely, pulling the bread apart to study it.

"Pimiento cheese? I wouldn't eat that if I were you," Gordon warned, before leaning back and grabbing a paper bag. "I've got some fresh cherries from home if you want some. They taste like summer. They might tide you over until dinner. Watch out for the pits."

"Thanks," Willo said, grabbing a cherry and popping the fruit off its stem, spitting the leftover pit into the sand.

"Very ladylike," he said.

"I'm from Michigan," she said. "Gotta know how to spit a pit."

Gordon laughed. "You seem like a woman filled with unexpected surprises," he said.

Unexpected surprises, Willo thought. *How refreshing to hear.*

"Cherries remind me of one of my grandmother's favorite desserts," she said. "Cherry chip cake."

"Sounds delicious," Gordon said. "Is that in your recipe box?"

Willo smiled and nodded. "Actually, it is."

"I love cherries, and I love cake."

"It has this wonderfully rich frosting, and the cake is filled with cherries," she said. "It was actually the wedding cake for my grand-parents and parents."

"Life on an orchard," Gordon said, his voice wistful. "Hope I get to try that cake someday."

Willo blushed, and she was glad her cheeks were already red from the sun.

Gordon walked Willo home and then picked her up for dinner on a bike for two. She liked his father, who talked with love and passion about his family, boats, his business, fishing, and his wife.

When Gordon dropped her off, it was twilight, and they stood in the shadow cast from the lighthouse. Willo felt drawn to him, a familiar and deep connection like they had met before and were destined to meet again.

Why now? Willo wondered.

"It was nice to meet you," Gordon said, extending his hand.

A gentleman, Willo thought.

"If you ever get over to Traverse City,"

Gordon added shyly, "make sure to stop and say hi. I'd like to meet your husband."

He turned and got onto his bike. "Better go before it's too dark to get home."

Gordon began to pedal away, waving at Willo. She waved good-bye. His bike slowed, and he suddenly did a U-turn on the dirt road.

"The only constant in life is change, Willo," he said. "Remember that."

Willo could feel her heart pound in her chest. And, with that, Gordon took off, dust billowing from the back wheel of the bike.

Willo turned, in shock, and walked toward the shore. She stopped at the stone wall and again read the plaque, thinking again of those who had left never to return.

Will Gordon ever return? Willo thought. *And why does my heart ache for someone I just met and barely know?*

She turned toward the lighthouse and looked up at it. "Help me, Elizabeth," she whispered. "What should I do? How did you bear losing the one great love of your life? How did you go on?"

Willo faced the water, inhaling the fresh, unsalted scent of Lake Michigan. She then lifted her head to look at the lighthouse one last time before going inside to bed.

As she did, light began to illuminate the

top of the lighthouse, the ceiling red, a bright beacon suddenly shining forth toward the water.

Willo stopped cold, but she wasn't afraid. Instead, she took the ghostly light as a sign, a beacon of hope.

The only constant in life is change.

"Thank you," she said to the lighthouse. "Thank you, Elizabeth."

NINE

Sam lifted the bottle of wine to her lips. Willo saw it was now half empty.

"I forgot it was that good of a story," Willo quipped.

"I'm a little bit in shock here, Grandma! You mean, you weren't supposed to marry Grandpa?" Sam gasped, her voice husky and a bit slurred, shaking her grandmother's leg with her free arm. "You cheated with Grandpa?"

Willo stiffened, and she bristled. "Of course not," she said. "I would never. I broke it off with Fred and dated Gordon for a long while before we married. Fred actually ended up meeting and marrying a very nice woman, and they were married over fifty years, like your grandfather and I were. It turned out to have a happy ending for everyone."

"Is that why you told me this story? So I would believe in happy endings?" she asked.

"Or did you just want me to be scared of ghosts forever?"

Willo looked into her granddaughter's eyes and shook her head. "I want you to understand that change can be good, and it's sometimes completely unexpected." Willo hesitated. "One of my greatest hopes is that you find love like I did."

Sam matched her grandmother's concentrated stare. She nodded but said very firmly, "I just don't think I need a man in my life, Grandma. I don't need someone telling me what to do, how to act, where to live."

"No, you don't," Willo said. "You need someone who complements you, challenges you, brings out the very best in you, and adores even the most irritating qualities about you. Love isn't a game in which you give up control. It's a partnership."

Sam stopped and dropped her head, her eyes searching the wood planks in front of her. "But that story? It sounds like you fell head over heels for Grandpa, but you altered your life for him. You didn't leave Michigan and explore the world. You didn't have a career. You stayed right here on the orchard. You altered your life for a man. Same goes for Mom."

Willo *tsk-tsk*ed under her breath. "Oh,

Sam," she said, her voice filled with sadness. "I never realized you felt that way." She stopped. "But you're wrong, my dear."

"Am I?"

"Yes," Willo said, her voice stern. "Completely. And completely out of line, too. I didn't bend to meet your grandfather's needs."

"But you stayed here."

"I *wanted* to," Willo said, her voice rising. "That's what you're missing." She took a deep breath and slowed her words. "I had a challenging career . . . I still do. Women saved this orchard. Women made this a successful business. Your mother and I changed your history. You are a chef because of the decisions we made. Are you unhappy with that?"

Sam looked at her grandmother. Her heart raced. "No," she said, her voice suddenly shaky. "I'm just . . . unhappy right now."

Willo put her arm around Sam and drew her close. "We can all see that," she said. "But for now, we're not asking. Your happiness is of the utmost importance to all of us."

She squeezed her granddaughter. "The reason I shared that story with you is that only you can decide what makes you happy. Don't let anyone else do that for you, or you never will be happy. And promise me you're running *to* something and not from something."

"I promise, Grandma," Sam said.

"Falling in love is like looking in a mirror," Willo said. "It's a reflection of who we are. Choose wisely and you'll cherish seeing your reflection, no matter how much it changes over the years. Because all you'll see is joy.

"No more moping then," Willo concluded, standing slowly and extending her hand to Sam. "Oh, my legs are a little shaky from the wine." She laughed. "I better make dinner," she added, nodding toward the deck. "They will turn into an angry mob if they don't get some food soon. How's goop sound? I know how much you all love it."

Sam winced but didn't say a word.

Willo's "goops" were essentially what Sam's mother called "everything-but-the-kitchen-sink casseroles" in confidence to her daughter. Willo's goops consisted largely of Velveeta cheese, white rice, and cans of alphabet and cream of mushroom soup, and the end result did resemble, well, a glob of goop.

And tasted like it, too, Sam thought, forcing a smile and a nod at her grandmother.

To Sam, the biggest irony surrounding

Willo was that she was a wonderful baker but far from even an average cook. For decades, the family had to endure dinner in order to get to dessert.

Sort of the way kids have to endure math to get to recess, Sam thought.

"Why don't I make dinner?" Sam asked.

"You sober enough?" Willo teased.

"I'm a city girl now, Grandma," Sam joked back. "It takes more than a few sips of wine to throw me off my game."

"Show me your skills," Willo said.

"Skills?" Sam asked. "You're very hip, Grandma."

"I work alongside a lot of high school and college kids," she said. "I have to stay up on my lingo."

"You show me your skills then," Sam said. "How long does it take to make the cherry chip cake?"

"A while," Willo said.

Sam suddenly zipped around the kitchen, a spring in her step. She opened the refrigerator, filling her arms with a variety of produce, and then scanned the counters.

"I'll whip up a fast dinner," she said, eyeing ingredients she haphazardly tossed onto the island. "I'll roast this peaches-and-cream corn with a fresh herbed butter alongside some foiled potatoes with chopped onion. While those grill, I'll prep this yummy salmon Dad caught with lots of lemon and herbs, and I'll make a salad with fresh tomatoes, radish, carrots, and some chèvre. Will take a few minutes to pull together if you help me." She turned to Willo. "And then I can help you make the cherry chip cake."

Willo's face broke into a wide smile. "I'd be honored," she said.

Willo walked to the stove and pulled her daughter's recipe box off a pretty shelf. She pulled a necklace from around her neck and grabbed the key that hung at the end. "I got one just like yours," she laughed. "And it fits every recipe box." She put her finger over her mouth. "Sssshhh. Your mom doesn't know." She looked at Sam and touched her key. "Nice to keep this close to your heart, isn't it? Makes you feel safe and protected, even when you might not, huh?"

Sam's mind was immediately flooded with the scene of her walking out on Chef Dimples. She nodded.

Willo flipped through the index cards in the recipe box. "Here it is!" she said, pulling a card forth.

Sam walked over and studied the card, flecked with pink spots.

Willo watched her granddaughter and

smiled. *Maybe one day I'll make this for your wedding,* she thought.

"This is going to take some time," she said, studying the ingredients and directions.

Willo nodded toward the wine fridge and then toward the deck. "We'll just give them another bottle of wine . . . no, make it two . . . that way they won't care when everything is ready."

Sam laughed and grabbed some wine.

"You don't like my goop, do you?" Willo asked.

"What?" Sam asked, tilting her head, acting as if she couldn't hear her. "What?"

"You heard me," Willo said.

"What do you mean?" Sam asked, lifting her shoulders, acting innocent.

Willo laughed. "I always had a hunch," she said, "since I found so much of it hidden in napkins."

Sam chuckled. As she turned, light poured through the kitchen window, a ghostly beacon of pinkish red as it filtered through the clouds on the horizon.

I wonder if that is the same light my grandma saw on Beaver Island? Sam thought. She shook her head. *Wine has gone to my head.*

The only constant in life is change, Sam then heard a voice whisper to her.

She looked again at the light, searching it, her heart racing.

"Did you say something, Grandma?" Sam asked.

Willo shook her head.

Someone is definitely trying to tell me something, Sam thought.

Cherry Chip Cake With Cherry Vanilla Buttercream

Ingredients for Cake

1 10-ounce jar maraschino cherries (about 30 cherries)

10 to 15 large fresh cherries, pitted and finely chopped

1/2 cup unsalted butter, room temperature

1 1/2 cups granulated sugar

4 large egg whites

1 teaspoon vanilla extract

1/4 teaspoon almond extract

2 cups cake flour

2 teaspoons baking powder

1/2 teaspoon baking soda

1/2 teaspoon salt

1 1/3 cups buttermilk

4 tablespoons maraschino cherry juice

Ingredients for Frosting

1/4 teaspoon vanilla extract

3/4 cup salted butter, room temperature

3 1/2 cups powdered sugar

1/4 cup heavy whipping cream

4 tablespoons maraschino cherry juice

Ingredients for Garnish (if desired)

Pitted fresh cherries and maraschino cherries

Directions for Cake

Preheat the oven to 350°F. Butter and flour two 8-inch round cake pans and line the bottoms with parchment paper.

Drain the maraschino cherries, reserving the juice. In a food processor or with a sharp knife, finely chop the fresh cherries. Set aside.

In the bowl of a stand mixer fitted with a paddle attachment, or in a large bowl using a handheld mixer, beat the butter and sugar at high speed until light and fluffy, about 5 minutes. Scrape down the bowl and add the egg whites one at a time, mixing after each. Add the vanilla and almond extracts and mix until combined.

In a separate bowl, combine the cake flour, baking powder, baking soda, and salt. In a smaller bowl, combine the buttermilk and cherry juice. Add the flour mixture to the mixer in three additions, alternating with the buttermilk mixture. Mix after each addition and scrape down the bowl as necessary. Stir in the chopped cherries and maraschino cherries.

Divide the batter evenly between the cake pans and bake 30 to 35 minutes, until a toothpick inserted into the center comes out with a few moist crumbs. Let cool in the pans 10 minutes, then transfer to a wire rack to cool completely.

Directions for Frosting

In the bowl of a stand mixer fitted with a paddle attachment, beat the vanilla and butter about 1 minute at medium speed. Add the powdered sugar and mix at low speed until the sugar is completely incorporated. Add the whipping cream and cherry juice. Increase the speed to medium and beat 1 to 2 minutes, or until light and fluffy.

Assembly

Place one cake layer on a plate or cake stand. Cover with 1/2 cup of the buttercream frosting. Place the second cake layer on top and cover the top and sides with the remaining buttercream. If desired, ring the top of the cake with pitted fresh cherries or maraschino cherries (or both).

Let the cake firm for a few minutes at room temperature before serving.

Yields one 8-inch layer cake

■ ■ ■ ■

PART FOUR:
TRIPLE BERRY
GALETTE

■ ■ ■ ■

TEN

Summer 2017

The early-morning light illuminated Sam's childhood bedroom in a shocking, too-bright glow, as if she were waking up in the middle of Times Square.

Sam opened her eyes, the light blaring directly into them. She shut her eyes again quickly and rubbed her head, which was aching slightly from the previous evening's wine. She leaned up and looked over at the pink Hello Kitty clock that still sat on her nightstand: 5:37 A.M.

That's why, Sam thought, rubbing her eyes. *Stupid light in Michigan. Comes up too early.*

She sat up on her elbows, and a photo of her on the wall as a little girl in a little chef's hat and Mullins apron crimping pies in the bakery seemed to be staring at her.

Too early to wake up, she thought. *Too late to grow up.*

Summer's dawn broke in Michigan around five A.M., and dark didn't descend until well after eleven P.M. The state was constantly glowing in light, a contrast to its long winters of dark hibernation.

Which is nice when you're not exhausted, a little depressed, and hungover, Sam thought.

She heard a rustling in her parents' kitchen — the faucet running, the crinkle of a coffee filter, the grinding of beans — and, after a few seconds, she could hear the pot percolating and the smell of freshly brewing coffee filled the air.

She finally eased herself straight up in bed, stood, stretched, and walked to her window. For a moment, she experienced a flashback from her routine of just a few days ago. Sam expected to smell the spices from the Indian restaurant, Naan Better, that occupied the ground floor of her Brooklyn apartment building and to see a brick wall across the narrow street that served as a sort of Broadway backdrop to the choreographed chaos of the city streets that greeted her every morning: people scurrying to work, cab horns blaring, sirens whirring, a world of music echoing up to her.

This is a different world, Sam thought, the serenity of Suttons Bay greeting her instead.

The bay was quiet, save for the fishermen

whose johnboats were already positioned in their lucky spots: the glacier rocks that jutted out on the east side of the bay, the shallows near Old Mission Peninsula, the clear, deep spots in the middle where the bay merged into Lake Michigan.

I'd forgotten how beautiful this is, Sam thought. *It looks like a painting. One my grandma might do.*

Sam's mind suddenly went to her grandmother, to the story she had shared.

How well do I know the women in my family? Sam wondered.

All of a sudden, she checked her childhood clock again.

No, Sam thought. *She couldn't still be doing that, could she?*

Sam quickly scoured through her suitcase, yanking out a Tigers T-shirt and pair of running shorts, clothes tumbling onto the floor. She plucked a pair of running socks off the carpet and grabbed her tennis shoes and went scurrying out of her room and down the stairs, running a hand through her blond hair and blowing her bangs out of her eyes.

She rounded the stairs and headed into the kitchen. It was quiet, the coffeepot still on, sputtering every few seconds. Sam walked to the kitchen window, leaned forward over the sink, and scanned the hillside that led up to the orchards. Sam's house and her grandmother's home both shared views of the orchard, albeit from opposite ends and different perspectives.

From this vantage point, Sam's view was pastoral. Rabbits and squirrels scurried on the hillside, while birds darted in and out of the orchard's trees and bushes. The morning's low light illuminated the world from one side in a dramatic way: apples were split in two, red and black; halves of trees were luminescent and green, while the other halves were dark and brooding.

Life is divided into shadow and light, Sam thought. *You can see it either way, based on your own perspective.* Sam stopped and considered that, before adjusting her thought. *Based on your own light level.*

Two long figures, shadows cast down the hillside and as tall as giraffes, caught Sam's eye. She scanned the orchard to see her mother and grandmother walking.

A smile crossed Sam's face, and she hurriedly found a travel mug in the back of a kitchen cupboard, filled it with coffee, pulled on her tennis shoes, and went running out of the house.

Although Sam was tired, the sight of her mom and grandma walking filled her soul. For as long as Sam could remember — and as long as Deana could recall — Willo and Gordon had walked the orchards every single morning at dawn, no matter the weather. They trudged through the snow, in boots, on snowshoes, or sporting cross-country skis. They slogged through the rain and mud in waders and wellies. Sam's grandfather used to joke that he and his wife were personally responsible for tucking the orchards into bed for the winter, waking them up in the spring, and playing with them in the summer and fall.

After her grandfather had died, Sam had wondered if her grandmother's routine would continue.

"Hey," Sam said, jogging up behind her mom and grandma, out of breath and trying to keep her coffee level.

"Well, this is a surprise," Willo said, her face breaking into a big smile.

"Especially after all that wine," Deana joked, the two chuckling.

"It wasn't *that* much wine," Sam said, before her mom added, "For a rhino."

"I pulled off dinner," Sam protested.

"It was marvelous, honey," her mom said.

"And Grandma, the cherry chip cake was" — Sam searched for the right word — "magical. I might have to steal it."

"No need to steal it. It's in your recipe

box," Willo said. "Just promise me you wouldn't dare ever give it to that evil chef of yours."

The outside world suddenly came tumbling into this one, and Sam nervously took a sip of coffee. "I would never," she said quietly.

Willo glanced at Deana, and the three walked in silence.

Dew dampened the grass and shimmered on the apples. From a distance, the blueberry bushes glistened as if encased in frost, and the trees looked as if they had been cloaked in ice.

Walking through the orchards was comforting to Sam, nearly as comforting as baking. There was a precision in both endeavors, which brought a sense of order to the world, and yet each was filled with new surprises and revelations every day.

The trees lined up like hunchback sentinels, seeming to protect the women as they walked the land. The paths between the trees were grassy but worn, showing where tourists and U-Pickers had trod in straight lines before veering left or right. Every so often, the earth had been upended by moles, muddy earthquakes left in the wake of their own underground walks.

"Grandpa hated moles, didn't he?" Sam

asked out of the blue.

"With a passion," Willo said, touched that Sam remembered an innocuous fact about her grandfather from long ago.

It was even cooler as the three went deeper into the heart of the orchards, mist dancing in between the rows of trees and the lake glistening beyond like a mirage. It was magical, mysterious, a lost world.

I always feel like I've been transported to the world depicted in Lord of the Rings, Sam thought.

Sam slowed to take a sip of coffee, dropping slightly behind her mom and grandma. She smiled as she watched the two of them walk.

*They look so much alik*e, she thought. She tried to stop the next thought from entering her mind but couldn't. *Apple doesn't fall far from the tree.*

Sam looked at the ground, at their shadows moving through the orchards, this ground that had connected generations, served as the foundation of family, produced fruit that helped feed countless people.

"Remember how you played in these orchards as young girls?" Willo asked Deana and Sam.

Deana turned to look at Sam, and the two smiled. "We do," they said at the same time.

These orchards had been their playground as girls.

Sam slowed even more and studied the orchards carefully.

I ran, played hide-and-seek, caught fireflies, scaled trees, picked apples and peaches straight off the tree, launched pits from sling-shots, and danced in the sprinklers here, Sam thought. *Moreover, I learned about plants and science: I understood the seasons, when to plant trees and seeds, how to nurture them and protect them from insects, what to feed the deer in winter and the hummingbirds in summer.*

Sam again thought of her grandpa.

If we're good to Mother Nature, she will be good to us, he always used to tell her. *Same goes for people.*

Sam's mind went back to Chef Dimples, and her stomach lurched.

He made goodness seem like a scam, she thought. *He made men seem . . . well, not like my father or grandfather.*

Without thinking, Sam said, "I didn't know if you'd continue walking after Grandpa was gone. I was sort of surprised to see you out here this morning."

Willo slowed as they came out of the orchards and rounded a corner near the hillside that overlooked the bay. A small

186

patch of raised, bermed land sat at the end of the hillside, surrounded by a deer fence and marked with a sign: WILLO'S PILLOW.

The ground did, indeed, resemble a fluffy pillow, rising from the earth like a peaceful place for a giant to rest his head. For as long as Sam could remember, her grandma and grandpa had overseen this chunk of land at the end of the orchard as their own garden, to grow the other bounties of summer the orchard didn't produce.

The long rows were marked with labels that read *Rhubarb, Lettuce, Tomatoes, Strawberries, Asparagus, Green Beans, Peppers.* A teak bench sat in the corner next to a small potting shed. And a plaque was attached to the door of a pretty painted garden gate, thick with old coats of green paint, pink roses climbing the trellis that flanked it.

Willo walked up to the plaque and began to read, smiling as she recited the lines of a simple poem about the beauty and importance of what lies beyond a garden gate. Her voice grew husky as she read the final lines:

But if you'd have a mind at peace and a
    heart that cannot harden,

Go find a gate that opens wide upon a little garden.

Willo finally turned to Sam, a melancholy smile on her face. "Your grandfather made that plaque for me," she said. "He saw the poem in an old newspaper, attributed to E. M. Boult. My mom started this garden after her mother died. Alice had a little garden up by their old log cabin that my mom let go to seed after she passed. One winter my mom was going through her recipe box, and there were so many old-fashioned recipes in it that called for fresh produce. She wanted to honor her legacy — and feed her family in hard times — so she started it again, right here, in one of the prettiest spots on the whole orchard. This is where my mom loved to sit and watch the sunset, or read a book, a big glass of sun tea right beside her."

Willo took Sam's free hand in hers and gripped it tightly. "To answer your question: I won't — and never will — stop walking these orchards every morning, unless I'm unable to do so. This is how I talk to your grandfather," she said, a mist forming in her eyes matching the mist in the air. Willo hesitated and turned to scan the orchard. "I can't stop because he's still here . . . in every leaf and branch and apple and blade of grass. I can see him, smell him, talk to him, hear him."

Willo took Sam's hand. "Listen," she whispered. "Shut your eyes. Be still. Sssshhh."

Sam closed her eyes, feeling silly for a moment, as she had when she first started doing yoga. But slowly her mind stilled, and her own thoughts stopped talking back to her and cluttering her head. Birds sang happily, the wind sighed, the bay lapped in the distance, and in every single sound, Sam indeed could hear her grandfather's voice.

Hi, Grandpa, she said to herself. *You're right beside me, aren't you?* She stopped and exhaled. *You always have been, haven't you?*

Sam opened her eyes when Willo tightened her grip on her hand. "Your great-great-grandmother and grandfather did the same thing, as did your great-grandma and grandpa," Willo continued. "They walked these orchards every single day. My mom used to tell me they had all made a pact to get to know each other as well as they knew the land, to never start a day on the wrong foot, to make sure they were moving ahead on the very same path."

Willo stopped and looked at Sam, giving her hand a little shake, and then looked at

Deana. "They had nothing but this orchard and each other. And they cared for them with great love and respect."

Willo glanced at her garden, vines covered in tomatoes and strawberries, asparagus that resembled spiderwebs as the morning sun shone through their misty tops.

"When we walk these orchards, we follow in the steps of our ancestors," Willo said. "And that is an honor and a privilege."

ELEVEN

Winter 1942

Madge and Wilbur Beck stopped in the middle of the orchard, snow falling hard all around them. They lifted their noses, their yellow Lab, Babe, following suit.

The whole world smelled like popcorn.

The couple looked at one another, and Madge's eyes filled with tears.

"Please don't, sweetheart," Wilbur said softly. He pulled his wife into his arms, before Babe nestled between their legs and then crawled up their bodies to join the hug. Madge emitted a tiny laugh through her tears.

My mother, my father, the Depression, and now this, Madge thought, trying hard not to collapse into tears yet again. *How much can I endure?*

Madge and Wilbur had returned to the orchard to care for her mother after she was stricken with ovarian cancer.

191

The silent killer, Madge thought. *Undetected. She didn't know until it was too late.*

Her father had died of heartbreak two years later.

They never even knew about you, Madge thought, rubbing her expanding stomach and suddenly bursting into tears.

"Oh, honey," Wilbur whispered.

The Depression and the war had been hard enough on their little orchard, but the economy was now about to put them under. Her parents had worked hard to produce big crops during the war, but now prices had fallen and the harder they worked, the further they fell behind. The price of a bushel of corn was just eight cents, and many families were burning their own corn because it was cheaper than coal in their stoves.

"They're burning their own livelihood," Madge said in a shaky voice, again sniffing the air. "They're burning their own history. It's not fair."

"No, it's not," Wilbur said. "But people have to survive somehow."

"What about us?" she asked. "If we lose this?"

Wilbur remained silent. Madge looked down and rubbed her stomach once more, tears again filling her eyes. "What will happen to our baby if we lose this? What will our child have?"

Wilbur pulled his wife close and hugged her, stroking her head with his gloved hands. "Us," he said softly. "Us."

Madge looked up and into her husband's eyes. "I can't imagine life somewhere else anymore, now that we're back."

"Then don't," Wilbur said. "And remember, we're still better off than a lot of city folk."

Babe barked and took off in a flash after a rabbit, his body flying through the snow, powder flying into the air, making it look as if a truck had just driven down a dry gravel road.

Madge took her husband's hand, and the two continued to walk.

He's right, Madge thought, looking around the orchard, barren and dark in the winter, wet, black limbs covered in snow, the whole world resembling a paint-by-numbers picture. The couple rounded a corner, and there — on a hillside overlooking the bay — sat the garden they had started after Alice had died. *At least we can produce some of our own food.*

Nearly every farm and orchard in the area did double duty or traded with one another, raising large gardens with vegetables and canning fruit from the orchards. Most kept dairy cattle and chickens. Madge bought sugar and flour in fifty-pound sacks, baked her own bread, and then made clothing from the flour and feed sacks. She made one-dish suppers, and the women in her church organized potlucks to share food and have a little fun.

We've learned how to get by with very little, Madge thought. *But how far can a little go?*

Madge stretched her food and budget with what she liked to call "goop," casseroles that filled the belly but did little for the taste buds.

That's why I love to bake, she thought. *I can't wait for apples . . . and apple crisp.*

Her soul suddenly felt as warm as a hot oven, and she again rubbed her stomach.

"When I think about apple crisp, the baby kicks," Madge said, her breath coming out in little puffs.

"So does mine," Wilbur laughed as Babe came sprinting back up to them, tongue hanging, his face a happy smile. Wilbur reached down and petted the dog. "Atta-boy," he said, brushing a layer of snow off the dog. "Gotta learn to be like Babe. Happy and grateful for the smallest things in this world."

As the couple continued walking through

the orchard, hushed and quiet in the insulation of snow, Madge looked at her husband surveying their land. He had taken every penny he had and purchased even more land after her father had died in order to expand what her family had passed on to them. He had worked tirelessly. In the spring, lugs of apples would be loaded onto horse-drawn wagons and pulled into the barn on the far side of the orchard. The apples were washed and wrapped in tissue paper before being placed in handmade wooden boxes for distribution. Even at the lowest of times, Wilbur had never considered quitting or cutting back. He added peach and cherry trees to the orchard, blueberry bushes, pumpkins.

"We can't be one season," he had said. "We must be three. It's a long winter."

Wilbur now wanted to can and sell his produce. He had considered having people come and pick their own fruit. He had even asked Madge to sell her pies and cakes at church socials and to local restaurants.

The couple navigated the edge of the orchard overlooking the bay, which was frozen as far as the eye could see, and then cut right into the middle of the trees. Snow was piled in deep pillows, the glow from the icy bay faded, and their world grew even darker.

It's becoming harder to see our future, Madge thought.

Wilbur slowed and then stopped. "Look," he said, his voice echoing in the grove of bare trees. "What do you see?"

Madge looked around. "Nothing," she said.

"Look harder."

She scanned the orchards. They were bare. She searched the hillside, the limbs, the barn in the distance. Nothing. Even the birds had hunkered down in the snow. Madge was about to answer, but then her eyes did a final scan of the land, and she saw it.

"Our footsteps," she said.

Wilbur smiled. "Our history," he said in a raw voice. "Us." He hesitated and grabbed her hand. "I want this orchard to be our place . . . not just where we work, but where we come to be together. Let's try to walk this orchard every day, to get to know not only the land better but each other better. Let's talk as we walk, figure things out, make plans . . . and, more often than not, just be at one with each other and our land. Be thankful for what God has blessed us with . . . land, nature, a child, each other."

He turned and looked his wife in the eyes. "I want our children to run through these orchards. I want to hear them laugh. I want to see them pick apples and spit peach pits. I want them to grow old here, like us. I want them to leave footsteps, a history."

Wilbur pulled her into him. "This is all we have to connect us, the only thing any of us have: the earth and family. It's all that will remain after we're gone, but it will tell our history, repeat our stories, vibrate with the impressions left by our footsteps. Your recipes do the same. Your imprint will be left on the world. All of this is our legacy."

Madge got onto her tiptoes and kissed her husband deeply. "So is our baby," she added, putting her husband's hand on her stomach.

"I just felt a kick," he said. "Time for some dessert."

"It's barely dawn, Wilbur," she said, hitting him playfully on the chest. But then she thought of what he'd just said, about her recipes being a legacy, and she added, "But I have an idea."

When they got home, Madge turned on her oven and began to pull sugar and flour from her cupboard. She stopped.

I have no fresh fruit, she thought. *Only what I've canned or preserved.*

Madge thought of what she could make for Wilbur and her baby — a mix of breakfast and dessert, a sort of early-morning crisp — and thoughts of her mom baking filled her mind.

What was that recipe called? Madge wondered, racking her brain. *What was it?*

Madge shut her eyes tightly and was transported back in time. She could see herself sitting, legs crossed, on the floor of her parents' old log cabin kitchen, wearing a little dress and drawing.

"I'm going to make something very special for breakfast this morning," she could recall her mother saying. "It's your father's birthday, and although we don't have a lot of money, I want you to learn that you can make a meal fit for royalty with what we have right here, all around us."

"How?" Madge asked, standing up, eyes now wide.

"Follow me," her mother said, grabbing a colander and her daughter's hand and heading outside.

She took her into the backyard and to the edge of the woods that bordered it.

"What do you see?" Alice asked.

"Weeds," Madge said. "Chiggers."

Alice smiled. "Look harder," she said, edging into the bramble and holding up a thorny branch. "Now what do you see?"

"Raspberries."

"You love raspberries, like your dad," she said, picking the red fruit. "Life is a lot like this bush right now: thorny and difficult to navigate, but there's always beauty to be found. Sometimes you just have to look really hard." She turned and looked at her daughter. "I hope you never forget that."

She waded a little deeper into the woods and began picking some blackberries, before freeing herself from a few thorns and heading toward the orchard, where they picked fresh blueberries.

When the two returned to the kitchen, Alice pulled over a small, upholstered footstool she kept nearby for her daughter to stand on. "You can help me measure all the ingredients, OK?"

"OK!"

"We're going to make a triple berry tart," her mom said.

"What's that?" Madge asked.

"It's sort of like an open-faced sandwich," her mom explained. "We make a crust for the bottom, but it's open on the top, so you can see all the fruit, everything that's inside."

She continued. "And remember how I said this was fit for royalty? I have a poem for you, so you'll always remember what we're making. It goes like this:

"The Queen of Hearts
She made some tarts . . ."

"What's that mean?" Madge asked when she was done. "And why did that mean person steal them?"

Her mother laughed. "It means that tarts are for royalty," she said. "They're rich and beautiful, just like a queen. And . . ." Her mother stopped and leaned in to her daughter to whisper, "It means that you should never let anyone steal your tarts." She laughed again, tickling her daughter. "And don't let anyone steal our recipes. Remember our little poem when you need to remember how to make the recipe."

Babe barked, knocking Madge from her memory. She walked over to her cabinet, pulled down her recipe box, and inserted the key that she kept on a chain near her heart. She unlocked the recipe box and began to thumb through the cards, smiling as soon as she found the recipe.

I forgot I had drawn on it, she thought, her face breaking into a big smile. *A crown for a queen.*

Madge went to her freezer and found

some frozen blueberries, blackberries, and raspberries.

"The Queen of Hearts, she made some tarts, all on a winter's day," she sang to herself, altering the verse to match the season.

She looked over at her husband and dog. *They're right,* she thought. *I need to be grateful for the simplest of things. Worry takes you out of the moment.*

As she ran hot water in the kitchen sink to begin thawing the berries, she looked out the window, smiled, and leaned even closer.

Their family footsteps remained, firm in the snow and crisscrossed like birds' tracks, leading from home to orchard and back again. As her eyes tracked to the apple trees, which would soon be filled again with fruit, Madge felt her baby kick.

TWELVE

"I still love apples," Willo said with a laugh. "And apple crisp most of all."

She scanned the orchard and continued. "This was my playground, too, just like yours. I used to pick blueberries and blackberries, hide in the trees, catch lightning bugs in mason jars at dusk, and play in the sprinklers, just like both of you." Willo stopped and looked at Sam. "You used to run these orchards — back and forth, row by row — when you were training for cross-country in high school. You left a lot of footprints here."

Sam scanned the path between a row of trees, thick with apples, that they had just walked. All of their footprints were visible in the dew, soft outlines as if they had just stepped in wet concrete.

My footprints are everywhere, Sam thought. *These may dry, but they will never go away.* She stopped and looked at her mom and grandma. *Unless I do.*

"Sam?" she heard her mother ask. "Are you OK?"

"Who's hungry?" Sam asked out of the blue.

"Starving," Willo said. "We can have some donuts when we get to the bakery."

"Mind if I whip something up this morning?" Sam asked.

"Oh, honey," Deana said. "You made dinner last night. And you got up so early. You must be tired still."

Sam inhaled deeply, the smell of apples and grass, wood and water filling her senses. A cloud of fog danced in the orchards, a ghostly image that seemed to hug every tree. The sun suddenly clipped the edges of the orchard, brightening the world inch by inch. Sam watched the fog dissipate in front of her eyes, vanish slowly and then nearly all at once, leaving behind its dewy kiss on everything.

"I actually feel quite alive," Sam said. "I used to get up before dawn every morning for my job anyway, remember."

Sam's stomach dropped as soon as she said it. The words *used to* hung in the air and seemed to echo. She could feel herself try to reel them back in, turn back time, but she watched as her mom and grandma glanced at one another in slow motion.

"Still do," Sam said too cheerily and quickly. "Already used to being on vacation. See" — she laughed giddily — "I just said 'used to' again."

I sound insane, she thought.

"It would be lovely for you to make us breakfast," Willo said, acting as if nothing had happened, just like she did when customers would fight in front of her over what kind of pie they wanted to take home. "What time should I come over? I need to stop by the bakery first and check in on everything."

"I was hoping I might be able to come over to your house and bake," Sam said. "I just wanted to . . ." Sam hesitated, unsure of how to explain her emotions. ". . . be there."

Willo beamed. "I would love nothing more."

The three headed toward the pie pantry, and Willo and Deana peeled off at the entrance. "You go get started," Willo said. "We'll be there in a few. Get some coffee brewing."

Sam nodded and took off up the little dirt driveway that led past the entrance to the orchard and restaurant and to her grandmother's house.

"It's unlocked," Willo called.

Sam smiled. *Things you never yell in the city,* she thought with a laugh. She passed by the old log cabin and Ford pickup, waving at a yawning teen who was shuffling, still half asleep, toward the little shed while texting on his phone. Sam watched the boy, all gangly limbs and shiny hair like a pony, unlock the shed, open the homemade curtains, and then shuffle toward the pie pantry to pick up a batch of misfits for early-morning visitors, still texting.

Sam immediately felt for her pocket. *I didn't even bring my cell,* she thought. *What's wrong with me?* She hesitated, slowed, and looked around. *Maybe that's why I'm noticing everything. I don't need to distract myself here.*

Sam crossed the little dirt road — waving at her father, always a blur of motion in the summer, who honked in his old pickup as he headed into the orchard — and headed up the curving flagstone walkway to her grandmother's home. The old farmhouse looked just the same: bright red shutters with apple cutouts smiled down on her, and the wide wooden planks of the front porch squeaked in exactly the same place when Sam stepped on them. Sam opened the front door, and the smells of her childhood immediately overwhelmed her.

Grandma's house smells like cinnamon and freshly baked cookies, she thought.

A narrow staircase with an ornately carved handrail and shiny spindles led upstairs, the entire wall filled with family photos. Sam took the first step and stared at a photo, into the eyes of her grandfather.

I miss you, Grandpa, Sam said to the picture. *I never knew your secret history with Grandma. You were quite the romantic.*

Sam looked up at the collage of family photos filling the staircase wall.

History, she thought. *Footsteps.*

Sam walked into the kitchen and smiled. The kitchen was sunny and bright, and it, too, was filled with her grandparents' history. Her grandmother's watercolors of the orchards and bay dotted the walls, colanders and kitchen utensils dangled haphazardly from hooks, speckled enamelware bowls were stacked on the cabinets, and McCoy cookie jars in a variety of colors and shapes — from wise old owls to, of course, apples — lined the tops of the cupboards.

Sam ran her hand over the smooth, worn edge of the old farm sink, deep and white, with a grooved, angled side where a wooden drying rack always sat. She looked out the window, and her heart jumped: the expanse of the pie pantry and orchard shimmered in the early-morning light in front of her, the bay and Lake Michigan glimmering in the distance. To Sam, it looked as if one of her grandmother's paintings had come to life: red apples bobbed as tree limbs swayed in the breeze; bushes thick with the bluest of blueberries shimmied; peaches, fuzzy and bright, nestled snugly against branches; shiny cars and people dressed in bright T-shirts and caps danced into the pie pantry and into the orchards; in the near distance, the cornfields seemed to move as if they were doing the wave at a football game, while cherry trees dotted with the deep red fruit resembled holly bushes out of season.

And yet there was an incredible uniformity to the scene despite the visual overload: everything was lined up in neat rows, as if each tree, bush, and person understood its purpose at this very moment.

I've forgotten this view, Sam thought, recalling the one from her own bedroom window earlier in the morning. *There is an order to life's chaos, be it the city or country, if we just stop for a moment and see it.*

Not that long ago, Sam had always thought it odd that her grandparents' kitchen sat in the front of the house, but now she understood why.

This view, Sam thought. *It's my grandmother's entire world.* She stopped and reconsidered that. *No, it's been my family's entire world for a long time.*

The grandfather clock in the living room chimed, its deep voice reverberating through the house and Sam's body. *I better get started on breakfast,* she thought, counting the chimes. *I didn't realize we'd been walking and talking so long.*

She scanned the countertops, where blueberries, apples, peaches, and rhubarb sat in little baskets and bowls. *So many options with all the fresh fruit,* she thought. Sam turned to open the refrigerator and threw open the doors too quickly. They swung out of her hands, the freezer door bumping the tall cabinet.

Thwack!

"Ooops," Sam said, grabbing the door and shutting it, the cabinet suddenly grabbing her attention.

The ancient cabinet, now white but painted so many colors so many times over the years, had stood in the same place for ages. Sam looked down; even the floor looked as if it had sunk over time from the cabinet's weight.

The cabinet featured pretty finials at the

top and bottom, and its warped wooden shelves were stacked with Michigan knick-knacks and tchotchkes, more photos and cookie jars, antiques and cookbooks.

And then Sam finally saw it: her grandmother's recipe box sat right in front of her, nearly at eye level, staring at her. Sam picked it up and ran her fingers over the burnished wood and the carved letters that read *RECIPE BOX.* She took it over to the counter, set it down, and began to open it. She stopped, seeing the lock.

"I wonder if," she said to herself as she grabbed the key dangling on her necklace that she never took off. She put it into the old lock, which immediately popped open. "Grandma," Sam said to herself with a smile. "You were either teasing me or testing me last night. We're all equals in this, aren't we?"

For some reason, Sam held her breath as she opened the box, almost as if a genie were to be released into the world.

The smell of wood, of the outdoors, of the orchards, seemed to be released into the air when she opened it.

Sam rifled her fingers through the index cards, calling out the colorful tabs that demarcated different sections of the recipe box.

"Breads, muffins, cookies, pies, cakes," Sam said to herself.

Her finger stopped on a card that felt thicker than the others, and when she pulled it free, it read *Alice Mullins's Secret Family Apple Crisp!* The card had flour embedded into its outer edges and was dotted with stains, vanilla and oil, which had made clear circles all over the card. The handwriting was looped and curving, smeared and ghosted, but it was deeply faded — hard to read — and Sam held it up in front of her eyes.

Oh, my gosh! Is this my great-great-grandmother's original recipe? she wondered. *The handwriting looks just like my grandmother's. And it's written in pencil.*

Did she see this same view while she baked from her cabin? Sam wondered, peering out the kitchen window. *What must it have looked like then?*

Sam put the index card back in the box. She stopped and looked out the kitchen window again.

Am I seeing what you did? Sam thought, picturing her great-great-grandmother from the photos on the wall. She then thought of her great-grandmother and her view from this very spot. *Help me, please, ladies. Guide me. I need to make the right decisions in my life.*

As if playing a game of chance, Sam shut her eyes and flicked her fingers through the cards again. Sam suddenly stopped, plucking a recipe completely at random from the middle. She opened her eyes and smiled.

Madge's Summer Tart

"A tart!" Sam said excitedly, leaning against the cabinet and reading the recipe card, which was decorated with a little crown that had been drawn by a child. "From Grandma's mom!"

Sam was quickly transported back to New York. She thought of her days in culinary school and working alongside Trisha at Chef Dimples's bakery. Her mind whirred thinking of all the various tarts she had made, savory and sweet.

But it seems like Michigan baking should be a little less fussy, Sam thought.

She glanced out the window again and an even bigger smile overtook her face. "Do you mind if I make a slight change to your recipe?" Sam asked the card.

And then she set to work, washing fresh blueberries that sat on the counter, before grabbing a big colander. Sam headed into the backyard, whose lawn backed acres of woods. Blackberries and raspberries grew wild and thick in the brambles that sat at the edge of the woods. Sam carefully navigated her way through the thorny vines, her thin running shirt catching and snagging on a thorn.

"Darn it," she mumbled.

Blackberries are red when they're green, she could hear her grandfather telling her when they used to pick the fruit. But today, a brilliant summer day, the blackberries were deep purple, almost black, and each one resembled a mini beehive.

Sam plucked and popped a fresh blackberry, already warm from the sun, into her mouth, savoring the natural sweetness, and picked until her colander was half full before easing her way through the woods to find a raspberry bush thick with fruit. She navigated her way out of the brambles and headed back to the kitchen, where she preheated the oven and began to wash the blackberries and raspberries.

Sam pulled cold, unsalted butter from the fridge and began to cube it, some flour and sugar from the cupboard, a large bowl, and then she located her grandmother's old pastry blender.

Sam made the crust and then rolled it into

a ball, lightly flouring it and wrapping it in plastic before placing it in the refrigerator. Then she started in on the filling, mixing the berries, sugar, flour, and fresh orange juice. She was in the middle of tossing the fruit when her mother and grandmother walked into the house.

"I don't smell coffee," her grandma called.

Sam shrugged, her hands deep in the bowl of berries. "I forgot."

"No problem," her grandma said, grabbing a filter and a bag of local coffee. "You have your hands full . . . literally." She added the coffee without measuring. "That looks like quite a production."

"Actually, it's pretty easy," Sam said. "And I had a little help and inspiration."

"Oh, Sam," her mom and grandma both said at the same time. Deana picked up the recipe card. "I haven't made this in forever."

"Well, I'm changing it up a bit, giving it a more modern flair," Sam said. "I don't think we have oleo in the fridge anyway." Sam chuckled and then stopped, looking at her mom and grandma intently. "I hope that's OK."

"Oh, sweetheart, my mom would be so honored and so proud," Willo said. "I actually remember her making this for my dad's birthday." Willo shut her eyes and then said:

"The Queen of Hearts
She made some tarts,
All on a summer's day;
The Knave of Hearts
He stole those tarts,
And took them clean away."

"Mean ol' knave," Sam said. "Whatever that is."

"My mom told me that's how I'd remember to make it," Willo said. "I used to make this for your grandfather occasionally, before we got so busy at the pie pantry. How are you changing it?"

Sam stirred the bowl of fruit and then set it aside. "I'm making a galette instead of a tart," Sam said.

"Fancy," Deana said.

"Actually, it's not," Sam said. "It's more rustic. More fitting of Michigan, I thought."

Willo pulled three mugs — all mismatched — from her cupboard and poured three cups of coffee.

"In school, I learned that a galette is sort of the offspring of a pie and a tart — halfway between homespun and fancy — but easier to make than its parents. The biggest difference is that a galette is a free-form pastry, baked without a pie pan or tart ring. It's rustic. And it's forgiving. You just roll it out flat and then fold it in roughly around the filling." Sam stopped and sipped her coffee. "The wonderful thing is that you can't mess it up; the crust will tear and be a little more done in places, the juices will leak, but as long as you use really fresh ingredients, like the fruit we have here, and real butter for the dough, it bakes into something magical. Making a galette really gave me confidence to try trickier desserts. But it's still one of my favorites. And you can make sweet or savory galettes. I made two crusts today. I thought I'd turn one into a savory galette for dinner. I have a recipe for an asparagus, mushroom, goat cheese, and bacon galette I think I'll make."

Sam looked at her mom and grandma, who were staring at her openmouthed. "I never realized how accomplished you were," Deana said. "But I knew you had — what did we call it, Mom?"

"The gift," Willo said. "You've always had the desire and talent to bake." Willo took a sip of coffee and continued. "You know, you're standing in the exact same place where my mom, your mom, and I have baked so many desserts and cooked so many meals," she said. "It's the place where we've experimented, too, the place where we've planned this orchard's future. You're a part of history."

What if I don't want to be a part of this history? Sam thought, immediately furious at herself that this was the first thing to cross her mind. *What if I want to make my own history?*

As if reading her daughter's mind, Deana said, "We define our own history, Sam."

"Where's your recipe box?" Willo asked out of the blue.

Sam's heart raced when she turned to discover her grandmother staring at her, her head cocked, her crocheted cap at an angle. "I think it's in the attic." Sam stumbled, her face turning red. "I think I packed it up when I left for school, along with all my high school stuff."

"You didn't take it with you to New York?" Willo asked. "Why?"

Sam didn't answer, and for a few seconds, an awkward silence ensued, before Deana chirped, "Why don't we eat in the orchard this morning? Make it a picnic. How's that sound?"

"Great," Sam said a bit too quickly and happily.

"Mom, you want to help me?" Deana asked. "Let's get a quilt and some plates. Honey, we'll check in at the pie pantry again and let you finish up here. Just come over when you're done, OK?"

"OK," Sam said.

When they had left and the galette was baking, Sam again picked up the recipe box and began to look through the cards, studying the recipes of the women who came before her.

Everything is online now, Sam thought, touching the handwriting on the cards. *But this just feels different, personal . . . It feels more important . . . like history.*

She hesitated. *Why did I leave my recipe box at home?* Sam wondered. *You know why. You thought the recipes weren't good enough.*

The smell of the baking galette transported Sam, and she thought of the slab pie she had made before walking out of her job.

Or did I? she thought. *Maybe I didn't really leave it behind.*

Sam glanced out the window. Her mom and grandma were making their way back to the pie pantry, their bodies casting long shadows in the sun.

That's the thing about baking, Sam thought. *You bake for someone because it is familial and familiar, new yet ancestral, a way of connecting generations.*

As the pair made their way past the pickup and log cabin, their shadows grew smaller and finally disappeared. The simple scene made Sam's heart race, and when she turned away from the window, she realized she was clutching the recipe card for the tart tightly to her chest, a drawing of a crown done by a little girl resting atop a key that little girl had grown up to give her own granddaughter.

TRIPLE BERRY GALETTE

Ingredients for Crust

1 cup all-purpose flour

1 teaspoon kosher salt

2 tablespoons superfine sugar

1/4 teaspoon baking spice

1/2 cup chilled unsalted butter, cut into small cubes

3 tablespoons ice water

Brown sugar and ground cinnamon, for dusting

Ingredients for Filling

3/4 cup blueberries

3/4 heaping cup blackberries

3/4 heaping cup raspberries

1/2 teaspoon fresh lemon juice

2 tablespoons granulated sugar

1 tablespoon dark brown sugar, packed

2 tablespoons all-purpose flour

1/2 teaspoon baking spice

1/2 teaspoon orange juice

1 tablespoon butter, room temperature

Directions for Crust

In a large bowl, combine the flour, salt, superfine sugar, and baking spice. Blend together with a fork.

Break apart the cubes of chilled butter and add slowly, a few at a time, to the flour mixture, quickly coating each cube with a fork or your fingers.

Cut the chilled butter into the flour mixture with a pastry cutter, rotating the bowl as you go and scraping the butter off the cutter as needed, until the mixture resembles small crumbles or pea-sized gravel.

Slowly drizzle the ice water into the bowl, 1 tablespoon at a time, mixing until a dough forms (add additional water if necessary).

Form the dough into a ball with your hands. Lightly dust with flour and wrap in plastic wrap. Refrigerate the dough for at least 1 hour.

Directions for Filling

In a large mixing bowl, combine the blueberries, blackberries, and raspberries.

Add the lemon juice and granulated sugar and stir with a spoon.

Add the brown sugar and stir.

Add the flour and stir.

Add the baking spice and stir.

Add the orange juice and stir.

Dot the fruit with butter and mix.

Assembly

Preheat the oven to 450°F.

Place the dough ball on lightly floured waxed paper.

Roll the dough out into a 10-inch circle, using a lightly floured rolling pin.

Transfer the dough to an air bake sheet.

Lightly dust the dough with brown sugar and cinnamon.

Place the fruit in the center of the pastry, leaving a 2-inch border. Sprinkle the fruit with more sugar and cinnamon.

Fold the edge of the crust inward toward the fruit (not covering it), pinching the corners to seal as you go (this is a rustic dough, so the edges will resemble pizza dough; the center of the fruit is not covered).

Reduce the oven temperature to 425°F before placing the galette in the oven. Bake 25 minutes. Let the galette cool for 5 minutes before serving.

Serves 6 to 8

■ ■ ■ ■

PART FIVE:
THUMBPRINT
COOKIES

■ ■ ■ ■

THIRTEEN

Summer 2017

Sam was lying on a swim platform that was floating in the bay at the end of her parents' long dock. Her eyes were closed, the water was flat as glass, and the soft waves — which gently slapped at the platform's side — were lulling her to sleep. But every few minutes, a boat or Jet-Ski whizzed by in the near distance, and Sam's back would stiffen. She'd grip the bottom of the giant, inflated platform to try to ride out the wake. The platform bobbed, sometimes violently, and waves crashed over its lip, dousing Sam with chilly Michigan lake water. When the same two Jet-Skis continued to circle near her, Sam sat up on her knees and yelled, "NO WAKE ZONE!"

But just as she would settle back down, the same thing would happen again.

Sam rolled over on her towel, the sun immediately warming her back. She picked up a paperback of an old Agatha Christie novel, its pages yellow and warped by water, that she had found at her grandmother's. Sand poured from the pages of the book.

This book must have a history, Sam thought, the word *history* sticking in her head. *A lot of history around here.*

Sam looked up at the Michigan landscape. *A lot of history here, too,* she thought.

Glaciers had sculpted the land thousands of years ago into an object of stunning beauty. *God is an artist,* her grandmother always said. *A painter, sculptor, musician, writer.*

Sam had a 360-degree perspective of all that made Michigan so beautiful in the summer. The majesty of Lake Michigan — stunning blues and greens — shimmered beyond the bay, which was tucked into a sandy corner of a lush green hillside, the thick boughs of towering pines waving at her. Cottages of all sizes dotted the hillside, windows making them resemble happy faces, long docks jutting into the water. The orchards, colorful and symmetrical, sat atop the hill.

The cherry on top of the cake, Sam mused. *Or apple on top of the pie.*

Sam thought of her trip to the Hamptons just a few weeks ago. Its beauty rivaled Suttons Bay, but — despite all the resorters from Chicago, Detroit, and St. Louis — a decided edge and urban electricity was missing in Michigan.

Do I miss that edge? Sam wondered.

Sam's cell trilled, and she quickly fumbled through her beach bag — digging through lotions and magazines — to find it. The cell said, "Incoming Call — Trish," and Sam had tagged Trish's contact information with a photo she had taken when the two worked together, a smiling Trish wearing a tall white hat emblazoned with DIMPLES BAKERY tilted on her head.

"OMG, girlfriend! I literally just heard about your epic mic drop at Chef Jackass's!" Trish exclaimed in her New York accent. "You made my walkout seem like amateur hour. I'm so proud of you."

Sam laughed, and it echoed back to her off the water. "Thanks," she said. "I think."

"You're the talk of the town. Honestly," Trish said. "Everyone in the industry is talking about it. People are proud of you. I'm proud of you. And supposedly a producer from *GMA* said some pie you made was the best they'd ever had."

Sam smiled, and she could feel her body flush with pride.

"That girl is on fire," Trish began to sing,

a bit off-key.

"That's enough, Alicia Off-Keys," Sam joked.

"Where are you?" Trish asked.

Sam hesitated. "Home," she said. "Michigan."

"Michigan?" Trish exclaimed. "Where? What? Why?"

"I needed a break," Sam said. "That job — that man — nearly broke me. I'm just . . ." She hesitated again, searching for the right word. "Lost."

"Well, I'm your compass," Trish said. "I have a job for you."

"What?" Sam said. "Where?"

"We're asking a lot of the same questions today," Trish laughed. "I just started at Doux Souvenirs."

"Two souvenirs?" Sam asked, confused.

Trish laughed. "No, it's French for Sweet Memories. The pastry chef from the Ritz in Paris just opened her own shop in Midtown. She's an amazing pastry chef and even better person." Trish took a deep breath and then said, her voice rising, "And she wants to talk with you."

"What? When?" Sam asked.

"You're starting to sound like a recording," Trish said. "I have her number. I told her you would call."

Sam didn't respond.

"So call," Trish said.

"OK," Sam said.

"And," Trish continued, her voice even higher, "I happened to see Angelo at Doux Souvenirs."

"You did?" Sam said, sitting taller on the swim platform. "What did he say?"

"Well, he's the one who told me how you walked out on Chef Narcissist," she said. "And he told me how much he misses you. Sam, he really likes you."

Sam didn't respond.

"Anyway, he said he had your number, and that he'd texted you," Trish said casually. "He said you sent him a thumbs-up emoji or something completely third grade. I told him you were probably off your meds . . ." She hesitated. "And I told him to call."

"You what? Trish, he's so different. He's a Jersey delivery guy."

"And you're a Michigan farm girl."

"Ouch."

"Sam, that's not a bad thing," Trish said. "You need to stop apologizing for your past. For who you are. You're a wonderful person and a wonderful pastry chef. And you don't need to run from men."

"I'm not running," she said.

"Not all men are like your high school boyfriend or Chef Boyardumb," Trish said. "Believe it or not, a lot of guys actually love strong, smart women who follow their passion." She hesitated. "But, unfortunately, a lot of strong, smart women don't give them a chance because they don't believe in themselves."

"Ouch again."

"So you're going to call Colette and listen to Angelo, right?"

Sam didn't respond.

"Right?"

"Right as rain."

"You country people with your cute country phrases," Trish laughed.

"And you city people with your cute city phrases," Sam repeated.

"You mean like, 'Get outta my way!' or 'Stupid cabdriver!' " Trish said. "Speaking of which, I gotta go catch the subway. Love you."

"Love you back," Sam said.

She had just hung up the phone when it rang again, and Sam answered it immediately.

"What now?" Sam asked, thinking it was Trish again.

"That's a nice greeting."

"Who is this?" Sam asked upon hearing a

man's voice. She pulled her cell back and squinted in the sun, trying to make out the number.

"It's Angelo. Angelo Morelli." He hesitated. "You've already forgotten my voice, Michigan?"

Trish! You didn't tell me he was calling immediately, Sam thought, her pulse quickening. She sat up straight on the swim platform, smoothed her hair, blew her bangs out of her eyes, and sucked in her stomach, as if she were on FaceTime.

"Oh, hey, Jersey," she said casually. "How are you?"

"I'm good," he said. "It's nice to hear your voice. The bigger question is, 'How are *you*?' "

There was something familiar and comforting about hearing Angelo's rugged voice and East Coast accent, like hearing the loons calling at dusk in the bay or the gentle slapping of the waves on the platform. Sam found herself smiling.

"I'm good," she said.

"Really?" Angelo asked.

"Really," Sam repeated.

"Last time I saw you wasn't so good," Angelo said. "And then, poof, you were gone. You ghosted . . . disappeared without a word." Angelo paused, and his voice

231

wavered. "I feel like I got . . . left behind."

Sam's heart dropped at the emotion in his voice.

"I didn't know we were dating," Sam said. She said it gently, but still wished she could take the words back as soon as she said them.

"I tried," Angelo said. "I asked you to dinner, to ball games . . . even said I'd cook for you if you brought dessert."

Sam's heart dropped again.

"Maybe I got ghosted from the beginning, and I was just too dumb to know it," he said softly.

"I'm sorry," Sam said. "The job just got me in such a bad space. I was worried I'd get fired if I did something he didn't approve of." She paused. "I didn't mean to ghost. I just had to get out of there . . . out of New York for a while."

"I get it," Angelo said. "Speaking of which, I'm getting out of the city for a while, too." He hesitated. "I'm coming to Michigan."

"You're what?" Sam said, her voice suddenly loud and booming off the water.

"You don't sound too happy about that," Angelo said with a little laugh.

"It's just that . . ." Sam couldn't find the words. "Why?"

"I have to work over Labor Day, and I have a few vacation days I need to take or I'll lose them, so I decided to be impulsive."

"Why here?" Sam asked a bit too icily.

"You were always talking about how beautiful Michigan was, especially in the summer," Angelo said. "You said it was like heaven, as pretty as the Hamptons. So I thought I'd check it out." He paused, took a breath, and continued. "I trust you, Sam. You're . . . real." He stopped for a long few seconds as if searching for the right thing to say. "You put your thumbprint on a lot of people's hearts in New York . . . including mine."

Sam didn't say a word.

"You don't have to see me," Angelo said to fill the silence, his voice filled with hurt. "Really. I just wanted you to know. And I just wanted to see how you were doing."

Sam opened her mouth to say she was sorry, to tell Angelo about the potential job, to tell him something, anything, but instead, he said, "Later, Michigan," and hung up.

Sam stared at her cell, expecting it to ring again. When it didn't, she dropped her head as if it were too heavy for her shoulders and stared at the water underneath the webbing of the platform.

Maybe my view of the world is too narrow,

233

she thought. *Maybe I'm seeing everything from the wrong perspective?*

Sam tucked her cell into the beach bag, stood on the platform, steadying her legs, and then dove into the lake.

She opened her eyes as she knifed through the water, and the underwater world danced in light: the sandy bottom shimmered, and beautiful lake stones — Leland blues, agate, chert, jasper, and Petoskey stones — dotted the depths like forgotten gemstones.

Sam popped up, her skin covered in goose pimples, and the world sparkled, her family's orchard towering over the bay. Sam grabbed the dock and pulled herself onto it to sit. She steadied the still-bobbing swim platform with her feet and then eased back into it. When she looked up, Sam could see her wet fingerprints on the dock, each wavy line clearly defined, the lifeline on her palm snaking in different directions. Sam glanced up one more time at the orchard. When she looked down at the platform again, her fingerprints were gone, dried quickly in the sun, as if they had never been there.

FOURTEEN

The pie pantry had a familiar scent, warm and earthy like flour, yeast, and dough, with top notes of apples and spices.

Sam unconsciously wrapped her arms around her body — the smells greeting her like a warm hug — and smiled.

I actually just used the words "top notes," Sam laughed to herself, thinking of her roommate, Lily, who had worked at Yankee Candle while in college, and — although she never purchased a single grocery item save for Oreos — bought candles for their tiny apartment constantly, describing the scents in flowery, over-the-top descriptions.

A cinnamon stick candle didn't just smell like cinnamon, Sam mused, trying to remember how Lily had described it. *Oh, yes: its top notes were cinnamon, its middle notes were clove and cardamom, and its base notes were cedarwood and bay leaf.*

The pie pantry was overflowing with summer tourists, a line snaking out the door and down the driveway, misfits being handed out left and right, along with Dixie cups of fresh apple cider.

Resorters were mesmerized by the nostalgic kitsch of the old barn: the antique farm and baking implements and utensils, Willo's watercolors and paintings on the floor, the Ball jars filled with homemade jams, jellies, caramel, and fudge. Sticky-fingered children wiped their hands on their T-shirts, parents held stacks of pies to buy, while waitresses juggled trays teetering with sloppy joes, mugs of cider, and slabs of pie covered in melting apple cider ice cream.

This is like Mayberry, Sam thought. *This is the world people want to re-create for their families.*

The word *families* reverberated in Sam's head, and she thought of her own. She sneaked a peek through the packed dining room, and she could see her grandmother at the register checking out customers at the wooden counter as if she knew each of them personally, while her mother scurried from oven to oven, checking pies, and then to the kitchen, checking receipts.

The ultimate expediter, Sam thought, a term she had learned in school about the person in a restaurant who keeps order and ensures efficient movement behind the scenes. *She's been that way with our family. Little credit for hard work. Always behind the scenes.*

Again, the word *family* stuck in Sam's head, and, for some reason, she turned and scanned the line of diners.

All families, Sam finally realized. *No younger, single couples. No girls' weekend groups. No dating couples out of the city for a few days of stress relief. Where were they?* Sam wondered. *The wineries? The nicer restaurants in Traverse City?*

Change is the only constant had been a mantra from one of Sam's professors in culinary school, a successful restaurateur who taught business to aspiring chefs. *You must adapt, be it McDonald's or a small bakery.*

"Cider?"

Sam jumped at a squeaky voice. A young girl, probably from a local high school, was holding a tray filled with little sips of cider. The girl was cute as a button, almost like a girlfriend to Alvin or one of the chipmunks.

"Oh," Sam said. "Thanks."

Sam took the cup and downed it in one shot. Drinking the cider was like sipping directly from a freshly picked apple that had been filled with sugar and spices.

How different from hard cider, Sam thought, thinking of the newly popular drink that was now rivaling fine wine and craft beer with hipsters and urbanites alike.

"You're already getting brown as a berry," Willo said, catching Sam off guard again. "Did you have a relaxing morning on the lake?"

Sam nodded. *My lies continue,* she thought.

"How's the cider?" Willo asked.

"Like heaven," Sam said with a smile. "They should start offering this at communion. So much better than grape juice."

Willo laughed. "Hadn't considered churches for the marketing and sales plan yet." She stopped and considered her granddaughter carefully. "Any other ideas? Looked like something was on your mind when I startled you. Very deep in thought."

Sam ducked her eyes. "No," she said. "All good."

"OK then," Willo said, before changing the subject. "Wanna help us out in back for a while? We could use it. This place is insane today."

Sam nodded and followed Willo into the back, where she began to shadow her grandmother and mother, filling in as needed, checking people out at the register, pulling pies from the oven, prepping plates, stirring the pots of chili, cutting a variety of apples into pretty slices, which customers received as an "orchard amuse-bouche."

When the crowds thinned, Sam, Deana, and Willo took a seat at a booth at the back of the restaurant. The wooden benches were filled with mismatched cushions and pillows Sam's grandmother and great-grandmother had made. The same chipper girl who had been serving apple cider to the masses earlier came to their table, the same big smile on her face. She poured three big glasses of cider, along with three glasses of water.

"It's nice to get served, Amanda," Willo said to the girl. "Thank you."

"It's nice to be of service." The girl winked. "Especially to the Mullins matriarchs." She pulled her shoulders back and looked around the restaurant. "Such history here. My mom was so happy when I got this job. She said she felt like our family has been eating with your family forever."

When the girl was out of earshot, Sam said, "Matriarchs? We sound like dying royalty."

"I think she meant it as a compliment," Deana said. "You OK? You've been a little edgy since you got home."

Sam watched Amanda happily serve the tables around them. The words *happy, history,* and *family* rang in her ears. Sam wanted to deny and deflect yet again, but as she started to open her mouth, "Young at Heart" by Frank Sinatra — one of her grandmother's favorite songs — came on the stereo and poured softly through the restaurant. Her grandmother tilted her head, smiled, and sang the lyrics:

"You can go to extremes with impossible
    schemes
You can laugh when your dreams fall apart
    at the seams"

The lyrics sliced Sam's heart, and she burst into tears, lowering her head onto the table and sobbing.

"I'll come back," Amanda said, stopping quickly and retreating, menus still in hand.

"Sam? Honey?" Deana asked. "What's going on?"

She pulled her daughter into her arms and looked at Willo as Sam sobbed. When she had finished, Deana handed her daughter a napkin.

"She might need another one," Willo said, holding out hers.

Her joke broke the tension, and a wee smile appeared at the edges of Sam's mouth. She let out a little laugh, and wet tears flew off her face like a sprinkler. Willo dabbed at her face as if to dry it, and Sam's shoulders seemed to ease. She took a deep breath and then spilled her guts, telling her mother and grandmother everything that had occurred: her walking out on Chef Dimples, her surprise return home, her flirtations with Angelo and his phone call, as well as the call from Trish about a possible job interview in New York.

When she had finished, Willo reached over the table and clasped her granddaughter's hands. "Thank you for telling us," she said. "Thank you for trusting us."

Sam nodded and tucked herself even tighter into her mother's side, feeling — for once in a long time — safe and relieved but also completely exhausted.

The three ordered huge slices of pie — apple, cherry, blueberry — topped in apple cider ice cream and whipped cream.

"I think I'm dizzy from the sugar," Sam said after they'd polished off their desserts. She yawned and blinked slowly, once, twice, three times, her lids feeling like concrete.

"Nothing like sweets to ease the pain of a tough day, is there?" Willo asked. "I think you need to take a nap."

Sam yawned again and nodded.

"Before you do, can I show you something?" Willo asked.

She led Sam and Deana to the tiny office stuffed in the back of the kitchen. The desk held a laptop and a little lamp and was stacked with papers: order sheets, deliveries, bills. An old wooden credenza sat behind the desk. On top, in the midst of even more papers, were a few family photos. Willo walked to the credenza, pushed aside some papers, and turned around holding a recipe box.

"You know this is the original one, right?" Willo asked. "The others are replicas that were made for me, and for your mom and for you on our thirteenth birthdays. But this," she said, rubbing her hands over the wood box, "was the one your great-great-grandfather made for your great-great-grandmother." She stopped. "That's a lot of greats."

Willo took a seat in the swivel chair and set the box down on the cluttered desk. "And I still have the original key to this," she said with a wink, "but it's in a special place at home." She inserted the key that dangled around her own neck and opened it. She smiled and began to flick through the index cards, rifling through them quickly and stopping, as if she had each one memorized in order.

"Here it is," she said, holding it out for Sam. "I wanted you to see it."

"Thumbprint cookies?" Sam asked, reading the card, her face scrunched in confusion. "I haven't had these in ages." She hesitated and then looked at her mom and grandma. "OK. What am I missing?"

"What do you see?"

Sam looked at the recipe card and read the ingredients.

"I see that you can use fresh strawberry, raspberry, or apricot jam," she said. "I love all of them. We make and sell all of them."

"Keep looking," Willo urged.

"Oh," Sam said, squinting and holding the card even closer to her face. "What is that? It's really faded. Is that a thumbprint?"

Willo smiled. "It is," she said, standing. "It's your great-great-grandmother's thumbprint. Looks like she covered it in ink, or maybe pencil lead, and imprinted it on the recipe card."

"That's amazing it's lasted so long," Sam said. "Very cool."

"I want you to see something else before you get some rest," Willo said, standing and leading them out of the office, through the back door of the pie pantry, and around the barn to the front entrance. She stopped and pointed at the stone foundation of the old barn. A concrete cornerstone, smooth and cracked, jutted out. Grass grew all around it, while clover and dandelions — happy and yellow — poked up through the cracks.

"Why have I never noticed this before?" Sam asked. "My whole life?"

She crouched down and studied the cornerstone. " 'Built 1927,' " she read. " 'For Alice: The Apple of My Eye.' "

"My grandpa built this for her about a decade after they started the orchard," Willo said.

Sam ran her hand over the cornerstone, stopping and looking even closer. She then began to clear the clover and dandelions, and rub the dirt off the old concrete. That was when it became clear. Three faded handprints, of different sizes and shapes, were visible in the concrete: those of a man and a woman, along with the paw print of a dog.

"I don't understand," Sam said.

"I think you do," Willo replied.

Sam took a seat on the ground, continuing to run her hand over the stone. "I do," she said softly. "They left their mark, and it still remains. Not only in this stone but in this orchard."

"And you will too, Sam," Deana said. "I know you're confused about where your life is headed right now, but you need to know that you can only leave a lasting imprint when you're happy."

"You need to decide what will make you happy," Willo said.

"What if I don't know?" Sam asked.

"Then you don't know," Deana said. "But don't turn your back on any opportunity that might provide the answer. If you want to interview for that job in New York, you should."

"If you want to see Angelo, you should," Willo said. "But don't live with regret, sweetheart. You never want to look back at your life and say you should've done this or that, because you'll never get another chance to be young or to do it."

"But right now, you should probably go take that nap," Deana said, holding out her hands and helping her daughter to her feet. "Can't make important decisions exhausted."

Sam looked at the cornerstone and then at her mom and grandma. "Actually, I'd rather make some cookies with you, if you don't mind. Some thumbprints."

Willo and Deana smiled. "We'd love to,"

they said in unison.

"What flavor?" Deana asked.

"Apricot? Raspberry? Strawberry?" Willo asked.

"All of them," Sam replied.

Thumbprint Cookies (With Fresh Apricot, Strawberry, or Raspberry Jam)

Ingredients for Dough

2/3 cup granulated sugar
1 cup butter, room temperature
1/2 teaspoon vanilla extract
2 cups all-purpose flour

Ingredients for Jam

1/2 cup apricot jam, strawberry jam, or seedless raspberry jam (use your favorite flavor jam, or make your own jam or freezer jam . . . delicious!)

Ingredients for Icing

1 cup powdered sugar
1 1/2 teaspoons vanilla extract
2 to 3 teaspoons water

Directions for Dough

In a small mixing bowl, combine the sugar, butter, and vanilla. Beat at medium speed until creamy, 2 to 3 minutes.

Add the flour and mix 2 to 3 minutes.

Form the dough into a ball, wrap in plastic wrap, and refrigerate at least 1 hour.

Assembly

Preheat the oven to 350°F.

Shape the dough into 1-inch balls. Place the balls 2 inches apart on an ungreased cookie sheet. Make an indentation with your thumb in the center of each cookie; the edges will crack.

Fill each cookie with 1/4 teaspoon jam.

Bake 14 to 18 minutes.

Cool completely.

In a small bowl, combine the icing ingredients and drizzle the icing over the cooled cookies.

(Note: Use different jams, so everyone has a favorite!)

Makes about 3 1/2 dozen cookies

■ ■ ■ ■

PART SIX:
ICE CREAM
SANDWICHES WITH
MAPLE SPICE
CHOCOLATE
CHIP–CHERRY
CHUNK COOKIES

■ ■ ■ ■

FIFTEEN

Summer 2017

The sun was filtering through the apple trees, angled shafts of light on the grassy orchard floor. Sam's father was standing in the light and, to Sam, he looked like an actor about to deliver a heartfelt monologue on Broadway.

He's still so handsome, Sam thought.

Most people love summer, especially Michiganders who wait all year for a respite from winter, but growing up, Sam had had mixed feelings about the season. Her father constantly worked in the summer months, waking early, coming home late, eating on the run. He was so busy with the orchard that — in Sam's summer memories — he was . . .

A blur, Sam thought as she continued to stare at him. *No, a ghost.*

Her father's shaggy blond hair ruffled in the breeze. His face and neck were deeply tanned from days working in the sun, his hands dusty and callused. Sam used to make fun of her father's "farmer's tan" growing up, but now she understood he never had a chance to slow down, even as she had just done earlier in the day. A pang of guilt caused her stomach to clench, and that feeling rose as she realized her dad — who looked just like her brother — had aged a bit since she'd last seen him.

Just like Grandma, she thought.

Gary Nelson turned in the light, as if he knew his daughter was near, and smiled as brightly as the beam of sun in which he was standing.

My baby, Sam could see him mouth, holding out his arms.

Sam ran to her father, and he hugged her tightly, his embrace erasing her exhaustion, making her feel as if there were no one else in the world but the two of them. He held her, and they rocked back and forth, in and out of the sunlight.

"I missed you," Gary said.

"I missed you, too," Sam said.

"So happy that you're home for a little while," he said.

He smells just the same, she thought. *Like sunshine and apples.* She stopped. *Like home.*

252

"Oh, I brought cookies," Sam said, letting go of her dad and holding out a square of tinfoil.

"A bribe?" her father asked, noisily unwrapping the foil.

"How did you know?" she said.

"A father knows everything." He winked. "Thumbprint cookies? Wow. Your mom and grandma haven't made these in a month of Sundays."

"Actually, I made them."

Gary raised his sun-bleached eyebrows and took a bite of a cookie. He shut his eyes and smiled. "Apricot," he sighed. "Better than I remembered." He opened his eyes, which danced even bluer in the sunlight. "You are a talent."

"Thanks, Dad," Sam said.

Gary grabbed his daughter's hand and took her into the middle of a row of trees, away from the crowds. They sat down under an apple tree, her father leaning against its trunk.

"The bribe worked," he said, downing another cookie. "I'm ready. So spill the beans. Why are you home?"

Sam told him everything, just as she had done with her mom and grandma earlier. Her father never said a word, simply listening intently, until she had finished and he had eaten all of the thumbprint cookies Sam had brought.

"You did the right thing quitting that job," he finally said. "You know that, right?"

"I do," she said. "But I still feel like such a failure."

"You're anything but," he said. "You're an amazing young woman, filled with intelligence, talent, and passion. That's all a parent can wish for in this world. I'm so, so proud of you."

"Thank you, Dad," Sam said. She stopped and kicked at the ground with her tennis shoe. "For some reason, though, I never feel proud of myself."

Gary wiped his hands on his jeans and eased his back against the trunk again. He searched the limbs and the skies, and then searched his daughter's eyes.

"You've always put such pressure on yourself," he said quietly. "Ever since you were a little girl. You wanted to be the fastest runner. You wanted to be the smartest in your class. You wanted to be the best baker." He stopped. "And I feel a lot of guilt about that."

"Why, Dad?" Sam asked.

"This is a family that never gives up or gives in. We push ourselves to succeed, every day. It's in our blood. But that's not always a good thing. We forget to take a break . . . we forget to give ourselves a break."

He inhaled deeply and then gently shooed along a bee that was buzzing around his face.

"This family is just like bees," he said. "Always on the move." He hesitated. "I just feel like I missed so much of your childhood, and I can never get that back."

"You had a business to run," she said. "It's OK."

Gary looked at his daughter. "Actually, it's not. I'm sorry."

He hesitated again. "Can I ask you a personal question?"

Sam nodded.

"And I don't want you to take it the wrong way."

Sam's eyes widened. "Oh, boy."

"Why do you knowingly seem to pick guys who make you unhappy — personally and professionally — even when you know it's not going to end well from the very beginning?"

Sam's face flushed with shock. "What are you implying, Dad?"

"I knew I'd upset you," he said. "And that's not my intention. But I want to talk about why you seem to get yourself into relationships with men who you know in your heart are not right for you."

"Like?" Sam asked, her eyes flashing.

"Like Connor," he said. "You two were as different as night and day, and still you dated him — all through high school and college, even when we all knew you would eventually leave home."

"Dad," Sam said, "I did love him . . . in my own way."

"Did you?" he asked. "Or was he safe? Like that little blanket you carried around until you started first grade."

Sam's eyes rimmed with tears.

"And Chef Dimples," Gary continued. "Why would you work for a man like that?"

"It was a great opportunity, Dad," she said. "It's not easy to find jobs like that in New York. It was a gift. And it's leading to other opportunities now." She could feel her anger rising at her father's inquiry. "You wouldn't understand."

"I wouldn't?" he asked, his voice icier than Sam had heard it in ages. An apple thumped beside him, shiny and bright, too heavy to remain on the tree. He picked it up, rubbed it on his jeans, and then took a big bite.

"You know, most people think that summer is a respite from all the hard work for us: the trees produce fruit, we pick it and sell it, end of story. But the work here is never done." He took another bite of the apple and then looked at it. "We had such stellar spring and summer weather, which resulted in a bumper crop of produce. But now we can barely get all the fruit off the trees."

Gary scanned the orchard; migrant workers were lined up picking apples.

"This isn't an easy life for this family," he continued. "But imagine what it's like for their families. The backbreaking work for not much money. The lack of benefits. Trying to bridge a gap between their culture and ours. No permanent home, always on the move looking for seasonal work. Just trying to survive. But knowing they're giving their children a better chance at a better future."

"I know," she said. "I see it in the city, too."

"They just want the dream we all have," he said, "and they will kill themselves to achieve it." He hesitated. "That's why I didn't know if I wanted to sign up for all this, Sam," her dad continued quietly. "I saw what Deana's family went through, their years of struggle, of little money, of worry and wondering how they could keep this going.

"I wanted to be a civil engineer. You knew

that, right? I wanted to move far away from Michigan and work on roads, bridges, and buildings in the city," he said. "And then I met your mother."

"So you sold out for love?" Sam asked.

Her father shook his head before finishing the apple and setting the core beside him. "No, that's what I'm trying to tell you," he said. "I didn't sell out. I found myself. And that's what you need to do eventually."

"But . . ." Sam started.

"I don't mean to sound harsh, I really don't," he said. "I'm so, so proud of you. You will have an amazing life and career, but I just don't want you falling into a trap of doing the same thing over and over. I think you seek out men like Connor and Chef Dimples because they allow you to keep running and not commit."

"Dad," Sam protested. "That's not nice. Are you trying to be mean?"

"I'm not, honey," he said, grabbing her hand. "Honestly. I just think you've been torn much of your life like I was."

"Torn?"

"Between wanting to be here and wanting to run as far away as possible," he said. "To reinvent yourself. And I get that. But stop picking guys as safety nets from allowing yourself to make that decision. It's unhealthy."

Gary stopped and picked up the apple core. He wound his arm back and flung it into the distance, the core bouncing until it disappeared. "It's OK to find yourself. Take all the time you need. Travel. Try different jobs. Bounce all over the world. But stop picking the wrong guys as ellipses in your life. Pick someone who is an exclamation point to your life."

He continued. "When I met your mother, she made everything clear. I knew I wanted to stay here. I knew I wanted to continue what her grandparents had started. I knew I wanted to embrace and improve their legacy. Your mother and I talked about leaving."

"Why didn't you?" Sam asked.

"I'd been trying to convince myself that this wasn't good enough for me," he said. "That staying would be a cop-out. But one Sunday afternoon, I watched your grandmother teaching your mom a recipe in the kitchen, and I started crying."

"Dad," Sam started softly, reaching out for his hand.

"It was such a simple moment but such an important and beautiful one," he said. "Willo was teaching your mom how to make ice cream sandwiches with her favorite cookies. And watching them, I had to ask myself what I really wanted in my life. What was I missing? What was I seeking? Love? Adventure? Affirmation? Challenging career? I had all of those things. And that's when I realized I hadn't been asking the right question of myself."

"Which was?" Sam asked.

"What would be my biggest regret in my life if I were to die tomorrow?"

"And what was that?" she asked.

"Leaving," he said.

SIXTEEN

Summer 1988

Gordon's beloved La-Z-Boy was rocking violently. He was watching the Detroit Tigers pummel the Boston Red Sox, putting an end to Boston's twenty-four-game home winning streak at Fenway Park, and he kept jumping out of his chair with each run the Tigers scored. Every time he stood, their Jack Russell, Peachy, would jump onto the chair — riding it as if he were on a surf board — waiting for it to slow and then curling up into the warm seat that had been vacated.

"Honey, you're going to have a heart attack," Willo said. "Calm down."

Peachy jumped back off as Gordon sat back down in his corduroy rocker. He took off his Detroit ball cap and waved off his wife as if she were a bothersome mosquito. "I never thought they'd lose at home again," he said. "Tigers did it." He stopped and put

261

his cap back on, adjusting it just so on his tanned, balding head.

"Mind bringing me a beer to celebrate?" he asked Willo.

"What did you celebrate with the first two beers?" she asked.

The windows were open in their farmhouse, and a warm summer breeze was tossing the curtains around. Willo looked at her husband, who had returned his focus to the game, and smiled.

"Been a hot summer," she said, thinking of how hard her husband had toiled in the muggy weather. "You deserve it."

She returned with an ice-cold beer for him and a Vernors for herself.

"Cheers to the Tigers," she said, nodding at the TV, clinking her husband's beer with her own ginger ale.

Gordon caught his wife's eye and stared intently at her, nodding at her. "Back atcha," he said, his voice suddenly emotional.

Willo leaned in, pulled off her husband's ball cap, and gave him a peck on top of the head. "I think I'll bake something while you finish watching the game," she said, replacing his cap.

"How about some ice cream sandwiches?" she asked. "Made with your favorite cookies."

"Your secret maple spice chocolate chip–cherry chunk cookies?" he asked. "I won't fight you on that." Gordon laughed and rubbed his tummy.

Gary watched his in-laws in silence from the staircase in the foyer. He had made it halfway downstairs from the bedroom he and Deana had shared in their house since they graduated college and recently married, but the sweet scene had compelled him to stop and watch. Peachy — constantly on the prowl for unwanted varmints and visitors in the orchard and at home — suddenly scampered into the foyer and caught Gary sitting there. Peachy's wiry body stiffened, and he hunched his back to bark.

"Peachy!" Gary said in a hushed yet forceful whisper. "No bark!"

Peachy stared at Gary, as if to say, *You're the visitor now,* and again hunched his back.

"You wanna cookie?" Gary whispered in a singsong voice, offering the dog a fake treat. "C'mere."

Peachy scampered up the steps and stood in front of Gary, his tail wagging uncontrollably. But when Gary offered nothing, the dog barked his disapproval, and Gary jumped.

"Peachy!" Gordon called from the living room. "What is it? You get 'im."

Peachy went running to Gordon, and Gary watched the dog jump onto his father-in-law's lap and circle round and round for a moment, before curling into a ball and falling immediately asleep.

I wish life were so simple, Gary thought.

He looked down at the letter in his hand, the words blurring in front of his eyes.

Dear Mr. Nelson:

Essex Engineering is pleased to offer you the position of assistant project engineer at our company headquarters in San Francisco, California. Mr. Essex, a fellow University of Michigan engineering graduate, feels your education and qualifications would make you . . .

Gordon yelled excitedly, and Gary jumped. He watched his father-in-law get back out of his recliner, take a sip of his beer, and then settle back into the rocker, Peachy settling back into his lap once again.

Do I want life to follow the same routine? Gary thought. *The same, never-ending pattern of orchard life — season by season, tied to this place, this house — over and over and over again?*

Gary thought of his own parents, who had worked in the auto industry in Detroit their whole lives, also doing the same thing every single day. Gordon and Willo wanted Gary and Deana to continue their legacy . . .

But do we want that? he thought. *We haven't even started our lives, and everyone wants to define them for us.*

Gary nervously turned the letter over in his hands, the paper becoming more and more crinkled. He set it on the step and then looked at his own hands. Since graduating from college, he and Deana had returned home to work on the orchard and live until they figured things out. His hands had gone from smooth to deeply callused, and the daily labor had shifted from mind to body. The orchard was growing — more people were traveling to and discovering the beauty of northern Michigan — but the profits were small, the work monumental.

Gary turned and looked at the family photos that spanned the staircase wall. Their lives had all been marked by the orchard and Michigan's seasons: peach blossoms and blizzards, apple picking and pumpkins. Gary's heart began to race, and he had the urge to run before this small world and home collapsed on top of him.

"What are you doing?"

Gary's panic subsided as soon as he heard his new wife's voice.

"I'm making some ice cream sandwiches," Willo said, her voice reverberating into the hallway. "Want to help?"

"I'd love to," Deana said.

"How's the guest room?" Willo asked. "Are you and Gary comfortable? I know it's small. I know it's not your own home."

"Mom, stop," Deana said. "It's wonderful. We can never thank you enough."

Gary had asked Deana to marry him at halftime of the Michigan–Michigan State game. It might not have sounded romantic to other people, but to true Michiganders this was the equivalent of being proposed to in front of the Eiffel Tower in Paris while an orchestra played.

"You're more than my son-in-law," Willo had told Gary over Christmas. "You're like my son. Never had a boy, so it's nice to have one around for a change. For some reason, the women in our family can never give birth to a boy. I think it has something to do with our recipe box . . . I think there was some secret pact made long ago, so we could pass it on forever. You should know, that's the joke around these parts, by the way: 'What are the two things you can't get at Mullins Orchards? A bad pie and a baby boy.' "

Gary had laughed, but Willo had been

serious. "You and Deana will have a girl, I promise," she said. "But maybe you can break the streak."

The two had ended up talking about the future that Christmas, whether he and Deana might move from Michigan and where they might end up, and Gary had shared the list of interviews he had lined up for the spring with Deana and her parents.

But not this letter, he thought.

Gary quietly scooted himself up the stairs a few steps, like a reverse Slinky, giving himself a better angle into the kitchen. He watched Willo and Deana assemble ingredients for the ice cream, fudge, and caramel. They pulled butter from the refrigerator, a mix of chocolate chips and cocoa powder along with flour and white and brown sugar from the pantry, vanilla and maple spice from the spice drawer.

"And the pièce de résistance?" Willo asked. "Voilà."

She held up a bag of cherries the orchard had dried.

Deana stuck her hand into the bag and popped a few into her mouth. "These taste like heaven," she said.

Gary heard the women shuffle around the kitchen, talking and laughing as they mixed ingredients. Their voices drifted up to him, along with the evening sounds of life along the bay and orchard: birds calling, cicadas chirping, frogs moaning, the ball game playing, the dull roar of boats and lawn mowers.

"The secret is in the cherries and the maple spice," Willo told her daughter. "It's such a perfect combination with the chocolate and the ice cream."

"Ice cream sandwiches," Deana said. "Reminds me of being a kid. They are quintessential summer."

The sounds of his wife and mother-in-law talking were comforting, like the play-by-play of the baseball game.

She is right, Gary thought. *All of this is quintessential.*

Gary watched the duo skitter around the kitchen, eating as much of the chocolate chips as they put into the batter, talking nonstop as they did, Willo imparting knowledge through old stories, just as she did in the pie pantry.

When his mother-in-law pulled the old recipe box from the cabinet, Gary remembered once joking that the cabinet was so big he believed the farmhouse had been built around it. Willo opened the recipe box with a key she always wore around her neck and, as if by memory, went directly to an index card, pulling it from the box.

"Look at the card for these cookies," Willo said to Deana. "It's covered with chocolate fingerprints."

"It looks like a Dalmatian," Deana laughed. "Spots everywhere. Now there's some history."

"And some old DNA," Willo laughed. "And listen to this. I just love your grandmother's directions. 'Drop by heaping teaspoons onto an ungreased cookie sheet . . . and then into your mouth.' Or this at the bottom of the card: 'Eat warm cookies immediately with grandchildren.' "

Gary watched Willo pull another index card from the recipe box.

"Not only are all of her recipes incredible, but most of them have her own special directions on them. That's why I love this recipe box so much. It's like she's still here, right now, with us."

"I believe that," Deana said. "I can feel her cooking with us."

"Oh, and look at this," Willo said. "One of her friends from church gave her a family gelatin recipe — she used to call them her 'Sunday salads' although they didn't have one leaf of lettuce or anything healthy in them — and at the end it says, 'Shake until it doesn't shake anymore . . . unlike my thighs.' Another gelatin recipe says, 'Jiggle 'til it doesn't wiggle.' "

The two roared in laughter.

As the two laughed, Gary's heart rose into his throat, and he felt as if he might cry. Watching the two share beloved recipes moved Gary and caused him to see his mother-in-law — and his new family — in a new light.

"Why don't you add these items to the restaurant?" Deana suddenly said.

"What do you mean?" Willo asked.

"Ice cream represents summer," Deana said. "It should be on the menu at the pie pantry. People would go crazy. You could even package and sell the ice cream and ice cream sandwiches. I mean, what if we developed our own flavors, like apple cider ice cream?"

"I've never thought of that," Willo said. "Just when you think you've thought of it all. How would we do it?"

"I'll pull together a model and forecast," Deana said. "Let's sit down tomorrow and break down cost, how we would make them, package them, what equipment we'd need, what health codes we'd need to meet." She stopped. "All of this is why people come here. I know there will be some logistical and business hoops to jump through, but I think it makes sense."

This time, Gary's eyes filled with tears as his business-major wife excitedly shared a new vision about . . .

Our business, Gary said to himself.

"What do you enjoy most about studying business?" Willo asked Deana.

"Being an entrepreneur," she said. "What do you enjoy most about running a business?"

"Same," Willo said. "I love seeing people smile. I love living off of the land that our family started. I love doing it for ourselves. It's our company. At the end of every single day, Gordon and I can look at each other and say, 'We gave it our all.' What more can you ask?"

Willo hesitated, and continued. "And at the end of my life, I know I can look back and say I had no regrets. I think that's the secret to a happy and long life: being able to look back — be it at the very end of a day or at the very end of life — and say, 'I did it. I don't regret a darn thing.' Too many people end their lives wishing they had done this, or done that, and they are filled with regret. I don't want that for you or Gary. You two need to do what will make you the happiest."

Gary watched the two hug.

"Oh, I think the cookies are ready," Willo said. "Grab the ice cream."

Willo continued: "You know it's fitting we're making ice cream sandwiches, isn't it? Each component complements the other, makes it better . . . complete. Just like us." She laughed as she began assembling them, putting a big scoop of cold ice cream between two warm cookies. "Ice cream sandwiches are like the teamwork of dessert."

We are a good team, Gary thought. We all do make each other better and more complete. His soul suddenly filled with pride at how much Deana's parents and grandparents — as well as his own — had achieved and at his wife's vision for the future. *They do have a good life.*

Gary scanned the wall of family photos, his eyes locking with the orchard's ancestors.

We *do have a good life,* he said, altering his thought.

A good life. Maybe it is that simple, Gary thought. *Maybe that's really all there is to life.*

Gary looked at the letter in his hands. As he stared at the job offer, the opportunity for a new life somewhere far from here, his eyes couldn't help but keep changing the name Essex for Nelson.

Will I regret staying? Gary wondered.

"Who wants ice cream sandwiches?" he heard Willo yell.

No, he realized. *I'll regret leaving.*

Gary reread the letter, one last time, and then he folded it into a tiny square and put it in a secret compartment in his wallet, where it would remain hidden forever.

"I do," Gary suddenly yelled, standing and coming down the stairs. "Make it two!"

SEVENTEEN

"Live without any regrets, Sam," Gary said. "That's the only advice I can give to you. Life goes by so fast — in one blink of God's eye, as your grandmother likes to say — so make sure you have no regrets. Do what makes you happy."

He stopped and pulled out his wallet, whose black leather had been worn nearly clear on both sides. He opened it and pulled from a small compartment the letter he'd received decades ago.

"You know what this means, don't you?" her father asked.

"That you need a new wallet," Sam said, and laughed.

"I had convinced myself not only that this life wasn't good enough — this place, this job — but that I wasn't good enough," he said. "I was. You are. No matter where you land."

He hesitated. "One of the hardest things

about being a parent is letting go," he said. "Doing everything you believe is right, and then trusting you've done a good enough job and just . . . letting go." Gary looked at his daughter. "One of the hardest things I've ever done was kissing you good-bye, right here in this orchard, and letting you go off to college in New York. The hardest thing for your mom and grandma was leaving you there, letting you be on your own . . . letting you be an adult, letting you make your own decisions, letting you soar." He stopped. "But I didn't have children to be replicas of myself."

He folded the letter and returned it to his wallet. "Parents should be respected but not idolized."

"I idolize you, Dad," Sam said softly. "I always have."

"Don't," Gary said, looking his daughter directly in the eye. "Parents are human, just like you. We make good decisions and bad ones. We are flawed. But I didn't have children who only did what I said, or wanted to be like I was. And I will die with regret if I ever felt you or your brother lived only to please your mother and me." He stopped and watched the workers pick fruit. "We have choices. They often don't. We're blessed in so many ways. So, please, I beg you, be who you want to be. Whether it's here or New York, whether it's alone or with someone . . . but don't let guilt force you into a life you don't want. I love you, and I'll always love you no matter what decisions you make, because you're an amazing person. I just want you to believe that you're an amazing person."

"Dad," Sam said softly.

"And one last thing," he said. "You know I ran cross-country in high school, too. It's a tough sport, isn't it?"

Sam nodded, remembering her days of training, running hills, often running alone.

"When we run, the only people we have to rely on are ourselves," Gary said. "When I ran on sunny days, I would often talk to my shadow. My shadow stayed in lockstep with me, never leaving my side. I always believed I'd have to do everything on my own. When I met your mother on a sunny day in college, we took a walk and talked. I remember looking at our shadows as we walked."

"I don't think I'm following, Dad," Sam said, a quizzical look on her face.

"I had met my shadow," he said softly. "I'd met the person I knew would be in lockstep with me the rest of my life. Your shadow is out there, Sam. Maybe it's this Angelo fellow. Who knows? But it's hard to keep running a marathon like life, especially when you're alone."

Gary leaned over and hugged Sam. "Back to work," he said, standing. "Thanks for the cookies."

"Thanks for the pep talk," Sam said.

Her father winked. "Love you," he said.

"Me, too," Sam said.

She watched her father walk away and start picking apples alongside the workers. She watched the workers, considered the sacrifices they made every day, the uncertainties they faced and their children faced.

An apple thumped beside her, just as one had done moments earlier beside her father. She picked it up, wiped it on her shorts, and then took a big bite. Sam considered the apple, how its beauty and simplicity — like the beauty and simplicity of this land — had made her want to be a pastry chef.

Sam stood, her legs feeling shaky.

This land grounds me and yet feels like quicksand, Sam thought, taking a bite of apple. *Have I always been running?*

Sam finished her apple and then walked over, picked up a basket, and put it around her neck. She found a tree and began to pick apples alongside the other workers. Sam chatted with them in the broken Spanish she knew.

"Gracias," a young woman said to her.

Sam's heart broke. "No," Sam said. *"Usted . . . gracias. Por . . ."* Sam stopped, searching her mind for the word. *"Todo."*

The woman smiled, her dark eyes twinkling, her hands in motion, never slowing. She looked at Sam and said, *"La vida es bella. Familia lo es todo."*

Sam cocked her head, trying to translate in her mind. The woman looked at a man next to her, and he nodded. "She said, 'Life is beautiful. Family is everything.' "

Sam's eyes widened, and her heart jumped. *"Gracias,"* she said.

Sam glanced over, and her father was watching her, smiling, still caught in a shaft of light, his shadow as long as the apple trees. Sam picked another apple and when she turned again, her father was gone, but the light remained.

Ice Cream Sandwiches With Maple Spice Chocolate Chip–Cherry Chunk Cookies

Ingredients

1/2 cup plus 1 tablespoon butter, room temperature
1/2 cup granulated sugar
1/4 cup dark brown sugar, packed
1 large egg
1 teaspoon vanilla extract
1 teaspoon maple extract
1 1/2 cups all-purpose flour
1/2 teaspoon baking soda
1/4 teaspoon salt
1 1/2 tablespoons cocoa powder
1/2 12-ounce bag semisweet chocolate chips
1/2 12-ounce bag white chocolate chips
1/4 cup flaked coconut
1/2 cup dried cherries or cranberries
Vanilla ice cream

Directions

Preheat the oven to 350°F.

In a large mixing bowl, cream the butter, gradually adding the granulated sugar and brown sugar. Slowly add the egg, vanilla, and maple extract and cream together.

Sift together the flour, baking soda, salt, and cocoa powder into a separate bowl. Slowly add the flour mixture to the butter mixture and combine (don't overmix, just enough to moisten).

Stir in the semisweet chocolate chips, white chocolate chips, coconut, and dried cherries.

Drop the dough by heaping teaspoons onto an ungreased cookie sheet. Bake 10 to 12 minutes, or until lightly golden.

Let cookies cool for an hour. Place one scoop of vanilla ice cream (or your favorite flavor! Or make your own homemade ice cream, which is THE best!) between two cookies and press together carefully to form a sandwich. You may eat immediately, or wrap in plastic wrap and freeze.

Yields about a dozen ice cream sandwiches

■ ■ ■ ■

PART SEVEN:
THE PERFECT
PIE CRUST

■ ■ ■ ■

EIGHTEEN

Summer 2017

Sam awoke with a start. She sat straight up in bed, confused and in a panic. Her hair was over her eyes, and she brushed it back, but the world was still dark. And then lightning flashed, just outside her bedroom window, and seconds later . . . *BOOM!*

Sam jumped.

Lightning again flashed, and Sam counted — just as her mom and dad had taught her — until thunder boomed again.

The storm is on top of us, Sam thought.

She checked her Hello Kitty clock, which read 6:08 A.M., slowly got out of bed, and shuffled toward her window.

BOOM!

The house shook. In fact, the whole world seemed to tremble. Thunder echoed off the hillside of the orchard and rolled, like a timpani drum, down into the bay, where the rumble seemed to drift across the water and out into Lake Michigan like the final rousing note of a symphony.

It was dark, but the lightning illuminated the world in flashes. It reminded Sam of a nightclub in the city her friends loved to frequent on Saturday nights.

Sam had been in the middle of a dream when the thunder woke her. She had been picking apples when the whole world began to collapse, the earth all around her dropping away in big chunks — the orchard, her grandma's farmhouse, the pie pantry, the bay, until only she remained on a tiny crag of land clutching the limb of an apple tree, the only thing that kept her from falling into nothingness.

Sam shuffled toward the bathroom and washed her face in cold water.

Maybe it wasn't a dream, Sam thought, drying her face and then staring at her tired reflection in the mirror. *Maybe it was a premonition. Maybe my whole world — my future and my family — is disintegrating in front of me, and there's nothing I can do to stop it.*

Sam thought of her father's letter and of the workers who labored on the orchard.

Does God give us free will? she wondered. *Or is everything predestined?*

Sam dabbed some eye cream and moisturizer onto her face before running a brush through her hair.

Is my fate already sealed?

Sam pulled on some jeans and a long-sleeved T-shirt, then walked downstairs into the kitchen. The house was quiet. She leaned into the window and scanned the orchard for her mom and grandma.

Weather must have kept them from walking, she thought. *Bet they're already at the pie pantry.*

Sam headed out the door and stopped.

No key, she suddenly remembered.

Then she shook her head, realizing there wasn't a need for one. Her parents never locked their house or their car doors, and she didn't even know if her grandmother had a key for anything but her recipe box.

Sam took off jogging up the hill and into the orchard. It was beginning to sprinkle, the wind was gusting, and it was chilly — almost cold — the temperature having dropped precipitously overnight.

Sam slowed as she made it into the orchard. It was only August, but the rapid drop in temperature reminded Sam that snow could be falling here in just a few weeks.

Lots of winter coats worn over my Halloween costumes growing up, Sam thought.

Northern Michigan was another world in winter, stunningly beautiful but shockingly desolate.

"Like *The Shining,*" Sam said out loud to the trees with a knowing laugh.

Sam preferred New York in the winter. It was cold but bustling, and she loved tucking herself into cozy coffee shops and tiny cafés. After the resorters left Michigan, only the die-hard locals remained. The holidays were certainly cute — as the town draped itself in lights — but January through March was a dark, challenging trek, only for the hardiest of souls, bodies, and hearts.

In the near distance, the lights from the pie pantry twinkled in the dark. The old barn looked as if it were smiling and bright-eyed, ready for the day ahead.

It's like my family's soul is alive in there, Sam thought.

The heavy wooden front door was unlocked, and Sam grunted as she pulled it open. The pie pantry was warm and welcoming, and her grandmother's watercolors on the floor happily greeted Sam.

She couldn't help but smile.

She headed toward the kitchen, stopping in front of the long, barn-wood counter and hiding behind a huge beam that ran from the floor to the rafters. Sam watched the bakers work.

For decades, nearly the same group of women had gathered to bake at dawn. They worked alongside one another at islands and stainless steel tables, clad in jeans and Mullins aprons, smiles on their faces, their hands, bodies, and mouths in constant motion, working independently and yet in unison, telling stories and sharing secrets about life and baking.

Over the years, a good chunk of the labor had been mechanized — cherries were pitted and apples were skinned and cored by large machines. And industrial-sized ovens could now bake many pies at once.

But the pie pantry still prided itself on its "handmade" moniker. Each and every pie and dessert was handmade, meaning the crusts were individually made, rolled, and hand-crimped, and the fillings were made in small batches so they could be spiced to perfection.

"People know when something is made with love," Willo always said. "You can taste the effort . . . and the love."

Sam believed that. She believed that simple ingredients and careful preparation always yielded the best food.

You don't have to cook fancy or complicated masterpieces, just good food from fresh ingre-

dients, Sam remembered Julia Child once saying, a philosophy that was also taught in culinary school. Sam watched the women twirl around the kitchen, and she remembered another Julia quote, a plaque that she had in her apartment in New York: *Until I discovered cooking, I was never really interested in anything.*

It was the same with Sam. It was the same with this core group of women: their lives seemed to revolve around a joy for baking. While Deana and Willo buzzed around the kitchen like bees, overseeing the work, double-checking outgoing deliveries, Sam watched three women calmly work alongside one another as if they were the eye of a hurricane, calm amid the chaos.

Donna, Debbie, and DeDe Cupertino were known in the pie pantry — and all around Suttons Bay — as the "D Cups," a source of never-ending laughter, as the triplets were wirier than a cooling rack and thinner than a pie shell. Donna and Debbie had each had six boys, and DeDe had had five girls, enough kids, Donna joked, "to field two basketball teams, a football team, and all the cheerleaders."

The women were all around the age of Sam's mom, but they looked much older: no makeup, gray hair parted down the middle and pulled back, baggy shirts. The Cupertino family had not had the easiest of lives, but they truly loved working at the pie pantry, and Willo treated them like family. They were the first to receive health benefits, and Willo employed them year round, even in the winter, as they made all the desserts for the holidays, from Christmas to Valentine's.

Sam had gone to school with many of their kids, who often kept Sam at arm's length, treating her as if she were better than they were, a surrogate employer, like Willo and Deana were to their mothers. It had made Sam uncomfortable. But for many of the kids in Sam's high school, like the Cupertinos, college wasn't an option. Leaving northern Michigan wasn't an option either.

There was an undercurrent town-gown rivalry that occurred between those in the area who owned small businesses and those who worked for them. Many people considered Sam to be better than they were for leaving town, and many of her high school friends had stopped talking to her when she left for New York. Sam had tried to tell them she wasn't abandoning them, but that she simply wanted to learn about what she loved most from those who knew it best.

Maybe I was *abandoning them, though,*

Sam thought, watching the sisters work.

"Well, look who the cat drug in!"

Sam jumped, just as she had earlier at the thunder, at the sound of DeDe's booming voice.

"If it ain't Julia Child," she continued.

Sam simultaneously bristled and enjoyed the comparison.

"Willo and Deana said you were in town," Donna said. "Must have missed you when you arrived."

The sisters worked similar hours to what Sam had in New York, but even earlier here, often arriving at three A.M. to prep dough.

Sam walked into the kitchen, and the sisters hugged her, followed by those who had yet to see her.

"How's New York?" Debbie asked. "Been mugged yet?"

Everyone laughed, but Sam hated such simplistic clichés.

People who have never been to New York make snap judgments of the city, Sam thought, bristling again.

"Ever been to New York?" Sam asked a bit too curtly.

Willo shot her granddaughter a stern look, stopping and wiping her hands on her apron.

Debbie's tired face drooped even more,

the bags under her eyes twitching. "No," she said. "Just Traverse City a few times a year."

Sam's stomach clenched, and she thought of what her father had said about being alone.

I do keep people at arm's distance, she thought. *Why?*

"I hope you get there someday," Sam said softly, smiling at Debbie. "You'd love it. And even the food on the street is good."

"Tell us about it," they all said, smiling, returning to work. "Tell us about working with that famous TV star."

Sam did, and the women's faces dropped again with disappointment as she shared what it was really like.

"But there were some really good stories," Sam added to perk them up, telling them about the celebrities and bachelorettes who used to come into the shop, as well as explaining how morning TV shows like *Good Morning America* worked.

"*GMA* should come here," DeDe said, standing tall, her shoulders back, her voice filling with pride. "This is a *real* bakery."

Everyone nodded and agreed, as Willo said, "Now, now."

The kitchen was teeming with activity, and Sam had to admit she missed working with a bigger team. There was a sense of excitement when she was in school and in her internship, a sense of camaraderie of working with a team, everyone flying, on their toes, working on deadlines. Sam loved working with Trish, but working at Dimples Bakery was little fun and highly controlled.

Watching this group work, Sam finally realized how well trained the bakers were at the pie pantry, something she had never noticed growing up. They knew the important basics in the kitchen: they understood the recipes and had made them over and over again, perfecting them as they went. The pie pantry had digital scales to weigh ingredients, which were more accurate than measuring cups. Her mom and grandma had invested in expensive mixers with dough hooks and paddles. And they all talked about the recipes as they went along, asking if a little more nutmeg might add depth to a certain dessert.

The kitchen was hot and cold: steamy from the ovens and the work at hand, cool from the chilly breeze that blew in through the barn windows and open doors. Outside, lightning flashed. Inside, pie pans, knives, and countertops gleamed.

"Teach us something, Julia Child," DeDe boomed, knocking Sam from her thoughts.

"What?" Sam asked.

"You went to that fancy school, and it's about time we all took a break," DeDe said. "Teach us something you learned."

Sam's heart raced. She felt as if she had been transported back to school, and a professor had called on her to make a sauce for the class.

"Everyone's so busy," she said. "I haven't even had any coffee."

"Here's some coffee," Willo said, walking over with a steaming mug and an apple cider donut.

"I'd like to see what I paid for," Deana said with a wink, walking over to nudge Sam with her elbow. "Honestly, we'd all love to learn something new."

Sam took a big sip from the mug, the hot coffee burning her tongue. She looked outside as the lightning flashed, and an idea came to her.

"*Pâte brisée sucrée,*" she said.

"What's that?" Willo asked.

"It literally means broken sweet dough," Sam explained. "But it's essentially the perfect pie crust."

This time, Willo's face fell. "I thought we already made the perfect pie crust here," she said.

"Oh, Grandma, I didn't mean it that way,"

Sam said. "Your pie crust is amazing. This is just the way I was taught." She looked at DeDe. "This was how Julia Child made it, and our instructors taught us."

She hesitated and reached out to touch her grandma's arm. "I promise you'll like it," she said. "And you can make it in a food processor, too." Sam stopped and looked at her mom and grandma. "You've shared so much with me through your recipe boxes. Let me share something with you."

The two nodded. Sam smiled, took another swig of coffee, then tied on an apron.

She began to assemble ingredients — flour, sugar, salt, shortening — talking excitedly about the first time she learned the recipe.

"I was taught by my mom and grandma that a great pie is like a great family," Sam said. "It must have a great foundation to work."

Willo and Deana beamed.

"The key to a great *pate brisée sucrée* is chilled butter and cold water." The women gathered around as Sam mixed the ingredients by hand, rubbing the butter and shortening into the dry ingredients with the tips of her fingers, adding cold water, forming the dough into a ball.

"But the most important part of a perfect

crust is the *fraisage*," Sam said.

"The what?" Deana asked, moving closer.

"It literally means milling, but it's the final blending of the dough," Sam explained. She placed the dough on a lightly floured surface and used the heel of her hand to swiftly press little circles of dough away from her until the ball was flat. "The reason you do it like this, in small increments, is to incorporate the butter evenly through the dough. That's what creates a flaky crust."

Sam pulled the dough into a ball again, wrapped it in plastic wrap, and placed it in one of the kitchen's refrigerators. "Now it needs to rest," she said.

"Can we try?" Debbie asked, looking at Sam and then Willo.

"Of course," Willo said. "It's nice to learn something new."

As Sam began to walk the bakers through the recipe, moving around to instruct each person as she'd been taught and as she had done in New York, a cold wind gusted through the kitchen.

"North wind," Willo said. "Farmer's almanac already portends a cold winter."

"Same every year," DeDe laughed.

Willo's eyes scanned the kitchen, and she smiled at the band of women working happily as one.

She watched her granddaughter, and her heart swelled with love.

Will she stay? Willo wondered. *Or will my independent girl blow away like this wind?*

Willo stopped for a moment and pulled her arms around herself, the cold wind and the strength and camaraderie of the women transporting her.

She sidled up to Sam. "Mind if I tell you a story as we bake?"

Sam shook her head. "It's nice to learn something new." She smiled.

"Women saved this orchard," Willo said. "On a cold day just like this. You need to know that."

NINETEEN

March 1967

The apple blossoms were in full bloom, and the orchard looked as if it had been dusted in pink snow. Every few seconds, a gusty, warm wind bellowed down the hillside and into the bay, a roar followed by a brief silence in which another sound would emerge: the hum of bees on the blossoms.

"Reminds me of *The Wizard of Oz* when the movie turned into Technicolor," Willo said, pushing up the sleeves on her long-sleeved shirt. "Feels like May."

Madge took off her jacket and tied it around her waist, while Wilbur and Gordon were ahead of them in the orchard, stopping, pointing, inspecting branches.

"Birdie!" Deana screeched, letting go of her mother's and grandmother's hands and pointing at a cardinal in the quickly greening orchard grass. She watched the bird and then looked at the trees. "Apples!"

"Let's hope," Madge said to herself, mussing Deana's blond hair. They walked for another moment until Madge stopped and looked at Willo. "It's March, and it's almost eighty degrees. This is bad. Very bad."

Spring had sprung in the middle of winter. Northern Michigan was experiencing record-breaking warmth at a time when heavy snow and icy cold typically blanketed the entire state.

"Pray this holds," Madge continued. It was only then that Willo noticed that her mom's voice was shaky. When she looked closely at her, she realized her cheeks were quivering.

"Are you OK?" Willo asked.

"No," Madge said.

For days, the family stayed glued to the local weather forecast. They visited other orchards, talked to other farmers. They got on their knees before bed and prayed for a miracle, that Michigan weather would not return to normal.

But the temperatures, like their spirits, quickly began to drop, from the seventies to the forties. And then they heard the local meteorologist say that a Canadian cold front — the coldest of the winter, one of the coldest in decades — would be sweeping into Michigan, bringing below-freezing temperatures and snow.

"Will it really be that bad?" asked Willo, who was feeding Deana. "Don't we have insurance to cover everything?"

Madge smiled at her child's unwavering innocence and optimism.

I used to be like that, she thought, *but the pressures of the orchard have muted those traits.*

Although Willo had grown up on the orchard, being a kid had meant she only had cursory experience with the real work of the orchard. Then she had gone to college, met and married Gordon, and then her new marriage, pregnancy, and nearly two-year-old daughter kept her preoccupied. Gordon, Wilbur, and Madge carried the load.

"Crop insurance will only recover a little of our losses if it's bad," Madge said. "It's very expensive, Willo. We couldn't even afford to cover the new trees we put in over the last few years."

"What's that mean?" Willo asked, cocking her head.

Madge looked at Willo and then Deana, and her heart broke. Their faces were so young, so hopeful, so innocent.

"I don't know," Madge lied.

The next morning, the skies turned gray,

storm clouds rolled in like angry tumble-weeds, and the north wind began to blow so hard the pine trees bent, shuddered, and creaked. Snow blew sideways, flakes no bigger than a speck, but slowly they grew thicker, wetter, denser. Madge held her mug of coffee close to her face and stared out the kitchen window; snow began to cover the snowdrops and daffodils that had bloomed too early, and she could actually see them droop in the cold.

"No," she said, her breath leaving a sad O on the window. "Noooo."

The snow was melting on the road and the grass, but when Madge squinted, it looked as if the sky was snowing pink flakes.

The apple blossoms are freezing and blowing away, she thought.

Two figures moved like ghosts in the snow. Madge squinted again, and she could see her husband and son-in-law jogging toward the house, zipping up coats, yelling to one another, their faces red. They rushed into the house, the cold wind following.

"We haven't been able to find any buds that haven't been frozen," Wilbur said, taking off his gloves and blowing on his hands.

"Have you checked them all?" Madge asked.

"There's millions of buds. You can't check

them all," Wilbur said. "The ones we checked . . ." He stopped and looked at Gordon.

"We haven't found any that weren't damaged," Gordon finished, his eyes down.

Madge didn't know what to say or do. She turned, pulled two mugs from the cupboard, filled them with coffee, and handed them to her son-in-law and husband. Deana toddled into the room, followed by Willo, and Madge suddenly burst into tears.

"Oh, honey," Wilbur said. He set his coffee down and pulled his wife close. She cried into his shoulder.

"What about heaters?" she finally asked, a hopeful tone in her voice.

"No money for heaters," he said. "We're not like the big guys who can rent heaters, or helicopters, or wind machines to stave off the frost."

Madge watched Willo pull Deana into her arms, and she felt as if their futures were freezing in front of her, blowing away in the cruel winter wind.

"So . . . ?" she asked her husband, her voice trembling. "Some of the apples? Galas? Granny Smiths? Red Delicious? What about the peaches? Anything?"

"Honey," Wilbur said softly. "We didn't find any buds that weren't frozen. This will

301

be the first year in our history that the entire crop will be killed off."

Madge's sobs echoed throughout the house.

Deana began to cry, too, and Willo could see the impact of this on families everywhere, from orchard owners to the summer workers who tended, picked, and packaged the fruit.

"Will we . . . ?" Madge started, unable to finish the sentence with "survive."

"I don't know," Wilbur whispered in a husky voice. "Gordon and I are meeting some farmers at the feed store to talk about what's next. We'll be back soon." He kissed his wife on the cheek. "We won't give up, you hear me? We survived more than a cold snap before."

Madge didn't say anything. Gordon gave her shoulders a gentle shake. "Right?"

"Right," she said in an unconvincing whisper.

The two departed, Gordon giving his wife and daughter a kiss as he left, forcing a smile at Madge. As Deana's cries subsided, the wind howled outside and buffeted the house.

"What can I do for you, Mom?" Willo asked.

Madge turned and watched Wilbur's truck

pull out of the driveway. The lights shone brightly into the house and then dimmed. The orchard looked even bleaker, the pinks and greens fading, like a beautiful new watercolor on an easel that had been left in the rain.

"I don't know," Madge said. "I don't know. I feel so lost and useless. Decades of work gone in the blink of an eye."

"Dad said we've almost lost the orchard before," Willo said. "That there were times when we didn't know if we'd make it through the winter, or if we could compete with other orchards, or if anyone would buy our fruit. How did we do it then?"

"I don't know," Madge said. "We were younger. Stupid optimism, I guess."

She wanted to take the words back as soon as she'd said them. The last thing she wanted to do was dent Willo's constantly sunny demeanor.

"Let's say a prayer then," Willo said. She put Deana on the floor, grabbed her and her mother's hands and bowed her head. "God, please help us in our time of need. I know we too often pray when we need something, and I'm sorry about that, but we truly need a miracle. We need a sign, an idea, a little bit of hope for this orchard. We'll do all the heavy lifting, just, please, give us a sign. In God's name we pray. Amen."

"All gone," Deana said happily, using two of the few words she'd recently learned and loved to repeat, especially at mealtime.

Madge finally smiled. "Close, baby girl," she said, her face breaking into a smile. "But it's *amen*. Can you say *amen*?"

"All gone," Deana said again.

Madge smiled and looked out the window, the orchard in the near distance, and suddenly her granddaughter's words rang even truer.

All gone, she thought. *You're right, little one.*

"I'm going to make some more coffee, just to get our juices flowing a little better," Willo said, rubbing her mom's shoulder.

Willo walked into the kitchen, grabbed the pot, and rinsed it out. She dumped the coffee grounds in the trash, found a coffee filter, and headed toward the pantry to grab the coffee. As she did, Willo bumped into the large cabinet that had sat in the kitchen for as long as she could remember.

"Ouch," she said to herself, her shoulder already throbbing, a framed photo falling over with a loud *thud.* "Clumsy."

She stopped to stand up the photo. When she turned it upright, she smiled; it was a black-and-white picture of her mom and grandma, who had started the orchard with her grandpa, proudly showing off a home-made pie, a blue ribbon sitting on top of the crust. Willo placed the photo back in the cabinet at an angle and, as she did, something else caught her eye: her mom's recipe box.

"I should tape a BE CAREFUL sign to that cabinet," Madge said, walking over to Willo. "Are you OK, honey?"

Sign, Willo thought, her heart racing. She remembered her prayer. *It is a sign!*

"More than OK," Willo suddenly yelled, her voice high-pitched and excited. She grabbed the recipe box. "Follow me, Mom," she continued, hurriedly tossing coats, gloves, and stocking caps on Deana and herself.

"Where are we going?" Madge asked. "What about the coffee? What are we do-ing?"

"We're going to save this orchard," Willo said with a determined nod. "C'mon. Time's a-wastin'."

Madge followed Willo out the door, trying to keep up with her daughter, who was mov-ing faster than a jackrabbit all while jug-gling the recipe box and her granddaughter.

"Willo?" Madge called in the hissing snow. "Have you gone mad?"

Willo flew into the old barn that the family now used as a packing and storage facility for the fruit and equipment. Shelves of canned and preserved fruit lined the walls. A freezer and cold storage were enclosed and off to one side, but the rest of the old barn was wide open.

"Willo?" Madge repeated as soon as they were in the barn. "What on earth are you doing?"

Willo sat Deana down on the concrete floor and then shook the recipe box at her mom. "When we prayed, I asked for a sign," Willo said, shaking the recipe box even harder at Madge. "This is it. This . . . is . . . it!"

Willo's sparkly eyes were watery, and tears were running down her cheeks. At first, Madge thought her daughter's eyes were watering from the cold, but she realized she was crying.

Willo went over to a picnic table where the workers often ate their lunches, and sat down. Madge followed, and Willo inserted the key she wore around her neck into the recipe box.

"The orchard isn't the only legacy in this family," Willo said.

"What do you mean?"

"This," Willo said, running her hand over

the box's wood, "is *our* legacy."

"It's a recipe box," Madge said gently, not following.

"No, it's not," Willo said. "Why do you think you gave it to me when I turned thirteen? Why did Grandma start this? It's the legacy of the women in our family. And it's what will save this orchard."

She opened the recipe box and began plucking out index cards. "Look," she said, reading the recipes aloud to her mother. "Apple pie, peach pie, cherry pie, strawberry-rhubarb pie, blueberry pie, cherry-berry pie, red raspberry pie, pumpkin pie, caramel apple pie, apple crisp, cherry crisp, apricot bars, apple-walnut cake, cherry turnovers, coffee cakes, cookies . . ."

"Willo," Madge said, reaching out to stop her daughter's hand, which was tossing index cards left and right as if she were dealing a deck of cards. "What are you doing? I still don't understand."

"Grandma's recipes are a tribute to this orchard and a gift to this family," Willo said. She stood like a bolt, still holding a few cards in her hand, and began to pace in front of Madge, gesturing wildly every few seconds. "What if you and I began to bake pies and sell them? Look at all the canned and frozen fruit we have from last season. We can make pies, sell some to local restaurants, but freeze most of them and sell them this summer. People already love our pies. We win every contest we enter at church and the county fairs. People ask for these recipes. They *beg* for our pies." She stopped to catch her breath. "What do you think?"

"That's not possible," Madge said, shaking her head. "We don't have the right equipment. We'd probably need approval from the county. You're busy with a toddler. We'll have to work all summer to get the orchard in shape for next season. We'll need to invest in equipment so we don't go through this again. We . . ."

Willo walked over to her mother and stood in front of her. "We can do this," she said, her voice firm. She looked into her mother's eyes and repeated, "We. Can. Do. This. Mom."

Willo took her mom's hand and led her over to the canned fruit. "Look at this bounty," she said, pulling mason jars off the shelves. "And look at *this* bounty," she repeated, shaking the cards still in her hand. "Grandma left these for us — for future generations — for a reason. She wanted to share her secrets with us."

"And they should remain secrets," Madge

protested.

"They will," said Willo. "No one will know the recipes. We'll just be sharing the wonderful end product. Think about it. How much is flour, sugar, butter, and eggs? Maybe we can barter with other farmers, or the grocery? We can make a little profit. Maybe enough to tide us until next year."

"Where do we sell them?" Madge asked, suddenly becoming swept up in her daughter's unbridled enthusiasm. "How do we sell them?"

Willo rotated in a circle, like a top that just wouldn't stop spinning. She stopped, midspin, her eyes as big as the barn lights that dangled behind her. "What if we moved Grandma and Grandpa's old log cabin to the front of the property?" she asked. "It's just sitting there empty now. You said it would cost too much now to update and renovate. It doesn't even have central air or heat. Mom, there's still an outhouse."

Madge shook her head. "No," she said. "It's . . . my history."

"Let's keep it that way then," Willo said. "If we moved it to the front of the orchard, we could put up a plaque about its history, and people would learn the history of the people who founded it. We could sell pies out of it. We'll advertise. Put up a billboard."

Willo suddenly leapt into the air. "And what if we made the orchard a U-Pick next year? People in the city love driving into the Michigan countryside to pick their own fruit, get pumpkins in the fall, all that fun stuff. That way, there would be multiple streams of income always coming into the business: fruit, food, U-Pick. We wouldn't be reliant on one thing anymore should disaster strike again."

"I need to think about this," Madge said. "We'll need to talk to Wilbur and Gordon."

"I know," Willo said. She looked intently at her mom and then walked over to the picnic table, where she began to put the index cards back into the recipe box. "Mom, we're at war. People need some happiness and nostalgia in their lives. I really think this could work."

Madge walked over and handed the recipe cards she was holding to her daughter. Suddenly, she stopped, her face as frozen as the weather outside.

"I don't ever remember seeing this card before," she said. "It must have been tucked in the back or something."

"What's the recipe?"

"It's not a recipe," said Madge, looking at the card.

"What is it then?"

"A sign," Madge said. "From my mother." Her eyes filled with tears. She wiped them away and read the card. *" 'You bake for someone because it is an act of love.' "*

Madge stopped and picked up her granddaughter, giving her a big kiss on the top of her head. She looked at Willo. "I think this could work," she said.

Madge began to twist like a top, just as Willo had done moments before. "I make the best pies in the world, thanks to my mom. And we have the best pie crust recipe ever." She lifted Deana into the air and laughed. Then she turned to Willo and said, "Your grandma was tough as nails. She and your grandpa worked themselves to death to pass this orchard along to their family. I will not let them down." She hesitated, and her voice became emotional. "The women of this family *will* save this orchard."

"Let's go bake some pies then," Willo said.

Twenty

"Why didn't you ever tell me all that before?" Sam asked her grandma when she had finished her story. She looked at her mom. "Why didn't you?"

The two women looked at one another. "You always wanted to know the recipes," her mother said, "but not the history behind them."

"You were always looking ahead," Willo said. "But sometimes looking back is what gives you perspective."

Sam's heart sank, and she thought of her talk with her father.

"There is no limit to what this place can be," Deana said. "In many ways, your grandma and I feel we've only scratched the surface."

Sam was cleaning up but stopped. "I thought this was a well-oiled machine? That the orchard and pie pantry were exactly the way you wanted it?"

"We've built a successful small business," Willo said, "but that doesn't mean it's the way *you* would want it."

"What?"

"I think you tend to look at this place like you do your high school yearbook," Willo said. "It's a relic. A thing of the past. Something you remember fondly but have stored away and don't really care to revisit."

"Grandma," Sam started, thinking of her own recipe box.

"It's OK," she said. "I understand. I think sometimes people need to leave the place they were raised in, in order to reinvent themselves. Fresh start, right?" She hesitated. A wry smile eased onto her face. "But without that history, you can become a ghost of who you were, a mirage of who you want to become."

Sam's hand tightened around the dishcloth she was holding.

"I think it's time we get your crusts in the oven," Willo said, changing the subject. "What do you suggest we fill them with?"

"One of everything?" Sam suggested.

"I think that's a lovely idea," Willo said.

Each of the women made her own pies — an apple, peach, cherry, strawberry-rhubarb, blueberry, cherry-berry, red raspberry, four-berry — and slid them into the oven. When they came out to cool, Deana said, "Let's have a tasting party."

The women pulled out some homemade ice cream and whipped cream, sampled pies, and talked — all before morning had even started for most people. As they ate, Willo whispered to Sam, "This is a wonderful crust. Flaky, buttery . . . thank you for teaching us something new."

Laughter shot across the kitchen, and Sam watched her mother joke with the bakers. They were back to their routines, making batter, crimping, frying donuts.

These women, Sam thought, *have more baking experience than I will ever have in my whole life. Where did they learn? Here. In their own homes. Trial and error.*

Just like me, she added.

Another Julia Child quote floated into Sam's head: *You'll never know everything about anything, especially something you love.*

Sam finally realized if she could teach them things, they could teach her, too.

All I have to do is ask, she thought. *Why is that so hard for me?*

"Your turn," Sam said, walking toward the bakers.

Their faces lifted in shock.

"What?" asked Donna.

"It's your turn to teach me something."

"What do we know?" DeDe asked, her face flushing.

"A lot," Sam said. "You're the experts. Now it's my turn to watch, listen, and learn."

Slowly, one at a time, their faces exploded in smiles. The D Cups looked at one another and began tossing out recipes, thoughts, ideas.

"I know," DeDe finally yelled over the others. "Your family pie crust! How long has it been since you made it?"

Sam's face flushed, and she shrugged. "Your grandma taught us your family crust, and it's similar to the one our mom and grandma made, isn't it, girls?"

Donna and Debbie nodded excitedly, big smiles on their faces.

"Mom and Grandma Eleanor just mixed everything together, rolled it out, filled it, and baked it!" DeDe continued. "They didn't have time to fuss around." She glanced at Sam. "Yours is great, don't get me wrong, but they had lots of kids to feed. No time for fancy."

"My grandma used to make an all-lard crust," Willo said. "But I ended up adapting ours because I like a little butter flavor, too. I ran out of lard one day and panicked, so I experimented with butter. I was the first woman to add a little butter to the secret crust. It's even better than the original, I think."

"Ready?" DeDe asked Sam.

Sam smiled and listened closely as DeDe showed her how to make the pie crust.

Why haven't I made this in forever? Sam wondered, the word *fancy* floating in her head. *Do I think I'm fancy? Have I always thought, maybe in the back of my mind, that I am a bit better than everyone else?* Her heart dropped. *Shame on you, Sam.*

As Sam started to make her crust, Willo standing guard, her face lit with a big smile, Donna sidled over to Sam, rubbed her arm, and said very quietly, "Thank you for asking."

Sam's heart felt as if it were going to explode.

When the crusts were ready, they again filled them with different fruits and slid them into the oven.

"I'll repeat what Sam said earlier," Willo said. "As my grandmother taught me, you can't have a great life, a great home, a great family, or a great pie without a great foundation. This crust — this place — is a great foundation. I hope you think so, too."

When the pies came out of the oven and Sam tasted the crust, she looked over at her grandmother, her face beaming. "Julia Child's got nothin' on you," she said. "Or any of my fancy teachers."

Sam tore off an end piece of the rich crust and popped it into her mouth. "Amazing," she said to the bakers. "Just like you. What else can you show me?"

"Enough about baking," DeDe bellowed, waving off Sam's suggestion as if she were a bothersome mosquito. "Let's cut to the chase. Tell us about this Angelo we've been hearing about."

The bakers began to shout, "Yeah!"

Sam shot her mom and grandma a look, but they both shrugged innocently and took another bite from the pies in front of them.

"Spill the blueberries, as we say around here," DeDe said.

Sam rolled her eyes and exhaled. "Well, we never went out on a date," she said. "My boss wouldn't have allowed it. Not that it matters now."

Sam watched their faces droop. There was something about the comfort and closeness of the women and the warmth and communal nature of the kitchen on a cold day that softened Sam's shell.

"He's really dreamy," she then said in a rush of breath and, feeling a little silly, realized she sounded just like a teenager.

"Dark hair and eyes, dimples that go on for days, and his body . . . it's like Zac Efron's."

"OK," DeDe said, fanning her face with her apron. "Open another window."

The women roared.

"Even though we never went out," Sam said, "we talked nearly every day at dawn for a year when he'd drop off the fresh fruit." She hesitated and looked out the window. "It was really the only thing I looked forward to every day," she continued softly, as if to herself.

The woman all cooed like a chorus of doves.

"Every character in every romantic movie and book always falls in love," DeDe said, as she returned to chopping apples. "But you know the thing about falling? It usually hurts. The nice thing is to walk into love, to be best friends with someone, to want to wake up knowing they're the best thing about your day. Then, when you fall, you realize it happened in slow motion."

The women again oohed and aahed.

"Wow," Willo said, her eyes wide in surprise at the sisters' atypical soft and romantic tone.

"Is that how it happened with you and your husband?" Sam asked.

"No," DeDe rumbled, her voice returning

to its normal decibel level. "I got pregnant in high school."

The woman roared, and Sam realized she was laughing along with them, enjoying their company, and baking again felt like a joy and discovery.

Sam broke off another piece of her family pie crust and took a bite of the warm, flaky dough, which melted in her mouth. Sam closed her eyes as she ate and exhaled contentedly. When she opened her eyes, she could feel someone watching her, and when she turned, her grandmother was smiling, her fingers crimping a crust.

AUNT ELEANOR'S TWO-CRUST PASTRY

Ingredients

2 1/2 cups all-purpose flour
1 teaspoon salt
1/2 cup cold butter, cut into 1/2-inch cubes
1/4 cup cold lard, cut into 1/2-inch cubes
5 to 6 tablespoons ice water

Directions

In a large bowl, combine the flour and salt. Add the butter and lard, cutting it into the flour mixture until pea-sized lumps form. Add the ice water, 1 tablespoon at a time, mixing with a fork until a dough forms, adding additional water if necessary.

Form the dough into a ball. Divide the ball in half. Flatten each half into disks; wrap each disk in plastic wrap. Refrigerate at least 1 hour or overnight. Roll out the dough on a floured surface and use in your favorite recipe.

■ ■ ■ ■

PART EIGHT:
STRAWBERRY
SHORTCAKES

■ ■ ■ ■

Twenty-One

Summer 2017

Sam caught her reflection in the glass on the arrivals and departures monitor. She was more tan, her blond hair already bleached blonder from the sun, and she was wearing a touch of makeup that made her skin glimmer. She leaned into the monitor and looked even closer.

"It might be easier to read if you took off your sunglasses, sweetie."

Sam turned, and an elderly woman wearing cataract glasses was staring at her.

"I can't take mine off, but you can," she said. "You look nervous. Bet you're meeting someone special."

She patted Sam on the back and tottered away.

Someone special? Sam thought, taking off her sunglasses and putting them in her purse. *Am I?*

Sam raced toward the gate to wait, arriving in a few seconds, forgetting she was in the Traverse City airport and not LaGuardia. She took a seat, sipped the coffee she was holding, crossed and uncrossed her legs, stood and then sat down again.

A man looked up from his cell, watching her suspiciously, and then moved seats as far away from Sam as he could get.

Looking at her Starbucks cup, she wondered, *Why did I get an extra shot of espresso?*

Though it had only been a few days since she'd flown back home unannounced, it seemed like forever to Sam.

And did I fly back home for a visit? she asked herself. *Or did I run like my dad said?*

Sam twisted her cup in her hands and stopped midmotion.

Sad had been marked on her cup by a barista, rather than her name, *Sam.*

Sad? Sam thought. *Seriously? Do they do that on purpose? Talk about a sign, Grandma.*

"Hey there, Michigan!"

Sam jumped, and a mini geyser of coffee spewed from the opening.

"Didn't mean to startle you," Angelo said. "Can you believe it? I'm actually in Michigan, Michigan."

Sam stood to greet Angelo and, for a second, felt frozen, as if she were in one of those old-fashioned romantic movies where time stops, and the actors move in super slow motion. Angelo's dark curly hair was longer and even more lustrous, and the gold in his dark eyes sparkled under the airport lights. Even though he had shaved and it was still morning, a five-o'clock shadow already cast through his smooth, dark skin and highlighted his strong jaw. He was wearing dark jeans, a black belt, and a form-fitting polo — tucked just so behind the belt's buckle — and high-top Converse Chuck Taylor sneakers.

And those dimples, Sam thought, as he smiled at her. *Were you this good-looking in New York?*

"Hi, Jersey," Sam squeaked.

"You look . . ." Angelo stopped, and an even bigger smile lit his face, making his dimples look even more adorable. ". . . amazing."

He reached over to hug her and pulled her close. "Thank you for doing this," he said. "I needed to get out of the city for a bit. Just like you."

Angelo smelled like soap, leather and spice, the city and the outdoors, the familiar and unfamiliar. Sam's heart leapt.

Lily would have a field day trying to determine his top notes, Sam thought, inhaling his scent and thinking of her roommate's love of Yankee candles.

Angelo held Sam at arm's length. "Miss me?" he asked.

"I've been busy," she said, wondering why she said it as soon as the words left her mouth. "Preoccupied."

Angelo's smile faded, and his dimples retreated.

"That didn't come out right," Sam finally said. "I have missed you. I miss the city and my roommates."

"I certainly miss seeing you every day," he said. "It's just not the same."

Sam's face flushed, and goose bumps covered her arms. "Did you check any bags?" she asked, to cover.

"No," he said, nudging the bag on his shoulder up a bit and nodding to a small suitcase on wheels beside him. "Just this stuff. I'm a light traveler. Just some jeans, shorts, swimsuit . . . summer stuff."

Swimsuit, Sam thought, feeling suddenly woozy.

"Well, you just missed a cold snap," she said. "It's really warming back up. You picked the right time for a vacation."

"Let's see Michigan, Michigan," Angelo said with a laugh.

"Follow me," Sam said, heading toward

the exit.

The two got in Sam's rental car, and she navigated through Traverse City and onto M-22, Angelo making her stop or slow down so he could take pictures of the lake and bay.

The windows were down, and a warm wind filled the car, along with an unsettling silence. Sam reached over to turn on the radio to fill the quiet. It was still tuned to the oldies station she'd discovered when she first arrived.

"I didn't know that about you." Angelo laughed, his dark hair ruffled by the breeze. "You're old-school." He turned and looked at Sam. "*Real* old-school."

Sam wanted to laugh, knew she should laugh, but her nerves got the best of her and instead she looked straight ahead as she drove and said, "There's a lot you don't know about me." Angelo turned to her, a surprised and shocked look apparent on his face. "This is a little awkward, isn't it?" Sam asked. "You have to admit that."

She wished she could take the words back, but it was too late.

Angelo chuckled softly, and it slowly grew into a laugh.

"Is something wrong?" Sam asked.

"It's just vintage you," he said.

"What's that mean?" she asked. "You do barely know me."

Angelo's face was turned toward the bay, which paralleled the winding, two-lane road. Cottages were tucked in dense pines along the water, and each passing scene resembled a beautiful watercolor vignette.

"It doesn't even look real," Angelo muttered to himself. He turned to Sam. "Do you mind pulling over so I can get a few quick pictures? I'd like to get some without the passenger mirror in them."

Don't answer me, Sam thought. *Fine.*

"Sure," she said, instead. Sam found a little scenic overlook — nothing more than a half-circle graveled turnaround — that held a stunning view of the bay, much like the one she'd stopped at when she first arrived. Angelo got out of the car, went over to stand atop a lone picnic table, and began angling his body and camera this way and that. Finally, he sat down on top of the table.

"You want to join me?" he called to Sam without turning around.

Sam shook her head and sat in the car for a second before getting out and taking a seat on the picnic bench. The two sat in silence staring at the summer scene.

"No, I don't think this is awkward," Angelo finally said, still not turning to look at Sam. "I feel like I know you really well. We talked every day for over a year. I've told you things I've never told some of my friends and family. You were the one who encouraged me to go back to school. You told me I could do and be anything, just like you." He turned and looked at Sam. The sun was angled just so on his handsome face, making his cheeks glow red and his golden skin match the sand. "I work nonstop. I finished finals. I'm tired and just needed a break." He smiled sadly at Sam. "So give me a break, OK?"

Sam ducked her head.

"You don't have to see me while I'm here," he said. "I mean, I was surprised when you texted me and said you'd pick me up at the airport after our last conversation." He hesitated. "Just drop me off at my hotel, and I'll take a cab everywhere."

Sam looked at him. A smile slowly emerged on her face, and a little laugh sneaked out. "We don't have cabs," she said. "This is northern Michigan. We might have a pedi-cab with a keg on it."

Angelo laughed as a group of white swans and quacking ducks paddled toward them thinking they might have food. "You're an interesting bird," he said, watching them. "You do this a lot, don't you?"

"Do what?"

"This," he said. "This push-pull. This let-you-in-but-keep-you-at-arm's-length game."

"I don't play games," Sam said, her voice rising.

"You don't?" Angelo asked. "OK. It's just . . . I'm from a loud Italian family. We say what we feel and what we mean."

"My family is the same," Sam protested.

"I think you're used to trying to make everyone happy. But no one ends up that way because you're not really happy."

"That's not fair," Sam said.

"Are you happy?" he asked.

Sam looked at him and shook her head. "No."

"Why?"

"I don't know."

"You do," he said.

Angelo scooted off the table and onto the bench next to Sam. "Bakers are fascinating people," he said.

"I'm a pastry chef," Sam said, correcting him.

"Oooh, sorry," he joked. "You say potayto, I say potahto."

"Talk about old-school," Sam said.

"Baking — being a pastry chef, excuse me — is largely about following directions, right? Baking is science in many ways. There are precise directions to follow, measurements must be perfect . . . you follow the rules. That's the way you've always been in life, isn't it? Straight As. High achieving. Perfection."

Angelo looked at Sam. "Keep going," she said.

"You have a plan in your head, and you can't deviate from it or you'll be wrong. Imperfect. A disappointment," he said in a deep voice. "But who's setting those rules? You are. And chances are you will never meet those expectations. You know what my mom tells me, don't you? Expectations are just preconceived resentments. You set yourself up to fail even when you don't do anything wrong."

Sam dipped her head and traced her fingers over the names of young lovers — enclosed in hearts — that had been carved into the picnic table over the years. To Sam, the table looked like a work of art, intricately designed. She suddenly remembered Connor having carved their names into this table, ages ago. Her eyes nervously scanned the tabletop, and, there, on the far edge nearest her, were their names, faded, worn, dulled but still there.

I set myself up to fail with him, Sam

thought. *Whose rules was I following?*

Angelo looked toward Sam, his bare arm brushing hers. Her heart raced, her body stiffened, and she moved her arm, imperceptibly but ever so slightly, closer to his.

"You're also an artist, Sam," Angelo continued. "You follow those rules in baking, but you also live to reinvent and re-imagine recipes. You take risks. And that's the perfect balance in life, if you can only allow yourself to see that and embrace that. So you need to ask yourself, 'What balances risk with my love of baking?' How do you marry the two?"

Who is this person? Sam thought. *A Zen deliveryman?*

The swans and ducks waddled their way up the embankment and surrounded Sam and Angelo. They squawked and began to peck at Sam and Angelo's legs. Realizing they had no food, they finally honked their disappointment and waddled back toward the water. As they were swimming away, Sam turned, extended her hand, and said, "Hi, I'm Sam, and I'd like to start over."

Angelo turned, extended his hand, and said — a thousand-watt smile beaming on his face as bright as the sun behind him — "Hi, I'm Angelo, and it's really nice to meet you, Sam."

"Wanna see where I'm from?" Sam asked, standing.

"Why do you think I'm here?" Angelo asked.

TWENTY-TWO

"Grandma . . . Mom," Sam said. "This is Angelo. Angelo, this is Deana and Willo."

"It's nice to meet you," Deana said, giving him a hug. "Welcome to Michigan!"

"So this is the famous Angelo?" Willo said, smiling broadly.

"Famous?" Angelo asked, turning toward Sam. "You've talked about me?"

"She baked for you," Willo said, a mischievous look in her eyes. "Even better." Willo leaned and pulled Angelo in for a big bear hug. "And, yes, she's talked about you," she whispered in his ear. "Come, come," Willo said, ushering him into the pie pantry. "This is where Sam grew up."

Angelo turned, his eyes trying to take in every nuance of the place: the soaring roof, the rugged beams, the expansive barn-wood counter, the open kitchen buzzing with activity, the shelves, cases, and freezers filled with pies.

Angelo smiled. "Now I know where she gets all of her talent and passion," he said in a voice filled with emotion. "I finally get it."

Willo and Deana exchanged glances and surprised smiles, and Sam ducked her head in embarrassment.

"It smells like heaven in here," he said. "And who did all the paintings on the floor? They are amazing . . . so full of happiness and joy."

"I did." Willo beamed. "I think this young man just earned himself a free piece of pie. Your choice?"

He smiled and scanned the expansive chalkboard menu, which was as long as the checkout counter. The chalkboard was replete with endless food and dessert options along with cute, colorful drawings of happy fruit and dancing pies, as well as funny quips and phrases, like *What did the apple say to the farmer? Stop picking on me!*

"I think it has to be apple," he said, "with apple cider ice cream."

"A man after my own heart," Willo said. "Back in a flash."

"So what brings you to Michigan, Angelo?" Deana asked, her head bobbing between Angelo and Sam, who was giving her mom a *Stop it already* glare.

"I needed a mini vacation from work and

school," he said.

"Sam said you deliver wonderful fruit and produce to some of New York's best restaurants?" Deana said.

"Yes," he said. "But I want to do more."

"I think anything having to do with fresh fruit is top of the tree," Deana said with a wink. "What are you studying in school?"

"Business," Angelo said.

"That's what I studied in school," she said.

"It was your daughter who encouraged me to go back to college."

"She did?" Deana asked, looking at Sam, whose face was already turning red.

"Isn't that right, Michigan?" Angelo asked.

"That's right, Jersey," Sam said.

Willo returned with a slice of hot apple pie topped with melting ice cream on an old green Depression glass plate. "Thank you," Angelo said, immediately taking a bite. He shut his eyes and chewed. "Wow. This is the best pie I've ever had in my life," he said. "No wonder you walked out on Chef Dimples. This place is so much better than his overpriced celebrity Southern Gothic hangout."

"A man who speaks his mind and loves our pie," Willo said. "I think I already like you."

"Thanks," Angelo said, his mouth full. He

locked in on the plate and began devouring the pie as if his life depended on it.

"You eat this week?" Willo asked with a laugh.

"Bag of pretzels on the plane just didn't cut it," he said. "Do you mind if I see the orchard?"

"Sure," Sam said, as Deana took his plate. She began to lead Angelo out the doors.

"They already have nicknames for one another," Deana whispered to her mom. " 'Michigan' and 'Jersey.' It's so cute."

"You coming, Gossip Girls?" Sam asked, hearing their hushed whispers.

"Right behind you," Willo said in a chirp.

Sam led Angelo out of the pie pantry, down the gravel path, and into the orchard, which was overflowing with U-Pickers on a magical summer day. Gary saw them and came rushing over, hand extended.

"Angelo, I assume," he said. "I'm Gary Nelson, Sam's father."

"It's a pleasure to meet you, sir."

"No *sir,*" Gary said. "Just Mr. Nelson."

"Dad," Sam said.

"Just teasing. Call me Gary. And welcome to our orchard."

"I hear you have a big anniversary coming up?" Angelo asked. "And a big birthday, too."

Willo beamed. "Seventy-five and one hundred," she said. "I'm turning seventy-five, in case you were wondering."

Angelo laughed. "I would have guessed you were just turning legal drinking age," he said.

Willo laughed in unison with him. "Honey, then that means I've been drinking illegally for decades."

"Want a tour?" Gary asked.

Angelo nodded. As the five walked through the midst of the orchard, Angelo's head turned this way and that, up and down.

"It's so . . ." He stopped, searching for the right word. "Green."

"It certainly is," Deana said.

"Living in New York, I'm so used to everything being gray: concrete and steel, construction and trucks," Angelo said. He stopped and walked over to an apple tree. "I deliver these," he said, his eyes wide in wonder. "But I never see it grow, live . . . I never see where it comes from. This is the real deal." He turned and looked at the family. "It's magical."

"A city boy who loves the country," Gary said.

"My family once had a small vineyard and farm in Italy," he said. "My grandparents sold it and moved here. It's in my blood, I think." His eyes scanned the orchard, the fruit, the hillside and bay. "I wonder what my life would have been like if they had kept it. It's not easy to keep something like this going in a family for so long." Angelo turned to Sam. "You're really lucky."

Sam nodded. "We better get you checked into your inn," she said. "Don't want you to lose your room. It's crazy around here on the weekends."

They turned and headed toward the barn.

"Where are you staying?" Deana asked.

"The Bayview Inn," Angelo said. "Sam suggested it. The inn looks very nice."

"That's just silly," Willo said. She turned to Sam. "Why didn't you tell us earlier he was coming?" Suddenly, her face lit up. "Aaron is away at college. Angelo could stay in his room."

"Grandma," Sam said, the word filled with tension.

"No, it's OK, ma'am," Angelo said.

"You're working and going to school," Willo said. "It's silly for you to spend your hard-earned cash on a hotel if you don't need to."

"He'll lose his deposit anyway," Sam said.

"Sylvia at the Bayview Inn has been one of my dear friends forever," Willo said. "I'll just call her." Willo stopped and her face lit up again. "Listen, if Sam thinks it's too awkward for you to stay in her house . . ."

"Grandma!"

"Well, that's what you're thinking, isn't it?" she asked. "Then stay with me. I have so much room, and it's just me toddling about in that old farmhouse. It'd be nice to have some company for a couple of days."

"I couldn't, ma'am," Angelo said.

"There is no discussion," she said. "And stop calling me ma'am, or you won't get any more pie."

Angelo laughed, and Sam shot her grandma a dirty look. Willo laughed in delight.

"OK, let me call Sylvia and get you set up in the spare room," Willo said. "Then why don't you two take the boat out. It's a beautiful day, and there is no better way to see Michigan than from the water. Right, Sam?"

"It's all gassed up," Gary said. "And Sam is a very good captain."

"And she already made dessert for you," Willo added. "Follow me."

She took Angelo's hand, and Sam drifted back, watching her grandma chat with Angelo as her parents followed. Their long shadows were cast behind them, as if Sam were walking alongside their ghosts. All at once, Sam felt overcome with emotion. While no one was looking, Sam reached out and grabbed Angelo's shadowy hand with her real one, as though this were their orchard and they were on their morning walk. As if he could feel her invisible touch, Angelo turned and smiled at Sam.

Twenty-Three

The aqua-and-white ski boat sliced through the water of the bay.

"Hold on!" Sam yelled to Angelo.

The boat hit a wake that had been produced by a large boat headed in the other direction and suddenly took flight. The boat landed with a *thunk,* Sam bouncing in the captain's seat. When she turned to check on Angelo, he was white-knuckling the seat of the boat, and his sunglasses had bounced down his nose, his eyes wide with surprise.

Sam laughed.

"It's like a pothole, but in the water," Angelo yelled. Sam laughed, nodded, and headed the twenty-seven-foot fun boat through the middle of the open bay.

The bay is, essentially, like a watery interstate, Sam thought as she steered the boat, her blond hair swirling all around her head in the wind.

Sam used to Jet-Ski with her mom, dad,

and brother over to Elk Rapids, another resort town across the bay, and have week-end brunch. She used to anchor the boat at Old Mission Peninsula and have lunch at a winery. And the harbor was packed with beaches — public and private — where she could either party with friends or sneak away to tan and read a book.

Michigan was a boater's paradise. "Longest freshwater coastline in the continental U.S.," Willo always told customers from out of state, "and second longest next to Alaska."

Though Sam was surrounded by water in New York, she felt a bit removed from it. But now that she was back home and driving a boat, a sense of calm returned.

Angelo smiled as he watched Sam behind the wheel, her skin shining, her hair a whip of blond.

She looks so at home here, he thought. *As if she dropped the shell and persona she wore in the city.*

The boat slowed, and Angelo finally noticed that the water was as flat as glass.

"Over there," Sam yelled, pointing and wagging her finger. Angelo scanned the distance and squinted through his sunglasses to try to distinguish the blue water from the blue horizon, the world drenched in sparkling light. As the boat continued to motor forward, Angelo finally was able to make out a densely treed island, wide and round, surrounded by what looked like hundreds of boats. As Sam steered closer, Angelo could see it was a virtual party cove of boats, all anchored around the island, people swimming, tanning, drinking. Music, screams, and laughter echoed over the water and the boat's engine.

"Power Island," Sam yelled to him. "Thought it would be a fun place."

Sam slowed the engine even more and checked the depth gauge: ten feet, five feet, three feet. She killed the motor, stood, and peered over the front of the boat and then both sides, carefully steering the boat over the shallow waters, the sandy bottom now clearly visible. Sam found a spot near a group of bigger boats and dropped anchor, giving herself a wide enough berth so that her boat could swing in the wind. She turned on the radio and pop music filled the air. Sam flipped up one of the seat cushions and pulled out a cooler, freeing two Oberons and handing one to Angelo.

"I think you've done this before," Angelo said.

"A time or two," Sam said with a wink.

She pulled off her tank top and wriggled

out of her jean shorts, revealing an electric-
yellow bikini. Sam opened the little door on
the back of the boat that led to the swim
platform, took a seat, and hopped into the
water with a yell, all while holding her beer.

Wow, Angelo thought, unable to avert his
eyes from Sam's lithe body and tan skin.

Sam turned and busted him staring.

"I'll repeat what I just said," Angelo said,
trying to cover.

"Summer in Michigan," she said. "You
wanted to experience it. This is what it's all
about. You getting in?"

Angelo set his beer down in a cup holder,
pulled off his T-shirt, and stepped out of his
board shorts to show off a pair of orange
box cut swim trunks covered in miniature
Mets baseball team logos.

This time, Sam couldn't avert her eyes.
Angelo wasn't just in good shape, he was
ripped.

That's not a six-pack, Sam thought, actually counting the muscles in his stomach.
*That's an eight-pack. His body might be bet-
ter than Zac Efron's.*

Angelo's skin was golden and, in the sun,
he looked almost like an animated movie
hero.

*And his dimples are bigger than Mario Lo-
pez's,* Sam thought.

Angelo caught Sam staring and smiled, his dimples widening.

"You can take the boy out of New York, but you can't take New York out of the boy," Sam said, taking a sip of her beer and nodding at his swim trunks, trying to cover this time around.

Angelo grabbed his beer and hopped into the water. He took a drink and teasingly splashed Sam, which elicited a little yelp.

"Water's cold in Michigan, Michigan," he said, laughing.

"Just like the beer," she said. Sam reached out her beer in salute, and Angelo clinked her bottle. "Cheers. Welcome to Michigan, Jersey."

"What is all this?" Angelo asked, nodding at all the boats surrounding the little island.

"This is Power Island," Sam said. "It's where all the locals come. The island was once owned by Henry Ford. Has a little bit of a party history, which is why I think people like to come here. Fun is in the air."

"Really?" Angelo said, staring at the island. "Tell me about it."

"Well," Sam started, "the island used to have a giant dance pavilion, and steamships would bring out an entire orchestra to play for these crazy dances that lasted all night. Ford purchased the island in the early

1900s, and he used to dock his yacht in Grand Traverse Bay and bring friends like Thomas Edison here. Legend has it that Ford kicked Babe Ruth off the island following a drunken night."

"Wow," Angelo said. "I bet he could put down some liquor."

Sam continued, "Native American legend has it the island is haunted, but that never seemed to stop Michiganders from flocking to it. Now the island has some campsites, but it's completely undeveloped. Quite a history."

Sam took a sip of beer and stared intently at the island. "My grandma used to bring me out here and tell me all the legends," she said. "I dreamed of what it must have been like to be a Ford, or one of the socialites who came over to dance on the island."

"Have you always dreamed of being someone else?" Angelo asked, watching Sam closely.

Sam turned and cocked her head. Suddenly, she sank into the lake, holding her beer above the water, before coming up for air. She ran her hand through her hair, slicking it back, and took a sip from her Oberon as water dripped off her face and body.

"I guess so," she finally said. "You live so long in the shadow of a family like mine.

The orchard has a storied history just like this island." She stopped and looked at Angelo. "But sometimes you feel like you need a new script, or you just want to be a character in a different story for once. Does that make sense?"

"It does," Angelo said. "I mean, that's what my grandparents did. They set out for a new life in America in order to rewrite their lives. They weren't unhappy, they always told me, they just felt like they wanted . . . more."

"That's how I've always felt," Sam said.

"They wanted opportunity and freedom," Angelo said. "What do you want?"

"I want to make my mark in the world, but I don't want to be tied down to the same thing every day."

"Or the same guy?" he asked.

Sam looked at him, took a sip of her beer, but didn't answer.

"I get it," Angelo said, "but life — no matter where you are — is largely routine."

"No, it's not," Sam said.

"What did you do in New York?" Angelo asked. "You got up, you went to work, you worked out, you went home."

"That's not fair," Sam said. "I had the entire world at my feet when I wasn't working."

"Or tired," Angelo asked. "How many times a month did time and money allow you to go out and explore the city?"

Sam took a sip of her beer and shot Angelo a dirty look. "You don't need money to explore the city."

"No, you don't," Angelo said. "I've been doing it my whole life."

Sam laughed. "I understand what you're saying. We all tend to run in concentric circles no matter where we live. But I don't know if I can run in concentric circles here. It sort of feels like, well, a dog chasing its own tail. I mean, the orchard is the way it is. It'll never change."

"How do you know?" Angelo asked. "Have you asked your family if they would be open to changes?"

"A little," Sam said.

"Have you had a courageous conversation?"

"A what?" Sam asked.

"My mom is a teacher." Angelo laughed. "She is all about courageous conversations . . . about students, teachers, and parents having the courage to talk with someone about something that bothers or upsets them, rather than just letting it fester."

"You mean I should ask my parents why

they named me Sam?" she asked. "To find out they wanted a boy? Or ask them if they would consider making their menu hipper or more trendy?"

"Why not?" Angelo asked. "Sometimes you have to reveal your soul for the world to see."

"Have you done that with your parents?" Sam asked.

Angelo nodded. "I told them I might leave the city one day," he said. "For the right opportunity." He hesitated. "Or the right girl."

"You'd move?" Sam asked. "For someone?"

"Of course," he said. "Wouldn't you?"

Sam felt as if she'd been hit by a brick. She looked at Angelo, and then at Power Island, and everything appeared off-kilter, as if she'd just emerged from a roller coaster.

Sam finished the rest of her beer, set it on the swim platform, and walked a few feet away from the boat, then dove into the water. When she came up, everything had returned to normal, until Sam saw a familiar-looking boat dropping anchor not far from her.

Connor's Honor read the name on the back of the boat.

No, Sam thought, quickly diving back under the water.

"Sam?" she immediately heard when she surfaced.

Connor was standing on the back of his boat. As water cascaded over her eyes, Sam could still picture herself on it, as if she were watching an old movie reel.

"Sam," Angelo said, repeating her name in stereo. "I think that guy is yelling for you."

"Who?" Sam asked. "What? Where?"

"Are you trying to act like a journalist?" Angelo joked, pointing at Connor in front of the whole world. "That guy. Right there."

"Oh," Sam said. "Right."

"Sam?" Connor called again. "What are you doing here?"

Sam trudged through the shallow water until she was a few feet from her former boyfriend. He looked the same as he always had — boyish, blond, and happy as a Lab — although he'd gained a bit of weight over the years. A little boy and a little girl ran around on the boat, and a woman was trying to capture them.

"Wow," Connor said. "I never thought . . ." He let his sentence trail off, shaking his head. "How's New York?"

"Great," Sam said. "Great job. Great friends. Everything's amazing."

"I'm happy for you," Connor said.

"How are you?"

"Good," he said. "Busy. Summer season is bonkers for the fishing charters . . . well, your family knows how summer is. Took a mental health day." He turned and nodded at the boat. "Brought my wife and two kids."

Sam smiled. "I heard. I'm so happy for you," she said, echoing Connor's words.

His kids screamed as his wife — a friendly-looking woman Sam didn't know — slathered suntan lotion over their bodies, their arms outstretched.

Sam turned and looked at Angelo, who had jumped onto the back of the swim platform and lay flat to catch some rays.

Courageous conversation, Sam could hear him say.

"I'm not so great actually," Sam heard herself saying. "I finished culinary school and got a great job with a not-so-great boss . . . I quit. And I came back here to sort of lick my wounds."

Sam hesitated. "And there's something else," she started. "I'm sorry."

Connor's eyes grew wide.

"For pretty much everything," she continued. "Stringing you along. Not being the person you wanted me to be. Not being the person I wanted to be."

"You don't have to apologize," Connor

said. "Water under the boat," he added with a smile.

"No, I do," she said. "I'm finding I tend to get into situations I know aren't exactly right, and then I . . . well, run."

"Did you run home?"

She nodded.

"Are you running from that guy over there?"

Sam nodded again.

Connor's face grew calm. His eyes scanned the water, the island, the horizon. He kneeled down on the back of the boat, looked Sam in the eyes, and said, "Don't. Remember cross-country?"

Sam nodded once more.

"Beautiful scenery," he said. "But you don't really notice it when you're in full sprint." He stopped and smiled at her. "You can have a nice life here. You can have a nice life in New York. That's not settling, Sam. It's just understanding what you want and need to be happy."

"Daddy!" the little boy suddenly screamed. "Swim!"

"You're being summoned," Sam laughed.

"So are you," Connor said, nodding somewhere in the distance.

Sam turned, looking at Angelo, the lake, Michigan, the sky.

"It was good to see you, Sam."

"You, too."

Sam began to make her way through the water when Connor called, "Thank you." She turned and smiled.

"By the way, is that the necklace I gave you on your thirteenth birthday?" he asked.

Sam looked down at the necklace around her neck. "It is," she said. "Now I wear the key to my recipe box on it." She stopped. "Which I got on my thirteenth birthday, too."

Connor stood on the back of the boat and took the hands of his children. "You're not running from everything," he said, "if you always keep a piece of home near your heart." He smiled. "Say hi to Miss Nelson," Connor said to his kids.

"Hi!" they yelled. "Swim now, Daddy!"

Sam watched Connor get in the water and then help his kids in one at a time.

Sam waved to them and then quietly sneaked up on Angelo, humming the creepy soundtrack to *Jaws* as she got within a few feet of him. He sat up quickly, as if he had been napping, his stomach hardening. Before he could do anything, Sam was splashing him.

Angelo jumped into the water, hunkered into the chilly lake, and began to approach

Sam, one hand imitating the fin of a shark.

"Dun-duh," he hummed, turning the tables on Sam. "Dun-duh."

As he got closer, the humming intensified — just as it had in the movie.

Sam screamed and began to swim away, but Angelo lunged and caught her leg. He began to fake-bite at her ankle, but Sam kicked to try to get away, and Angelo groaned in pain, reaching for his lip.

"Ow," he said, before noticing a small trickle of blood in the water. "This is just like *Jaws*. I better get out before I really get hurt."

"Oh, no," Sam said, standing and following him back to the boat. "I'm sorry." She stopped. "I'm saying that a lot today."

Sam jumped onto the boat, followed by Angelo, and grabbed a towel. Angelo pressed it to his lip for a second. "No damage," he said. "I'm New York tough." He smiled. "I take it you apologized to the guy on the boat?"

"Connor," she said. "My ex."

Angelo pressed the towel to his lip again. "Did you do this much damage to him?"

Sam nodded. "Worse," she said. "Hurt his heart a lot, I think."

Angelo walked over to Sam. "You had a

courageous conversation," he said with a smile.

"I did," she said. "I listened to you."

For a second, the two stared into each other's eyes. The sun warmed their bodies, relaxing Sam, and she felt — for the first time in ages — a desire not to run, but to be still, to be here, just in the moment. Angelo leaned forward, his body edging toward Sam's. She moved her face toward his.

Is this it? she wondered. *Our first kiss?*

A boat suddenly honked its horn, and both of them jumped, the top of Sam's head hitting Angelo's chin and lip, causing him to grunt again in pain.

"Are you OK?" she asked, looking closely at his lip.

"Yes," he said. "I think you're trying to tell me something."

"I'm so sorry," Sam said. "See, I said it again."

Angelo smiled. "Ow," he said.

Sam reached into the cooler and grabbed another bottle of beer. "Maybe this will help," she said.

Angelo put the cold bottle against his lip, wincing at first before his face relaxed a bit. "Better," he said. He then opened the beer and began to take a sip, wincing again as the bottle touched his lip, before downing half the Oberon. "Much better," he said.

Sam laughed. She turned to crank up the radio but stopped when she saw Connor and his children — both bobbing happily in their life jackets and splashing their father — playing in the lake.

"Are you OK?" Angelo asked.

Sometimes you have to reveal your soul for the world to see, Sam could hear him say to her.

"There's something I want to show you," Sam said, immediately starting the boat.

"Actually, it's something I need to say," she said to herself, the engine drowning out her words before they could reach Angelo.

Sam guided the boat to a remote inlet that led to a bay, which was sheltered on three sides by a parenthesis-shaped slice of land.

"Looks like an episode of *Lost,*" Angelo said.

"I think both of us watch too many old movies and TV shows," Sam laughed.

The bay was quiet, silent compared to Power Island, and the boat's engine echoed off the surrounding dunes and trees, causing birds to take flight. Sam shut off the engine and looked over the edge of the boat, steering this way and that.

"There!" she finally said excitedly. "Look."

At first, Angelo searched the shoreline and then the surface of the water, but he couldn't understand what Sam was wanting him to see. But then he saw it: the wooden bones of an old shipwreck sat at the bottom of the clear water. The ribs of the ship were splayed open, like those of a long-dead animal in the middle of the desert. Massive beams lay between those wooden slats, and a giant mast sat cockeyed in the sand. The entire ship was illuminated by the sun, which filtered through the lake like prismed spotlights, and magnified by the water as if it were under a microscope.

"Wow," Angelo said. "What happened?"

"Kids found this when I was a little girl," Sam said, staring into the water. "They thought it was a hot tub, or something silly like that. Turns out it was a shipwreck from the 1800s, a schooner supposedly carrying wheat and beer."

"Let's go," Angelo joked, acting as if he were ready to dive off the edge of the boat.

Sam laughed. "Want to see it up close? We can snorkel."

"Sure," Angelo said excitedly. Sam pulled out the gear; they sat on the swim platform and put on life jackets and flippers, then hopped into the water.

Sam held up her mask.

"Before you put on the mask, blow into it like this first," Sam said, demonstrating to Angelo and then pulling hers over her eyes. "Keeps it from fogging up."

She watched Angelo mimic what she had just done.

"Ready?" Sam asked, putting in her snorkel and going face-first into the water.

The two swam over the top of the shipwreck. Seaweed and moss undulated off the wooden beams and ribs. Fish of all colors and sizes darted around the old ship. This underwater world reminded Sam of her life in Michigan: quiet and stunningly beautiful yet haunting, unmoving, never changing. Sam heard a rumbling and came to the surface to find Angelo talking nonstop.

"It's so beautiful," he was saying. "How deep is this? What happened?"

Sam smiled at his childlike inquiries and began to answer them all.

"This belongs to the state of Michigan," Sam said. "No one can touch or move any part. There are shipwrecks like this all over the coastline." She realized she still had her mask on and sounded as if she had a cold. Sam removed her mask and looked at Angelo. "Haunting, isn't it? The past, just stuck in place."

Angelo took his mask off, a raccoonlike

ring remaining around his eyes, and tilted his head, water dripping from the ends of his dark curls. "It's also sort of romantic, too," he said. "There's a wonderful history that people are reminded of when they see this, a way of life that has passed but was rich and fascinating and beautiful. It reminds me of going into those old restaurants in New York, buildings that have been around for centuries. You can almost hear the walls talk." He looked at Sam. "There's something important about history. My family's past — my mother's heirlooms from Italy and her parents — mean the world. We are who we are based on the history and sacrifices of all those who came before us."

The orchard, Sam thought. *The recipe box.*

Angelo looked down at the ship's skeleton once again and, as if on cue, said, "Sometimes you have to reveal your soul for the world to see."

Sam playfully splashed Angelo. "What is it with you?" she asked. "You always know the right thing to say."

"Maybe I'm just a nice guy," he said.

Maybe, Sam thought. *Just maybe.*

"Now, according to your grandma, I heard you baked something extra special for me," he said, and winked. "I'm getting hungry."

"Follow me," Sam said, swimming to the boat, taking off her snorkeling gear, and heading for the cooler. "My family's strawberry shortcakes."

She pulled a few shortcakes from a bag, put them in a bowl, and then opened a Tupperware container and spooned out deep red strawberries along with their sugary juice. She handed Angelo a bowl and a spoon. He took a bite, shut his eyes, and groaned. "So good," he said. "Tastes like summer."

"Fresh strawberries from my grandma's garden," Sam said. "My family shortcake recipe with my own twist."

"What's the twist?" he asked.

"I like more of a biscuity shortcake," Sam said. "They stand up well to the firm strawberries but are still tender enough to soak up all that juice."

"See?" Angelo said. "You can honor your history and still write your own."

"There you go again," she said, digging into her own bowl. She shook her head. "Aren't we supposed to be young and having fun on a summer day?"

"I'm down for that," he said. "Hand me another beer."

Sam popped open a beer, took a swig, and handed it to him.

"I think I like Michigan, Michigan," he said with a sexy wink, his dark lashes falling heavily.

And I think I might like you, Jersey, Sam thought, as the two floated above the skeleton of the old ship.

STRAWBERRY SHORTCAKES WITH FRESH STRAWBERRY SAUCE

Ingredients for Shortcake

2 cups all-purpose flour
1/4 cup granulated sugar
1 tablespoon baking powder
1 teaspoon salt
1 1/2 cups heavy whipping cream, cold
Cinnamon sugar

Ingredients for Sauce

1 pint fresh strawberries
1/4 cup granulated sugar, or to taste

Directions

Preheat the oven to 350°F.

In a large bowl, combine the flour, granulated sugar, baking powder, and salt.

Gently stirring with a fork, gradually mix in the whipping cream until combined. The mixture should hold together, but barely.

Form the dough into eight 2- to 3-inch balls using your hands.

Roll the dough in the cinnamon sugar.

Place the balls 3 inches apart on an ungreased baking sheet. Bake 25 to 30 minutes, until golden brown.

Cut the tops off the strawberries and slice them. Add the sugar. Let the berries meld with the sugar to form juice while the shortcakes bake.

Top the shortcakes (served warm or cool) with the strawberry mixture and whipped cream or ice cream.

■ ■ ■ ■

PART NINE: RHUBARB SOUR CREAM COFFEE CAKE WITH CINNAMON STREUSEL TOPPING

■ ■ ■ ■

TWENTY-FOUR

Summer 2017

"How was your day?" Willo asked, when the two returned to the pie pantry. "You both look rested and all cleaned up."

"Looks like you got some sun," Deana added.

"It was amazing," Angelo said. "Sam took me to Power Island and then to see an old shipwreck. And, best of all, she made me strawberry shortcakes." He hesitated and a mischievous twinkle came into his dark eyes. "Oh, and she apologized to an old boyfriend."

"Connor?" Deana and Willo gasped at the same time.

Sam playfully hit Angelo in the shoulder. "I did," she said. "Total coincidence. His boat anchored near ours off Power Island. He was there with his family." She hesitated and looked at Angelo. "Something Angelo

367

said made me want to clear the slate. Move on."

Willo walked over to Angelo and put her arm around his back, giving him a sweet side hug. "Attaboy," she said. "I think you've earned another free piece of pie."

"I think I might need some dinner first," he said. "I'm full of beer and strawberries."

"Not a bad combination," Willo joked.

"Hey, it's so pretty out," Deana said. "We were thinking of going to the Sunset Inn for some fresh fish and . . ." She stopped and nudged Angelo. ". . . more beer. Your dad is joining us."

"I was thinking maybe we'd just get a pizza and head to the beach to watch the sunset, if that's OK with you." Sam ducked her head and looked at Angelo, who smiled sweetly at her. "He's had a long first day. Thought it might be nice to chill. Rain check for tomorrow?"

"Sounds good," Deana said.

Willo looked at Angelo. "Your curfew is ten P.M., young man," she teased. "I have rules at my house."

"The sun isn't even really gone at ten," Sam said.

"I'm just pulling his leg," Willo said. "See you later."

When they had walked out, Angelo said,

"Your grandma is something else. And so is this place. Do you mind giving me a little tour? I was so excited to eat the pie and see the orchard that I missed this."

"Really?" Sam asked. "OK."

Before she had even gotten to the kitchen, the D Cups hooted and hollered, "This must be Angelo." DeDe zipped over with a spatula, swatted Angelo on the behind, and said in her husky voice, "They grow 'em nice in Jersey."

Angelo laughed. "They grow 'em nice in Michigan, too." He bent over. "Swat me again."

DeDe roared and smacked him again. "I think this pie's ready," she laughed. "Seems firm to the touch."

"I don't want to scare him off yet," Sam said.

"That'd be a first," DeDe said to raucous laughter.

"What are you making?" Angelo asked the bakers.

"Lots of apple pies," Debbie said. "Fresh off the tree."

"Trying to get as many made as possible before the big anniversary party for the orchard and your grandma on Labor Day weekend," Debbie said. "Working OT."

"I remember you talking about that,"

Angelo said to Sam. "That's amazing. What's your involvement?"

His question stopped Sam cold.

I've been so caught up in my own life, I haven't even asked about that, Sam thought, guilt rising in the pit of her stomach. *Will I even be here? Will I have a new job by then?* She thought of the call she had made to Colette on the drive to pick up Angelo.

She said she'd call to schedule the interview, Sam thought. *I feel like such a traitor.*

"Maybe a new recipe for the party?" DeDe said, saving Sam. "A mix of the old and the new, like these pies and your pie crust?" DeDe hesitated and tried to act very demure, but she dissolved into a fit of giggles and could barely get out, "Or like me and Angelo."

"I better get you out of here before it's too late," Sam said.

"We're headed out in just a bit," Donna called as Sam began to usher Angelo out of the kitchen. "Long day."

"OK," Sam said. "I can shut everything down."

The pie pantry was beginning to slow for the day. Some of the waitresses had taken seats at a back table and were eating sandwiches and divvying up their tip money. They were chatting about their day, with piles of dollar bills and plates filled with pie and ice cream crammed into the middle of an old Formica table.

Angelo stopped every few feet to study the historic memorabilia that lined every nook and cranny of the restaurant. He read old newspaper headlines about the war, and the great spring freeze that nearly killed Michigan's orchards. He touched old baking utensils and was fascinated by the antique orchard ladders that lined the walls. He partially climbed one of the old, short, wooden ladders — carefully testing each rickety step — before turning to Sam and saying, "Take my picture."

She took his camera and snapped a shot before saying, "I'm ordering the pizza . . . before someone gets hurt."

"OK," Angelo said, as if in a trance. "This stuff is fascinating."

It is? Sam thought, as she called to order the pizza. When she was done, she stood beside Angelo and tried to see what he was seeing: this place through his eyes, for the first time. Slowly, as his enthusiasm began to affect her, she became more engaged, telling him about the history of the memorabilia.

"What's this?" he asked as they returned toward the front of the pie pantry near the kitchen. A glass door — frosted over as if it were the middle of winter — sat adjacent to two large stainless steel doors, both of which were also cold to the touch.

"Oh, that's our cold storage," Sam said. She opened the first door, gesturing for Angelo to go in.

"You locking me up?" he asked. "Already done with me?"

"Not yet," Sam laughed. The room was lined with small crates filled with apples, while shelves held gallons of cider. "This is where we keep the apples and cider that we use on a daily and weekly basis. You probably saw our waitresses dash in and out of here to get apples for customers or to serve cider."

Sam spread out her arms.

"It's bigger than my whole apartment in New York," Sam said. "Warmer, too."

Angelo laughed. "So true. You take that for granted being here. Having so much room to breathe is a gift."

"Speaking of breath," Sam said, exhaling a puff of white into the chilly air. "We better get out of here before ours freezes."

They walked out of the cold storage, and a din of noise echoed through the pie pantry. The four waitresses who had been counting their tip money earlier were now attempting to navigate a big dolly lined with folding tables through the restaurant. One uncooperative wheel on the dolly, however, didn't even touch the concrete floor and simply spun in a circle like those on a bad shopping cart. The four young women groaned to keep it going the right way on the wavy, sloping concrete floor.

"What are you doing, Mandy?" Sam asked one of the women.

"Oh," said the waitress. "Didn't see you, Sam. Your grandma wanted us to start hauling these tables out to the orchard barn before we left. She wants to get a jump-start on the party planning. She's very excited. And excited the forecast isn't calling for rain."

Sam smiled despite feeling a pang of guilt. "I know," she said. "But you all have had such a long day. Just deal with it tomorrow."

"But . . ." Mandy started.

"And I'll deal with my grandma," Sam added with a laugh.

"Thanks," the waitress said. "The D Cups just left . . . Want us to shut all the lights off and lock up, or do you want to do that when you leave?"

"I'll do it, Mandy," Sam said. "Thanks.

We're leaving in a second. Have a good night."

Mandy waved and walked out with her friends, leaving the dolly. Sam opened the larger doors. Angelo peeked his head inside.

"This is our large cold storage room," Sam said.

"For really big apples?" Angelo laughed. "Mind if I peek?"

Sam shook her head and dropped the tote she was carrying.

Angelo walked into the giant freezer, and Sam followed. Apples of all colors and varieties had been sorted into larger and smaller wooden crates. "We sort them into half pecks, pecks, and bushels to sell to grocery stores and restaurants," Sam said, "as well as baskets to sell to customers."

"Sounds like a country song," Angelo said, beginning to croon off-key and acting as if he were strumming a guitar. "Bushels and pecks . . . my life is a wreck . . . now that the apple of my eye has turned to mush."

Sam laughed. "Did you make up those lyrics on the spot?"

Angelo nodded proudly.

"Impressive . . . although I wouldn't quit your day job just yet," she said with a smile. "Although there is something catchy about your lyrics. And truthful. Cold storage keeps the apples from turning into mush."

Angelo walked over, picked up an apple, and took a big bite.

"Hey," Sam said. "Don't eat our profit."

"I deliver fruit for a living," he said. "I know exactly how much profit I'm eating." He took another bite of apple, chewed, and shut his eyes. "I ate about one thirty-second of your peck profit."

"Wow," Sam said. "You're right. A peck is about thirty-two apples, or twelve pounds, and a bushel is a hundred twenty-six apples, or forty-eight pounds." She looked around the big storage unit. "Cold apple storage is a boon for keeping income generated for us during the leaner winter months. My grandpa said we used to lose apples before they even got off the tree. Now, we can control the temperature and oxygen concentration to perfection." Sam walked over and picked up a beautiful, red, shiny apple. "This baby," she said, "will be a birthday apple."

"A what?" Angelo asked.

"A birthday apple," Sam said. "In about a year, someone might buy this at a grocery store, a year after it's been picked. But it will still be as delicious as it is right now." She took a big bite. "Many of these will go to our apple corer and be used for pies, and many of these will be mashed in the press for cider. A lot will be sold to stores. And a lot will be eaten right here." Sam took another bite.

"Speaking of eating," she said, "our pizza should be about ready." She rubbed her hands over her bare arms, which were covered in goose bumps. "And I'm not ready to be freeze-dried."

Sam pushed the door, but it wouldn't open. She tried again, to no avail.

"That's weird," she said. "What's going on?"

"You need a big strong Jersey man," Angelo said with a wink.

"Where can I find one in here?" Sam joked.

"Very funny," he said. Angelo walked over and gave the door a big push, but it didn't budge. He tried harder. Nothing. He then cemented his feet into the ground, angled his body, and ran into the door with all his might, his shoulder bouncing off the steel door.

Angelo put one eye to the crack and strained to see something, anything.

"You don't think . . ." Sam started.

"I don't," Angelo said. "That's how I've made it this far."

"You don't think the dolly rolled in front of the door, do you? The old floors in here are so warped. They go uphill and downhill. What if the dolly with all those tables has us trapped in here?"

Angelo walked over and shook his head, trying to look calm. "Don't worry," he said, putting his arm around Sam. "Lucy and Ethel got out of way worse."

Sam couldn't help but laugh. "See?" she said. "You really are an old soul."

"My parents love Lucy," he said. "Now, what would they do to get out of such a mess?"

Sam scrunched her face. It suddenly lit up. "Use their cell phones!" Sam said.

"They didn't have cell phones," Angelo said.

"No, but we do," she said. They both immediately pulled their cells out, but their faces dropped in disappointment. "No service in here. Walls are too thick."

Sam looked at Angelo, her face turning into that of a kid who was genuinely scared. "Sam, it's going to be OK," he said. "Don't worry." Angelo walked to the door and began to pound on it. "Hello?" he yelled. "We're stuck in here! Help! Anyone?"

He stopped and panted, his breath coming out in frosty puffs.

"Don't worry," he said again, although this time Sam could tell he didn't sound as convinced.

Angelo walked over to a closed crate, took a seat, and patted the wooden top next to him. Sam walked over, head down, and sat down beside him.

"What if we never get out of here?" she asked, her eyes wide. "What if this is it? What if they find our bodies frozen in here?"

"Sam, you're overreacting," Angelo said.

"Am I?" she asked again, her voice rising. Angelo put his arm around her, and Sam took a deep breath.

"What would you regret?" Angelo asked out of the blue. When Sam turned with a confused look, he added, "If this *were* it. What would you regret?"

"Now you're scaring me," Sam said.

"I don't mean to," he said. "But sometimes — at the strangest times — I think God forces us to stop for a moment, be still and reflect on our lives. Either we choose to pay attention, or we don't . . . and I think that often determines the path our lives will take."

"Old soul," Sam said, repeating what she'd said earlier. "Mind giving me an example?"

Angelo chuckled. "Sure," he said. "When

you told me I should go to college. Most guys I know my age would have laughed it off. They would have said they were too busy working, having fun, dating . . . that the course of their lives was already set."

"But you?" Sam asked.

"I thought, 'Why is this smart, driven person taking an interest in me? Why is she telling me this?' And I believe it's because I needed to hear it. My mom told me the same thing, but I never listened until you said it." He hesitated. "I love my friends, but so many aren't ever going to change. They're going to do the same job for the next forty years, but when you said that, I realized I wanted something more. I don't want to be a deliveryman when I'm forty."

"That's how I felt, too," Sam said. "That's a big reason I moved to New York. I didn't want the same thing."

"I think you are very blessed to have a family like yours who supports you without question, and to be a part of a place like this with so much history and opportunity," Angelo said quietly.

"Opportunity?" Sam asked. "For me?"

"Yes," Angelo said. "Have you ever considered that you could bring New York here?"

"What?" Sam asked. "Is your brain already freezing?"

"I just see so much opportunity here, Sam," Angelo said, suddenly standing and walking around the freezer. "I mean, just think about what's hot in New York right now . . . pardon the pun again." He picked up an apple. "Have you or your family ever considered making your own hard cider, or starting your own winery?"

"What?" Sam asked. "We're known for our sweet cider. We don't even serve soda here. There are tons of wineries around us."

"And what makes the best cider?" he asked, tossing the apple into the air and catching it. "The best fruit."

Sam cocked her head, considering Angelo's words.

"And what's the hottest thing in New York right now?" he asked. "Every bar serves high-end hard cider. It's like the new craft beer."

"Go on," Sam said.

"You could reach an entirely new market," Angelo said, "without losing your current one. You could have concerts in the orchards in the evening."

Sam immediately thought of when she surveyed the pie pantry's crowd and wondered where the younger customers were.

"And so many people love quality, high-end comfort food these days," he continued.

"What if the pie pantry added a country poutine, or veggie pot pies with your special crusts? What if your new takes on old-fashioned desserts were a part of a new menu?"

"People who come here would never go for that," Sam said. "This is tradition. It's like your friends. Some things will never change."

"How do you know if you don't ever try?" he said. "I didn't know what I could do until you said something to me, and I finally listened."

Sam smiled. "That's sweet, but . . ."

"Just think about it," he said. "You're the strong one, Sam. You just need to realize that. You can be a great pastry chef in Paris, or New York, or here. But you can't be you everywhere, or you'll never make a mark."

Sam thought of the pie pantry's cornerstone, of the thumbprint cookies she'd made, of the footsteps she, her mom, and her grandma had left in the orchard.

Angelo walked over and sat again by Sam on the crate. He put his arm around her to warm her up, rubbing her shoulders. "You know what I would regret if we froze to death in here?" Sam asked.

"We're not going to freeze to death," Angelo insisted.

"I'd regret being a failure," she said.

"You're not," he said. "Why do you think that?"

"I don't know," she said. "I just feel that whatever I do isn't good enough."

"You're putting that pressure on yourself," he said.

"I know," Sam said. "I just want people to remember my food."

"They will," Angelo said. "But remember that food is connected to our hearts and our histories, our souls as much as our taste buds. When my mom makes one of her grandmother's favorite recipes, she says it's as though she's still with her in the kitchen."

"You have that here," he added.

"What would you regret if we froze to death in here?" Sam asked.

"We're *not* freezing to death in here, Sam," Angelo said, giving her a gentle shake.

"Just asking," she said.

"I'd regret not doing this," Angelo said. He leaned in and kissed Sam on the lips, gently at first, then harder, their mouths — cool at first — suddenly hot. Sam felt her body go from ice-cold to red hot, and she moved closer to Angelo, running her hands through his dark locks. His lips were smooth and large, and Sam leaned her head back, and Angelo kissed her neck, as Sam's body exploded again in goose bumps.

Sam opened her eyes, and she realized Angelo's dark eyes were staring back, seeming to search her soul.

"I like you, Sam," he said, his breath coming out hot, the words trembling. "A lot."

"We haven't even had a proper first date yet," Sam said demurely.

"I've been courting you forever," he said.

There was something about that word — *courting* — that Sam loved.

It's so old-fashioned, genuine and sweet, Sam thought. *The way he says it is respectful and honest.*

"I like being courted," Sam said. She stopped and put her hands on Angelo's face, her heart stopping at how handsome he was.

"My first kiss obviously didn't do enough," Angelo said. "You still have goose bumps."

"That's because you gave me the chills," Sam whispered in a husky voice.

"That might just be the room," he said. "I'm trying to give you the hots."

He leaned in and kissed her again, when the door suddenly opened.

"What's going on in here?" Willo asked.

Angelo and Sam bolted upright, as if they were kids busted sneaking into the movie theater. Their sudden movement caused the crate of apples on which they were sitting to tumble, and apples rolled across the cold floor.

Willo smiled.

"Grandma!" Sam exclaimed, rushing over to hug her. "Thank you. We could have died in here."

"You look just fine to me," Willo said.

Sam looked outside the door. "No, really. The dolly rolled in front of the door and blocked us in. We could have frozen to death."

"With all that body heat," Willo continued to tease.

"Grandma," Sam said.

"Well, I'm glad I noticed the lights on in here before I left to meet your folks for dinner," she said. "Goodness knows what might have happened."

Willo stepped to the door and picked up Sam's tote. "I also saw your bag sitting outside the door. I'm a regular Perry Mason."

Sam and Angelo cocked their heads. "Who?" they asked at the same time.

"Never mind," Willo said. She shot her eyes from Angelo to Sam, a mischievous smile growing on her face. "Want me to shut the door behind me, leave you two alone a while longer?"

"OK, Grandma, that's enough," Sam said, rolling her eyes, as Angelo began picking up all the apples. "Go to dinner. We'll lock up."

"Lock lips, you mean," Willo whispered to her granddaughter. "Have fun on the beach." She turned and looked at Angelo. "Curfew is ten P.M., young man."

"Yes, ma'am," Angelo said with a laugh.

When Willo had departed and they had picked up all the apples, Sam shut the doors to the cold storage unit. Despite her skin being chilled from being locked inside, Sam felt as if she were on fire, burning inside from the kiss with Angelo. She leaned against the doors to cool her desire and then turned and ran her hands over the chilly steel, smiling to herself as if she were locking away a precious memory she wanted to keep as fresh and preserved as the apples inside.

"Ready?" Angelo asked.

Sam shook off the irony of the question, nodded, and turned off the lights of the pie pantry.

TWENTY-FIVE

"How did you sleep?"

Angelo walked into Willo's kitchen and rubbed his eyes.

"Like a dream," Angelo said, feeling the most rested he had in ages. "Nice to have the windows open, to feel a summer breeze, to hear nothing but crickets and birds and the lake."

Before he could say another word, Willo winked at him and said, "I'm sure you had a lot to dream about."

Angelo began to protest. "I don't know what you think you saw," he started.

"I may be about to turn seventy-five," Willo said, "but my eyesight is still twenty-twenty."

Angelo's cheeks flushed, and he began to stammer for words.

"I'm just teasing you," Willo said. "Actually, I can barely see a thing anymore." She winked. "Come. Sit. Coffee?" Angelo nodded and took a seat at the little table next to the kitchen. Willo brought him a mug. "Cream? Sugar?"

Angelo shook his head.

"Man after my own heart," she said. "I always figure I live in a world glittered with sugar, so I don't need any extra in my coffee."

Angelo smiled and took a sip. Although he had been sleepy seconds ago, Willo's teasing now made him feel awake, on his toes. He sat upright, nearly rigid, in the wooden chair, his back pressed against the slats.

"No need to be embarrassed," Willo said. She filled her own mug and sat at the table. "I'm happy that Sam seems to have met a nice young man."

"Thank you," he said.

"But you know she's not your average person," Willo said. She took a sip of coffee and looked at Angelo. "She's determined. She's hard to tie down."

"I don't want to tie her down," Angelo said. "I want her to fly."

Willo could feel her heart flutter at the conviction and passion of his words, just like the wings of the hummingbird that levitated at the red feeder outside her patio door, its throat the color of a ruby, its wings as luminescent as an emerald.

"And what if she wants to fly on her own?" Willo asked.

Angelo considered Willo's words, took another sip of coffee, and then followed her gaze toward the hummingbird. "My grandma used to tell me this story of two hummingbirds that she said returned to her home every year," he said. "She firmly believed she witnessed the first time the two birds fell in love." He laughed and shut his eyes for a second before returning his gaze to the patio. "My grandma said humming-birds do this thing called a courtship dive, where the male ascends a very long distance before suddenly diving over an interested female at a high rate of speed. She said it was akin to a dive bomber, and that the g-force acceleration was so severe that it would have caused loss of consciousness in fighter pilots." Angelo laughed again and took a sip of coffee. "My grandma seemed to always know the strangest information. Like the difference between a hare and a rabbit, or the only city with three dotted letters in a row? Anyway . . ."

"What *is* the only city with three dotted letters in a row?" Willo interrupted.

"Beijing," Angelo laughed.

"Now I know," Willo smiled. "Go on."

"I guess when diving, the flow of air through the tail feathers produces a high-pitched sound that's similar to a loud, longing chirp. A couple of years later, after my grandmother had just washed all the windows, the female hummingbird flew into the kitchen window so hard my grandma heard it over the TV. She ran outside, and it was lying on the grass. At first, she thought it was dead, but then she could see it breathing, its little chest barely moving. She didn't touch it, but she brought it some sugar water in a little bowl, stood guard over it, and prayed that it wouldn't die."

Angelo stopped and looked outside at the feeder, where the one hummingbird was now joined by a second, their long beaks positioned into holes in the middle of little plastic flowers.

"The entire time she was watching over it, the other hummingbird was right there, too, darting around like crazy at first," he continued. "But eventually it sat on the end of an olive tree branch, watching. My grandma said it was the longest she'd ever seen a hummingbird be still. For the longest time, the injured bird lay on the ground, and my grandmother eventually lay down beside it, her face next to the bird. Its breathing slowed so much, my grandma thought it was taking its final breaths. Finally, around dusk, the bird sort of sat up, drank some water, tested its wings and tail, stood for a while without moving, and then, suddenly, took off, darting around her yard. As it did, the male ascended to a great height — just as it had done years before — and dove toward her, emitting the most joyous sound my grandma had ever heard."

Angelo stopped, turned from the birds, and looked at Willo. "If Sam flies, I fly," he said.

Tears immediately popped into Willo's eyes. "Allergies," she said, reaching for a napkin.

"You know," Angelo said, "we haven't even really been on a proper date yet. This is probably the most unusual dating I've ever done. I'm sort of following her lead."

"But you came to Michigan to see her, didn't you?" Willo asked. "It wasn't just to see the state of Michigan. It was to see Michigan, wasn't it, Jersey?"

Angelo shook his head. "You're as honest as my family," he said. "No stone is left un-turned." He stopped and looked directly at Willo. "I did. I felt such a void in my life after she quit her job. I don't blame her — Chef Dimples was an awful person — but I missed her passion and enthusiasm. I . . ."

He hesitated. "I just missed her."

Willo smiled.

"The women in my family are similar to the women in your family, I think," he said. "Smart, driven . . . their sacrifices helped our family to get to where we are today. My mom is a teacher. My grandmother passed away a few years ago, but she was the force who got my family to America." Angelo looked at Willo. "I just want Sam to know being strong and independent doesn't mean being alone. I don't know if she understands that."

"I don't either," Willo said. "OK, enough seriousness. I have an idea. Do you want to help me make something for breakfast? We can surprise Sam. Bake something for her. Let's show her you know your way around a kitchen as well as you know your way around a woman's heart. My gut tells me you do."

Angelo hesitated. "I live with two other guys in a tiny apartment," he laughed. "We can pour a mean bowl of cereal and order pizza like a pro, but that's about it."

"What about your grandmother?" Willo asked. "She must have had a favorite recipe."

"She did," Angelo said immediately.

Willo sat up in her chair. "I knew it. What was it?"

"She made this incredible Sicilian cannoli," he said, "with fresh ricotta and goat cheese, and fried dough that was as light as air. Sort of like your donuts."

"I actually have some ricotta," Willo said, her voice rising. "And there's a little goat farm up the road that sells the freshest goat cheese. Let me get ready."

"Hold on, hold on," Angelo said. "My grandma brought this to nearly every Sunday dinner for dessert. Everyone would rush through dinner just to get to her cannoli. She acted like it was a huge secret, and she refused to share the recipe with anyone. When she got sick, my mom begged her, finally, to share the recipe with her and to show her how to make it before it was too late. 'Get me a pen,' my grandma whispered to my mom. My mom brought her a pen and a pad of paper. With a shaky hand, my grandma wrote *Nana's Cannoli* and below it *Farrelli's.* 'What does this mean?' my mom asked her. 'I don't understand.' 'I buy the cannoli at Farrelli's Bakery in Bensonhurst,' my grandma told her."

Willo burst out laughing.

"It was never a secret family recipe," Angelo said. "Just like her famous Sunday gravy, which is what every Italian family calls its special homemade spaghetti sauce. My mom learned it was just sausage, hamburger meat, and Ragu."

Willo laughed again.

"You want to know the weird thing?" Angelo asked. "Even though her recipes weren't passed down or true heirlooms, the cannoli and gravy we have now just don't taste the same. They're not as good, even though we go to all the effort to make them by hand."

"You know why, don't you?" Willo asked.

Angelo shook his head.

"There's one missing ingredient," she continued. "Your grandma."

Angelo ducked his head, and Willo reached out to take his hand in hers. "Thank you," he said. "I miss her."

"I know," Willo said softly.

She gave his hand a gentle squeeze and continued. "Even though every dessert we make at the pie pantry is a family recipe, and I think they're the best in the world, I also know that it's the memories people are buying: the smells of cinnamon, nutmeg, and apples baking in the oven, the taste of a homemade crust or streusel topping . . . those trigger memories of your mom and grandma baking in the kitchen, of the holidays, of summers at a beloved cabin. They remind us of a time when we were safe, warm, and loved. We need even more of that today. That's what baking is: recreating beautiful memories."

"You know that's why Sam is a pastry chef?" Angelo asked.

"I've always hoped so," Willo said.

"You know she made your special slab pie for *Good Morning America,* don't you? It was the day Trish, the pastry chef, walked out. I think it was Sam's way of paying homage to you while also . . . well . . . how can I put this gingerly?" Angelo stopped and thought for a second, his long, dark lashes fluttering as he did. "While also giving Chef Dimples the middle finger."

"That's my girl." Willo laughed. "Well, let me teach you something my family has made for years . . . it's one of the oldest recipes in our family recipe box."

"What is it?" Angelo asked.

"It's a rhubarb sour cream coffee cake with a cinnamon streusel topping," she said. "My mouth is already watering. My family has made it forever. My mom said a great recipe box should always have a great coffee cake recipe. This was our go-to on weekends." She stood and reached out her hand to Angelo, who took it and joined her in the kitchen. Willo pulled the recipe from the box and showed it to Angelo.

"The handwriting," Angelo started, "the age of the card. It's like a piece of history."

"And you can bring it to life every time you make it," she said as she began to pull ingredients from the refrigerator and cabinet. She placed a clump of rhubarb onto the little island. "From my garden this morning. You should know your way around these," she said. "Get to dicing."

As Willo prepared the batter, Angelo began slicing up the stalks of pretty red rhubarb. She then showed him how to make the streusel topping, cutting the brown sugar into the butter and then sprinkling it over the batter. When Willo slid the cake into the oven, she turned to Angelo and said, "See? It's quick and fills the house with the best smells."

As the coffee cake baked, Angelo helped Willo clean up the kitchen. "Are you excited about your and the orchard's big birthdays?" he asked.

"Every birthday is big when you get to be my age," Willo said as she washed a bowl in the big farm sink. "But, yes, I am." She hesitated, her eyes searching the orchard outside the kitchen window. She flicked some soap suds off her hands and seemed to mutter to herself, "I just hope Sam's here for it."

"Me, too," Angelo said. Willo's eyes opened, as if she had forgotten he was in the kitchen with her. She dried her hands, picked up the recipe card, and placed it back in the box.

"You know, my grandma kept her recipe box under lock and key," Willo said. "She believed — besides her family and the orchard — it was the most valuable item in her possession. She never wanted anyone to have her recipes except her family. And, although we all still lock ours up out of tradition, I always sort of felt that those secrets should be shared with the world. What do we have if we don't share our gifts with the world? It would be a pretty lonely place. You can't keep everything locked away."

Suddenly, Willo stopped and looked at Angelo. "Keep an eye on the coffee cake," she said. "I'll be back in a flash." Suddenly, Willo jogged out of the kitchen and up the stairs. Angelo could hear her footsteps overhead and a series of thumps and clatters. Willo returned to the kitchen out of breath, her hands behind her back.

"Hold out your hands," she said, still

breathing heavily. "I want to give you something."

Angelo's face was etched with a quizzical expression, but he held out his hands. Willo brought her hands from behind her back and placed a tiny, old key in his hands.

"This is the key to my grandma's original recipe box," she said, her voice thick with emotion. Willo showed Angelo the key she wore around her neck. "This is just a replica, like the one Sam wears, too." She stopped and smiled. "You know, my mom said my grandma used to wear it on a chain around her neck, too, just like we all do now. I think it's in our DNA. She believed that that way no one would ever be able to steal it, and it would always be close to her heart." Willo hesitated, and Angelo could see her blue eyes fill with tears. "I'm hoping you can unlock Sam's heart."

She wrapped Angelo's fingers around the key. "I can't take this," he said.

"Yes, you can," Willo said. "You have my blessing. And . . ." She hesitated. "I need you to take it." She stopped. "I trust you. I know you'll do the right thing with it . . . and with Sam."

Angelo opened his arms and hugged Willo. "Thank you," he said, before placing the key into his wallet.

"No, thank *you,*" Willo echoed. The oven timer buzzed, and Willo opened the door. She grabbed an oven mitt and toothpick, slid out the rack, and turned to Angelo. "Here's how you test to see if it's done," she said, sticking the toothpick into the middle of the coffee cake. "If it comes out clean, it's ready. And it's ready!"

She set the pan on top of the oven and grabbed two plates and a knife. She cut big wedges for both of them and put the plates on the table. "Mind refreshing our coffee?" she asked Angelo.

The two took a seat at the table and dug into the steaming fluffy white cake, which was spotted red from the rhubarb, the streusel topping thick and crumbly.

Angelo's eyes widened as he took a bite, and then another. "This is the best coffee cake of my life," he said.

"You're right. It is," Willo said quietly with a chuckle. She then leaned toward Angelo and whispered conspiratorially, "But if you're in a bind and want to impress your roommates, you can always make Betty Crocker in honor of your grandma."

Angelo laughed. "They probably wouldn't know the difference anyway, especially when they were hungover."

Willo laughed, and the pair ate another

slice of the coffee cake as humingbirds darted around the patio.

"Why is this so good?" Angelo asked, shoveling forkfuls of the coffee cake into his mouth. "I mean, come on . . . this is crazy good."

"It's the love," Willo said, before adding with a laugh, "actually, it's the butter. And the sugar." She stopped. "It's always the butter and sugar."

Angelo laughed and went back for more.

"I think we might have to make another one," he mumbled, taking another bite.

TWENTY-SIX

"Might as well take an apple for the road," Sam said. "Or twenty. We've got plenty."

She reached up and plucked an apple from the tree and tossed it Angelo's way without any warning. He stuck a hand out at the last minute to nab it before it sailed past him.

"You've got quite the arm on you, Michigan," he laughed. "You should pitch for the Mets. We need the help."

"Tigers," she said. "I only pitch for the Tigers, Jersey."

Angelo laughed, walked up to Sam, and kissed her.

"You gave me less warning than I gave you," she said, a smile crossing her face.

Angelo kept his face close to hers and whispered in a husky tone, "I thought I should get a second chance after being interrupted by your grandmother. And I kind of wanted my first kiss to give you the chills, but I think you nearly got pneumonia instead."

Sam laughed and then touched his face, her fingertips trailing over his sexy stubble. Angelo inhaled at her touch, his dimples deepening. Sam kissed him, softly at first, and then harder. "Hope that was hotter," she said.

"It was," Angelo said.

"I hate to do this, but," Sam said, checking the time, her voice dropping in disappointment, "we better go. Airport will be a madhouse today."

"Can I show you something before we go?" Angelo asked.

Sam's eyes widened.

"Nothing bad," Angelo said, pulling out his wallet.

"Are you paying me?" she asked. "Like *Pretty Woman*?"

"Your grandma gave me this," Angelo said, showing her the key.

"That's her grandma's recipe box key," Sam said, her voice now rising in surprise. "When did she give you this? *Why* did she give you this?"

"She gave it to me when she showed me how to make the coffee cake," Angelo explained. "She said she trusted me and wanted me to have it so that . . ." Angelo hesitated. "So that I could unlock your heart."

Sam took a step back. "Angelo, that's very sweet, but this all seems to be moving a little too quickly. You came here on a whim . . ."

"I came here to see you," he said, his face dropping. "I came here because I missed you."

"I'm in no-man's-land right now," Sam said. "I'm the outfielder who loses the ball in the lights and doesn't know which way to go. I'm headed to New York for another interview for what could be a dream job. I miss the city. I miss my roommates. I miss making my mark on the world."

"Sam, you can make your mark on the world anywhere," he said. "Paris. New York. Suttons Bay. But you can't be *you* everywhere."

"Angelo, I'm not sure I'm even ready for a relationship," she said. "I really wasn't looking."

Angelo smiled in a sad way, his dimples deepening. "You're always looking," he said. "For something. Sometimes, though, when you're always looking ahead, you miss what you already have."

Sam checked her cell again.

"I'm ready," Angelo said. "Let me know when you head back to the city. I'd love to see you. You know that." He began to walk toward the barn. He stopped and turned to take in the expanse: the orchard, the bay, the lake, the sky. "Michigan is just as beautiful and beguiling as you, Michigan."

Angelo held out his hand for Sam to take. *Take it, Sam,* she thought. *Take his hand.*

Instead, she acted as if she didn't see it and reached over to pick another apple. "You might need an extra for the drive," she said, her voice falsely chipper.

Angelo nodded and took the apple, his dimples disappearing.

Rhubarb Sour Cream Coffee Cake with Cinnamon Streusel Topping

Ingredients for Coffee Cake

1 1/3 cups granulated sugar

1/2 cup butter, room temperature

1/4 teaspoon maple extract

1 teaspoon vanilla extract

1 large egg

1 cup sour cream

1 teaspoon baking soda

Dash of salt

2 cups all-purpose flour

2 cups rhubarb, chopped into 1/4-inch pieces (let rest on paper towels and then blot dry)

Ingredients for Topping

1/2 cup brown sugar, packed

1 tablespoon butter, room temperature

1 teaspoon ground cinnamon

Directions for Coffee Cake

Preheat the oven to 350°F.

In a large mixing bowl, cream the sugar, butter, maple extract, and vanilla. Add the egg and mix on high.

Reduce the mixer speed to low, add the sour cream, and mix to combine.

In a separate bowl, combine the baking

soda, salt, and flour with a fork.

Slowly add the flour mixture to the butter mixture and mix on low, just until combined. Do not overmix.

Remove the bowl from the mixer and slowly fold in the rhubarb with a spatula.

Directions for Topping

Place the topping ingredients in a small bowl and cut with a pastry cutter into crumbly pea-sized pieces.

Assembly

Pour the batter into a buttered 9 × 13-inch glass baking dish. Sprinkle the topping over the batter.

Bake 40 minutes, or until a toothpick inserted in the center of the cake comes out clean.

Serves 12 to 14

■ ■ ■ ■

PART TEN:
APPLE AND CHERRY
TURNOVERS

■ ■ ■ ■

Twenty-Seven

Summer 2017

Willo had a vision. And a megaphone.

"A little more to the left," she said, her voice booming through the megaphone and reverberating across the orchard. "Higher. Higher!"

Six workers on ladders were holding a giant, double-sided banner in midair and attempting to hang it over the entrance to the orchards and pie pantry. It read:

HAPPY BIRTHDAY TO . . . US!

CELEBRATE OUR CENTENNIAL
(AND GRANDMA WILLO'S BIRTHDAY)!

MULLINS FAMILY ORCHARDS & PIE
PANTRY IS TURNING 100! AND OUR
MATRIARCH IS TURNING 75!

WE HOPE YOUR FAMILY WILL JOIN

OURS FOR THIS ONCE-IN-A-LIFETIME CELEBRATION!

PI=3.14159
(WHO ARE WE KIDDING? PIE=LOVE!)

"Grandma, people in Traverse City can hear you," Sam said. "And everyone has cell phones now. You can just text them instead of scaring half of Michigan."

Willo shot her a withering glance.

"And I haven't seen an actual megaphone since, well, ever," Sam continued, pushing her grandmother's buttons.

Willo laughed. "It's nice to have you home," she said. Willo meant to say it softly, sweetly, but her mouth was still up to the megaphone, and her voice again boomed.

"It's nice to be home," Sam yelled back, causing her grandmother to dissolve into a fit of giggles.

"We have so much work to do for the party," Willo said. "It's nice to have your help. And it will be so great having you home for the celebration." She stopped. "And my birthday."

Sam looked at her grandmother, and her heart sank knowing she had the interview coming up for a job that would carry her away.

Sam turned, acting as if she were looking out over the orchards, and, as she did, her cell vibrated. She pulled it from the pocket of her shorts and saw that there was a voice mail. Sam took a few steps away and listened.

"Hi, Sam," the message started, "this is Colette from Doux Souvenirs. Listen, I hate to do this last minute, but I was hoping we might be able to schedule your interview for this weekend. I know it's Labor Day, but we're getting busier and busier, and I need to hire a pastry chef to assist me and Trish before fall and the holiday season kicks into high gear. Trish said you were sort of between things right now, and you'd be free to talk. Would you be available Friday? Call me when you can. Thanks. Bye."

Though it was a bright morning, a gloomy feeling was suddenly cast over the day.

Sam turned, and her grandmother was watching her closely. A sad smile crept over Willo's face, and her shoulders drooped in disappointment until her back was shaped like a comma.

"Don't tell me right now," she said in a soft voice, her head shaking, the green stem on her cap trembling.

"How did . . ." Sam started.

"Grandma's intuition," Willo said, cutting her off before she could finish. "Let's go make something for the party. Together. And then you tell me, OK?"

Sam could feel her lip quiver, and she blinked hard — once, twice — to keep tears at bay. "OK, Grandma," she said. "OK."

TWENTY-EIGHT

"Don't you want to bake in the pie pantry?" Sam asked as they passed it and headed toward Willo's house.

"No," Willo said without turning around. "I wanted to bake with you at home. Just us."

"Like you did with Angelo?" Sam asked.

Willo turned and smiled. "A kitchen should be buzzing with activity," she said. "Mine has been quiet lately." She looked at Sam. "I'm not saying that to make you feel guilty either. I just want to be a little bit selfish. Have you all to myself right now." She hesitated. "While I have the chance."

Sam nodded at her grandmother and then looked away.

"It was nice to bake with Angelo," Willo said, opening her front door and heading directly into the kitchen. "He's a very nice young man. Very grounded."

Alex, I'll take Guilt for a thousand, Sam

thought.

"What do you want to make?" Sam asked instead, trying to change the subject.

"It's National Cherry Turnover Day," Willo said. "August twenty-eighth. So I thought we'd make turnovers."

"How do you know these things?" Sam asked in a happy voice, trying to lessen her guilt.

"I run a pie pantry," Willo said, pulling flour and butter from the cupboard and refrigerator. "I have to know these things."

"Why aren't turnovers on the menu?" Sam asked. "I've always wondered."

"Well, that's something you need to know as well," Willo said, putting down the butter and looking at Sam. "It's the one recipe I've never shared. Until today."

Willo walked over to the cabinet, retrieved her recipe box, and unlocked it. Without warning, she turned it upside down, and all the recipe cards came tumbling out onto the counter.

"Grandma," Sam yelled. "What are you doing?"

The recipe cards were of every variety: index cards with handwritten recipes and index cards with typewritten recipes; cards that featured photos and drawings of the recipe, and cards that had recipes from magazines taped onto them; many cards that were emblematic of different eras in American culture and design. Cards from the 1950s featured pretty little borders around the edges, while cards from the 1970s featured funky typefaces and art of fish, onions, and mushrooms. Most read *Recipe* or *Here's What's Cookin'* at the top with *From the Kitchen of* or *Recipe From* directly underneath. Many index cards just had lines on which to write, while some were more specific and read *Cooking Time, Oven Temp, Serves, Ingredients,* and *Instructions.*

But Sam quickly noticed they all had one thing in common: all the index cards were stained, dotted, worn. Butter, gravy, icing, sticky fingerprints were present on every card, revealing not just a recipe but a history.

A family's history, Sam thought. *Flecked with love.*

"Here it is," Willo said, her voice high, shaking the now-empty recipe box.

"Did you miss your meds this morning?" Sam asked with a laugh.

"Look!"

Willo held out the recipe box and there — stuck in the very bottom like a forgotten blanket at the bottom of a chest — was a single card. Willo grabbed a fork from the utensil drawer and popped it free. She handed the card to Sam.

"Apple turnovers," Sam said, her voice rising.

"Turn it over," Willo said.

"Cherry turnovers," Sam added. She looked at her grandma. "I'm so confused."

"The two recipes I never shared," she said. "My favorites. They remind me of my mom. We each felt we had the best turnover recipe: my mom's is the apple turnovers, mine is the cherry. We used to have bake-offs. Both were so good. Everyone in the family was scared to choose a favorite, especially your mom, and I never really could; I loved them both." She hesitated. "They're so special to me that I could never include them on the menu at the pie pantry."

"Why?" Sam asked. "Especially if it means so much, and the recipes are so good. You've always felt it was important to share our gifts with the world."

Willo nodded, looked at the kitchen window, and smiled. Sam followed her gaze. There was nothing outside, save for the usual summer buzz of tourists entering the orchard.

"Turnover," Willo whispered to herself. "Life is filled with turnover."

Twenty-Nine

Fall 1975

Deana sat in a cushioned chair by the bedroom window trying to do her schoolwork, but it couldn't divert her attention. Her mother held a cold washcloth to her grandmother's head, whispering, "It's OK, Mom. It's all going to be OK."

That's a lie, Deana thought. *It's not going to be OK.*

Her grandmother's eyes were closed. She was pale, her skin dry; sores were present under her nose, and she was so thin Deana could see the outline of her bones underneath her pajamas, blue veins present on her arms, legs and face like highways on a map.

She doesn't look like herself anymore, Deana thought.

Deana had heard the word *cancer* in church and in school, but now it had come to invade her home and her family.

It has come to steal my grandma, Deana thought. *Ovarian cancer. Just like my grandma's mom.*

She stared at her math textbook. The numbers and symbols blurred in front of her eyes, and she didn't realize she was crying until teardrops plopped onto the pages. She put her pencil between her teeth and chewed on it, hard, to stop her emotions.

It was a beautiful fall day, crisp but still warm. The sugar maples that surrounded her grandmother's house were turning color — brilliant orange, crimson, gold — and it lit the dreary bedroom in saturated tones. The world was alive, filled with color, and yet her grandmother was dying.

It's not fair, Deana thought. *It's not fair.*

"How many tablespoons in a stick of butter?"

Deana lifted her head. Her grandmother's eyes fluttered, steadied, and focused.

"How many tablespoons in a stick of butter?" Madge repeated.

Deana shook her head, the pencil still in her mouth, not comprehending. She blinked hard, a lone tear trailing down her face.

"That's real math," her grandma said in a weak voice. "The kind of math you're going to have to do here. You should know that by now."

Willo turned and looked at her daughter, a smile etched on her exhausted face. *Eight,* she mouthed.

Deana removed the pencil from her mouth. "Eight," she said.

Her grandmother's face slowly worked itself into a smile, as if God Himself had grabbed the edges of her mouth and lifted them for all the world to see.

"Recipe box," her grandmother said in a hoarse voice. Willo nodded and retreated, returning with the box. She placed it gingerly atop her mother's lap and opened it with the key around her neck. With great effort, Madge picked up the recipe box and promptly turned it upside down.

"Mom?" Willo asked. "What are you doing? Are you OK?"

Madge laid the box back atop her lap and pointed a trembling finger at it. "Look inside," she said.

Willo picked it up, looked, and then shot a questioning glance at her mother. She dug her hand into the box and jiggled it around as if trying to free something, then pulled out a recipe card.

"Read it," her mom said.

"Apple turnovers," Willo read.

"Turn over the turnover," Madge said, a slight lilt in her voice.

"Cherry turnovers," Willo read. Slowly, Willo's face changed from confusion to joy. "These are our turnover recipes," she said, her voice shaky.

Her mother nodded.

"Why did you hide them?"

"One of the first recipes we made together," she said. "Our secret."

"Mom," Willo whispered, leaning down to kiss her mother softly on the cheek. She walked over to Deana and kneeled beside her, showing her daughter the recipe card. "This is her apple turnover recipe," she explained, before flipping the card over. "And this is mine."

She continued. "Your great-grandmother was known for making apple crisp," she said. "She made it for church socials and picnics, and people around here begged for the recipe. But she would never give it away. She said it was meant to share only with family. Your grandmother wanted to make her own mark, and she came up with this apple turnover recipe. It was the very first thing I remember making with her. Everyone around here loved it, too. When I got older, I wanted to make my own mark, just like she did, so I came up with my own cherry turnover recipe. It's a little easier than hers — my gosh, I think I was just a teenager when I came up with it — but it's so delicious, too. One day, we had a bake-off, and we tasted each other's recipes."

"What happened?" Deana asked, eyes wide.

"It was a draw," her grandmother said with a smile.

"We wrote our recipes on this card, and your grandma must have hidden it after that," she said. "I could make these from memory." She turned to look at her mom. "Why did you hide these?"

"Family treasure," she said. Slowly, she pushed herself up in bed, straining, using all her might to get on her elbows. "Bake-off," she said, winded. "Final time."

"Mom," Willo started. "You're too weak. You can't . . ."

"No, but Deana can," she said with a definitive nod. "She needs to learn this recipe. Otherwise . . ." She stopped, her voice emotional. "Won't be around to see her get the recipe box at thirteen."

Deana's eyes grew wider, and she held back her tears. "OK," she said, standing up, chest out, acting strong. "I'm ready."

"Help me into my wheelchair," Madge said.

"Mom," Willo started again.

"Get me into my wheelchair," she repeated

with force, her jaw clenched.

The two helped her into her wheelchair, an inch at a time, stopping every few seconds to allow the pain to subside just enough to start again. When she was in her wheelchair, Willo pushed her mother into the kitchen, Deana following with the index card.

Willo put the card into a stand on the counter. "I'll bake my cherry turnovers, and your grandma will teach you how to make her apple turnovers. Just listen carefully and do everything she says."

Deana nodded.

"The secret's in the syrup, the crust, and the apples," her grandmother said. "Run out and pick six of the prettiest apples you can find, OK? A mix of tart and sweet. Hurry." Deana darted out the door with a basket and ran to the orchard, dashing from tree to tree in the quickening twilight to pick the prettiest, juiciest apples. She sprinted back into the kitchen, out of breath, showing her apples to her grandmother. "Perfect," she said. "First, the crust."

Slowly, her grandmother walked Deana through the recipe. As her granddaughter measured, peeled, and sliced, the smells transported Madge. She could feel her hands in the flour, turning the dough. She could feel the glossy peel of the apples in her hands. She could sense that just an extra dash of cinnamon was needed.

When the turnovers went into the oven, Deana and Willo got Madge back into bed. Though her face was racked with pain and exhaustion, she kept her eyes open until the timer rang. Willo brought her a dish: on one side were the apple turnovers, on the other were the cherry, whipped cream dolloped on each.

Willo scooped a bite of the apple onto a spoon and fed her mom. She then did the same with the cherry.

"What's the verdict?" Willo asked.

Her mother smiled. "Tie," she said, looking at her daughter. "Thank you."

Suddenly, her face sagged, and her eyes grew heavy.

Willo's cheeks quivered. She nodded and kissed her mom. "I'll clean up," she said. "You get some sleep."

When Willo left, Madge wagged a finger at Deana, who was finishing her turnovers. Deana set her plate down, walked over, and sat on the edge of her grandmother's bed.

"Ours was better," she whispered in a voice that was barely audible. She held a trembling finger over her mouth and smiled. "Sssshhh. Don't ever tell your mom."

Deana giggled.

For a few moments, there was silence. Her grandmother watched the last of the day's light fill the bedroom and then turned to watch her granddaughter beside her, taking in every nuance of her beautiful face.

"Turnover," Madge finally whispered. "The world is filled with turnover."

Deana cocked her head, confused, leaning closer to her grandma.

"Only constant in life is change," she whispered. "Constant turnover." She stopped and coughed. "But turnover can be sweet, unexpected, just like the ones we made." She held out her hand for Deana to take, and she gripped it with all her strength. "Don't be sad when I'm gone. Celebrate me when you bake. That's how I'll live on forever."

Her grandmother's pale eyes filled with tears. "I love you," she said.

"I love you, too," Deana said.

Her grandmother's eyes grew heavy, and she blinked hard to stay awake and stare at her granddaughter. Eventually, she fell asleep, just as the sun began to set, her breathing labored. Deana watched her grandmother sleep for a few moments, still gripping her hand as the color in the room, the color in her face, slowly faded to gray.

And then she went into the kitchen, found the index card still on the stand, retrieved the recipe box, and hid the turnover recipe back in the bottom of the box, just as her grandmother had done.

THIRTY

"Oh, Grandma," Sam said. "I'm so sorry. And my mom's heart must have broken."

"*Turnover* is an interesting word, isn't it?" she asked as she pared apples. "It means a lot of things . . . professional turnover, be it loss of a job, like you just experienced, or personal loss, such as the death of loved ones, like we've both experienced. We use *turnover* in running our orchard and pie pantry. It means the amount of money that we've received in sales." She stopped as Sam continued to make the dough. "My mother was right: the only constant in life is change. Turnover is continual."

Willo set down her knife, reached out, and touched Sam's arm.

"Good luck on your interview," she said.

"Grandma," Sam said, her eyes wide. "How did you know?"

"Not rocket science," she said. She stopped and searched Sam's eyes.

"Oh, Grandma," Sam said in a wavering voice.

"When is it?"

Sam cast her eyes to the floor. "Friday. I didn't know how to tell you. It's a great opportunity with a renowned pastry chef who's running her own show now. I'd be reunited with Trish. I'd be back in the city with my friends."

"You'd see Angelo," Willo said.

"Perhaps," Sam said, again ducking her eyes. She returned to the dough, nervously pushing it back and forth. "I'm going to miss your birthday." She turned and fought back guilty tears.

"You have my blessing," Willo said.

"I do?" Sam asked.

"Always," she said. "No regrets, my beautiful girl. No regrets."

The two worked in silence to finish the apple and cherry turnovers. They slid them into the oven and started work on the whipped cream. When the turnovers came out of the oven, they took one of each, plopped on some whipped cream, and took a seat at the kitchen table.

"Which do you like better?" Willo finally asked.

"Tie," Sam said with a smile. "Different, but equally delicious."

Willo winked. "After my mom died, I sort of went mad," she said, suddenly very serious. "I would go into the pie pantry and make hundreds of crusts, but I never finished a pie. I never put anything in them. I felt as empty and unfulfilled as they were. One day, I picked up the recipe box and flung it across the room. All of the cards took flight, like little butterflies. I fell to the floor and cried like a baby. As I was sitting in the midst of all the cards, I remembered what Deana had told me that my mom had said, that we shouldn't be sad when she was gone, that we should celebrate her through our baking, and that was how she'd live on forever. When I began to pick up and sort all the index cards, I found the turnover recipe still stuck in the bottom of the box, right where your mom had left it. I started laughing like a madwoman. And we both decided never to share it." Willo hesitated. "There's one stuck in the bottom of your recipe box, too," she continued. "I bet you never found it."

Sam shook her head. "No," she said, reaching out for her grandma's hand. "I think maybe it's time you made these for the big celebration, don't you? I think your mom would love that."

"She would," Willo said.

"Thank you for sharing that story with me. Thank you for sharing all of the family recipes with me. And thank you for inspiring me to become a pastry chef." Sam hesitated. "But most of all, thank you for your blessing."

The two hugged and returned to the kitchen. Willo began to pick up and clean the mixing bowls and dishes, while Sam began to reorganize the recipe box. As she did, a flash of orange caught her eye. Sam scanned the recipe and as she did, her heart began to race with excitement.

Sounds amazing, she thought. *Why have I never made this?*

She glanced nervously at her grandma and again felt the familiar pang of guilt in her stomach.

Too simple, she thought. *I always thought this wasn't fancy enough even though I loved eating it.*

Sam began to place the card back into the recipe box, but stopped. When her grandmother bent down to load the dishwasher, Sam folded the card in half and secretly stashed the recipe in her pocket.

Apple Turnovers

Ingredients for Turnovers

2 cups all-purpose flour
2 teaspoons baking powder
1 teaspoon salt
3/4 cup shortening
1/2 cup whole milk
6 medium baking apples, peeled, cored, and cut into quarters
6 tablespoons sugar
Ground cinnamon
Ground nutmeg

Ingredients for Syrup

2 cups granulated sugar
1/4 teaspoon ground cinnamon
1/4 teaspoon ground nutmeg
2 cups water
1/4 cup unsalted butter

Directions for Turnovers

Preheat the oven to 375°F.

In a large mixing bowl, combine the flour, baking powder, and salt. Cut in the shortening until crumbly. Add the milk and stir until all of the flour is moistened.

Form the dough into a ball. Using a floured rolling pin, roll two-thirds of the dough into a 14-inch square on a generously floured, cloth-covered board. Cut into 4 squares.

Roll the remaining dough into a 14 × 7-inch rectangle. Cut into 2 squares.

Place 4 apple quarters on each pastry square. Sprinkle each square with 1 tablespoon sugar and a sprinkle of cinnamon and nutmeg. Bring the corners of each pastry up over the apple quarters and press together.

Directions for Syrup

In a medium saucepan over medium-high heat, bring the sugar, cinnamon, nutmeg, and water to a boil. Remove from the heat and stir in the butter.

Assembly

Place the turnovers in a buttered 9 × 13-inch baking dish. Pour the syrup over the turnovers (reserve some for later). Bake about 45 minutes, until the crust is golden and the apples are tender. Spoon the remaining syrup over the turnovers. Serve warm with Heavenly Homemade Whipped Cream (recipe follows).

Serves 6

CHERRY TURNOVERS

Ingredients

3 cups all-purpose flour

3 tablespoons granulated sugar

1 1/2 teaspoons salt

1/2 teaspoon ground cinnamon

1 1/4 cups shortening

5 to 6 tablespoons cold water

1 can cherry pie filling (add 3 tablespoons granulated sugar) OR 1 pound fresh cherries, pitted and chopped (add granulated sugar to taste)

Directions

Preheat the oven to 425°F.

In a large mixing bowl, combine the flour, sugar, salt, and cinnamon. Cut in the shortening with a pastry blender until the mixture is pea-sized in consistency (don't over-blend; make sure the mixture remains loose). Sprinkle mixture with cold water, 1 tablespoon at a time, until the dough has formed.

Form the dough into a ball. Divide the dough in half. Using a floured rolling pin, roll each ball of dough into a 10 × 15-inch rectangle on a floured surface. Cut into six 5-inch squares. Put 2 tablespoons of fruit in the center of each square.

Moisten the edges with water and fold over to form a triangle. Seal with a fork and prick the top to vent. Place the turnovers on an ungreased cookie sheet and bake 12 to 15 minutes or until lightly golden.

Serves 6 to 8

HEAVENLY HOMEMADE WHIPPED CREAM

Ingredients

2 cups heavy whipping cream, cold

8 to 9 tablespoons powdered sugar (regular sugar can be used, but can be grainy; powdered sugar incorporates more evenly)

1 teaspoon vanilla extract

Directions

Pour the whipping cream into a large mixing bowl.

Mix on low, adding powdered sugar 1 tablespoon at a time.

When the sugar is incorporated, beat on high, adding vanilla toward the end, until fluffy.

(Note: Recipe can be cut in half.)

■ ■ ■ ■

PART ELEVEN: PUMPKIN BARS WITH CREAM CHEESE FROSTING

■ ■ ■ ■

THIRTY-ONE

Labor Day Weekend 2017

The Brooklyn Bridge was sweltering and jammed.

Sam snaked her way between tourists who were walking slower than the zombies on *The Walking Dead,* stopping every few feet to take photos, buy water from pop-up vendors for $3 a bottle, or FaceTime with friends from Singapore to St. Louis.

The pace, the people, the diversity, the heat, the smells, Sam thought as she juked left and right between tourists. *I've missed this.*

She heard the chime of a bell, and a man behind her yelled, "On your left!" Sam quickened her pace and stepped farther to the right. When she looked up, an elderly man and woman were stopped in the middle of the bridge licking ice cream cones, the hordes moving around them as if they were a boulder in the middle of a roaring stream. Sam heard the bell behind her chime again, this time over and over, and the man yelled, "Move!" Sam scrambled forward, arms out like a net, and moved the couple a few feet over just as the bicyclist — a man outfitted in a blue gingham jumper, puffy white shirt, red sequined shoes, a double-braided wig, and full beard, complete with a live cairn terrier in the bike's basket — whizzed by at a high rate of speed.

"Damn tourists!" he yelled. "There's no place like home . . . so go home!"

"I'm not a tourist, Dorothy!" Sam yelled back.

"Thank you," the wild-eyed woman said to Sam, ice cream dripping down her arm. "You gotta love New York."

"You do," Sam laughed.

As Sam crossed the bridge, she glanced out at the expanse of Manhattan and Brooklyn — water, bridges, and traffic below her — and slowed for just a second. She tried to stop the thought from forming in her head, but she couldn't.

There's no place like home, she thought.

In the distance, Sam could see the *Wizard of Oz* bicyclist disappear into the crowd, and she suddenly remembered the biker who had yelled at her the last day of her job at Chef Dimples.

"You the last virgin in the city?" a man

had screamed as he zipped by on his bike.

"You wish!" Sam had replied.

My grandma taught me to be tough, Sam thought. *To bend but never break, just like a willow tree.*

Sam shook her head, checked her cell, and picked up her pace.

As she approached the middle of the iconic bridge, a mass of people was huddled, again taking pictures, many trying to capture the panorama of the view, many reading the plaques about the bridge's history and construction. Even in the sea of people, Sam spotted Angelo. He was standing atop a pillar above the crowd waving his arm. Angelo was wearing a tank top, his body covered in sweat from the heat, his muscles glistening in the sun. Sam gulped. His curly hair was a sexy mop, and he was beaming as brightly as the sun, his dimples as big as commas on a Broadway marquee.

Sam could feel her entire body flush from excitement.

I didn't expect to feel this way, she thought.

"You made it!" Angelo yelled. He produced an iced latte from behind his back for Sam. "Better drink it fast," he said.

"Thanks," she said, taking a sip.

Angelo leaned in and hugged Sam. Her body was a bit stiff at first, the hug tentative, but then Angelo looked into her eyes and leaned in to kiss her, and Sam's body went limp, and she nearly dropped the iced coffee.

"Boy, it's good to see you again, Michigan," he said.

"It's only been a few days, Jersey," she said.

"I know, but still . . ." He smiled and ducked his head. "So, how have you been?"

"Good," Sam said hesitantly. "OK," she then hedged. "Preoccupied," she finally stated.

"OK then," Angelo said. "You've covered all the emotional bases."

Sam laughed and took another drink of her latte. "A lot on my mind," she said. "The interview tomorrow, missing my grandma's birthday and the orchard's big party . . ." She hesitated. ". . . You."

Angelo smiled.

Stop it with the dimples already, Sam thought.

"So, I bet you're wondering why I wanted to meet you here?"

"Not really," Sam said nonchalantly, although she had wondered just that about a hundred times since he'd asked her to meet him.

"You're a good liar, Michigan," Angelo

laughed.

"OK, maybe I have wondered why," she said.

Angelo walked to the center of the bridge and gestured at a commemorative plaque.

"Did you know the Brooklyn Bridge was once called 'The Eighth Wonder of the World'?" Angelo asked. Sam shook her head. "Its length, steel suspension architecture, and design beauty with two towers made it an engineering wonder." Angelo stopped and looked at Sam. "The broad promenade on which we're standing above the highways was designed solely for pedestrian use. This bridge has such a great history."

He walked over to the railing and scanned the city. "It's also the great connector between Brooklyn and Manhattan," he continued. He gestured toward the Statue of Liberty in the distance. "I used to come here when I was younger and just stare at her. I thought about how far my family had come, what they went through to get to America and make their way here, what my life would be like." He hesitated. "Even though the bridge connected the two boroughs, it seemed like such a huge distance to me. I wanted to make it in Manhattan." He turned to Sam, who came over to him.

He slipped his arm around her back. "My job was a way to get there," he said, nodding his head toward Manhattan. "And then I met you. And you helped me realize that education was the key to take me anywhere, that I could do anything."

Angelo's voice was thick with emotion, and he was staring hard at the Statue of Liberty, the muscles in his face clenched, as if he didn't want to cry.

"I want to show you something," he finally said. He took Sam's hand and led her along the bridge in the direction of Brooklyn. He finally stopped in front of a section of the bridge whose crisscross steel railing was covered in locks. Some of the locks were painted colors or decorated with hearts, while some featured handmade signs that said, *I will love you, forever* or *To the moon and back,* and others simply were emblazoned with the name of a man or woman.

"This started in Italy," Angelo said. "They're known as love locks. Love-struck New Yorkers and tourists hang these locks here and then throw the keys into the East River. It's symbolic . . . it means they have locked their hearts forever and thrown away the key, so they can never be reopened."

"I read about that in the *Times,* I think,"

Sam said. "It all started with a book, didn't it?"

Angelo nodded. "The city is starting to cut all the padlocks off now," he said. "They're worried they pose a safety hazard if they fall onto a pedestrian or car below, and they're also worried about the overall weight of thousands of locks on the bridge."

He stopped and looked at Sam. "So I figured I didn't have much time," he said.

"For what?" Sam asked, tilting her head, her voice rising.

"Look hard," Angelo said. "Might take a while."

"What did you do?" Sam asked, her voice sounding both exasperated and excited. "What's going on?"

"This is like hide-and-seek," Angelo said with a wry smile. "I've hidden something. You have to find it."

Sam took a big drink of her latte. "Hold this," she said, handing the cup to him and beginning to scan the railings, which were dense with locks. She walked left and right. She kneeled and studied. After a few minutes, she said, "This could take months. You're going to have to help me a little bit, Jersey. Say, 'You're getting hot,' or something."

"You're definitely hot," he said in a lusty

voice, with a wink. "Or something."

"Stop it," she said, putting her hands on her hips. Sam took off her sunglasses and put them on top of her head. She looked again and laughed. "Is this it?" she asked, pointing at a sign a New Yorker had obviously placed that read NO MORE LOCKS! beside which another New Yorker had written WHAT ABOUT LOCKS & BAGELS?

"You're cold," Angelo said with a big laugh. "Just like the salmon."

Sam walked quickly toward Angelo. "Cold," he said. "Freezing. Icy."

She skipped the other way, Angelo following. "Still cold," he said, as she continued to move across the bridge toward Brooklyn. "Tepid. Lukewarm. Warm. Hot. Hotter. OK, you're red hot. Literally on fire."

Sam stopped and began to scan the railing in front of her. She looked left, right, high, low, and then there it was, staring directly at her: a lock featuring a sticker of Michigan was holding a recipe box to the railing. Sam turned, her eyes wide.

"What is this?"

"What do you think this is?"

"Are you a Sphinx?" Sam asked. "What's this mean?"

Angelo walked up to Sam, set her coffee down on the pavement, and put his hands

444

on her shoulders.

"I didn't know what to do with the key that Willo gave me," he said in a quiet voice. "It just meant so much to me. I felt as if I had been entrusted not only with your family's history but also its heart." He stopped. "When I got back to New York, the weight and importance of the key weighed on me. I was walking the bridge a few days back, saw the railings filled with locks, and it finally hit me."

"What hit you?" Sam asked.

"I don't hold the key to your heart or your life," he said, his voice serious and strong but filled with emotion. "And your family doesn't hold the key, either."

Sam shook her head. "I'm confused," she said. "Then who does?"

"You do," Angelo said with a knowing smile. "You do, Sam."

He reached into his pocket, grabbed Sam's hand, placed something into her palm, and closed her hand. When Sam opened her hand, the key her grandmother had given him to the original recipe box was there.

"It's your decision what to do with the key," he said. "No one else's."

Sam stood there, tears in her eyes, shaking her head, her knees feeling as if they were going to buckle.

"I had a lock made that fits this key," he said. "And I filled the recipe box with some . . . let's just say, surprises. If you want to be with me, you have the key . . . you can use it to unlock the recipe box and discover what's inside. If not, just leave it here."

A lone tear trailed down Sam's cheek. "Angelo," she started.

"You hold the key to your own happiness, Sam," he said. "And once you unlock that, you'll know what to do."

"I don't know what to say," she said, her voice wavering.

"You don't have to say anything," Angelo said, his dimples flashing. "I'm going to go." He leaned in and kissed her gently on the cheek. "Good luck on the interview, Michigan. You're going to knock 'em dead." Angelo walked toward the edge of the railing and acted as if he were going to climb over and jump. "Just don't leave me hangin', Michigan, OK?"

Sam smiled and shook her head. "OK," she said.

Angelo waved good-bye, but he turned one last time and yelled, "Just a week before this bridge opened in 1884, P. T. Barnum led twenty-one elephants over it to prove that it was stable."

Sam shrugged and made a face. "What are you talking about?"

"Sometimes you just have to trust everything's going to work out," he called, "whether you've actually crossed that bridge or not."

Sam laughed. "You're crazy," she called.

"I know," Angelo said with a backward wave.

Sam watched him walk across the bridge, his body becoming smaller and smaller until he was just a dot among the masses.

Sam turned and looked at the lock and the recipe box. Just over the railing, in the distance, the Statue of Liberty stood tall, holding up her torch for the world to see.

So strong, beautiful, proud, independent, Sam thought.

And yet, Sam couldn't help but also think, *she's all alone out there.*

Sam stood on the bridge, turning the key over and over and over again in her hands.

THIRTY-TWO

Willo awoke with a start. She leaned up in bed and looked at the clock on her nightstand. The red numbers flashed in the still-black night: 4:35. Willo smiled to herself in the dark, the clock's numbers conveying a not-so-hidden message: $4 + 3 = 7$, followed by 5.

"Happy birthday, old gal," Willo said to herself. "You made it to seventy-five." She stopped and added with a chuckle, "Somehow." Her laugh echoed in the still of her bedroom.

For the past few months, Willo had experienced difficulty sleeping. At first, she believed it was merely her excitement at what lay ahead: her and the orchard's dueling birthdays and celebrations, and the planning and execution that entailed. Despite getting a handle on those details, Willo still found herself waking up in the middle of the night, her heart racing, near panic.

Willo went to the doctor worried, but she was told that this condition was normal as people aged.

"The older we get, the more prominent sleep problems can become," her doctor said. "Waking before sunrise, unable to fall back asleep. Getting up several times during the night. For many adults over fifty, sleep issues can disrupt everyday life and leave you more exhausted."

Her doctor urged her not to nap or disrupt her normal sleep pattern. She had suggested some sleeping aids, but Willo had demurred. She was proud that her daily regimen of medication consisted solely of vitamins and a pill for her arthritis. Many of her friends took fistfuls of pills, carried around boxes crammed with pills for every hour of the day.

Hour, Willo thought, checking the time again and shaking her head. *Big day. Might as well get it started now.*

She clicked on the little lamp on her nightstand — a pink ceramic base topped by a vintage shade dotted, of course, with little apples — and reached for her reading glasses, knocking over a small plaque as she did. Willo put on her glasses and reached over to set it upright, smiling at its message: GRAY HAIR IS A CROWN OF SPLENDOR.

PROVERBS 16:31.

"What about gray hair that's been colored a bit?" she asked the plaque with a chuckle. "I even think the color is called Splendiferously Salt and Pepper."

Willo picked up a book on her nightstand — essays by Anne Lamott, whose wisdom and insights about surviving the daily hardships of life provided her with comfort and strength — and stopped cold when she read the bookmark: *Fear doesn't prevent death. It prevents life. Naguib Mahfouz.*

Sam had given the bookmark to Willo years back, and it had marked every single book Willo read over the years, still standing proud and firm like a literary friend and sentinel.

How true, Willo thought, rereading the bookmark.

Suddenly, Willo sat up straight in bed.

That's it, she thought. *It's not because I'm older, or worried about all the planning. I haven't been sleeping because I've been afraid.*

Willo placed the book in her lap and looked around her bedroom. It was adorned with the history of her life and the history of her family's life: photos of her husband and daughter, grandparents and parents, the orchard and pie pantry. Scanning the framed pictures on her walls was like watching an old film reel: babies being born, growing up, going off into the world, having kids of their own, aging and . . .

Willo stopped and shut her eyes. *I'm next,* she thought. *There is no one standing before me in line any longer, is there, God?*

She opened her eyes again, and black-and-white photos of the orchard turned to color pictures, saplings turned into trees, buildings expanded.

I'm not afraid of my own death, Willo thought. *I'm afraid of the death of what my family started. Is that selfish?*

Willo looked at photos of Sam and her brother, Aaron. *What if my grandchildren don't want the orchard? What if they sell out to a company or larger farm? What if . . .*

A voice inside Willo's head called to her. It was that of her mother, standing with her in the kitchen, teaching her how to bake.

"What if the cookies don't turn out?" Willo had asked her mom over and over in the kitchen. *"What if we didn't add enough sugar?"*

"You can't control any of that, Willo," her mother had explained. *"You've followed the recipe. You've even added your own spin on it: cherries in the chocolate chunk cookies.*

You've done everything you can; now you just have to trust that it will all turn out."

"*Sometimes,*" her mom had added, picking Willo up into her arms, "*you can be too careful, you can worry too much. Sometimes, your grandma once told me, you have to approach love and life differently than baking: with more abandon.*"

Willo pulled on a pink chenille robe and fuzzy bunny slippers.

"What would life be like without bunny slippers?" Willo asked the happy little faces. She whispered into their soft ears, "Ready for some coffee?"

She padded down the stairs and into the kitchen, turning on lights along the way. Willo started the coffee and impatiently tapped her fingers on the counter, waiting until the pot was full enough that she could pour her first cup. She nabbed her favorite mug, which read *Baking Is Love Made Visible,* and filled it to the brim.

"I love you, coffee," she whispered to the mug.

Willo moved toward the kitchen table to take a seat, but stopped on her way, plucking the recipe box from the old cabinet along the way.

Should I bake something this morning? she thought. *A special treat for everyone who's working so hard to set everything up? Start on those turnovers?*

She glanced at the kitchen clock, which was shaped like a pie, the hands moving across a lattice crust, one piece of apple pie missing. *I certainly have enough time,* she thought.

She sat and opened the box, perusing and plucking cards as if she were turning the pages of a newspaper. As she did, memories came flooding back, just as they had moments ago when she'd looked at the photos in her bedroom.

All the birthday cakes and holiday pies, ice cream on warm summer nights, and warm, gooey treats on cold snowy days, Willo thought. *Cookies, cupcakes, chocolate, and coffee cakes.*

Willo stopped and ran her hand over the box's burnished wood.

This is a history of my family, Willo thought. *This tells the story of who we are.*

Willo lost track of time scanning the recipes, until a peek of light appeared outside. She stood and walked to the kitchen window. Beyond the orchard, in the distance over the bay, Willo could see the first light of her seventy-fifth birthday squeezing over the northeastern edge of the bay.

An unexpected thrill enveloped Willo's

body, and she crossed her arms around herself, burying her hands in the plush of the chenille. The dawn's light was orange, and the horizon looked as if a giant Creamsicle had melted over it.

How many beautiful sunrises have I witnessed in my life? Willo wondered. *How many stunning sunsets?* And though she tried to stop it, another question entered her mind: *And how many more will I see?*

Willo began to turn, but as she did, a lone leaf caught her attention in the blush of morning light. It was a sugar maple leaf dangling from a high branch, twirling in the breeze, round and round, as if it were a Cirque du Soleil performer. The leaf was bright orange, a hue even more beautiful than dawn over the horizon, and it stuck out like an oriole in a chorus line of bluebirds.

A harbinger of fall, Willo thought. *A harbinger of change.*

Every year, one branch of Willo's beloved towering sugar maple thumbed its nose at summer weeks before any signs of fall in northern Michigan had declared themselves. The leaves on the branch would turn a rainbow of colors while the rest of the leaves remained verdant. Willo would often sit on the patio and stare at the tree while she sipped her coffee or her wine, admiring the branch's bravado and coming to terms with the fact that another summer was ending, that fall was coming, that the seasons of life could never be slowed or stopped. Sometimes, the sun would blind Willo as she stared at the tree, and she would be forced to shut her eyes, and hundreds of mirror images of the tree would float in her viewfinder. She would pop open her eyes again, and the trees would still be there, this time moving, running, scampering around her yard, the hillside, and the orchard, like ghosts from her past and hopes for her future.

The leaf continued to twirl, performing only for Willo. Suddenly, an idea hit her. She scurried back to the kitchen table and began to rifle through the recipe box, looking for the flash of orange, just like the leaf.

Where is it? she wondered. *Where did it go?*

She sat, confused, and took a big sip of coffee to jolt her still sleepy mind awake.

Did I lose it?

Willo returned to the coffeepot and filled her mug, leaning out the kitchen window to look at the horizon and then at the leaf, still waving, still standing out proudly in the midst of a world that looked too much the same.

Willo's eyes widened, and she smiled to herself, finally understanding where the recipe had gone. She gave a little wave to the leaf.

Oh, Sam, Willo thought, shutting her eyes to say a little prayer. *Follow your true colors.*

THIRTY-THREE

Sam tossed and turned, and finally sat up in bed and checked the time on her cell: 4:35.

Happy birthday, Grandma, Sam thought. She considered texting her grandma an early birthday greeting but decided against it.

Too early, she thought. *And too early to wake up now, or my roommates will kill me.*

A trash truck clanged and clattered on a nearby block, the deafening noise echoing up the buildings as if they were a canyon.

Sam lay back down and covered her head with a pillow, trying to block out the city noise.

The city that never sleeps, Sam thought. *That's an understatement.*

Sam hadn't realized how accustomed she had grown to the city noise until she returned home. She'd been unable to sleep in Michigan at first because it was eerily quiet, but it had taken only a few days for Sam to readjust to the solitude. She quickly grew accustomed to an orchestra of owls and cicadas rather than the hard rock of trash trucks, police sirens, ambulances, music, and screaming New Yorkers. The noise was unrelenting; no matter the time of day, New York was awake.

With a vengeance, Sam thought, laying an arm over her pillow to muffle the noise of music blaring from a passing car. She tried to still her mind, but it was having none of it; her job interview was front and center.

I can't be exhausted for my interview, she thought. *Go back to sleep.*

But the more Sam repeated this mantra, the more amped up she got.

Will Colette be nice? Will she be a repeat of Chef Dimples? Sam wondered. *Will I like her? The job? What if she offers it to me? What if she doesn't?*

An image of her grandmother popped into Sam's head, and she forced the pillow more tightly across her face. Sam could hear her grandma saying the phrase she always repeated to her when she had worried about things she couldn't control growing up: "If *if*s and *but*s were candy and nuts, oh, what a Merry Christmas it would be!"

Nothing like Grandma's words of wisdom,

Sam thought. *If, if, if . . .*

A siren wailed by, and Sam's brief clarity was again shattered.

What if Colette asks me to make something for her on the spot? Sam wondered. *If so, what?*

Sam ran through options in her mind. *The galette would be ideal,* Sam thought. *But if Colette is the queen of French pastry, mine might not be up to her standards.*

I could make the slab pie, Sam continued. *But what if Trish already told her that was my mic drop moment at Chef Dimples?*

Sam's tired mind whirred, and then she remembered Colette saying she needed someone for fall. *Autumn,* Sam thought. *Scarves, sweaters, cute coats, and boots.*

Another image of Willo ran through Sam's mind. *That's why you stole that recipe, isn't it?* Sam asked herself.

She yanked the pillow off her face, the cool air sobering her, and she inhaled deeply. She reached over and grabbed her cell, flicking on the phone's flashlight. She shined the light around her bed and saw her purse sitting on a tiny folding chair. Sam stretched out her arms, not wanting to get out of bed, until her fingertips brushed her purse, and she was able to snag it and pull it to her. She opened it and inside was the index card that she had squirreled into her shorts when her grandma wasn't looking and then transferred to her purse before she headed back to New York. Sam illuminated the recipe with the tiny flashlight.

Willo's Fabulous Fall Pumpkin Bars with Cream Cheese Icing

Sam smiled in the dark. The recipe was written in orange marker in her grandma's slanted handwriting, the same cursive — tilted heavily toward the right as if the letters had been caught in a windstorm — that Sam and her mom used. The *F*s were fancy and flourished, just like schoolteachers used to teach, and Willo's *i*'s were dotted with hearts. Alongside the edges, Willo had drawn cute little pumpkins and fall leaves.

Sam laid the card flat on the bed and tried to smooth it out after her cat burglary. The card was wrinkled and bent, and Sam's heart sank. But the card had also seen better days; it was flecked with orange stains — from the pumpkin and the batter — and there were spots from the cream cheese icing, likely spun out of the mixer, covering some of the recipe's letters. Sam picked up the card and held it to her nose; it smelled like the wood of the recipe box.

It smells like home, Sam thought.

Sam scanned the ingredients and directions, trying to forge them into her mind in case she was asked to bake on the spot, but winced when she came upon an ingredient that stuck out like a sore thumb to her culinary training: Bisquick.

Grandma, Sam thought. *I forgot how much you love Bisquick.*

OK, Sam thought, staring at the recipe. *I can just rework it the old-fashioned way: flour, baking powder, salt, shortening or butter.*

Sam stopped. *What if it doesn't turn out, though?* she wondered. *What if . . .*

Sam suddenly shook her head and waved her arms in front of her body. "Stop it!" she said in the dark to herself. "Stop sabotaging everything before it's even happened."

As she did, the flashlight in her hand illuminated her bedroom walls like a strobe light. The tiny cube of a room brightened from left to right, as if a car were passing by at night, headlights on. When her hand stopped, the flashlight had settled on the wall in front of her and illuminated a plaque that her grandma had given to her when she first moved to New York.

Sure, you can mix the flour, baking soda,

salt, shortening and the whole nine yards, but why wouldn't you just pull out a box of Bisquick?

— Sandra Lee

Sam had nearly thrown the gift out when she received it.

"I can't put this up, Grandma," Sam had said. "My classmates would never let me live it down. A quote from the 'Semi-Homemade' chef? Really?"

"Lots of people are too busy to do what you do, and what we do at the pie pantry," said Willo, who loved watching the Food Network and its assortment of personalities. "Doesn't mean they don't want to bake or cook. They still want a good meal. They still want something more than fast food, a frozen pizza, or slice-and-bake cookies. But sometimes, they're just too busy to spend a lot of time. Shortcuts are OK as long as they're not compromises."

When Sam had hung the plaque, her classmates had goaded her, telling her about the reception Lee had received from celebrated chefs like Anthony Bourdain and asking her exactly what Bisquick was.

"Quick biscuits," Sam had said. And then she had surprised her classmates with fresh biscuits, which they'd raved about, none of them realizing they'd been made with Bisquick.

Sam picked up her phone, clicked off the flashlight, and began to text.

HAPPY BIRTHDAY, GRANDMA! Sam wrote, adding a gif of a cake featuring a flickering *75* candle. *I know you're not awake yet, but I'm thinking of you, I love you, and I miss you!*

Sam hit send and a minute later her phone trilled.

Thank you! I love you and am thinking of you, too! Up early watching the sun come up . . . it's the most glorious orange. Shine bright today and remember to show your true colors!

Sam immediately began to tear up, and she sent a series of heart emojis to her grandma, followed by a series of birthday balloons that floated across the screen.

If she's up, Sam thought, *I might as well get up, too. It's a big day for all of us.*

Sam stood, stretched, and looked out her bedroom window.

Hello, brick wall. Sam laughed, staring at the buildings that sat across the narrow alley from her own.

Without warning, the neon sign for the Indian restaurant below came to life. In the predawn dark, the sign illuminated the alley.

NAAN BETTER, the sign blinked, turning Sam's urban vista a bright, iridescent orange. Sam looked at the sign blinking, as bright orange as Indian spices, and blinked along with it.

I never realized, Sam thought, her eyes filled with orange. *What if the sign is a sign?*

THIRTY-FOUR

The orchard was teeming with activity.

Willo stood at the edge of the barn, surveying the celebration. The U-Pick was open, and every tree seemed to have someone underneath it, picking fruit. Kids' games were set up in the middle of the orchard: bobbing for apples, crafts, face painting. Food was being served outside the pie pantry, and smoke from the barbecue grills drifted lazily into the blue sky. Pie was being sold at makeshift tables, while a line of people waited to go inside the pantry for pie-making demonstrations and a line of cars snaked down the road waiting to enter.

"Hi, Willo!" a group of girls said as they passed, waving happily as they licked apple cider ice pops. "You look so pretty!"

"Thank you, girls," Willo said. She looked down and smoothed her skirt. Rather than her standard outfit, Willo was wearing a pretty blue dress that matched her eyes, she had curled her hair into soft waves, and she was wearing makeup.

"Happy birthday, Mom!"

Willo turned, and Deana and Gary were standing beside her. She hugged and kissed them both.

"You look beautiful," Gary said.

Willo did a little twirl. "Thank you," she said.

"As pretty as the weather," Deana added.

It was a perfect kickoff to Labor Day weekend in Suttons Bay, whose holiday forecast was usually more mixed than a triple berry galette. The weather on Labor Day weekend could be cold and rainy, cloudy and cool, or warm and sunny, but it varied greatly from year to year.

"We lucked out," Willo said. "Our prayers were answered."

The three stood in silence for a few seconds, the echoes of children's laughter and excited screams filling the air.

"I never dreamed . . ." Willo started, before stopping and clearing her throat. She started again, but her voice was thick with emotion.

"Oh, Mom," Deana said, slipping an arm around her mother's waist and pulling her close. "Are you OK?"

Willo nodded. "I just never dreamed that

our orchard would grow into something like this," she said, "or make it a hundred years. I'm very proud of what our family has done." She hesitated and turned to her daughter and son-in-law. "I'm very proud of both of you."

Deana and Gary smiled. "We wouldn't be here without you," Gary said. "I'm very proud of you. You are an amazing woman."

Willo's cheeks flushed crimson.

"Seventy-five," she said, shaking her head. "I don't feel seventy-five today. I still feel like one of the young girls here."

"You still act like one," Gary joked.

Willo smiled. "Life goes by so fast. I can remember standing here as a young girl, watching my parents when they weren't even your age. You can't stop time. You can only hope you use it wisely."

"You have, Mom," Deana said, her voice now emotional. "You have."

"I hope so," Willo said. "I don't have a lot of time left on this earth . . ."

"Mom, stop," Deana interrupted.

"Well, it's true. I'm sorry to say that," she said. "I'm not worried about my life ending. It's been a joyous ride."

Suddenly, a plump little boy in overall shorts, toddling barefoot unsteadily — his parents on each side of him, tightly gripping his hands and largely keeping him upright — came up to Willo.

"Jackson has something he wants to give you," his mom said, a big smile on her tan face. "You can give it to the nice lady now, Jackson."

His parents let go and Jackson stuck a chubby hand down the front of his overalls and produced an apple — as round, red, and handsome as his face. He giggled excitedly and then simply tossed the apple into the air, where it rolled toward Willo on the ground.

"Sorry," the boy's father said. "He's not so good at handing things to people yet."

"Can you say what you wanted to say?" his mom asked. "You can tell the nice lady."

"Hoppy bowfday!" Jackson said, jumping up and down after saying the words.

Willo kneeled and looked directly at the little boy. "Thank you, Jackson," she said. "Can I give you a hug?"

The boy looked up at his parents, who nodded their approval. Willo hugged Jackson and gave him a kiss on top of the head.

"My parents have brought me here every Labor Day weekend since I was a little girl," the woman said. "We're from Chicago and coming here makes our summer complete. We want to pass that along to our son. I just wanted to say thank you to you and your family, and wish you a happy birthday because you've given my family so many sweet memories over the years."

Willo could feel tears rise, and she willed them back, hugging the young woman.

"Thank you," she said. "From the bottom of my heart."

The family smiled and walked toward the pie pantry. Willo picked up the apple at her feet, rubbed it on her dress, and took a bite, the orchard reflected in the tears now rimming her eyes.

"It's this I don't want to end," Willo said in a whisper of a voice. "My family and my orchard are my legacies."

"Mom," Deana said. "It's all going to work out. Think of how many times our family has been challenged over the last century. Sometimes you just have to believe it will work out . . . and it will. That's what you taught us. Think of that family you just met, of all the people you've influenced over the years." Deana stopped and scratched her head. "What was that poem you used to recite to me when I complained about baking, or working here? Remember?"

"The 'Recipe for a Good Life'?" Willo said with a smile, remembering. "Take a few cups of kindness . . ."

"One dash of humility," Deana continued, as the two recited in unison the poem about how the ingredients of laughter, patience, forgiveness, love, faith, and courage should be combined equally in life and passed along to those you meet.

Willo leaned into her daughter when they had finished. "Thank you for reminding me of that," she said. "It's a poem from Muhammad Ali."

All of a sudden, Willo felt her feet go off the ground, and she was being spun around in a circle, the orchard flashing in front of her, then the barn, then Deana and Gary.

"Happy birthday, Grandma!"

Willo was back on the ground, the world still spinning. When she turned, Aaron was standing before her.

"My grandson!" she yelled. "It's so good to see you. What are you doing here?"

"I wouldn't miss this for the world," he said.

Willo looked at her grandson towering over her, the young boy she always saw now a grown man.

"I love you, Grandma," he said.

"I love you, too."

"So, Sam's back in New York?" he asked. Willo nodded. "She texted me earlier this week, but haven't heard from her since." He stopped. "Been sorta busy with fraternity rush."

Suddenly, a cymbal crashed in the distance.

"Speakin' a' which," Aaron said, pointing toward the edge of the orchard. "Surprise! I brought some friends who have a band in Ann Arbor. Thought it might be fun for them to play tonight."

"You should have asked us first," Gary said.

"Sorry," Aaron said. "I just wanted to give her a gift, too."

"It's OK," Willo said. "Thank you, Aaron. I love it. That'll be fun. As long as you will dance with me." Willo gave him a big wink.

"It would be my pleasure, Grandma," he said. "So, when do you want the band to play 'Happy Birthday'? We could do it now . . ."

Willo interrupted Aaron before he could finish. "Why don't we wait a while?" she said. "Everything is just gearing up."

"But we should do it while everyone's here, right?" he asked.

"It won't be dark for hours," Willo said. "We have plenty of time."

"OK," Aaron said, taking off. "I'm off to get some pie. On the house, right?"

Willo laughed. "First slice only!"

As her grandson jogged away, Willo laughed, belying what was really on her mind.

One of my birthday gifts is here, she thought. *But the other has yet to arrive.*

THIRTY-FIVE

"Don't be nervous."

Trish handed Sam an espresso in a little white cup.

"Are you trying to kill me?" Sam asked, looking at the espresso. "I've had an entire pot of coffee and a three-shot latte . . . I can't tell nervous from heart palpitations anymore."

Trish laughed. "Then sip it," she said. Trish put her hands on her friend's shoulders and gave her a gentle massage. "You got this."

"Thanks," Sam said.

"You'll love Colette. She's real and genuine. Everything Chef Narcissist wasn't."

Sam chuckled.

"I have to get back to work," Trish said. "I'll check in when you're done."

Sam looked around the little bakery in downtown Manhattan. Doux Souvenirs *was* real and genuine, everything Dimples Bakery wasn't. The small shop's brick walls were adorned with black-and-white photos of women baking. Despite Colette's renown, there were no celebrities in the bakery taking selfies or talking loudly on their cells, just an assortment of businessmen and women, a scattering of tourists, and some well-heeled uptown-looking women who must have read about the place and were checking it out.

"Those photographs are of my mother and my grandmother."

Sam jumped, and Colette appeared at her table.

"Mes excuses," she said in French. "My apologies. I did not mean to startle you."

Sam stood and extended her hand. "I'm Sam Nelson. Thank you for having me."

"Sit, sit," Colette said, waving her hand. *"S'il vous plaît."*

"I've had a bit of coffee in preparation for this interview," Sam said, lifting the espresso. "In advance, pardon my face twitching and non sequiturs."

Colette laughed. "No need to be nervous," she said. "I've heard wonderful things about you."

She gestured to the photos on the walls at which Sam had just been looking. "Those are family photos of me with my mother and grandmother in France," she said, before letting a small chuckle out. "Everyone in America says — how do they put it? — 'Your life is so *Chocolat*' — like the movie. But the women in my life taught me the art of baking, and the history of their family recipes." She stopped and smiled at the photos and then at Sam. "It's more than a passion to me. It's like . . . breathing. It's like . . . love."

Colette was lithe, fit, and impossibly pretty, one of those women with high cheekbones, flawless skin, and wide eyes who didn't have to wear much makeup to look gorgeous. She resembled the French actress Audrey Tautou in beauty, and yet her demeanor was unassuming and inviting, her smile like an open gate to a summer garden.

"Tell me a little about yourself." Colette stopped and smiled at Sam.

Sam began to talk about her culinary training, but Colette held up a finger. "I know all about that," she said sweetly. "It's a wonderful school. But I want to know *why* you bake. Tell me a story."

Despite the caffeine, Sam could feel her heart stop. She nodded, shut her eyes for a brief moment, and eased back in her chair.

"It's my grandmother's birthday," Sam started, her voice suddenly emotional.

"She's seventy-five. I grew up on a family orchard, where we run our own pie pantry, and . . ." Sam stopped and gestured at Colette's family photos. "Like you, my mother and grandmother taught me to bake."

Sam told Colette about the history of the orchard and pie pantry, the struggles and triumphs, of receiving the sacred family recipe box at thirteen, of loving home but needing to leave. When she finished, Colette held her petite hand out across the table, and she took Sam's in hers.

"We are kindred spirits," she said. "Raised and loved by wonderful women. Flour is in our blood.

"Why don't we head back to the kitchen now," Colette continued, standing. "I'd love it if you would bake something for me."

This time, Sam could feel her heart flutter. "Of course," Sam said.

As the two entered the kitchen, Colette handed Sam an apron, and she showed her around. "I won't hover, I promise," Colette said with a big smile. "Make me something that reminds you of home. You are cooking among friends," she continued.

"OK," Sam said, looking over at Trish, who mouthed, *You got this, girl!,* then made "snake eyes," pointing two fingers from her eyes toward Sam to give her strength, luck, and focus.

Sam took a deep breath and then subconsciously felt for the recipe card she had tucked into the back pocket of the black dress pants she'd worn to the interview.

Here goes nothin', Grandma, she thought.

Sam began weighing out the ingredients but stopped when she remembered that her family recipe called for Bisquick.

Do it the right way, Sam, she told herself, moving around the kitchen to gather flour, baking powder, salt, and butter.

Sam mixed the batter, added the spices, greased a 9-by-13-inch pan, and then slid the pumpkin bars into the oven.

I feel like I'm on Chopped, Sam thought, referring to the Food Network reality show where chefs compete against one another by making a three-course dinner using mystery ingredients pulled from a picnic basket in under thirty minutes. *What if I get chopped?*

Sam shook her head and started in on the cream cheese frosting while the pumpkin bars baked. She beat the dense, sweet topping until it was creamy, sticking a finger into the frosting at the end to taste.

A little more vanilla, she thought.

Sam checked the bars, sticking a toothpick

into the middle to see if they were fully baked, just as her grandma had taught her when she was young.

"Perfect," she said to herself.

When they were cool, Sam began to spread on the frosting, thick and heavy with a spatula, until the bars resembled a swirling cloud of sugar.

"It smells so wonderful," Colette said, walking over. "Is it OK to taste them now?"

Sam nodded. Colette grabbed a knife, coated it with cooking spray, and then wiped it clean before cutting a slice that slid out perfectly and evenly. She placed it on a pretty white plate and then repeated two more times, calling over Trish. Colette handed a plate to Sam. "A chef should always taste her own creation, yes?" she asked.

"Yes," Sam said.

Sam slid her fork through the pumpkin bar and lifted it to her mouth, chewing robotically, unable to taste it, waiting for Colette's reaction.

Colette shut her eyes as she chewed the dessert. She swallowed, smiled, and then tasted it again. In just a few seconds, the pumpkin bar was gone.

"Tastes like fall," she said. "Like home on a crisp autumn day. Just like something your grandma would make from an old recipe box."

Trish stood behind Colette nodding, then shot Sam another snake eyes and a big thumbs-up.

"Thank you," Sam said. "I don't know what to say. I didn't know what to make exactly, and I saw this recipe in my grandmother's recipe box when I was home. It reminded me of just what you said, of something your grandma would make."

"Tell me about the recipe," Colette asked. "How did you make it?"

"Well," Sam said, and laughed, "my grandma always made it with Bisquick, but I changed it to make it a little more refined."

"Why?" Colette asked.

Sam looked at her, eyes wide. "Well, I mean, it's Bisquick," she said, again with a nervous laugh. "Not a lot of Bisquick in culinary school."

Colette walked over to a large cupboard, opened the door, and turned. "Voilà!" She laughed, holding up a box of Bisquick, putting her finger over her mouth as if it were a secret. "Sssshhhh!"

Sam's eyes grew even wider.

"I . . . I . . . I . . ." Sam stuttered.

"Even trained pastry chefs take shortcuts sometimes," Colette said. "Not very often, but on occasion. We will never admit it in public, but we do sometimes." She returned the box to the cupboard and walked over to Sam, leaning against the marble counter.

"My mom would often use instant potatoes for her *hachis Parmentier,*" Colette said with a big smile. "I thought her shepherd's pie was the best in the world, and she used instant potatoes. I make it the same way for my family now. Sometimes, things are perfect as they are. Even if they're not perfect."

Sam smiled and nodded.

"Did you always want to own your own shop one day?" Sam asked.

"I did," Colette said. "I worked under some wonderful chefs, but I wanted to run my own business. I think that's what we all want in the end. To make our mark on the world."

"That's what I want, too," Sam said.

Colette walked over to Sam and touched her arm. "It sounds like you have that already," she said softly, before looking around her kitchen. "A corner shop on a street in New York, an old barn in Michigan, a stone kitchen in France. It doesn't matter where something is made, it matters who makes it and why."

She continued. "That's why I called my

shop Sweet Memories. I'm trying to re-create and recapture my childhood. People don't bake anymore. They don't spend time in kitchens with their family. If we can just give them a taste of that memory, a warm feeling, a delicious dessert, even an impetus to go home and bake in their kitchens with their own families, then our work is done."

Colette picked up her fork and dug into the pumpkin bars, as if she were alone at home in a robe eating with no one around to judge.

"This really is quite good," Colette said. "I'd love to add this to our menu here. It's perfect for fall." She stopped. "That is, if you're willing to part with a secret family recipe."

Colette leaned toward Sam, as if she were seeing her for the first time. "I just noticed what was around your neck," she said. "Is that a key?" She walked closer. "Two keys?"

Sam self-consciously felt for the keys around her neck. She had added the one Angelo had given her to the one she already had, and decided to wear them both this morning for good luck.

"Yes," Sam said.

"How pretty and unique," Colette said. "Where did you get them?"

"Long story," Sam said, "but one is the

original key to my great-great-grandmother's recipe box, and the other is the one to my recipe box."

"Incredible," Colette said, stepping forward to study the keys more closely. She looked at Sam. "I bet it has unlocked many sweet memories."

Sam smiled and nodded, feeling the keys.

"I would be honored if you would join me here," Colette said with a definitive nod. "I think we would make a great team."

"You're offering me a job?" Sam asked, her voice rising in excitement.

"I am," she said. "I will put together an offer and call you later today. Does that sound acceptable?"

"Yes," Sam said. "Yes! Of course. Thank you. Thank you."

Colette extended her hand. "No," she said. "Thank *you.*" She turned to Trish, who was listening closely but doing a bad job of acting as if she weren't. "And thank Trish, too."

"Thank you, Mrs. Kravitz," Sam said, laughing.

"I don't fully understand American humor," Colette said. "That will need some explaining."

Sam and Trish laughed. "I will call you later," Colette said. "I have a meeting, but

Trish will show you out when you're ready. Good-bye, Sam."

"Thank you," she said. "From the bottom of my heart."

Colette smiled at Sam and then glanced again at her keys. "You wear them close to your heart for a reason, don't you?" she asked.

Sam blushed and nodded.

As Colette exited, the kitchen door swung open. Beyond the shop's windows, Sam caught a glimpse of a tree. Her knees quaked, and she suddenly felt overcome with emotion and confusion.

Is that . . . ? Sam wondered, arcing her neck for a closer look as the door swung closed again. *It is. A willow.*

And I did wear these close to my heart for a reason, she thought, gripping the keys harder in her hands. *I just don't know right now if they're a talisman or an anchor.*

Thirty-Six

The orchard was aglow.

Lights twinkled from strands that had been strung between the rows of trees, the breeze making them sway. In the dark, the lights resembled thousands of fireflies. Lanterns lined the path between the trees, a lit highway that arced up and over the hillside before stopping. In the far distance, lights from boats that had gone for sunset sails looked like eyes that were attempting to sneak a peek into the party.

Willo stood at the edge of the barn as the band played and people danced, her eyes narrowed, scanning the darkness beyond the orchard.

"Grandma," Aaron said, startling her. "It's getting late. Can the band play 'Happy Birthday' now?"

Willo wanted to shake her head no, but she forced herself to nod.

"Cool," he said, blowing his blond bangs

out of his eyes, just as he'd done when he was little, just as his sister always did. "I'll let them know. Be ready with your speech and to take a bow, OK?"

He jogged off into the darkness.

"Mom," Deana said, approaching. "Are you OK? Seems like every time I've looked for you, you've been standing right here."

"I'm fine, sweetheart," she said. "Just a bit overwhelmed."

"I know," Deana said, pulling her mom close and giving her a hug. "Big day."

The music stopped, and Aaron's voice blared over the speakers. "Can I have your attention, please?"

He waited for the crowd to settle and quiet. "Thank you," he said. "And thank you all for coming. As you know, today is a day of monumental celebration for my family. It marks the one hundredth anniversary of our orchard, and my grandma's seventy-fifth birthday."

The crowd hooted and hollered, yelling, "Happy birthday!" into the night.

"My grandma wanted to say a few words before the band played 'Happy Birthday,' so if you'll turn your attention to the woman of the night — standing at the barn — the best pie maker, businesswoman, and grandma in the world . . . Willo!"

Deana handed Willo a microphone. She lifted it to her mouth when a spotlight suddenly clicked on, illuminating Willo, blinding her.

"Turn that thing off," Willo said into the mic. The crowd tittered, and Willo looked over at Gary, who was beaming as brightly as the light and shaking his head no.

"Speech!" someone yelled. "Speech!"

"Thank you all for coming tonight," she said, the speakers emitting an ear-piercing screech for a second. "That was my stomach . . . I'm a little nervous, and it's letting you know how I really feel right now," Willo adlibbed, and people laughed, breaking the tension.

She continued, "This orchard has not only been my home, it's also been your home. Our family has been your family. My grandparents had nothing but this land when they started, and they spent their whole lives building it. My mom and I started the pie pantry. This . . ." Willo stopped and swept her arms in front of her. ". . . you . . . have been my life, and I couldn't have been more blessed.

"My family taught me the reward of hard work, the need to dream, the strength of faith, and the simple beauty of a summer night in Michigan. My mother taught me that you bake for someone because it is a way of connecting family and generations." Willo hesitated, her voice thick with emotion.

"It's OK, Willo," someone yelled. People whooped in response.

Willo took a deep breath and continued. "My mother taught me that you bake for someone because it is an act of love. That's why I've done it my whole life. Because I love my family, and I love you."

"We love you, too, Willo!" people in the crowd began to yell.

"Thank you for bringing your family to celebrate with ours," she said.

The band immediately launched into "Happy Birthday," the crowd serenading her. Willo squinted, the spotlight still in her eyes, and she could see people swaying.

Suddenly, in the distance, Willo swore she could see something moving toward the orchard, something big, wide, and amorphous, lumbering slowly.

A bear, she thought. *What is that?*

As the crowd continued to sing, Willo stepped out of the spotlight and cupped her hands over her eyes. The figure grew closer and closer, moving up the hillside and toward the orchard, everyone's backs turned away from it.

Should I yell a warning? Willo thought.

Willo squinted even harder, and that was when the figure split into two.

Willo's heart began to race, and the two figures moved to the edge of the orchard.

Am I seeing things?

Willo took another step forward and could now distinguish that one figure was male with dark, curly hair and the other was female with long blond hair.

"Sam?" Willo asked into the microphone, her voice husky and choked with emotion.

"Happy birthday, dear Grandma . . ."

Willo heard Sam's voice singing.

Angelo joined her, his hand around Sam's waist.

"Happy birthday to you!"

Willo dropped the microphone with a resounding *thump* and went running, as fast as she could, down the orchard, the lights whirring around her, the memory of Sam's thirteenth birthday suddenly rushing into Willo's mind. She threw her arms around her granddaughter as the crowd erupted.

"I didn't want to have this day without you here," Willo said, her voice shaky.

"Happy birthday, Grandma," Sam whispered.

"You made it home," Willo said, collapsing into tears, which turned into heavy sobs.

"You made it home."

"I am home," Sam said, holding her tightly. Sam stopped, held her grandma at arm's length, and searched her eyes. "For good."

Willo's eyes widened and again filled with tears.

"What?" she asked. "You didn't get the job? Oh, Sam, I'm sorry. That's no reason to give up on your dream, though."

"Grandma," Sam said, "I was offered the job."

"I don't understand."

"I finally realized I already had the one I always wanted," she said.

"Sam," Willo started. "But how did you get here so fast?"

Sam smiled and pointed at Angelo. "This one," she said, as Angelo walked over to hug Willo.

"Happy birthday, Willo," he said.

"Sam!" Deana said, hugging her daughter.

"What a surprise," Gary said, following.

"What's cookin', sis?" Aaron said, walking over and giving Sam a bear hug. "You always know how to make an entrance, don't you?"

"You want me to drive you somewhere later?" Sam joked, referencing all the times she had served as her little brother's personal taxi.

"Depends on how much beer I have." He laughed.

"Hey, do you all mind if I steal Grandma away for a minute?" Sam asked. "I have a special birthday gift that I want to give her in private."

"Your presence is gift enough," Willo protested.

"Come on," Deana said to Angelo. "I bet you're hungry, and I think we can rustle up a piece of pie for you."

"Or an entire pie," Gary added.

"Bring it on," Angelo said. He leaned in and kissed Sam on the cheek, giving her a big wink as he walked away with her family.

Sam took Willo's hand in her own, and the two walked toward the barn.

"Where are we going?" Willo asked.

Sam didn't answer for a while. She simply gripped her grandmother's hand more tightly. When they passed the barn, turned up the gravel road, and headed toward Willo's house, Sam finally said, "It's your seventy-fifth birthday. I thought it would be nice to bake something together."

"Like your thirteenth birthday?" Willo asked, more memories flooding her mind. "Seems like yesterday."

The two walked into the house and

headed directly for the kitchen.

Sam immediately turned on the oven to preheat before removing the large leather shoulder bag she had crossed over her body. She pulled out a wrapped box and set it on the kitchen table.

"Take a seat," Sam said. "Open it."

"Sam," Willo said. "This isn't necessary."

"Actually," Sam said, "it is."

Willo unwrapped the box, and her eyes widened as she pulled the gift free.

"I don't understand," she said, cocking her head at Sam.

"Let me explain," Sam said, telling Willo of her meeting with Angelo on the Brooklyn Bridge and the love locks that were placed there. "He gave me the key you gave him, the key to your grandmother's original recipe box, and he told me before my interview that I held the key to my own happiness, and once I unlocked that, I'd know what to do."

Sam stopped and looked at her grandmother, her cheeks quivering. "He then made me find the love lock he'd made for me on the bridge. It was attached to . . ." Sam stopped, her eyes brimming with tears. ". . . a recipe box that he had made for me." Sam removed her necklace and showed her grandma the original key. "Angelo had a lock made that fit the key, and he'd locked the recipe box to the bridge. He told me if I wanted to be with him, I had the key to unlock the recipe box and discover what was inside. If I didn't, I could just leave it there. And then he just walked away."

"You unlocked it!" Willo said, her eyes, too, filling with tears. "You listened to your heart."

"When Colette called to go over her offer, I was already standing on the Brooklyn Bridge," Sam said. "I hesitated, and she knew immediately. Colette said, 'You wore those keys to the interview today for a reason. You already have your own sweet memories, don't you? Go unlock your destiny.' "

Sam continued: "As soon as I got off the phone with her, I slipped the key into the lock and freed the recipe box. Inside were two e-tickets to Michigan for this afternoon. A note said, 'There are two, but you may use only one if you wish. Just know you hold the key to my heart, and I would follow you anywhere in the world just to be with you.' "

"Oh, Sam," Willo said, tears trailing down her face.

"He made the recipe box for me, just like your grandpa did for your grandma," she said, showing it to Willo. "I'm just glad it didn't rain while it was on the bridge. I would have opened the box and found a pile of mush."

Although the box was new, its wood was reclaimed and burnished. Apples had been carved onto its top and then Angelo had hand-painted them, rubbing the paint to make it look worn. On the front of the box, underneath a small lock, was a little sign that read *RECIPE BOX.*

Sam took the key on her necklace and inserted it into the lock. Sam opened it, and though it was empty, it contained little hand-lettered cards that read: *PIES, COB-BLERS, DONUTS, COFFEE CAKES, COOK-IES, BARS,* and *JAMS AND JELLIES.*

"Look under *bars,*" Sam urged her grand-mother.

Willo moved the cards and there, sitting alone, was the sole recipe card in the box. Willo plucked it from the box and read it.

"Pumpkin bars," she said with a smile. "I knew it. I knew you'd taken it. I was going to make these this morning."

"I did," Sam smiled. "I made them for Colette. She loved them." Sam hesitated. "I actually altered the recipe so that it didn't use Bisquick, but when I left the interview, I realized that they were perfect exactly as they are." She stopped and reached out for her grandma's hand. "I realized I'm perfect exactly as I am."

Willo looked at her granddaughter and then at the recipe card. It was bent, smudged, and the recipe was written in the same cursive, looping style that every generation of women in their family had used. The ink had faded and smeared, the words ghosted next to each other. The card was flecked with flour, and there were darker stains from pumpkin as well as thick circles where frosting had been dropped.

"It tells a story, doesn't it?" Sam asked. "Like our orchard."

Willo shook her head, holding back tears. "Sam," she said. "Don't make an old woman weep."

"Someone once told me on my thirteenth birthday that a recipe box is the story of a family's life, of who we are, where we come from, how we got here, and where we are now."

Willo's faded blue eyes overflowed with tears.

"That special person also told me that the recipes that were passed down by the women who came before us aren't just recipes, they're our family history. There is nothing more important than family and food. Food represents how we celebrate, how we come together, how we rejoice, how we mourn, and how we remain one."

Sam squeezed her grandmother's hand. "This gift comes with a sacred pact. We must protect these and pass them on, because they can never be re-created."

Sam looked at her grandmother. "I am here because of your sacrifices. I am who I am because of your love. I do what I love because of family. I am blessed, and I am so honored to be your granddaughter."

Sam and Willo stood, hugging each other tightly. Then Sam reached back into her bag and pulled out a bottle of wine.

"You certainly come prepared," Willo said, laughing through her tears. "Do you have a masseuse in there, too?"

Sam rubbed her grandmother's shoulders. "I do," she said, before grabbing two glasses and opening the bottle.

"Cheers!" she said. "Happy birthday!"

Willo clinked glasses with Sam and took a healthy sip. "This isn't wine," she said. "It's hard cider."

"Angelo and I might have a few ideas to discuss with you," she said, holding up the bottle of hard cider. "We have the ability to use our fruit to make incredible ciders and wines. Sort of like you did with the pie pantry." Sam hesitated. "I think we could add this without losing who we are. The future is changing."

"It certainly is," Willo said. "And it looks very bright, not only for me and the orchard, but also for you and Angelo. Cheers."

"Cheers," Sam said, taking a sip of cider. "Ready to bake?"

"I'm guessing pumpkin bars?" Willo said.

"Second time today," Sam said with a laugh.

The two walked into the kitchen and began gathering ingredients. As they did, Sam stopped, walked back to the table, and returned holding a key.

"This belongs to you," Sam said. "Old key for a new recipe box."

Willo slipped off her necklace, and Sam added the key. Willo rubbed her fingers over both keys around her neck.

"I want to fill the new box with our own recipes," Sam said. "So I can pass it along to my daughters and granddaughters, too."

"I don't know what to say," Willo said.

"Don't say anything," Sam said, giving her a kiss on the cheek. "Except for where you keep the Bisquick."

Pumpkin Bars with Cream Cheese Frosting

Ingredients for Bars

2 cups granulated sugar
1/2 cup vegetable oil
1 16-ounce can pumpkin
4 large eggs, beaten
2 cups Bisquick
1 tablespoon ground cinnamon
1/2 teaspoon pumpkin pie spice
1/2 teaspoon ground mace
1 teaspoon ground nutmeg

Ingredients for Frosting

4 ounces cream cheese
1/3 cup butter, room temperature
3 1/2 cups powdered sugar
1 teaspoon vanilla extract

Directions for Bars

Preheat the oven to 350°F.

In a large mixing bowl, combine the sugar, oil, pumpkin, and eggs. Mix well.

Add the Bisquick, cinnamon, pumpkin pie spice, mace, and nutmeg. Mix well.

Pour the batter into a greased 9 × 13-inch baking dish. Bake 40 minutes, or until a toothpick inserted in the center of the pan comes out clean. Cool completely.

Directions for Frosting

In a small mixing bowl, combine the frosting ingredients and beat until creamy. Frost the cooled bars.

Serves 14 to 16

■ ■ ■ ■

EPILOGUE:
APPLE CRISP

■ ■ ■ ■

October 2068

The old woman washed her hands in the kitchen sink, looked out the window, and smiled.

The last of the mid-October day's light filtered through the brightly colored leaves of the sugar maples and sassafras, basking the kitchen in an otherworldly glow. One good storm off the lake, one sweeping windstorm, and the leaves would be gone, the trees would be bare, the orchard's twigs and limbs just silhouettes, and the land ready to hibernate once again.

But, for now, Sam thought, *the leaves remain, as do the apples.*

Two figures moved in the orchard, a man and a dog, and the angle of the sun cast their shadows down the hillside, making them both appear to be giants. The man held a basket, and when he reached to pick an apple, the light made it seem as if he

501

were hugging the tree, caressing its limbs, saying good night.

Just like he does with me, Sam thought, leaning even farther to look out the kitchen window.

She could feel the chill in the approaching night air creep through the farmhouse. And as the dog circled the man in delight, his barks echoing through the orchards causing birds to scatter, she turned on the oven to preheat.

She pulled a carving knife out of the kitchen drawer as well as a baking dish and red speckled enamelware bowl from the cupboard. Then she arranged flour, sugar, and cinnamon on the old counter. She checked the refrigerator for butter and then located her pastry blender.

Her husband came through the door and handed her a basket of apples.

"You don't have to do that," Angelo said, looking around the kitchen. His emerging smile, however, belied his words.

"I know," Sam said, "but I want to."

"OK then," Angelo said happily. "I'll build a fire. Getting chilly."

He started out the door with the dog, then turned and said, "We make a great team, don't we?"

"Like cinnamon and sugar?" she laughed.

"No," he said. "Marriage. Fifty years. We complement each other, bring out the best."

"Like cinnamon and sugar?" she repeated.

This time, he laughed. "Yes, like cinnamon and sugar. Come on, Jersey, let's go get some firewood."

The dog barked his approval, and the two ambled out the door. Sam started in on the apples, her knife pirouetting in quick circles, leaving curlicues of bright red and green skin that resembled wood carvings in the bowl. She sliced and diced the apples, and then stopped, before starting her streusel topping.

Although she knew the recipe by memory — had made it hundreds of times over the decades — she walked to the old cabinet. Sam ran her hand over the cabinet's smooth edges, stopping to look at a photo of her and her grandmother taken at Sam's wedding.

I look just like you now, Grandma, Sam thought.

Sam pulled the original family recipe box off the shelf and ran her hands over the burnished wood.

"And I still bake like you," Sam whispered.

She set the recipe box on the counter and felt for the key that rested at the end of her necklace. Sam's knuckles resembled the sassafras that sat just outside the kitchen window, and her skin was now like waxed paper, and she struggled to fit the key into the little lock.

She opened the recipe box, which was crammed with recipes. Her recipe box was not as neat or orderly as her mom and grandma had kept theirs. Instead, hers was a jumble of cards and paper, jutting this way and that, and yet Sam knew exactly where the recipe was hidden in the mess.

Alice Mullins's Secret Family Apple Crisp!

Sam pulled the recipe free and immediately smiled. The handwriting was the same as hers — the same as her mother's and grandmother's — same slant, same formal-looking *F*s, and *Q*s that looked like the number 2. Sam ran her fingers over her great-great-grandmother's notes: *May call for a few more dashes of cinnamon . . . If apples are tart, add another quarter cup of sugar.*

How many times did she make this? Sam wondered.

This dessert was still, bar none, the family favorite, the one everyone requested every fall weekend while the apples were fresh, ripe, and just off the tree.

Angelo came rushing back into the house carrying an armful of wood and twigs for the fireplace.

Sam finished the crisp and slid it into the oven, setting the timer.

I don't even need to time it, she thought. *I'll know when it's done by smell.*

Within minutes, the scent of apples, cinnamon, and sugar filled the house.

"Smells good," Angelo called from the front room, where he was sitting in his favorite chair by the stove, with Jersey curled up on a blanket in front of the fire.

"Soon," she called. "Be patient."

As Sam loaded the dishwasher, the sun slunk behind the orchard, and the world was suddenly cast in darkness. Sam searched the orchards — the apples set against the darkening sky — and an idea hit her out of the blue.

She pulled an index card and a pen from her junk drawer and began to write, making up a recipe on the spot:

Sam Morelli's Secret
Family Apple Chocolate Chip Cake

A big smile engulfed her face, and Sam added an exclamation point at the end, giggling at the audacity of it.

Sam Morelli's Secret
Family Apple Chocolate Chip Cake!

And then she wrote, step by step, ingredient by ingredient, a new recipe on the spot, adding her own notes at the end: *Shake in a few more chocolate chips just for good measure!*

When she finished, Sam gave the index card a little kiss.

"Another new recipe?" Angelo asked from the living room. Sam looked up, and he was watching her with a big smile. His curly hair was still thick but now white instead of dark.

But those dimples, Sam thought, inhaling. *They still take my breath away.*

Sam turned to the oven, opened it, and checked the crisp with a toothpick.

Perfect, she thought.

She pulled the dessert from the oven, set it on top of the oven to cool, and started in on some homemade whipped cream, adding a dash of vanilla and whipping it until it formed a soft peak and was as pretty as a cloud on a northern Michigan summer day. She dragged a finger through the whipped cream and tasted it, and then did it again, accidentally dropping a dollop onto the new

506

index card, the fat from the heavy whipping cream leaving an immediate circular stain in the middle.

Good, she thought. *Now it has some character.*

She grabbed two plates and cut a big piece for Angelo, the apples steaming and sliding to the sides, before topping it with whipped cream, which began to melt as soon as it hit the hot dessert. She made a plate for herself and then joined her husband by the fire.

He dragged his fork through the crisp, shut his eyes, and smiled like a child.

"You didn't have to do this," he said yet again.

"I know," she repeated. "But I wanted to."

She took a bite, sat back as the plate warmed her hands, the fire warmed her old body and the apple crisp warmed her soul, and watched her husband finish his dessert.

That's the thing about baking, she thought. *You bake for someone because it is familial and familiar, new yet ancestral, a way of connecting generations.*

Jersey sighed and rolled onto his side. Her husband lifted a fork filled with apples and streusel topping to his lips and again shut his eyes.

Sam took a bite of crisp.

How can the same recipe taste even better

every time? she wondered.

The two sat in silence finishing their desserts, when the doorbell rang. When Angelo opened the door, he said, "Sam, you gotta see this."

Sam got up and when she saw what was at the front door, she let out a big laugh.

"Oh, my gosh," she said. "What do we have here?"

Sam's granddaughter, Alice, was holding her daughter, who was dressed like a little apple for Halloween, her round body outfitted in a stuffed red plushy onesie, her beautiful face showing through a hat that wrapped around her head, a green stem smack-dab on top.

"Perfect!" Sam exclaimed. "My first great-grandchild is just perfect."

Alice held out the baby, and Sam took her, cooing and bouncing her.

"My grandma used to wear something just like this," Sam said to the baby. "And you now have her name. Willo. You will be strong just like her, you know that?"

"I wanted to give you a preview," Alice said to Sam. "I know we'll all be so busy this week with the big visit from *Good Morning America*. Do you know what you're going to make for their 'Fabulous Fall Food & Fun' segment?"

"I think I do," Sam said with a smile, her mouth already watering thinking of making another apple crisp.

Angelo pulled a cell from his pocket. "Smile," he said, taking pictures of Sam and Willo.

"Want to take some crisp home to John?" Sam asked.

"Of course," Alice said. "It's his favorite."

Sam handed Willo to Angelo, and she scurried into the kitchen to make a to-go package for Alice. "Here you go," she said when she returned.

"Thanks, Grandma," she said, giving her and Angelo a hug. "I'll see you bright and early in the morning."

When the two were alone again, Angelo pulled Sam into his arms and held her tightly, swaying back and forth, dancing with no music.

"We've had quite a life, haven't we?" he asked. "No regrets."

"Is that a statement or a question?" Sam said with a chuckle.

"Statement," he said.

"We have," Sam replied.

"I love you," he said.

"I love you, too."

They were silent for a moment, swaying in the farmhouse in front of the fire, their feet making the old wood floor creak, when Angelo whispered, "Mind if I have some more crisp?"

Sam laughed. "Is that why you married me?"

"Of course," he said.

Angelo stopped and held Sam at arm's length and then kissed her.

"You still take my breath away," he said.

"Back atcha," Sam said with a smile. "Be right back."

She returned with more apple crisp for her husband and herself, and as they ate in front of the fire, Sam looked at him, and then around the old farmhouse, and her heart filled with so much love it felt as it were going to shatter.

You bake for someone because it is an act of love, Sam thought. *And that love is renewed each and every time a favorite recipe is made.*

"I think this apple crisp is your best ever," Angelo said, his eyes shut as he savored the dessert.

"I think you're right," Sam said, taking another bite. "I think you're right."

AUTHOR'S NOTE

I spent much of my childhood in my grandma's country kitchen, tugging at the hem of her white aprons embroidered with bright strawberries or pretty flowers.

My tiny grandma and her little kitchen seemed larger than life to me as a child: a vintage oven anchored one side, while her sparkly countertops were engulfed by a bread box that held Little Debbies and Wonder Bread slices. But the most prized possession in her kitchen was her recipe box. A brilliant baker, my grandma cherished the burnished wood box jammed with beloved and secret family recipes, all organized into different categories — *Pies, Cakes, Cookies, Breads* — and all written in her looping cursive.

Her pink Formica table was the glamorous backdrop for her desserts: fresh fruit pies — apple, blueberry, cherry, strawberry-rhubarb — with golden crusts vented with a pretty *S* for *Shipman,* as well as lemon with mile-high meringue that resembled a heavenly cloud. And her cookies — chocolate chip, oatmeal, thumbprint filled with homemade jams — were devoured before they even had a chance to cool.

When my grandmother died, my mom inherited her recipes. After my mom passed, I became the keeper of those recipes and memories.

The Recipe Box is inspired by my grandmother's recipe box and recipes as well as her life, love, and lessons. This book is a tribute to our elders, especially the women in our lives whose voices were often overlooked in their lifetimes.

Food, recipes, baking, and cooking are what unite us, transport us, connect the past to our present. We all have special recipes, ones we make on holidays, special occasions; the ones we ask our moms, grandmas, sisters, and aunts to make because they capture treasured memories and transport us back in time.

The recipes in *The Recipe Box* are not only beloved family recipes but also beloved family recipes dear friends have shared with me. I'm honored to open the recipe boxes of my family and friends and share a slice of our lives — and our pies and cakes —

with you! I hope you will share in this tradition and pass along your heirloom recipes
to those you love.

XO,
Viola

FAMILY APPLE CRISP

My in-laws have made this apple crisp for
as long as I (and they) can remember. To
me, this is without a doubt one of the most
delicious desserts I've ever had in my
life . . . which is why I ask my husband,
Gary, or my mother-in-law to make it every
time it's apple season, summer through fall.
It's a mix of tart apples sweetened and
spiced to perfection with a hard crunch topping so sweet and rich it will make your
knees buckle . . . and then you'll head back
for seconds. You can also swap out the
apples for blueberries. And it's perfect to
top with homemade vanilla ice cream or
homemade whipped cream.

PEACH-BLUEBERRY SLAB PIE

This recipe was given to me by the wonderful Jeanne Ambrose, executive editor of
Trusted Media Brands, Inc. — which in-
cludes *Taste of Home* magazine — cookbook
author, and writer. Jeanne loved the concept
of *The Recipe Box* so much that she volun-

teered (OK, I begged!) a beloved family recipe with a wonderful history. As Jeanne told me, "Slab pie is a pastry baked in a jelly-roll pan and cut in slabs like a bar cookie. My grandfather was a baker in Chicago. He was German. I have a handful of his recipes from the bakery handwritten in German . . . Grandpa Schulz typically made apple slab pies or rhubarb slab pies for the bakery. I change up the fruit every season. I love this because it's not a typical pie . . . it's double crust and you can eat it by hand . . . plus there's icing on top." I've now made this pie — which is a bit like a pie sandwich — over and over. The fruit can be changed, depending on the season. In fact, Jeanne's raspberry-rhubarb version of slab pie has become one of *Taste of Home*'s most popular recipes and videos of all time. Here are the links to both:

https://www.tasteofhome.com/recipes/raspberry-rhubarb-slab-pie

https://www.tasteofhome.com/recipes/watch-us-make-raspberry-rhubarb-slab-pie

Thank you, Jeanne, from the bottom of my heart and stomach!

APPLE CIDER DONUTS

As I mention in my acknowledgments, the history of and family behind Crane's Pie

Pantry, Restaurant, Winery and U-Pick Orchards in Fennville, Michigan (just a beautiful bike ride away from where I live), were a main inspiration for *The Recipe Box*. The lives and love of Lue and Bob Crane and the story of the pie pantry and orchard — as shared by their daughter, Becky — formed much of the narrative in the novel. Of the endless desserts they serve (all of which are amazing!), their apple cider donuts immediately make my mouth water when I start heading in their direction. They're a treat, a throwback, a reminder that when I eat these donuts, or walk into Crane's, I am surrounded by family . . . and love.

Becky shared the apple cider donut recipe she believes her mom originated in the 1970s and that was the precursor to the cider donut recipe used today. There is just something about the sweetness of the apple cider in these donuts that make them the perfect treat for a cool weekend morning breakfast (no matter the season!) or a delightful dessert.

CHERRY CHIP CAKE

One of my most beloved recipes from my grandmother was her Cherry Chip Cake. I so loved it that I asked her to make it for me on every special occasion: my birthday, awards, holidays, a sunny day . . . but she pretty much just made it whenever she wanted me to know how much she loved me. It's not only rich and dreamy, but it's stunningly beautiful, a real showstopper of a dessert. And if you love cherries, this ain't the pits . . . it's as close to heaven as you can come! The sad thing is, when I went to look through my grandma's and my family's recipe boxes, I couldn't find it. I was heart-broken. I finally found the perfect cherry chip cake recipe from Annalise Sandberg at Completely Delicious, who agreed to let me use her cake recipe. I experimented with the icing to make it my own. The link to Annalise's recipe follows, and it is amazing!

http://www.completelydelicious.com/ cherry-chip-cake-with-whipped-vanilla-buttercream/

TRIPLE BERRY GALETTE

Another major inspiration behind this book were my dear friends, Kathy and Nancy, who live in a stunning home overlooking the bay in Suttons Bay, much like Sam and her family. Visiting their home in the sum-mer is Pure Michigan: boat rides, Jet-Skis, barbecues, cocktails on their deck watching the sunset, games, laughter, suntans, and, of course, baking. They made a galette one beautiful summer morning, and it remained with me forever. I asked for the recipe, which they graciously shared. They made a rhubarb galette, which was delicious, but since I use rhubarb in a coffee cake recipe later, we adapted their recipe to a three-berry galette, which sings *summer*!

The galette reminds me of the "breakfast pie" my Grandma Shipman used to make. It was essentially a galette, but she didn't use fancy words like that. She would lead me into her garden, or the woods and bramble that backed our house, and we'd pick fruit for her breakfast pie. The thorns would catch my shirt and often nick my bare legs, but my grandma would say the end result was worth the extra effort in life and baking. This is a perfect summer breakfast, and the fruit can be changed to fit the area where you live; I've added blueberries, which I can pick just out my Michigan back door. Today, I grow all the things my grandma did: rhubarb, strawberries — and my Michigan woods are filled with fresh, wild berries in the summer. My grandmothers always told me that the simplest things in life — family, friends, faith, fun, love, and a passion for what you do — were truly the grandest gifts. This included baking (creating something you could share) and using the simple ingredients that they grew and that surrounded them in the summer: rhubarb, strawberries, wild blackberries, and raspberries.

THUMBPRINT COOKIES

This is another family recipe with a sweet history. My family makes these a few times a year, but *always* at the holidays. It isn't Christmas unless we're all crammed into the kitchen, making dough and then imprinting them with our special touch (and favorite jam . . . make a homemade jam sometime, or even a freezer jam . . . it's *so* worth it!). These cookies are nostalgic, pretty, and delicately delicious.

ICE CREAM SANDWICHES WITH OZARKS MAPLE SPICE CHOCOLATE CHIP–CHERRY CHUNK COOKIES

I grew up spending my childhood summers at my grandparents' log cabin in the Missouri Ozarks. There was no TV, phone, or indoor shower/bath; all we had were fishing poles, inner tubes, books, food, and each other. It was quintessential summer. This is where I learned the stories of my family and where I learned that cooking was a team effort. These ice cream sandwiches are the perfect example of that. They defined summer at our cabin to me (and still do at my own Michigan summer cottage). The cookie dough is amazing — an amalgam, really, of favorite cookie doughs. When I was growing up, my dad always made the homemade ice cream. He loved making ice cream — vanilla was his favorite — and it was the heart of our ice cream sandwiches. We had an old hand-crank machine, and there was a dinner bell on the back of the cabin that my grandma rang to get everyone to come in for dinner off the beach/creek, and my dad would ring it when her shoulder got tired, and we'd all take our turns. My dad had two main vanilla ice cream recipes: one that is a custard-style (cooked) ice cream, and one that he re-created when machines got all newfangled (fewer ingredients). He also had a homemade caramel sauce that he liked to either drizzle in the ice cream at the end (so good!) or dab on the cookies before he put on the ice cream. It's best to eat these sandwiches in the summer heat, each bite cooling you as the ice cream melts down your arms. They make you feel like a kid again!

Aunt Eleanor's Two-Crust Pastry

As my grandmothers taught me, you can't have a great life, a great home, a great family, or a great pie without a great foundation . . . Jeanne Ambrose again helped me out, giving me a family recipe that closely replicated my own family's, which my grandma, mom, and dad all made with a mix of lard and butter. Jeanne's is one she tweaked from her aunt Eleanor (I, too, had an Aunt Eleanor!), who Jeanne said she was certain learned it from her mother, Creszentia Pfeiffer Schulz (who immigrated to the United States from Germany). Eleanor was a farmer's wife, so her original recipe made five crusts. Aunt Eleanor's recipe is probably from the 1950s, according to Jeanne, and she likely got it from her mother at least twenty-five years prior. "Grandma had eleven kids," says Jeanne. The pie crust is flaky and rich . . . and, as my grandmothers taught me, the perfect foundation!

Strawberry Shortcakes

I believe that my mom and my grandma made the best homemade strawberry shortcakes in the world. And I still do! But now Gary has even improved their recipe, taking part of a popular St. Louis recipe, mixing it with the Ozarks one, and adding his own inspiration. Growing up, my family would head out and pick strawberries in the heat of summer, putting a fair share directly into our mouths. But, besides the fresh strawberries, the shortcakes are the secret weapon, and people truly have their opinions on what makes the best shortcake! I tend to prefer a shortcake like my mom, grandma, and Gary make (of course!): one that is firm enough to complement the strawberries but soft enough to soak up all those delicious, sweet juices (which are the best!). These are a sort of biscuit-meets-shortcake.

RHUBARB SOUR CREAM COFFEE CAKE WITH CINNAMON STREUSEL TOPPING

Both of my grandmas believed, as I wrote in the book, that every recipe box should contain a coffee cake recipe. And this is a summer family favorite! We pick rhubarb fresh from our garden in Michigan and eat this fluffy cake topped with cinnamon streusel on our screened porch on summer weekends (with lots of coffee!). A version of this delicious recipe was reintroduced to us later in life by an innkeeper at a local Michigan B&B.

APPLE AND CHERRY TURNOVERS

These simple turnovers (OK, one is a bit more complicated to make) remind me of being a kid. And you can substitute nearly any fruit! My dad made the apple turnovers every single Christmas, and when I eat them, I remember his unabashed joy and childlike wonder that remained every holiday season, no matter his age. And the cherry turnovers — especially in Michigan in the summer — can't be beat. Make the apple turnovers when you have extra time, and the cherry ones when you're short on it.

PUMPKIN BARS WITH CREAM CHEESE FROSTING

When I say there is one family recipe that people go absolutely bonkers over, it's these pumpkin bars — created by Gary — with cream cheese frosting. They are decadent, to say the least, and embody the taste and spirit of autumn. They're incredible just out of the oven, but just as great the next day (if they last that long).

Happy Baking . . . and Eating!

ACKNOWLEDGMENTS

As always, heartfelt thanks to my agent, Wendy Sherman, who's been alongside me every step of this journey since day one. Her optimism, faith, and determination have allowed me to do things I never imagined I could.

Thank you to my editor, Laurie Chittenden, who makes each book infinitely better (and is also a blast to work with!); Lisa Bonvissuto, for her support and seamless assistance; my publicist, Katie Bassel; my publisher, Jen Enderlin; and the entire team at St. Martin's.

Huge hugs to Carol Fitzgerald and her team at The Book Report.

Thanks to Becky Crane and her sister, Laura Bale, for opening their hearts and their own recipe boxes to me. The stories of their lives growing up on an orchard with a pie pantry, as well as the stories, love, and relationship of their parents, Lue and Bob, informed the soul of this novel. I can never thank them and the Crane family enough for their support.

To my readers: Over the course of the last few years, you have attended events, sent emails, posted photos on social media, and essentially shared as much of your lives, families, histories, and elders with me as I have with you. That is a rare gift, and I know I'm blessed.

And to Gary. I would not be here — literally, figuratively, personally, professionally — without you. I'd start singing *Wind Beneath My Wings* now, but then you'd start crying, or dancing, or trying to call Bette Midler, and it would just deteriorate pretty quickly. I love you more than anything in this world.

ABOUT THE AUTHOR

Viola Shipman is a pen name for Wade Rouse, a popular, award-winning memoirist. Rouse chose his grandmother's name to honor the woman whose heirlooms and family stories inspire his fiction. To date, *The Charm Bracelet,* an Indie Next Pick, and *The Hope Chest* have been translated into over a dozen languages and become international bestsellers. *The Charm Bracelet* was named a 2017 Michigan Notable Book. Rouse lives in Michigan and writes regularly for *People, Good Housekeeping* and *Coastal Living,* among other places, and is a contributor to *All Things Considered.*

The employees of Thorndike Press hope you have enjoyed this Large Print book. All our Thorndike, Wheeler, and Kennebec Large Print titles are designed for easy reading, and all our books are made to last. Other Thorndike Press Large Print books are available at your library, through selected bookstores, or directly from us.

For information about titles, please call:
   (800) 223-1244

or visit our website at:
   gale.com/thorndike

To share your comments, please write:
   Publisher
   Thorndike Press
   10 Water St., Suite 310
   Waterville, ME 04901